Kim

A World of Difference

"What are you thinking, Conal?" she urged him to tell her and again he marvelled at her youth, for what mature woman would ask that of a man she had just met?

"That you must go home or there will be a hue and cry," he lied.

"No, you weren't. You were thinking of love. Of me and love."

He wondered at her perception, pulling her hard against him, tenderness flowing through him in overpowering waves. Tenderness and regret and . . . no . . . *no* . . . nothing else, he told himself as he put her from him.

"Go home, Jenna." His face was serious so that for a moment she felt a shaft of terror pierce her heart.

About the Author

Audrey Howard was born in Liverpool in 1929
and it is from that once great seaport that many
of the ideas for her books come. Before she
began to write she had a variety of jobs, among
them hairdresser, model, shop assistant, cleaner
and civil servant. In 1981, out of work and living
in Australia, she wrote the first of her thirteen
published novels. She was fifty-two. Her fourth
novel, *The Juniper Bush*, won the Boots Romantic
Novel of the Year Award in 1988. She now
lives in her childhood home, St Anne's on Sea,
Lancashire.

A World of Difference

Audrey Howard

CORONET BOOKS
Hodder and Stoughton

First published in Great Britain in 1995 by
Hodder and Stoughton
A division of Hodder Headline PLC
First published in paperback in 1996 by
Hodder and Stoughton
A Coronet Paperback

10 9 8 7 6 5 4

British Library Cataloguing in Publication Data

Howard, Audrey
World of Difference
I. Title
823.914 [F]

ISBN 0 340 63975 X

Typeset by Palimpsest Book Production Limited,
Polmont, Stirlingshire
Printed and bound in Great Britain by
Cox & Wyman Ltd, Reading, Berkshire

Hodder and Stoughton
A division of Hodder Headline PLC
338 Euston Road
London NW1 3BH

For the Procopides,
Margaret and Mum,
dear friends and good neighbours

The Fielden Family

Ezra and Agnes Fielden

Nella	Linnet – (twins) – Dove
m	m	m
Jonas	Sir	Sir
Townley	Julian	Edward
	Spencer	Faulkner

Jenna	Amy	Blake
Beth	Timothy	Christopher
Nancy	(twins)	Caroline
Rose		

Chapter One

When asked her age Jenna Townley declared that she
was eighteen years old. Well almost, she would add
stubbornly, narrowing her eyes, just as though daring
anyone to argue. She was eighteen years old, well almost,
when she met Conal Macrae.

It was the loveliest day. The sun shone from a cloudless
sky which was the bright, azure blue of a speedwell. It
had snowed during the night, only an inch or two, but
it had frozen hard, crisp and crunching underfoot. The
intense cold had petrified the remaining stalks of last
year's bracken to an inflexible rigidity, encasing each
one in ice, some straight and tall, others bowing towards
the hard ground as though at the weary weight of it.

The sun was not high yet. It hovered at the back of
the stark trees, its brilliance flashing in blinding glints
off the sparkle of pendant icicles, shattering into bright
fragments of iridescent light as it was reflected in the
glittering surface of the snow. It outlined the delicacy
of the white-laden branches, illuminating the frozen
tracery to a beauty which was breathtaking, darkening the
rough-textured brown of the tree trunks almost to black.
The trees flung deep shadows across the snow, fingers of
contrast in its sunlit dazzle and marked clearly between
them were the neat and purposeful prints of a fox. A mist,
knee-high, hung in whispers, still and mysterious, shifting
only as Jenna moved through it. She followed the trail the

fox had made, careful not to put her own feet where his paws had been, moving through the blinding radiance of the winter woodland, her eyes intent on his path.

There was a stream, clogged with the residue of what had been last autumn's glory, rotting leaves, fallen branches, feathers and twigs and across the water was a thin film of ice, broken where the fox, almost as though he sensed her on his trail, had artfully stepped into it, surprised perhaps when it did not bear his weight. He had moved upstream, splintering the ice, opening up the slow trickle of flesh-numbing water which flowed beneath it, and his trail was lost. Cunning as the fox, they said, and this one was no exception.

Jenna lost interest. She turned away from the stream, squinting into the radiance of the sunlight, smoothing her gloved hand up across her forehead and back over her crisply curling hair which fell to her waist. It was the exact colour of the fox whose trail she had been following, thick and heavy, long, soft corkscrews of flame, unrestrained by anything so tiresome as a ribbon or comb and if her governess had seen her she would have sighed in despair though she would not have been surprised.

Jenna tipped back her head, arching the lovely line of her chin and throat.

"Dory! Duff! Where are you?" she shouted impatiently, cupping her mouth with her hands, turning full circle. "Can't you smell the fox, you witless fools? Where the devil are you? I swear I'll have the pair of you put down if you don't come here to me at once," which was, of course, no more than Jenna's temper speaking for she loved her animals and would no more dream of thrashing them than she would any other living creature. "Here Dory, here Duff. Good boys, come here to me."

She waited for several impatient moments, her eyes darting from frosted bush to frosted bush, lifting and

2

turning her head to listen for the tell-tale excited crashing which would mark the dogs' passage through the crisp undergrowth towards her but there was no sound but the sweet, liquid song of a robin in a nearby thorn bush and the explosive shrillness of a peevish jay as it searched the woodland floor for acorns.

"Goddammit, where are you, you buffoons? I'm warning you that if I have to come searching for you I'll leather the pair of you. Come here to me at once. *At once*, I say."

Still there was no response and Jenna Townley stamped her foot in temper, the crusted snow breaking beneath her boot. There was no telling in which direction the wretches had gone while she had been studying the fox's trail. On through the woods perhaps? or back towards the house? though the latter seemed unlikely since they were always eager to explore whatever lay tantalisingly ahead of their questing noses.

She decided to go on, setting off towards Roundhill Pasture, lengthening her already long and boyish stride. She was tall for a girl, carrying herself bouyantly with a coltish grace which, if she heeded her mama and Miss Hammond's advice on the curbing of her tomboy ways, would develop into that womanly elegance so cherished in young females of good breeding.

There was no indication of it now as she headed towards the pasture which lay on the far side of Seven Cows Wood. Her jaw was set at a perilous angle which boded ill for the hapless Dory and Duff. Hitching up her skirt to her black stocking-clad knees, she broke into a headlong run, the sort of run which made those who had her in their charge throw up their hands in horror. They despaired of her, they said, her mama, her governess Miss Hammond, Molly who was ruler of the nursery, or had been when it was overflowing with babies. They asked one another, and *her*, several times a day what was to become of her, and if she didn't "shape" herself, Molly often muttered darkly, she'd not find herself a husband.

"I don't want to find myself a husband, Molly. At least not one who would throw a fit if I should break into a run."

"Now then, Miss Jenna, that's not the way a young lady should talk an' if tha' papa were to hear thi' he'd not care for it."

"Oh, stuff and nonsense, Molly. Papa doesn't give a fig for things like that. He's got more sense."

"Then why is Master Simeon allowed to gallop off on that wild beast yonder an' you're not, tell me that, Miss Jenna?"

"God knows," she would mutter mutinously, watching with envy as Simeon, two years younger than she was, swung himself into his saddle, put his heels to his roan's side and took off like a bird in flight, going only he knew where. Inclined to be a free spirit, was cousin Simeon when he was home from the school Papa had sent him to, which Jenna supposed was only natural, since he had no friends in Marfield. Now and again he brought home what he called a "chap" from his "dorm" and then the two of them would gallop off in the direction of Marfield. Up to no good, she'd be bound, but that was not often. He spent more time with his own sister than with anyone else which was a bit odd in a boy of fifteen, she supposed, but then what did she know of males of his age, having only sisters? Jenna envied him his freedom and whenever she could, which meant as soon as Mama, or Miss Hammond or Molly took their eyes off her for five minutes, she would escape herself. Not to follow Simeon, of course, for he was a thorn in Jenna's side, but to somewhere far away from Bank House, the family home, from the schoolroom and Miss Hammond, from Molly and the nursery and the thousand and one restrictions Jenna's position as Jonas

Townley's eldest daughter forced on her. A female of her class and position could forfeit not only her reputation but also her chance of a decent marriage which was her fate in life, or so Miss Hammond constantly told her, though she did not phrase it in exactly those words. She must not be seen stepping out of the decorous role her life had cast her in. Not a whisper of scandal, nor taint of gossip must brush against her, even the most innocent. She must never go about without a chaperone and to talk to a gentleman, even the most worthy, alone and unattended, or at least unwatched by another lady, preferably married, was to commit social suicide.

Sometimes, when Miss Hammond was in the school-room with Jenna's sisters and Molly dozed by the nursery fire; when Mama was down at Smithy Brow and there was no one to enquire where she was off to, Jenna would put on a pair of Simeon's breeches, those which she had filched from his wardrobe, pretending to join in the general hue and cry when he missed them, cram her hair into his old school cap, and go like the wind away from Bank House. She'd have had them on this morning, though it might have been tricky riding Simeon's roan Leander with the ground as it was. Besides which, Mama had sent Tilly to turn out Jenna's bedroom and there had been chance to do no more than fling on her warm, fur-lined cloak and stout walking boots and slip down the back stairs to the side door which led into the garden. From there it had been easy to follow the path skirting the vegetable garden out of sight of any disapproving eyes which might be glancing from a window at the front of the house, and through the little wicket gate which opened into Seven Cows Wood. Still on Papa's land, of course, which was not unusual since Papa owned most of the land for what seemed miles about Bank House and indeed surrounding the small township of Marfield itself, stretching to what was called the common.

The common, years ago, had belonged to the same agricultural scheme of life as the open field on which Jenna's ancestors had once raised their crops of corn. It was land where the men of Marfield, then no more than a hamlet, had grazed their cattle, their horses, their sheep and geese; on which pigs rooted and picked up acorns. The commoners' rights included the gathering of firewood, peat, bracken and nuts, a source not only of feed for their animals, but of life for themselves.

Now the common was covered with disused mine shafts, the old bell pits, so called because the shallow coal workings were the shape of a bell, some leading to short, shallow tunnels, to drift mines named adits or day-holes, with trees about them, said to have been planted to warn of the whereabouts and danger of the old shafts. Away from the trees were low hummocks and hollows with great open spaces where it was possible to race a pony as Simeon and the chap from his dorm did and which Jenna had always longed to do. Being a girl was the most trying, unendurable irritation in Jenna's young life!

Her papa's land, which did not include the common, consisted of hedged fields and rough pasture, four or five stretches of woodland where what Papa called a "bit of decent shooting" might be had, many old mine shafts, fenced for safety, rows of derelict cottages which he meant to pull down, the whole waiting for the right moment to sell which meant when the right profit might be made. There were wandering, narrow lanes, now used as short cuts by country folk, a stream by the name of Smithy Brook and another called Old Lady's Brook, both of them dashing cheerfully and erratically across shining, chuckling stones from here to there and going nowhere in particular. There was Heigh House on the far side of Beggars Wood where Papa's mine manager and his family lived and of course, well away from both Heigh

House and Bank House, the sprawling mass of the three collieries themselves from where the Townley wealth had first come.

None of this concerned Jenna Townley today as she jumped in one boyish bound over Old Lady's Brook, enjoying herself enormously now, despite the failure of her dogs to come to her call. She'd skin them alive, of course, the minute she found them, probably doing their idiotic best to get down a narrow rabbit burrow at one and the same time, but in the meanwhile the sheer exhilaration of racing across the dazzlingly white, dangerously slippery, snow-encrusted ground, legs flying, skirts held up to her stocking tops, her wayward hair streaming out like a bronzed banner behind her, brought a flush to her normally creamy pale skin and put a deep, iridescent gleam of a turquoise in her eyes. If only she had on her purloined breeches she could have gone even faster, lengthening her stride and covering the ground at twice the speed, she told herself. She forgot Dory and Duff, forgot where she was going or her purpose in going there – if she had one – carried on by her need to get away from the stifling strictures of her female life, to move more and more swiftly, her heart pumping, her breath forced in gasps from her lungs and from between her parted, hedge-berry lips in great swirls of vapour which lifted and dissipated on the frosted, wine-sweet air. Her boots were no more than a blur over the crisp snow as she left Seven Cows Wood, jumping again the frozen trickle of Old Lady's Brook which had turned back on itself, her long legs carrying her across the crunching grass of the wide pasture which, before Jenna Townley's father bought it, had grazed cattle.

She began to laugh with the sheer joy of it, a breathless laugh which echoed about the tall, winter-coated beauty of the frozen trees ahead of her, a laugh which lifted a flock of noisy rooks from their denuded branches and swirled them about the empty sky before they returned to the tree tops.

Beggars Wood lay ahead of her, dazzling and mysterious in its sunlit, white-silvered splendour. The sun was in her eyes, low in the sky, intense, blinding her and the fallen branch was almost hidden in the snow. When her toe caught it she went down as though a giant hand had punched her in the small of her back, measuring her length with a violence which forced every breath of air from her lungs.

"That was most spectacular," an amused male voice said. "I've no' seen a bonnier pair of legs, nor so *much* of them since my cousin Angus lost his kilt in a wrestling match on Glasgow Green. Now that was a fine sight, I can tell you, due for the most part to his lack of undergarments, but no' so fine as the one I'm studying just now. Will you be repeating the performance, d'you think, or will I commit it to memory in case I shouldna witness it again? Oh, and by the way, I heard you calling so I can take it these two daft beasties belong to you? I found them with their heads stuck down a rabbit hole, both of them determined to get into it at the same time and if I hadna come by when I did they'd have suffocated, the pair of them."

Slowly Jenna raised her nose an inch or two from the hard surface of the frozen snow. It was, without any doubt, well and truly broken, she told herself, and was that blood she could feel trickling across her chin? Dear God in heaven, Mama would throw a fit if she came home with a bloodied nose, perhaps a broken nose askew in the middle of her face, especially as they, Mama, Papa and herself, were to go to the ball to be held at the Assembly Rooms in Marfield tomorrow night to celebrate the birth of Her Majesty's first grandchild. Mama would be mortified and Papa livid if they were compelled to attend what amounted to a royal ball accompanied by their eldest daughter with a face on her that would not look amiss on that of a bare-fist prize fighter! If it came to that they would simply go alone, leaving her behind at Bank House with her younger sisters. Or worse still, they would take Beth who was nearly sixteen and almost ready for the grand affair the ball would undoubtedly be. And Jenna did so love to dance. Dammit, dammit, *Dammit!* She simply could not bear it if her own clumsiness caused her to miss it.

"Goddammit to hell and back," she groaned using one of her father's favourite expressions, sitting up awkwardly and putting a hesitant hand to her nose. She prodded it gently, grunting a little as the pain flared across her cheekbones. "Mama will kill me . . ."

"I shouldna be at all surprised if she heard you using language like that. I'd kill you myself if you were mine. May one ask where a lady would learn to curse so fluently?"

Jenna turned her head gingerly and looked at the pair of boots, planted wide apart in the snow, which were the first objects to swim into her line of vision. The soles and uppers were crusted with snow but from the ankle to the knee they were most elegantly polished. Next to the boots, sitting one on either side of them, were Duff and Dory, their short tails quivering apologetically, longing to leap at her with their usual boisterous rapture. Restraining them one to each collar, were a pair of slender brown hands. Fine hands, but strong with long fingers and well-tended fingernails, firm and conveying complete authority over her terriers. Dory and Duff were sitting in that state of absolute obedience she herself had never been able to instil in them, looking up at the man who bent over them as though at some omnipotent being, their keen dark eyes anxious, their heads cocked waiting for the words which would release them. They were Border terriers, their rough coats a rich wheaten colour. They had small, dropped ears and were as brave as lions but still with that endearing tendency to be daft as young dogs are.

For some reason the sight incensed her. Her eyes narrowed hazardously as they travelled up from the boots to the hands on the collars of *her* dogs, assessing unconsciously, for was she not Jonas Townley's daughter, the expensive leather of the footwear, the excellent quality and cut of the fine doeskin breeches which fitted snugly about the legs, the carelessly thrown back cape with its fur lining not unlike her own and which had cost her papa a pretty penny, the fine woollen jacket beneath it. Under a smooth-shaven and strong brown chin was an equally strong brown throat about which was wrapped a snowy white, immaculately laundered cravat.

Scrambling to her feet as he straightened she found herself glaring into a pair of smoky brown eyes, the depths of which were pricked with the most astonishing bright golden flecks. They were narrowed in laughter and the mouth, which she thought could be hard if provoked, was curved in a smile over even white teeth. The smile had a slant to it, giving the face a whimsical, lop-sided humour.

"Who the devil d'you think you are, standing there grinning like some half-witted fool?" were the first words Jenna Townley snapped at Conal Macrae. "And who gave you the right to handle my dogs? They would have come to my call if you'd left them alone and there is no need for you to drag them about by the scruff of their bloody necks."

The man shook his head in disbelief. "You really do have the foulest mouth on you, lassie," he remarked. "I believe I've heard no riper in a stable yard and as for these dogs they're the worst behaved I've come across in a long time so I'm not surprised to learn they're yours." He spoke with the great good humour which told her it was nothing to him, one way or the other, how she behaved *or* her dogs. He was just stating a fact! "You do well together. All three of you badly brought up which is a shame for they're grand little terriers. But a good thrashing would put the three of you to rights, I'd say." He grinned lazily.

"Is that so? I'll tell my father when next I see him but in the meanwhile I'd be obliged if you'd take your hands off them. How they, or I, behave is nothing to do with you so you'd best get back to wherever it is you came from. This is my father's land you're on and you are trespassing on it."

"Aye, so I believe," the man answered, unperturbed, still inclined to grin in that amiable manner adults assume when dealing with impudent children, "but just the same don't you think it might be best if I took you and these unruly animals home? You could do with that eye attending to and besides, God knows who might be lurking in these woods. A female such as yourself would be fair game to . . . well . . ." He gave her another engaging grin. "We'll say no more, shall we? We can just as easily continue this delightful exchange as we walk."

"Can we indeed?" She could feel the hot flare of her temper surge and yet at the same time she was quite astonished at the strength of it. The man had the manners of a boor, despite being quite obviously a gentleman and though he had overreached himself in assuming command of Duff and Dory and had been extremely rude on the matter of her fondness for her father's oaths, he had no right to say so.

"I have no intention of going home," she continued loftily, "and if I had I certainly have no need of you to escort me there. There is no danger to me here. This is my father's land." She lifted her chin with the imperious hauteur of a young princess whose father, the King, had every right to do as he pleased, and, as his daughter, so had she.

11

"So you keep telling me, lassie, but if I'm no' mistaken that eye of yours is beginning to swell up. It'll be a pretty colour within the hour if I'm any judge, which I am for I've had a few myself."

He spoke with a slight lilt in his voice which was very pleasing. A way of clipping the ends of words. She had no idea who he was, or where he had come from but his arrogant belief that he had a perfect right to be here, and to tell her what to do, infuriated her.

"Will you stop drivelling on about my face and my need to get myself home. I need neither your help nor advice. I'm perfectly all right, thank you."

"You don't look it but far be it for me to interfere."

"Indeed, so if you would release my dogs I'll be on my way. And you'd best get off my father's land as well. There is a gamekeeper about somewhere who would not hesitate to shoot you if he found you trespassing. He does not care for poachers."

He grinned lazily and something, some tiny core of female awareness, separate and capricious, which was beginning to bud in her speculated on the delightful slant of his smiling mouth, the narrowed glowing brown depths of his thickly lashed eyes, the smoothness of his clean-shaven face, which was unusual in itself, for most gentlemen of her acquaintance, at least of his age, wore whiskers of some sort. He aroused some . . . some pleasing emotion in her, something agreeable so that despite herself she wanted to return his smile and even – God in heaven – put up a hand to touch his cheek! His eyebrows were raised in crooked amusement which told her he was laughing at her and suddenly a fresh flare of temper disconcerted her again."

Why should this stranger have the power to annoy – and delight – her so? she asked herself irritably, for up to now she had been of the opinion that members of the male sex, with the exception of her father, were fools and bores.

He was a good deal taller than she was, wide-shouldered and yet not heavy like Papa. Slim-hipped, flat-bellied, long-legged, she could see that, even beneath the fullness of his winter cape, but despite his evident charm and apparent indolence there was something hidden in him, something beneath his engaging exterior which warned her that he was a man who did not suffer fools lightly, and she, in his opinion, was being foolish. He was old, at least thirty, she thought but what did that matter? What did he, or any of his opinions matter? He was where he had no right to be and she was not afraid to tell him so.

"Now what is it?" he asked amiably, ruefully.

"I beg your pardon!" She stiffened, her affront a visible thing warning him that she was Miss Jenna Townley of Bank House, a great heiress, the future keeper of not only this land on which they stood, but of all her father's considerable wealth and he'd best watch his manners.

"I can see you're going to upbraid me again."

"I mean to do no such thing," she snapped. "What you say or do, or even think, is a matter of supreme indifference to me."

"Then if that's the case and I have no reason to disbelieve you, won't you go home and have that eye seen to, child? You should be—"

"Dear God, I swear you're worse than my governess," she railed, then could have bitten her tongue. The "child" had rankled though she didn't know why it should. Now she had told him she still had a governess though strictly speaking Miss Hammond was governess only to her younger sisters and her cousin Bryony. She had left the schoolroom two years ago when she had reached the age of sixteen and though she had no idea why it mattered she found to her chagrin that it did.

The man was beginning to lose interest, she could tell that, held only by common courtesy but she raised her

head even higher with the defiant challenge that drove
her mama to distraction, throwing back the cloak of her
rippling russet hair. The sun caught it, burning streaks
of copper and gold down its length, the curling ends of
it crackling with fire and for the first time the man saw
her not as a child running with a child's delight across
the newly fallen, freshly crusted snow, not as a casualty
who, should it be needed must be given his assistance,
but as a young woman.

She was not a beauty in the classic sense of the word.
Her face was too strong for that, the jut of her small
chin diminishing any softness her gender might have
given her. There was insolence in her, arrogance, a
belief in her own importance and right to do as she
pleased which it seemed she did, for no young lady
of good family would be allowed to roam about the
fields and woodlands alone as this one was doing even
if, as she had told him several times, she was on her
father's land. No, her beauty lay in her colouring which
was quite magnificent. Her eyes, the vivid blue-green
of the Mediterranean seas across which he had sailed,
were set in thick, coppery-dark lashes, the golden-tipped
ends of which fanned the pale cream skin of her cheeks.
Many women with her colouring had skin which was
the flat white of . . . of snow, lifeless and somewhat
dead looking but hers was rich, like buttermilk with an
endearing scatter of freckles across her nose and a flush
of pale peach high on her cheekbone brought about by her
obvious temper, he was inclined to think. Her eyebrows
were delicately shaped in a fine winging arch, the same
dark copper as her lashes, swooping now in anger. She
was watching him as he allowed his curious male gaze to
run, somewhat impudently he supposed, down from her
face to the full curve of her young breasts. She was no
child, he could see that now, despite the bundling effect
of the thick and voluminous three-quarter-length cape she

wore. It successfully concealed her waist and hips but it could not disguise the high peak of her breasts.

"What the devil d'you think you're looking at?" she snapped, her eyes narrowing to ice-blue flint, her temper exploding to even greater heights as she watched where his gaze went.

"A man would no' be a man if he did not look at you, bonnie lassie." He smiled as he answered, amused at the hot flood of colour which washed beneath her skin. He did not mean to tease her for despite the curve of womanhood which bloomed beneath her cape, she was no more than a girl. And girls of her age and upbringing were vulnerable, unsure of themselves, unused to the pleasant flirtations which went on between the sexes. She would not like to be laughed at even in the most gentle way. She took herself very seriously, her furious glare told him and his attempt at humour, at lightening the stiff-necked atmosphere she was determined to create, had fallen on deaf ears.

"You are quite insufferably rude," she raged through clenched teeth, "and if my father heard you speak to me like that he would take a horsewhip to you."

"Perhaps he would be better employed keeping an eye on you. You shouldna be running about the countryside unattended and he should know that, if he wants to keep you out of trouble. There are men about who'd no' be so gentlemanly as myself." He grinned again, letting her know he meant her no harm; meant her no disrespect, his good humour restored, but Jenna Townley did not care to be told how to behave by her own mother, let alone this presumptuous stranger. A tiny glow of pleasure still warmed some place inside her, brought about by his reference to gentlemen looking at her, which included himself she supposed, but nevertheless he was mannerless to speak as he did and he had no right to criticise her Papa.

She tossed back her hair again, ready to give him

a piece of her mind which he richly deserved in her opinion, but he continued to speak, his eyes going to the living beauty of the fox red cape which coursed down her back.

"And if I were your father, I'd make damned sure your mother braided that hair of yours."

"Well, you're not my father, I'm glad to say, and what's wrong with my hair? Not that it's any of your business and not that I'm in the least bit interested."

Her eyes flashed dangerously, narrowing between the thick weight of her lashes and he could feel the exasperation begin to wash over him. She really was the most contentious young woman he had ever come across, he told himself, replying to everything he said with some defiant remark just as though she could bear no one to chide or restrain her. It was strange in a girl so young, as if there was something in her life that chafed her, turned what should have been sweet submission, which most young women of her class displayed, to a certain tartness. Oh, you could see she was spirited, my God, you could, but even so she was extraordinarily wilful. What would she be, sixteen, seventeen, he supposed, but then at his age any woman under twenty-five looked like a schoolgirl.

"You are quite the most ill-mannered man I have ever met. You stare at me like some country bumpkin," she went on, tossing her head in that irritating way she had.

"Really, and I've yet to meet a female who can fall into a tantrum as easily as you do, lassie. And if I was staring at you I apologise. That hair of yours is quite . . ."

"Dammit, I shall put up with your personal remarks no longer. If you refuse to get off my father's land I shall be forced to fetch the gamekeeper and have you thrown off."

The man's face hardened then and the humour disappeared entirely from his eyes. He'd had enough, his expression told her. Confound it, she was nothing but a spoiled child who needed a good tanning.

Just for a moment, to his own astonishment, the picture flashed into his mind of her over someone's knee, his, her skirts pulled up while the flat of someone's hand, his, administered the punishment, which would, of course, be no punishment at all but the prelude to some delightful lovemaking. He'd done it before with several willing young ladies, all part of love-play, naturally, which ended with the lady in question having her drawers removed and . . . Dear God, what was wrong with him? What was he thinking of ? She was no more than a schoolgirl, prattling in what she thought of as a grown-up manner, her silly, schoolgirl foolishness imbuing her with a need to challenge, as the young do, everything those older than themselves have to say.

"Well?" she demanded forcefully. "Are you going to leave these woods or will I have you thrown . . ."

"Lassie, will you no stop blethering in that childish way. You're only making a fool of yourself. I'm doing you, nor your father's land any harm so if you'd just take these two beasties off my hands I'll be on my way." His own sudden erotic image of her a moment ago made him sharp. Sharper than he meant to be and her mouth fell open in astonishment. She gave the impression that no one had ever spoken to her as he had done though, knowing who her father was, which he did, he was surprised. A man of forceful character with strong views of his own was Jonas Townley, so he had heard, whom nobody dared oppose, but then again, perhaps it was from her father that this arrogant young woman had inherited her disposition.

"Don't you speak to—"

"Oh, for God's sake, dinna start that again. Take your damned dogs and be off with you." He was furious at his own loss of temper and over nothing at all except the foolishness of a young girl's tantrum, which really meant nothing to him. If her father allowed her to prowl about alone but for these foolish animals then why should he be concerned and to prove it he took his hands off the dogs' collars and stepped back. With a curt nod he turned on his heel and strode off through the frozen woodland. Duff and Dory, released from his authority, began to chase one another about the clearing, young and excited and vastly relieved to be free.

"Well!" Jenna Townley said into the empty air, her hands on her hips, her face slack-jawed, then, feeling somewhat like a balloon which has been blown up far beyond its capacity and is now rapidly deflating, she turned about and began to wander aimlessly in the direction from which she had just come.

Chapter Two

As though to distract her father's attention from the purpling bruise which surrounded her eye and appeared to leak under her skin to her cheekbone, Jenna paid particular attention to the way in which she entered the dining-room that evening. Her sisters, gliding in the ladylike manner Miss Hammond had instilled in them from childhood, moved in front of her and she copied exactly what they did, allowing the full skirt of her gown no more than a slight, dipping sway. Her back was long and graceful, her head tilted with the luxuriant weight of her piled-up hair and though she really would have liked to keep her chin down, her face averted so that Papa would not see her eye, she did not do so. What was the use? He would notice it at once when they were seated so best to keep her behaviour flawless, her manner dignified and perhaps that would incline him to leniency when she explained to him how she had come by it. Mama had already scolded her, sending Maggie, the young kitchen maid, running down to Smithy Brow to beg an infusion of alder-buckthorn from Edda Singleton which would bring down the swelling, and it had to some extent, but she could not disguise the fact that she had a black eye.

A "shiner", as Simeon, who was still home from school on his Christmas "vac", had described it in that obnoxious manner he had and if Mama had not restrained her,

19

she would have clenched her fist and given him one to match hers.

"Where did you get that?" he had chortled. "And what does the other fellow look like? Knowing you, he will have two . . ."

"Be quiet, Simeon, or I swear I'll give you not only a black eye but knock your damn teeth down your throat as well."

"I'd like to see you try." Simeon Townley's eyes had gleamed with that brilliance which was as familiar to Jenna as the wicked glint in her own when she looked in her dressing-table mirror. Simeon Townley was, at least in the opinion of those with whom he shared a classroom, if not to Jenna, an engaging youth who was still at that stage in his masculine growth which his Uncle Jonas described as "high-spirited". There were those who would have characterised him in somewhat stronger terms. Wild was one of them. Unsteady was another, but a merry lad nevertheless, charming and for the most part good-humoured. Inclined to be undisciplined, they would have said, which was of course the fault of his indulgent guardian, but with no real bad in him. The lad had already been expelled from one school for some prank – his guardian's word – involving a game of cards and a local girl of loose character, the exact details of which had not been revealed. Boys will be boys, Jonas remarked, remembering perhaps his own headlong youthfulness. The lad had spirit, he said, one he did not wish to see broken as he whisked him off smartly to another boarding school which was known to be somewhat stricter in its guardianship of its pupils.

So far he had managed to keep out of any serious scrapes though Jenna did not care for the gleaming slant of his eyes, an expression resembling her own so accurately it was uncanny. Well, perhaps not uncanny, she supposed, since they were related in some distant degree though she was not awfully sure to what extent, but she cared nothing for that, only for the satisfaction of getting to grips with his taunting challenge. Her mama stopped them, of course, as she always did, stepping neatly between them, ordering Simeon to go and change for dinner which was at seven and it was almost that now, and really, when would Jenna learn to ignore Simeon's teasing?

Jonas Townley, who was already seated at the head of the table, rose courteously and so did Simeon on his left hand as his wife and the five young girls entered the dining-room. Jonas had driven down to the colliery at eight o'clock that morning, Simeon accompanying him which he did whenever he was home from school, for Jonas did not believe in young lads wasting their time galloping about the countryside with nothing to do but make trouble. Simeon, naturally as the ward of a wealthy gentleman, had a splendid mount of his own, a well-bred roan of smooth reddish-brown mixed with white with a magnificent mane and tail.

When he could lay his hands on Simeon Jonas would have him off to the pithead – and even the pitface on occasion – in an effort to cram into him the knowledge and experience he would need if he was to be concerned in the future running of the family business. He was fifteen now and in another year would leave school and the sooner he settled down to the employment which would be his, as a man, the better it would be in his guardian's opinion. The pair of them had spent the day at Fielden Colliery which had come to Jonas from his wife's side of the family, Nella having been Miss Prunella Fielden before he married her. Though he and Simeon shared a light meal at noon, Jonas was ravenously hungry. He had waited as patiently as it was in his nature to be for his wife and their daughters and for Simeon's sister, Bryony, but his expression was testy as he watched them

glide like swans on a lake to their places at the table. He
supposed you could describe the movement they made
as gliding, he thought wryly, though his wife, who was
woefully unconventional, and his eldest daughter, who
was the same, more often than not forgot they were
ladies and strode about with the graceful, long-legged
gait of young men.

Nella had always been so, caring not a tuppeny toss
for what anyone thought of her except him, she said
airily, and what's more meaning it, snapping her fingers
at those in Marfield who considered her to be as mad as a
hatter, shameless and improper. Years ago, after they had
been married for several months, she had opened what
she called a "shelter" for the wives and children of his
colliers, a place where they might obtain an hour's peace
and warmth away from the often brutish environment and
hardship of their own homes. Colliers were not the most
considerate of husbands and fathers, their own hard lot
deep underground inclining them to spend what they
laboriously earned underground at the Colliers Arms,
swilling down their parched throats the wages which
should have fed, housed and clothed their families, or
chucking it away at a cock-fight, or the dog-fights which
took place – illegally – in the torchlit yard at the back
of the inn. Full of checked caps and gaudy neckerchiefs
it was on those nights, and the pay packet which was
needed at home to buy food for undernourished children
was soon parted from them. Howling and swaying in the
garish light, avid in their excitement to see blood, to see
slaughter done before, their money gone, they staggered
home to get their worn-down, ground-down wives in the
family way again. A child every year most had, some
surviving, some not, and Jonas's wife had made up her
challenging mind, defying first her father, then him, that
these wives, these children, deserved better. A dispensary
where the healing and soothing potions made up from the

natural properties of living plants might be obtained free of charge. A school where children could, perhaps, learn to equip themselves for a better life than their parents had known; a parlour where a cup of hot, strong tea, or an encouraging bowl of broth could be enjoyed and by God, she'd made a success of it, his Nella, despite the hostility of the social class to which she herself belonged.

"What in God's name do you women do to yourselves before your mirrors that takes so long?" he scowled as they seated themselves. "Dinner's at seven sharp and it's ten past already. I could eat a bloody horse and so could the lad here. We've been waiting in the drawing-room . . ."

"I know, darling and I'm sorry but Beth's hair would just not go right, you know how straight and thick it is. Not that it isn't lovely," she added hastily, gazing affectionately at her second daughter whose hair was indeed so straight and heavy, so dark and lustrous it defied all Molly's efforts with the curling tongs and even the curling papers she twisted in it each night. Being female and contrary, which Jonas often remarked sardonically, women were, Beth was not satisfied with her own beautiful glossy hair but longed for the curls which her three sisters had. Four daughters and not one with the exact same colouring, all of them a mixture of himself and Nella. Jenna, a replica of her mother, with eyes which were never quite the same colour of blue, nor green, from hour to hour, depending on the light or Jenna's own mood. Hair, like Nella's the colour of a copper beech or the rippling fire of a fox, thick and twisting into tight curls which he would have thought to be more unmanageable than Beth's rich and gleaming locks which she got from him. Beth had Nella's green eyes, Nancy had hazel eyes with curly red hair, and Rose, his youngest, had hair of a pale, red-gold, almost the colour of an apricot, with eyes, like Jenna's, of a vivid blue-green.

Then there were Simeon and Bryony, both with ebony curls, both amber-skinned as their dead mother had been, both tall and beautiful but where Simeon's eyes were, like his own, a vivid and startling blue, Bryony's were a pale shade of brown, like honey, golden and slumbrous, again as her mother's had been, shaded with long, thick black lashes.

They took their places about the dinner table, his wife at the foot, Simeon, Nancy and Beth on his left, Jenna, Bryony and Rose opposite them. The air was fragrant with the aroma of the scented candles in the candle-lamps which shed pools of light down the polished length of the glowing mahogany table. Its clear surface reflected the faces of those about it and there appeared to be two of everything that stood on it, the silver, the fine crystal water glasses, the lamps and bowls of flowers, mirrored in its surface.

Jonas and Simeon were immaculately dressed in the well-cut, expensively tailored evening clothes Nella insisted upon each evening, for though she was inclined to be careless of the opinions of others there were certain standards she had been brought up to recognise, for her own mother had been gently bred. Dressing for dinner was one of them. Black dress coats, white waistcoats with an embroidered border, black trousers, silk stockings and black pumps, almost a uniform which all gentlemen of refinement wore, and though many of Jonas's business acquaintances, those who dined at Bank House and to whose homes he and Nella were invited, did not do so *en famille*, he and Nella had always kept up the pleasant custom.

The ladies, as he gallantly called them, lifting his glass to each one in turn, wore what exactly suited them and was correct for their age. Nella was the expert there for she had always been what was known as stylish – daring, some said – and had a talent for knowing what became her, in colour and in style, and she was the same with her daughters, and with Jonas's ward, Bryony Townley.

It was only in this past year that the youngest members of the family, Bryony and Rose, had been allowed from the schoolroom to dine with Jonas and Nella, and they, as was proper for thirteen-year-old girls, were in simple, short-sleeved, white organdie, unadorned but for a broad sash of raspberry pink velvet about their neat waists and slippers to match. At the back of each shining head was tied an enormous bow of the same colour and their long hair flowed smoothly down their straight young backs, ebony and pale red-gold.

Nancy, his third daughter, at almost fifteen and Beth, a year older, had been allowed to choose the colours of their gowns, providing they were appropriate, Mama had said. Nancy's was muslin, the palest lemon with a matching sash of satin, demure but very fetching, and an exact foil for her bright curls. Beth's was in a clear shade of a mignonette, the green matching her eyes. Jenna, almost eighteen, wore a pale, tawny-coloured silk. A gown with tiny puff sleeves and a bodice which was perhaps cut lower than her papa liked to see. Nevertheless it did show off the superb texture of her creamy skin and the wonderful fire of her hair. It was simple, elegant even, the skirt held out by a crinoline which, though wide, was modest compared to some, many measuring eighteen feet in circumference.

The Townley family applied themselves to Mrs Blaney's excellent Chantilly soup served to them by the maid-servants Dolly and Tilly and for several minutes there was silence as the head of the household took the edge off his appetite. A handsome man, Jonas Townley, in his fiftieth year but scarcely showing it, though his dark hair was streaked with white. He was well muscled, somewhat heavier than he once had been but still darkly attractive. He was a shrewd, well-respected businessman with an eye which missed nothing and when his voice spoke her name Jenna sighed with resignation for it seemed he had not missed her face nor the damage to it.

"And may one enquire, Jenna Townley, where you got that bruise about your eye?" His voice was deceptively mild. "Not taken up prize-fighting, I hope, though it wouldn't surprise me to hear you had, knowing your readiness to square up to anyone and anything that doesn't match your high standards. Who was it this time?"

"Papa, that's not fair. Anyone would think I got into a fight every day of the week!" Jenna's face was a picture of injured innocence.

"Oh, so it was a fight, was it? And who was your opponent? Not Simeon here, I trust, since he appears to be unmarked," turning a cool glance on the boy. "He seems to be your usual target, though from what I hear you don't mind who you pitch into. My over-viewer, making a joke of it of course, tells me he saw you lecturing a group of my colliers on the treatment of their ponies. They—"

"They were lowering one down the shaft all trussed up like a chicken ready for the oven, Papa, with belts and harnesses and the poor thing terrified out of its wits. It only needed one of them to go down with it, soothe it, give it confidence and I said so. I only told them—"

"I'm not really concerned with what you told them, Jenna. What does concern me is what you were doing at the pithead in the first place. It is no place for—"

"Papa, how am I to learn the running of the collieries if I'm not allowed to be a part of what goes on there?" Her voice was filled with passionate entreaty and her eyes burned into his. He sighed deeply, sitting back in his chair as Dolly removed his soup plate. He put his napkin to the corner of his mouth then replaced it in his lap. This was an old bone which was chewed over endlessly and tediously, by himself and Jenna, by himself and Nella who, naturally, could see no reason why a woman should

not do as well as a man in the matter of business. Women
had brains which, if allowed to develop as Jenna's had,
being curious and intelligent, could surely do exactly what
a man's did. Of course, Jenna could not go "inbye", as
a man would, her female strength being unequal to a
man's and there were sights unfit for women's eyes,
but in every other aspect she was as able, if not more
so, in Nella Townley's private opinion, though she had
not voiced this last to her husband, than the boy who had
no aptitude for it. She had a flair for figures, adding or
subtracting a column as fast as her eye could run down
it. She was shrewd and practical and had taught herself
from her father's engineering books in the library every
structure and phase of coal mining which could be learned
without actually hewing the coal. She had crammed her
head with facts and figures, probing her father's mind
when he would allow it, and was perfectly confident
that, since she would one day, as his eldest daughter,
own the mines, she would one day *run* the mines. She
was a fine-looking young woman, tall and graceful, or
would be when she got over her tendency to play hoyden,
as she had today. She had a brave, strong spirit and a
natural confidence which would see her through most
of life's emergencies but . . . but . . . she was a girl!
Female! Woman! Tied to a woman's biological cycle
and emotions and to the restrictions of today's society,
at least the one they moved in. It damned her to being
her husband's shadow, bearing his children and running
his household and how was Jenna Townley, who but for
her female body was a replica of Jonas Townley, to live
with that?

Her father shook his head, tapping his fingers in an
irritable tattoo on the shining surface of the table. He
was a strict man, and fair, but he was a man of his times
and the idea that Jenna, as she demanded passionately and
repeatedly that she be allowed to do, might take a hand

in the running of his business concerns was preposterous. He had told her she might spend some time in the colliery office which, though it was still highly improper, was at least manned by clerks who could be trusted to be respectful in the presence of a lady. She had done so and had learned it all so thoroughly she could quote, chapter and verse, his profits, his growth, his expenditure and had even had the temerity to question him on some of his methods and to suggest a few of her own.

But that was not the issue here this evening and he would not be sidetracked, kicking himself mentally for bringing up the question of the pony in the first place.

"Never mind the colliery now, Jenna. I put a question to you and I would like an answer. What have you done to your face? That was what I asked you and I would be obliged if you would give me an explanation."

From the other side of the table where he lounged, one arm along the back of Nancy's chair, one hand toying with a knife, Simeon grinned, his eyes sparkling with glee as he exchanged glances with his sister for there was nothing they enjoyed more than the sight of their cousin, or was she their second cousin, he could never remember, getting 'what for' from the man who was guardian to them both. He and Bryony were wards of Jonas Townley, their own parents having died when he himself was only eighteen months old and Bryony six months.

"I'm waiting, Jenna," her papa said ominously, signalling to Dolly, who had been about to serve the next course, a magnificent and succulent haunch of beef, to remain at the serving table for the time being.

"I . . . I fell, papa. I slipped in the snow this morning and I . . . fell." Jenna faced up to her father, her very defiance telling him that there was more to it than that. He wanted to smile. She was so transparent, so basically honest and when she tried to hide something as she was doing now she gave herself away by the very challenge she threw in his face. It was not in her to be deceitful and her every thought and emotion showed in her face. She was very dear to him but by God, she drove him to teeth-gritting distraction at times.

"I see, and where were you when this happened? And don't say in the garden because I can tell by your manner you were somewhere—"

"Oh, Jonas darling, does it matter?" his wife interrupted him lightly. "Dolly is waiting to serve the roast which will be cold if . . ."

"One moment, my love." Jonas and Nella were that strange complexity, at least to many of their friends, a happily married couple who loved one another devotedly and their children and servants were quite accustomed to their endearments and even the affection they showed to one another quite openly.

"Jenna?"

Jenna sighed. "Oh, all right papa, I was in Seven Cows Wood and I know I'm not supposed to go out alone but really, I had Dory and Duff with me."

"And a fat lot of good those two idiots would be if called upon to protect you," Simeon chortled. "No one would believe they came from decent stock to look at them. Just a couple of stray mongrels, Ben described them as. D'you want to know what he said, which I thought was hilarious—"

"No, we don't, for what you and Ben Parker think is hilarious, knowing your schoolboy sense of humour, is probably someone slipping on a—"

Jenna might not have spoken as Simeon continued. "He said they were just like mongrels which are known to be eternally cheerful, tireless and hopeless at anything but making friends with every one they meet. Some guard dogs, hey?"

He gazed round the table in triumph, his school friend's cleverness evidently a source of wonder to him but Jenna merely gave him the withering look she directed at all those she thought fools and imbeciles and there were many of those!

"Will you be quiet. Papa and I are having a serious conversation which has absolutely nothing to do with you, or Ben Parker. Mama, tell him to mind his own business, will you, or better still, leave the damned table and let—"

"Jenna, mind your language, if you please and Simeon, sit up straight and take your arm off Nancy's chair. Dolly, serve the damned roast . . ."

"Papa, you're allowed to swear and yet—"

"Jenna, will you be quiet!"

"But Papa . . ."

"Not another word from *anyone*, d'you hear?" he thundered, glaring round the table at his daughters, none of whom had spoken except Jenna, wondering as he did so why it was none of them could evoke the warmth and laughter in him that Jenna did. He was fond of them all but they lit nothing more than a paternal affection in him. Not like Jenna. She was not the same as the other girls. There was no pattern to her. She was as unpredictable as the weather in April, the month she was born, showing a restless quality, a brimming, inquisitive mind the others lacked and he loved her'. . . well, not as he loved his wife of course, who held him steady when memories came to haunt him, but in a way which delighted his gruff heart nevertheless.

Simeon, in many ways, was the same. Dark and handsome, high-spirited, constantly pleasure-seeking as young men are, adventurous, careless, but sweet-natured overall. He was still a boy and took but a small interest in the collieries at the moment, the collieries with which, as soon as he left school, he would be involved, but he would settle to it in time.

If only he could say the same of Jenna, not of the

collieries but of the life which young ladies such as herself would lead.

"Now then, young lady, what were you doing alone in Seven Cows Wood? Yes, yes, I know you had your dogs with you but as Simeon said they are young and untrained . . . no, don't interrupt. I have seen them myself prancing about the stable yard and generally causing havoc among the horses when they are let loose and unless you get them trained to instant obedience I shall get rid of them."

Jenna sighed and the rest of the family exchanged patient glances for they knew their father would do no such thing. His word was law, naturally, here and at the pit but Mama knew just how to handle him, soften the rigid disciplinarian pose he adopted and which was not real anyway. He was a disciplinarian, of course, but not an unjust one, nor cruel, and he would no more think about putting down Jenna's dogs, which she thought the world of, than he would one of his own children.

"I suppose they were fooling about and you, unable to restrain them, measured your length?"

"Something like that, Papa. I was . . . well, there was this fox's trail leading through the snow so I was following it . . ."

"Why, for God's sake?"

Jenna looked surprised as though to say "wouldn't anyone?" then, remembering that her sisters would think her mad, not only for being in the wood alone in the first place, and on a cold and inhospitable day such as this had been, but for concerning herself with something as foolish as the trail of a fox. How much more pleasant, they would say, to stay cosily by the fire, drinking hot chocolate, discussing the latest fashions and the older ones, Nancy and Beth, declaring at length, sighing with frustration, that they could not wait to go to their first ball.

"I was just . . . well, I couldn't help but think how hard it must be for the poor creature to find food at this time of the year and I was wondering where he was off to, to find it."

"Jenna, you are strange. Who else but you would care about such a thing?" It was Beth speaking, pretty Beth whose only concern, even at fifteen, was when she could reasonably expect to put on a flowery veil and share her hour of bridal glory with a bridegroom she had yet to meet. She was fashionably small, demure, longing to please her parents, even-tempered and submissive. The world in which she had been brought up did not demand cleverness in its women and she was not clever. She loved her papa, feeling secure in his absolute authority and the idea of flouting it – and constantly – as her older sister did, was an astonishment to her.

"I am interested in many things, Beth, and . . . oh, for God's sake, does it matter? The blasted dogs ran away . . ."

"Jenna, I will not tolerate such language in a girl so young and at the dinner table."

"I'm sorry, Papa, but I was trying to explain how I came to fall. I was looking for them, you see, running . . ."

"Yes, I can imagine," her father said, trying not to smile, sensing his wife's own amusement.

". . . and I tripped over a branch. That's all. The ground was frozen and I hit my face as I fell."

She smiled at him, believing he would understand, aware, as he was, of that special bond between them. He might not have taken the trouble to follow the trail of a fox, as his daughter had, even in his younger days, being concerned only with his pits and his profits and would consider it a waste of time to wander in the white frosted beauty of a crisp January morning, but he knew how she was and did his best to indulge her.

"I see, well, that eye is going to be a beauty, my lass, so you'd best heed your mother and put one of her 'witches' mixtures on it," smiling at his wife, her activities and interests at the women's shelter on Smithy Brow long accepted. "And the dogs came running back to your call, I suppose, or did they vanish completely?"

"No, when I lifted my head there they were sitting side by side—" She stopped speaking abruptly, her mouth faltering on the last word, for the picture which she had painted with those few words was a hard one to believe. Duff and Dory obediently sitting side by side! Obedient! Waiting for her! Her family could not believe it and their collective expression said so. She had not, of course and did not mean to mention the boots which had separated the dogs, nor the hands restraining them, but again her father knew when she was about to prevaricate and his expression told her she would do her cause no good by trying to pull the wool over his eyes.

She sighed deeply. "There was this man," she began, waiting for the explosion which, when it came, rocked her sisters in their chairs and drew up her mother to instant and anxious attention. Mama had been about to signal to Dolly to get on with the serving, or Mrs Blaney's superb meal would be ruined, but she froze, her hand in mid-air. Dolly and Tilly both sucked in their breath for they all knew in the house how particular the master was with his daughters and Simeon narrowed his eyes in sudden and alert interest.

"Man? What man?" Her father's voice was ice-cold and threatening and he leaned towards her as though he would draw the man's name from her by any means he thought best, fair or foul.

"Jonas, darling, it's all right, really it is," Mama said quickly. "She's all right, aren't you, Jenna? You were not . . . he did not . . . harm you?"

"Of course he didn't," Jenna said disgustedly, staring in amazement from her papa's face to her mama's, her own a picture of disbelief. Her father's reaction astounded her, though she had expected something, of course and her mother's attempt to calm him, just as though he was about to have an apoplectic fit, astounded her even further. She had expected his annoyance at her own flouting of his orders, but not this white-faced . . . Lord, she didn't know how to describe it. It was as though he had stumbled on a scene, a situation if you like, of such indescribable horror his mind could not cope with it and it frightened her.

"It's all right, Papa, really it is." She put a soothing hand on his rigid arm. "He was a gentleman, polite and . . . he brought Duff and Dory back to me. They were as good as gold for him." She tried to laugh and was relieved to see a lessening of the dreadful – what was it? – that had contorted his face. "He knew who I was and wanted to bring me home but I wouldn't let him."

She remembered for a split second her own obdurate displeasure, her wild show of temper, wondering even now why she had felt as she did. The stranger had offered her no threat, no offence, no harm beyond an inclination to laugh at her as though she was a precocious child and perhaps it was this which had incensed her. He had . . . looked at her . . . had he really admired her? as she realised now she had wanted him to, in the way a man admires a woman or, again, had he been laughing at her? Well, whatever had been in his mind it didn't matter but by God this did for if she could not convince papa that there was nothing to the incident, that she had been in no danger, it would be even more difficult than it was now, when the time came, to get out of the house, to get down to the colliery, to take up control of what was rightfully hers. Her father's pits!

"Papa, really, I was in no danger and came to no harm . . ."

"Who the bloody hell was he? I'll have him arrested and clapped in gaol for trespass."

"Papa! He was a gentleman. He had a strange accent as though he was not from these parts but really . . ."

Her mother sat back in her chair and a long sigh of relief eased from between her lips. She began to laugh and they all turned to stare at her. "And what is there to laugh at, may I ask, Nella Townley? Our daughter has been accosted . . ."

"Oh come now, Jonas. Hardly accosted. You heard what she said."

"She would say anything to get her own way, you know that. You're her mother and I'm sure you were the same at her age."

"Darling, calm yourself. You ought to know there's not one man in Marfield who would dare to set foot on your land, not without your permission. Dear God, they're well aware you'd skin them alive. I dare say there's a bit of poaching goes on but none would lay a hand on your daughter."

"Then who the hell was he, tell me that?"

Yes, oh yes, Mama, tell us that, her daughter's expressive face begged her. Jenna had no conception of the luminous interest in her eyes, nor realised that she was holding her breath as she waited for her mother's answer.

"Mark's brother, of course," her mother replied. "I told you he was coming to spend a few days. Laura—"

"Mark's brother! I didn't even know he had one."

"Jonas, my love. Do you ever listen to anything I say? Dear Heaven, I think I talk to myself at times. If it's not to do with the fetching of coal from the ground it's not worth speaking of in your opinion. Now then, can we resume our meal if you please? It will be quite cold if—"

"Would you like me to run back to the kitchen, ma'am, and get Mrs Blaney to warm up the gravy?" Dolly asked cheerfully, beckoning to Tilly to fetch the gravy boat and the enormous haunch of beef from where she had placed it on the serving table. "It'd take no more than a minute."

"No, I think not, Dolly. The master is hungry and . . ."

"Nella, will you please stop fiddling about with that blasted gravy boat and continue with what you were saying."

Jenna silently echoed her father's exasperated demand, leaning her elbows on the table to peer round Bryony and Rose in a way Miss Hammond would have deplored. She stared at her mother, willing her to speak.

"Could we not eat first, Jonas? The meal will—"

"Damn the meal, Nella. I want to know who is traipsing about my land, alarming my game birds, not to mention our daughter."

"I was not alarmed, Papa. Not at all. He was—"

"Jenna!"

Nella Townley sighed. "Very well, Jonas, if you insist but the meal will be quite ruined. The man is Mark's half-brother though he is a good deal younger than Mark. Laura told me he likes walking and asked me if you would mind if he took a turn in the woods. Heigh House is just on the other side of Seven Cows Wood—"

"Yes, Yes, I know that, woman."

"It would be told a good deal quicker if you would stop interrupting me, my love. Laura told me that when Mark's father died his mother married again. Mark, who was ten or eleven at the time remained with his maternal grandparents. He was at boarding school in Surrey or Sussex or somewhere and his mother married a Scottish gentleman so it was difficult for them to see one another when she went to live in Scotland and from what I gather his grandparents didn't encourage visits. Well, to cut a long story short, Mark's mother had another son and this is he."

"Does he have a name?"

"Conal Macrae."

"And what is he doing here? Is he in coal? And why have we not heard of him before?"

Simeon, who could see no romance in the story of Mark

Eason, his guardian's mine manager, and this long-lost half-brother of his, was clearly not interested. His sister and cousins, on the other hand, were quite spellbound but none so abundantly as Jenna Townley and if her papa had been looking in her direction and not that of his wife, his alarm, which had lessened and become relief, might have been considerably upset again.

"I will tell you all about him later," Mama said to Jenna's annoyance. "Now then, Dolly, let us continue our meal, if you please."

"That's all well and good, Nella," her husband interrupted her yet again, " and if the man really was Mark's half-brother then I suppose no harm has been done, except to this child's face—"

"I am not a child, Papa. I am almost eighteen."

Jonas cast his eyes ceilingwards. "Jenna, if you interrupt me once more I shall send you to your room."

"I'm sorry, Papa, but—"

"Jenna!"

"Yes, Papa."

"As I was saying, it seems no harm has come to our daughter apart from that black eye which brings me to the question of how she is to go out in society with a battered face—"

"Hardly battered, Papa. I would say it is no more—"

"What you have to say is of no concern to me, Jenna. Your mama and I would not dream of taking you to the ball in such a state."

"Why not, Uncle Jonas?" a quiet voice said from beside Jenna and they all turned to stare in astonishment at Bryony Townley.

"Why not, miss, why not?" Jonas Townley thundered. "Surely I do not have to explain why not, and what, by the way, has it to do with you?"

Bryony, who would be fourteen in March, was not intimidated.

"Nothing, Uncle, but it seems to me that there is no harm in Jenna taking her dogs for a walk. I do it myself."

"Not in those woods, you don't. You have the sense to stay in the grounds. I've seen you myself." Bryony smiled, a slow, rich smile that was curiously adult so that for a moment she looked the eldest of all the young people about the table.

"That's not to say I haven't been tempted."

"Have you indeed?"

"Oh yes, and after all it was not Jenna's fault that Mr Eason's brother was there at the time."

"Now look here, miss," Jonas blundered, but his face had softened and in his eyes was a look of something that said he was not really offended. Bryony was a self-contained child who had a tendency to listen to the others or not as the whim took her, saying little herself, as though what they did, or thought, meant little to her. She had no special friends and paired up with neither Nancy, Rose, Beth nor Jenna though there was a close bond between herself and her brother which was only natural. Now she was defending Jenna's actions and not only that, expressing her opinion that Jenna should not be punished.

"I'm sure Marian could disguise Jenna's bruised eye," she went on, "I could do it myself, in fact. I have a paste . . ." She turned sweetly to the woman at the foot of the table whose face was, for some reason, cool and without expression. "I hope you don't mind, Aunt Nella, but I found the remedy in that lovely book of yours, the one about plants and their medicinal properties. Marigold, the paste is made from. It will do wonders for bruising."

She looked about her, her smile containing nothing but innocent amiability. For several seconds there was silence. From his place next to his guardian Simeon regarded his sister with bewildered affection. What was she up to? his expression seemed to ask and so did Jenna's but she didn't care what it might be as long as it got Jenna Townley to the ball.

"Well, hmm, hmm." Jonas cleared his throat, tearing his gaze away from Bryony and fixing it on his wife. "We'll see, we'll see. Now what about that beef, Nella Townley?"

Chapter Three

"Mama, I swear if you try to stop me, or ask Papa to stop me, I'll never speak to you again."

Nella Townley smiled, well used to the dramatic statements her eldest daughter uttered and to the fiery upheaval she created out of the smallest incident.

"I was only remarking, sweetheart, that it is going to be hard to explain . . . well, we can only call it what it is, a black eye and in no way different to the one Jack Redman gives to his wife every Saturday night in his cups. It stands out like a plum in a bowl of apricots."

"Couldn't we . . . we . . . do what Bryony suggested perhaps, powder it or something, Mama, and besides, it doesn't bother me in the slightest. Who cares what other people think, if that's what you mean."

"Your father does, Jenna, and though it was come by innocently it is hardly what a young lady of fashion, or breeding, will be wearing. Can you imagine what everyone will be saying, especially your Aunt Linnet?"

"Since when has what Aunt Linnet had to say bothered you, Mama? You yourself have called her a fool and—"

"That's enough, Jenna. She is my sister and I will not have you speak so rudely of her. She is—"

"Nothing but a snob. I have heard you say so."

"Really, Jenna, you can be quite—"

"Insufferable, Mama?"

There was a moment's silence then mother and daughter exploded into infectious laughter, falling against one another in a way Nella's middle daughters could not quite understand, though Rose smiled. Of course Mama was as fond and affectionate with them as she was with Jenna but there was something about their older sister which they themselves failed to recognise, something which made Mama as foolish and high-spirited as Jenna was, larking about, shouting with laughter and generally, in Nancy and Beth's private opinion, making a fool of herself. Other girls' mamas were correct and dignified, softly spoken and gracious, impressing on their daughters the need to be the same. Their mama, on the other hand, did things which sometimes embarrassed them. For instance, her refusal to see the colliers' wives with whom she mixed at her shelter on Smithy Brow as other than simply women, like herself, or like she herself would be if she were not the owner's wife. They were not to be looked down on, nor despised, just because their circumstances were less fortunate than hers, or her daughters, and she told them so constantly, often in front of their friends which was worse still. She had a mind of her own, and used it, she said, and they, her daughters, must do the same. Jenna did and Rose was almost as bad, Beth and Nancy were forced to agree, but Rose was only thirteen and confined to the schoolroom a great deal and so was not in Mama's company as much as Jenna. Bryony was only distantly related and though she had been brought up with them since babyhood, was a solitary girl, inclined to wander off in the acres of Bank House with no one but her dog, an enormous thing she called Gilly, for company.

Of course Jenna had to have two, just to be different, but Nancy and Beth were close and alike and so, when the question of pets was broached had asked if they might have a kitten each. Nancy had chosen an enchanting little creature of grey velvet with transparent eyes of green and

Beth's was all white with an impish triangular face in which the bluest of eyes had twinkled. Snowy, she called him and Fluff was the name Nancy chose for hers. They had lived in the nursery, pampered in their satin-lined basket until one day, several months later, the basket had been alive with a further half-dozen wriggling grey and white kittens, much to Nancy and Beth's amazement. What a furore that had caused and it was not until Mama had explained to them, as gently as she knew how, that they understood.

Snowy and Fluff lived in the stables with the other animals from then on, producing a regular litter of further kittens which Daniels disposed of, one way or another, those which remained keeping down the population of rats and mice which tried to take up residence beside them.

Simeon's dog was a dangerous-looking Irish wolf-hound which scared the living daylights out of Nancy and Beth, *and* Fluff and Snowy, who kept well out of his way. Blarney, Simeon called him, which Mama and Jenna thought very whimsical, though the humour of it escaped Beth and Nancy.

"Well, I would not like to be seen at a ball with a black eye," said Beth primly, putting another immaculate stitch in the wisp of embroidery she held in her hands. Beth's embroidery was the envy of her sisters and peers and she was very proud of it. "And really, Jenna, I cannot imagine why you should want to go, looking as you do. In my opinion there is no way you can disguise it."

"Nobody asked you for your opinion so kindly keep it to yourself. This is between Mama and me. Anyway, I'm not going to try and disguise it, I've decided. I shall wear a black eye-patch instead, like a pirate. Everyone will talk about it" – airily tossing her head – "and every gentleman will want to dance with me if only to ask why I'm wearing it."

"Don't be silly, Jenna, an eye-patch indeed," her mother murmured, though Jenna could see she was amused just the same.

"Well, I think it's in very poor taste. No better than those women at Smithy Brow who think nothing of a black eye, or even two."

"Thank you, girls," their mother interrupted, "that is enough. And as for the ball it is up to your father whether you go or not, Jenna."

"No it's not, Mama. You know that if you say I may then he will agree. Oh please, Mama, please. I shall behave, really I will. I'll sit with you and Aunt Linnet and say not a word of which Papa would disapprove."

"I find that hard to believe, child. You are your father's daughter, and mine too and when have either of us known when to keep our opinions to ourselves?"

Jenna had to agree with her but that was not really the issue here. The ball was! Mr and Mrs Eason would be bound to be there. Mr Eason, as manager of Papa's three pits, had a position of some importance in Marfield and *all* gentlemen of importance would be there. Gentlemen of substance and their wives, the only ones who could afford the price of the ticket, the proceeds from the event to go to a worthy charity. And, of course, Mr Eason would not attend without his brother, would he? Jenna Townley did not mean to miss the opportunity to make herself known to the man she had met in Seven Cows Wood yesterday.

Conal Macrae! Even his name was different, exciting. A Scot, Mama had said, from somewhere up in the Highlands, the adventurous, wild Highlands which was anywhere north of the border and where the men wore kilts and plaids and were only a little more than half-tamed savages, Jenna had heard, not like the irksome, insipid sons of the gentlemen with whom her father did business. James Lockwood, still unmarried at thirty-two, the most eligible bachelor in Marfield since he was partner, with his married brother, in coal mining. Every mama with a daughter fluttered about him like cooing doves and he was without doubt the most obnoxious, vain, self-opinioned bore Jenna could conceive. Thomas Young was the same, a clever and prosperous solicitor with a career ahead of him in politics, she had heard her papa say approvingly. Then there was Frank Miller whose father had left him a thriving business in undertaking and whose eyes seemed to look at you as if he was measuring you for a coffin. Charles Graham, the banker's nephew, himself well on the way to becoming manager of his uncle's bank, all of them so insufferably tedious it was all Jenna could do not to yawn quite openly in their smoothly smiling and urbane faces. They would all be there and so would she, by God, even if she had to promise to behave exactly as her mama and papa expected her to behave for the rest of her life. No more slipping out into the woods alone but for Dory and Duff. No more saddling up Leander which, watching Simeon closely she had learned to do, and galloping off even before the grooms were out of their beds, making for the misted vastness of the common. No more exciting chases, leaping hedgerows and field gates with her dogs at her heels, or lazily swishing through the lush summer pastures, the tall grasses touching Leander's belly, rich with poppy and cornflower, the reins slack, her thoughts slow and dreaming as Dory and Duff scooted from one enchanting smell to another.

Not that Mama and Papa knew anything about this secret life of hers, a life which had begun on the day she left the schoolroom.

"I'm going to sit with Molly, Miss Hammond," she would say to the governess. "It will be quiet in the nursery so I'll take my book," and Miss Hammond would nod approvingly before turning back to Nancy, Rose, Beth and Bryony whose heads were bent industriously over the schoolroom table. The younger girls would remain there from nine in the morning until noon when they would take lunch together and then indulge in a walk round the garden and even into Seven Cows Wood where Miss Hammond would take the opportunity to instruct her charges in botany and modest biology as well as collecting flowers to press.

On two afternoons a week there would be dancing lessons and piano lessons, all very dreary and repetitious, Jenna knew, having suffered them for years. By the time they left the schoolroom her sisters, like herself, would be prepared for the activities which were such an important part of their social calendar. Dances and concerts, private musical soirées where they would be able to play and sing and entertain the guests as every young lady with the slightest pretence of talent was persuaded to do.

But in the meanwhile, as they were trained for it, it meant that Miss Hammond was in a predetermined place at the exact same time for the best part of each day and therefore easy to avoid.

"I'm going to help Miss Hammond in the schoolroom, Molly," she would say to the woman who had been her childhood nurse. Molly would eye her fondly from her warm spot before the cheerful nursery fire, her hands busy with a bit of darning or mending, dozing her life away in the comfort she so richly deserved, or so Mama said.

"Righto, lambkin," Molly would answer, smiling and rocking, a pastime she indulged in from morning until night, her uncritical mind not even considering her former charge's astounding statement. When had Jenna Townley ever willingly entered the schoolroom, it might have asked, particularly to give a hand to her governess?

With her mother at Smithy Brow and her father at the pit, with Miss Hammond believing she was in the nursery and Molly imagining her in the schoolroom, with the servants far too busy about their own tasks to wonder where Miss Jenna might be, it had been a simple matter to slip out of the side door, move stealthily in the shadow of the hedge to the small gate in the garden wall and be away free with not one soul in the house aware she had even left it. So far, keeping her fingers crossed as she said it, no one had found out, particularly with Simeon, who would, of course, have missed Leander, away at school.

It was odd, the way Papa kept her and her sisters so closely guarded, she had often mused. Naturally, all the young girls she knew were chaperoned wherever they went by a close male or female relative, or by some trusted family servant but Papa was quite a fanatic about it. Look at him last night when he heard she had met a stranger in the wood. She had, for a moment, been afraid of him, so fierce, so maddened had he been and had it not been for Mama who always managed to calm him, it seemed he might have exploded! It was as though he was afraid of something though the idea of Papa being afraid of anything was laughable. He had always seemed like some splendid being from another species to Jenna. A magnificent breed of men somewhat in the order of thoroughbred stallions, tall, handsome, brave and full of a spirit which outshone every man in whose company Jenna saw him. Not the ordinary kind of papa at all such as her cousin Caroline's papa, Jenna's uncle, Sir Edward Faulkner. He was kind and devoted to Caro but he was a mortal man despite being a baronet and had not a tenth of Papa's splendour.

Oh if only Papa, her wonderful papa, would overlook her bruised face and her behaviour which had so upset him and allow her to go to the ball.

The whole of Marfield appeared to be illuminated that night, the brilliance of the lighted Assembly Rooms spilling out into the crisp January darkness and spreading across the town. The entrance hall had been transformed into a flower garden, a profusion of red and white blossoms in swirling patterns apparently sprouting from the polished floor itself with vast arrangements cascading down each side of the stairs which led to the ballroom. The splendid event in honour of the royal family's newest member had been deliberately arranged so that it copied London's high society since Marfield did not mean to be outshone by anything St Helens, or even Manchester might put on. Mrs Frederick Lockwood, whose husband, after Jonas Townley, was the wealthiest and most influential coal owner in the district, and who had arranged the ball, in the absence of Mrs Jonas Townley who was too busy with her shelter on Smithy Brow, stood at the head of the stairs to welcome the guests. Having done all the planning, concerned herself with the preparation and worn herself out in the process, Mrs Lockwood felt it was only her due to play hostess. Privately she told her husband, she considered Nella Townley was too closely associated with those collier brats for folk, decent folk to be easy with her.

Mind you, she looked well enough as she came up the stairs, Mrs Lockwood had to concede, in her rich, blue silk brocade, her fine creamy shoulders rising from the somewhat low-cut bodice, her fine creamy neck adorned with the most magnificent triple strand of pearls Mrs Lockwood, or indeed anyone in Marfield had ever seen. Her vivid red hair had drifts of white in it but it was still thick and inclined to tumble about her ears and, though she did not say so to Frederick, if her husband looked at her as Jonas Townley looked at his wife she'd be hard put not to blush right down to her corsets.

Jenna's eye attracted a great deal of attention, causing her Papa to grit his teeth and mutter under his breath to her Mama that he knew it had been a mistake to bring her. That salve Nella had applied to the surrounding skin had

done no good at all and if his wife and daughter thought
he was to spend the whole evening explaining over and
over again how Jenna had come by it then they had been
misinformed. He was off to play cards with the other
gentlemen and Nella could send for him when they were
ready to leave. Her mother smiled at him, unperturbed
by his ill-humour and Jenna knew that within the hour
he and Mama would be dancing together, unconcerned
with the startled looks directed at them for no gentleman
here would think to dance with his *own* wife.

"Good evening," said James Lockwood. "You're looking very fine, Jenna, but may one ask what you have done
to your face?"

"No, one may not," she answered rudely, causing those
about them to stare as she and her mother made their way
towards the small tables and spindly legged gilt chairs
which had been set out for the ladies.

"Behave yourself, Jenna," her mother warned.

"Good evening," said Frank Miller. "A cold evening,
is it not?" and one which would be bound to bring him
custom since it was well known that January was a good
month in the funeral business. "And what have *you* been
up to, Miss Jenna?" smiling unctuously.

"Nothing that will need your services, Mr Miller," she
snapped, sailing past him with her head held high.

"Jenna, my darling, your papa will not like it if you
offend the business gentlemen of the town."

"Mama, you're a fine one to talk."

They both laughed, their faces so much alike in their
shared humour they might have been the same age. Even
their hair had the same lively tendency to go its own
riotous way, small corkscrews of leaping curls escaping
to bob endearingly about their foreheads, their neat ears
and graceful necks.

It was thus that Conal Macrae saw her for the second
time. Laughing, sparkling, vivid, a flame against which

every woman in the room – expect her own mama – looked as dim as a farthing rushlight. She wore a gown of pale tawny silk, the colour much favoured by her mother in her younger days, those who were old enough remembered. It shimmered as she moved, shot with colours of subtle copper, topaz and rose and yet it was none of these shades alone, the light from the dozens of hanging candelabra merging them into one glorious hue. The bodice was tight and cut very low, too low for a girl of her age, matrons muttered behind their fans, with a deep pointed waist. The sleeves were tiny and so was Jenna's waist, the double skirt enormous and looped up at one side to reveal a mass of rich creamy lace. About her neck she wore a narrow tawny velvet ribbon fastened at the back in a bow and another was tied to her wrist from which her dance card hung. There were swinging gold bobs in her ears and her hair was arranged in a careless tumble of curls held up by no more than a threaded ribbon to match the ones about her neck and wrist.

He could not take his eyes off her. She was magnificent, even the deep purpling of the bruise about her eye in no way detracting from her unusual beauty. And yet, he thought, she was not really beautiful. Her mouth was too wide, full, the colour of a ripe peach. She had golden freckles across her nose and cheeks. Her expression, now that the laughter had died away, was too forthright and her chin too square. The last time he had seen her she had appeared to be no more than a bad-tempered schoolgirl, truculent, scowling, her hair all over the place, a cloud of tangled curls, and though it was still almost as unfettered now, it was gleaming and rich under the lights, drawing his eyes, drawing his hands which he could imagine sinking into its undisciplined softness. She was smooth now, polished, her skin warm as clotted cream, a young lady from the tip of her velvet dancing slippers to the fragrant fox red of her hair. He was quite certain it would be fragrant!

He stood beside his brother Mark, and Mark's wife, Laura, listening politely to Laura as she pointed out the town's worthies, explaining who they were and what they did, smiling a little for his sister-in-law had an endearing sense of humour which was not in the least cruel. She was a kind woman and as far as he could tell in the short time he had known her had been a good wife and mother and was energetic in her charity work which included the management of a school for poor children of the mining community.

He let her talk, answering courteously when it was necessary but nine-tenths of his attention was directed towards the young woman he had met in Seven Cows Wood the day before. She had seated herself beside her mother after making her bob to several older woman, but she was restless, her foot tapping, her head constantly turning, her eyes darting across the polished floor of the ballroom, moving from one group of chatting people to another.

The orchestra was already playing in preparation for the dancing, seated on a raised dais at the end of the ballroom. Refreshments were set out in the small dining-room off the ballroom and would be served throughout the evening, claret and champagne, a vast array of confectionery, sorbets and ices of every sort, a never-ending flow of tea and coffee to strengthen the dancers and refresh the vigilant chaperones until supper was served.

Their eyes met just as Mrs Lockwood – who had worked so hard for it – and her husband opened the ball by taking a turn round the floor together. By the sudden still expression on Jenna Townley's face, which could not hide its emotions, he knew at once that she had been looking for him and he straightened his tall, lean frame. It was as though yesterday had never happened. It was as though this was their eyes' first meeting and the electric shock which passed from one to the other, that passed through them, blinding them with its force, taking away their senses and the breath from their lungs, must surely be noticed by every man and woman who stood in its path.

She remained frozen in anticipation, her young face dazzled and, for a moment, unsure. Her eyes became amazingly soft, a cloudy blue-green that was exactly the colour of a summer sky at sunset, just before the sun leaks into it. They clung to his and all about them was nothing but the hazed unreality of the whirling dancers who were filling the floor, of the chattering men and women whose voices rose to make themselves heard above the sound of the music and only they, Conal and Jenna, were clear, sharp, and only to each other.

"Excuse me," he murmured to Laura, who had launched into a humorous description of the social structure of Marfield. He smiled at her briefly and then began to make his way round the edge of the floor in the direction of Jenna Townley, leaving his brother and sister-in-law open-mouthed and speechless.

She saw him coming. This was not the first ball she had attended. She had been taught by her governess and by her Mama the unwritten guidelines to which a girl such as herself must adhere. At other balls and dances she had never lacked for partners and would not this evening. Though she was not the fashionable beauty gentlemen seemed to prefer, she was a good dancer, had a clever though sharp tongue, was lively and funny. She made her partners laugh and of course, she was an heiress. She was the eldest daughter of her father and everything he had would come to her. Her sisters, of course, would have splendid dowries, but most of what was Jonas Townley's would on the day he died, be hers. There was a row of chairs where girls who had neither looks, charm nor expectations sat for hours on end, hoping a brother or a father would conjure up a gentleman with whom they might take to the floor at least once, but Jenna Townley had never sat there.

Her eyes, which had begun to snap with excitement, her heart, which had begun to hammer with joy, her mind, which was blank with confusion, her whole being was occupied at that precise moment with one man, with Conal Macrae who was striding towards her mama with his purpose plain.

"Mrs Townley," he said courteously, bowing his head. Her mama looked up, startled, since they were not acquainted.

"Sir?"

"You don't know me, ma'am, but I would be glad if you would allow me to introduce myself. I am related to Mark Eason. His half-brother, Conal Macrae."

Jenna watched him, mesmerised and breathless.

"Of course, Mr Macrae. Laura has spoken of you." Her mama held out her hand and he bowed over it, bringing it to within half an inch of his lips. Still Jenna watched him, fascinated, wide-eyed, her lips parted in anticipation. He did not look at her and she was bewitched by his cleverness.

He smiled down at her mama, a lop-sided smile of such devastating charm Jenna felt her heart lurch in her breast.

"I almost feel as if I know you too, Mrs Townley, Laura sings your praises to such an extent. Your school and . . . shelter, do you call it? are very dear to her."

"And to me as well, Mr Macrae, and it is kind of you to say so, but is not Laura here, and Mark?"

"They are, and will be across presently, Laura said," the lie slipping easily from between his smiling lips.

"Well then, I must introduce you to Mrs Graham whose husband is Marfield's leading banker."

"Mrs Graham."

"And Mrs Hamilton. Mr Hamilton is a coal owner."

"Mrs Hamilton."

"And this is Mrs Ellison."

"Mrs Ellison."

"And this is my eldest daughter, Jenna. Jenna, may I introduce Mr Conal Macrae who is half-brother to Mr Eason." Her mama's eyes twinkled and for a scant second mother and daughter shared that bond of secret laughter which was special between them and which also said that Nella Townley was not born yesterday and saw through Conal Macrae's subterfuge as though it was made of glass.

"Miss Townley."

"Mr Macrae."

"Perhaps, Miss Townley, if you have a dance free we might—?"

"Yes," baldly interrupting his polite question.

She stood up, brushing past her mother's skirts and with an almost indecent haste and eagerness, Mrs Hamilton, Mrs Graham and Mrs Ellison agreed, moved into Mr Macrae's outstretched arms.

"I barely recognised you." He was smiling, his face so close to hers she could smell his breath which was fresh and yet contained the lingering masculine fragrance of cigars and brandy. His right arm was snug and tight across her lower back, holding her much too close for decency and his left hand clasped her right where it fitted perfectly. Her hair *was* fragrant, his senses told him as a wayward strand of it drifted across her mouth.

"I know." Her eyes were steady, without pretence or guile as they looked into his.

"You do?"

"Oh yes," for tonight she was a woman, and different.

"Your eye is very fetching." His narrowed eyes moved across her face in frank admiration.

She smiled at him without offence and from the edge of the ballroom where she sat, Nella Townley recognised the smile and felt the first stirring of disquiet move in her. She began to pray that Jonas would stay where he was in the card-room, at least until the dance was over for if he came out now and saw his daughter in the embrace – there could be no other word to describe it – of Mark Eason's brother, his anger would be dreadful. It was a waltz, slow and graceful, the couples floating and dipping but Mr Macrae and Jenna seemed to drift much, much slower than they should, their arms tight about one another, their faces close and surely, dear God, surely he was not about to kiss her? What was he thinking of? He must know that Jenna was an innocent, untried girl whose reputation must not be tarnished in any way; that the whole of Marfield was gawking at them, then at her, Jenna's mother, to see what she would do about it and what could she do short of stamping on to the ballroom floor and dragging her daughter from the man's arms, which would only make it worse. How could Jenna show her up like this? And him! He was a man of the world, probably about thirty by the look of him. He had a dark, determined face, a stubborn chin with a cleft in it, a humorous smile, good teeth, a fall of thick, dark hair; the sort of attractive whimsical man who would appeal to any woman and Jenna was no exception.

They did not speak much. Jenna was well aware of the furore this waltz with Conal Macrae would cause. She was also well aware of the peril she was putting herself, and him, in, for her papa's temper was hazardous and he was not in the least concerned with who might be watching it explode. He was, on the whole, a quiet man, sometimes going deep into silences which troubled his children but Mama had explained that Papa had suffered a great sorrow in his younger days, one which would never be talked about, by him or her but they must be

patient and kind with him and he would soon be himself
again, she told them. And so he was, but his temper was
short, especially where the safety of his daughters and
their cousin Bryony was concerned and she knew at the
furthest edges of her mind that he would not care for the
way in which Conal Macrae was dancing with her.

"Can we meet tomorrow?" she said abruptly as the
dance came to an end.

"I beg your pardon?" He was clearly startled.

"You heard me. Can we not meet . . . somewhere?"
Her gaze was intense, and from her chair at the side of
the ballroom her mother watched anxiously.

"Miss Townley . . . Jenna, you really must not . . . "

"Don't pretend, please. You asked me to dance and so
you must feel that . . . well . . . "

"What are you trying to say, lassie?" His voice
was gentle.

"Where we met yesterday . . . please. I just want to
talk." She had become breathless. "Please, Mr Macrae."

"Well, I dinna . . ."

"Please say yes."

"Your mama is . . . well, you must not look at me like
that, Jenna Townley or the whole town will be gossiping
even more than it already is. I'll take you back to your
mama before I do you more harm."

"Tomorrow . . . early?" Her voice was husky but he
did not answer.

She did not see him again that evening which she
passed through in a daze. The violins played their polkas,
their quadrilles and their waltzes and she danced every
one, laughing and brilliant, shimmering and sparkling so
that the young men were enchanted, clustering to dance
with her to the chagrin of every young lady present. It
would have been a triumph for her had it happened
last week, or the day before yesterday but she had no
thought in her head as they admired and flattered her

beyond her need to get it all over and done with so that tomorrow might soon be here. She was tireless as she circled the room with first one and then the other, captivating them all but as circumspect as even the most strict papa demanded. The appalling incident of her waltz with Mark Eason's relative was forgotten, or at least overlooked by those who had witnessed it and when her papa came from the card-room to dance with her mama he cast his fond look of approval on Jenna as she waltzed by with James Lockwood. It would suit her papa admirably to be allied, through her and James, with Fred Lockwood, a coal owner like himself. She smiled at the thought, a secret smile which intrigued James Lockwood to such an extent he took the unprecedented step of asking if he might call on her the next day.

"Will you not be at the colliery, James? Surely your papa does not allow you to gad about making afternoon calls? I know mine wouldn't," raising her eyebrows over his shoulder at her mama.

"I am not a boy, Jenna," James replied stiffly, "and my father is old. Jonathan and I" – Jonathan was James's married brother— "virtually run the colliery and I can certainly take some time off if I've a mind to."

"And you have a mind to call on me, have you?" she asked him flippantly dwelling still, not on this pompous ass who held her in his arms and who, he seemed to be telling her, was doing her some honour, but on the rapture of being in another man's arms before twenty-four hours had gone by. It had come on her so suddenly, this heavenly feeling, this exciting rush of her senses to meet his. Conal Macrae. Oh, sweet, sweet Jesus . . . she could hardly wait, smiling up into James Lockwood's face with such radiance he missed his step, wondering as he did so why he had not realised before the absolute rightness of bestowing on Miss Jenna Townley the undoubted privilege of paying her court.

Chapter Four

He was there, exactly where she had left him on the day she had fallen at his feet. He wore the same casual clothing and his hair fell across his forehead in a dark sweep.

"You managed to get away then?" was all he said in a lazy tone. He had his back to the broad trunk of an oak tree, his arms folded across his chest, indolently leaning as though she had come across him unexpectedly and his careless unconcern did not please her. Last night, surely, he had been more than curious about her; she had distinctly seen it in the depths of his eyes, despite her own inexperience of such things. A stirring of something, which he had not managed to hide, a warmth which had called to her own but now he was smiling at her as he had done at their first meeting.

She was not to know that Conal Macrae had spent an almost sleepless night going over and over in his mind the amazing depth and folly of his surprising interest in the seventeen-year-old daughter of the man who employed his own half-brother. It was folly which had begun only the day before yesterday; which had flowered as he took her in his arms last night, but which must be ended at once. It was going to be difficult when she was looking at him with those great shining turquoise eyes of hers, eyes which revealed everything he had awoken in her young woman's heart but it had to be done. Great God, she was

59

no more than a child, a schoolgirl, thirteen years younger than he was. He would need to be prudent, gentle even, for she was at that age when girls fall easily into love and could be badly hurt by it. What he felt was no more than what any man would feel when an attractive young female wanders across his path, he told himself and there had been more than a few of those in his life. Not as young as this one perhaps, for his taste was somewhat more sophisticated.

"Conal," she said slowly, ready to smile, relishing his name for the first time on her lips, at least out loud.

"Miss Townley." He grinned and, straightening up, bowed in her direction. "A pleasant morning, is it not?" which it was. A morning like the one on which they had met, white with hoar frost and the thin layer of snow that remained. She was in blue today, a rich blue cloak with a hood edged in soft white fur. Her face, rosy with the cold and with her excitement, was framed by it, snapping red curls caught in it and wisping back over the hood.

"I was only saying to Mark that it's just the day for a walk though I dare say we shall have more snow by nightfall."

The expression on her face changed. "What are you talking about the weather for?" she demanded abruptly. "We surely didn't arrange to meet just to exchange pleasantries on what sort of a day it was."

She moved a step closer to him and his heart surged amazingly towards her and yet at the same time sank to his boots. It was an exercise his inner mind felt the need to laugh at, or even sneer at for he was no callow youth to be talking of hearts and such romantic nonsense; nevertheless he experienced a surprising emotion he could not describe. It was not going to be easy, not with this headstrong, forthright girl who had no time, it seemed, for the rules which said the lady must let the gentleman take the lead. She said whatever came into her head. Last night was real to her and she would not be fobbed off with the pretence that it had been no more than a moment's flirtation. He had been a fool, worse, a damned fool, and cruel, to have agreed to a meeting but then last night his foolish male curiosity had ruled his head. There you go again, he told himself irritably, talking bloody nonsense when it was your flesh which led you into this. Your male flesh which had touched hers. Your eyes which looked at her and were pleased with what they saw and your masculinity which simply wanted to move on in the natural progression of what takes place between a man and a woman.

"Shall we walk?" he said, doing his best to ignore the sharp accusation in her voice and eyes.

"Why should we walk? I thought you wanted to kiss me?"

His insides melted into laughter and it was all he could do not to leap forward, pull her into his arms and kiss her, as she wanted him to, until she was breathless. She was quite unique, quite magnificent, honest and . . . and a woman it would be easy to love but he must not let her weaken him. He was to go home this afternoon though he did not intend to tell her so, cutting his stay with his brother short, but dear God, she was going to be hard to resist.

"Miss Townley," he laughed, "has your mama not told you that young ladies don't ask strange gentlemen to kiss them. Indeed if they did . . ."

"I have not discussed kissing with my mama, Conal. I have never been kissed, you see and I should like the first to be yours," and the last, her young heart whispered inside her, for already she knew even if he did not.

"Really, Miss—"

"Stop playing this game, Conal. My name is Jenna."

"Jenna, very well then. Come and walk with me, Jenna. You shall tell me all about yourself and I shall do the same. Let us at least start with the civilities. See, take my arm . . ."

"Dammit, Conal, don't do this. You are pretending you are a gentleman who has just met a lady and that you must treat her as though she was a ninny or a simpering mannequin who would faint if you so much as put a finger on her arm. I am neither of these and I will not faint."

She pushed back her hood, her hand somewhat unsteady. She had bundled her hair into a chenille net at the back of her head and the morning sun lit it to copper flame. The beauty of it, and of her imploring eyes caught his breath in his chest but he was beginning to feel impatience with her and with himself for being so affected by her.

"Good God, Jenna, what do you expect me to do? You must not act this way, really you must not. There are men who wouldna be so . . . so considerate with you, believe me. They would take advantage of . . . of your offer, and of your youth."

She smiled then and his damned heart trembled against his breastbone. He felt the uncertainty begin in him and he was aware that the difference in their ages no longer seemed to matter. He turned away so that she might not see his face. She was hot-tempered, imperious, arrogant, but she was sweet, so sweet and funny it was taking all his strength not to do as she asked. And she damn well knew it, that's why she was smiling. Sweet Jesus, the sooner he left Marfield the better and damn the impulse that had made him come in the first place.

He turned back to her, ready to be angry, to make her angry so that she would take offence and run off home to her mother but she was still smiling, a demure smile which should have warned him, he realised later. When was Jenna Townley ever demure? Even he, on the strength of only three meetings had come to know that.

She took his arm in a polite, ladylike gesture, her

demeanour as modest and innocent as any mama could ask for.

"Very well," she said, "let's walk. I should have brought Duff and Dory then you could have shown me how to get them to sit the way they did the other day. I must admit to being indulgent with them but they are such good-natured fools. Now then, won't you tell me about you and Mr Eason? He and Mrs Eason are great friends of ours and we none of us knew he had a brother."

"No, I don't suppose you would." He allowed her hand to rest in the crook of his arm while she led him on to the broad, frozen path which meandered through Seven Cows Wood, across Roundhill Pasture and on into Beggars Wood. They could have skirted it, keeping to the open field which stretched all the way to Heigh House where the Easons lived but Jenna, without his being aware of it since she knew these parts and he didn't, guided Conal into the wood where they would not be seen.

"How did it happen? You and Mr Eason, I mean."

He sighed, doing his best to ignore the pressure of her hand on his arm, then he began to talk.

"I was born in Scotland as I'm sure you can tell though I've no' as much Scots in my accent as I had."

Her eyes were soft as they looked up into his face, studying him unobserved as he stared off between the trees and back into his past.

"Mmm," she murmured encouragingly.

"Aye, well, I didna know of Mark until I was a lad of nine or ten when my mother, who was his mother too, thought I was old enough to understand, I suppose. My father was her second husband, d'you see? She was widowed young and being somewhat impoverished, from what I gathered, she lived with her first husband's parents who paid for Mark's education. She met my father, God knows how, for she was kept close by her in-laws. When she married him she went to live in Scotland with him, naturally. To give Mark a chance of a good education, for my father wouldna pay out good money for another man's son, she left him with his grandparents."

He paused, his face pensive as if his mother's pain, though he had not known of it then, was something he could well imagine.

"Was she . . . sad?"

"Och aye, times, for wouldna any mother be sad to lose a son, but she made no fuss of it. It wasn't until she died and I found a letter Mark had written to her that I knew his name or where he lived. My father wouldna have liked it, ye ken. He was a . . . a hard man."

Again he stopped, his thoughts far away, barely aware of her beside him as memory took him back to his boyhood. To the sad woman who had been his mother and the stern man who had made her that way.

"Mark must have been eleven or twelve when she married my father and I was born a year later," he went on, "and, as I said, my mother told me about him when I was ten or so. I was not then particularly interested in my 'foreign' half-brother who must have been in his twenties, I suppose . . ."

"Foreign?"

"Och aye." He grinned down at her. "Any man not born a Scot is a foreigner. A Sassenach."

"Pardon?"

"Sassenach. That's what a Scot calls an Englishman."

"Really, and what does an Englishman call a Scot?" she asked tartly. "I'm sure I could find a suitable title."

"Aye, I've no doubt, lassie." He stopped for a moment, turning her to face him. His face was serious again. His eyes searched hers then his gaze dropped to her mouth and her heart bounded. He was going to kiss her. He was . . . dear God . . . at last he was going to kiss her. She felt her body sway a little, eager to be next to his, to be as close as she could possibly get with nothing between them but the clothes they wore but suddenly his face changed, became sharp, hard even and he cleared his throat, blinking. Lifting his head he moved away from her and she had no choice but to follow, pushing her hand into the crook of his arm again. It seemed he had lost his place in his story, confused with something and she was not to know it was caused by the pounding in his blood and the glossy ripeness of her mouth pouting ready for his kiss, but she found it for him again.

"You were brought up in Scotland?" she questioned.

"Aye," he said thankfully, glad to have his mind put back on track. "My father was the second son of a Low-land laird. Macrae of Glencairn my grandfather is known as. The Macraes have land near the Loch of Glencairn in Renfrewshire and my Uncle Angus, who will be the next laird, and my father and aunts, seven in all, were born and brought up there. My uncle Angus, who was seven years older than my father, married young and his wife bore him five sons so you can see my father was well aware that there'd be no living for him or his sons off the land of Glencairn. He was nearly forty when he married my mother and, having always been interested in the ships which moved up and down the Clyde, only a hop and a jump from Glencairn, he persuaded my grandfather to help him set up in business there. The shipping business. Steamships. It began on the Clyde, you know. You'll not have heard of the *Charlotte Dundas* but she was the world's first successful steam-driven ship. March 1802 she was built in a workshop on the River Clyde and on her maiden trip towed two seventy-ton barges for a distance of twenty miles. Aye, a grand wee ship, my father said, for he saw her when he was a laddie. There were many steamships from then on, plying between Glasgow and Greenock, paddle steamers, pleasure boats, ye ken, but he began with only one small vessel, a freighter sailing from the Clyde down the coast, taking manufactured metals and ores, pig-iron and such like to Liverpool and fetching back anything he could get as cargo, anything from rock salt for the fishing industry to tobacco, palm oil and hemp."

He stopped walking and so did she, both of them leaning their backs against the trunk of an old sweet chestnut tree which was almost six feet wide at its base and a hundred feet tall. The massive trunk which extended right up into the crown of the tree was grey with age, its surface cracked into deep fissures which spiralled just as though the tree had slowly twisted as it grew. Their booted feet rested in its wide roots and all about them, spreading in a crisp, snapping sea of frost were mosses and fungus and wood sorrel crystallised in their winter coats. As old as the oldest tree in the country the chestnut was, standing for hundreds of years through the reigns of Henry VII, Henry VIII, Mary and Elizabeth and on until it still flourished in this reign of their good little Queen Victoria. Its branches were broad and bare in their black and white symmetry, a lace canopy over the heads of the absorbed man and woman.

Conal stared reflectively through the winter sunshine silhouetting the trunks of the widely spaced trees which made up the small and pretty woodland, some straight and tall as the masts on a sailing ship, others bent, their age forcing them into contorted shapes like old gentlemen suffering the distortion of rheumatism. Black and white and gold and beside him was the fiery helmet of the girl's hair, the vivid flowing blue of her cloak, the brilliance of her eyes. She was waiting for him to go on. She was interested, he could see that, and her interest was alive in those beautiful eyes.

Without thinking, almost without noticing he did it, he took her hand, watching with fascination the sable centre of her eyes dilate sharply at his touch. The blue around them became bluer as she blinked slowly, languorously, her long eyelashes creating a temporary shadow on her peached cheek.

"Go on," she said huskily.

"My father made a small success, enough to buy my mother a house on the banks of the Clyde where she and I used to watch the trading ships moving up and down the river. My father bought another small ship. He called her *Mary Macrae* for my mother. He did love her, you see. The first, purchased before he met her, was *Sea Serpent*. He did well enough, I suppose, but he was an ambitious and far-sighted man and he could see that though trading down to Liverpool and back was profitable, how much more lucrative if he traded *from* Liverpool and not just to it. Tentacles going from there up to the north of Scotland, to the coasts of Cumberland and Lancashire, to north and south Wales, to Bristol and Hayle and the ports of the south coast of England. Not just the main ones but to all those on the small creeks and estuaries where, as yet, there was no reliable railway system. Do you see?"

Indeed she did for was she not the daughter of Jonas Townley and as his daughter had she not been possessed from the moment she had realised what they were and who owned them with the working of her father's collieries? She could understand this canny Scot who was Conal Macrae's father for in his shoes she would do the same. Look for other markets, outlets where his cargoes would be welcome; look for cargoes which would bring the best return, expand, build more ships, steam or sail, wherever there was a need for anything she could carry, across the seas to America perhaps and even as far as . . .

"Aye, I see you do," Conal said softly as he watched the excitement, the interest, the wonder, the determination chase one another across her vivid face. "Well, so did my father and fourteen years ago, when I had finished my schooling, we moved to Liverpool. He rented premises on the corner of Chapel Street and New Quay so that he might watch his ships come in and out of George's Dock. I was taken into the business and for the next two years did my time on the decks of the cargo ships my father owned. The *Mary Macrae* first, then, when another steamship was purchased, named *Gem Star*, on her, steaming as far north as Bowmore and Tobermory and south to Truro and even Poole. I took to it. It was the kind of life a boy, and a young man, relishes, ye ken, and I did well. Then my mother died."

He put the back of her hand to his lips, his eyes unfocused, his breath warm on her skin. She shivered with the delight of it but he was not really aware of her and she could see that his mother's death had been a blow to him.

"It was then I found Mark's name and his address. A letter he had written in 1845. He had married and had a daughter and he wanted Mother to know, the letter said. Perhaps she had meant to go and see him. I dinna ken. The distance between Liverpool and Marfield is only ten miles or so . . . well, I shall never know."

There was a deep, sad silence and Jenna held her breath, wanting him to go on. To go on speaking so that she might hear the deep and pleasing resonance of his voice, the musical and lilting tones of his slight Scots accent. To go on staring out over her head so that she might watch the shifting emotions on his lean, brown face, the strength and humour of his slightly lop-sided mouth and feel the warmth of his lips and breath against the back of her hand.

"Why did you not get in touch with your brother then?" she murmured quietly so as not to break the spell.

"I don't know, really I don't. My father was more affected than I had anticipated by my mother's death and he needed me. We were expanding rapidly as the port of Liverpool itself expanded, as trade grew. The coasting trade had more than doubled since we had moved to Liverpool and our business doubled with it. I pushed Mark to the back of my mind because I was simply too busy to bother with him. My father died five years ago so I was even more involved with the business. Macrae and Son had grown to five ships, with managers and masters, crew and office staff all to be watched and supervised. I had a full life. I sometimes sailed up the coast to see my Scottish family, usually for Christmas or Hogmanay but this time, for some reason, Mark came into my mind and on a whim, nothing more, I wrote to him, He had, of course, been informed of our mother's death. He wrote back immediately and, well, you know the rest."

He continued to stare across the hazed and sun-dappled transparency of the glade in which they stood, his face pensive, dreaming, and it came to her then, from where she didn't know, just as though she could see into his mind, that he was at peace with himself. That, though he didn't voice it, or even acknowledge it, he had fulfilled a wish, a dream if you like, that had been his mother's. He had made a journey she had wanted to make, linked brother to brother and he was more complete because of it.

She watched him, unaware of what was in her face, in the luminous intensity of her eyes and when he looked down at her, smiling a little, she did nothing to hide it. For a full ten seconds their eyes clung then, groaning inwardly at the madness of it but unable to prevent it, he leaned towards her and placed his lips gently on hers, for this was her first kiss. Hers were closed, but warm and slightly moist, moving beneath his but not quite certain what to do next. Her first kiss, he whispered again to himself. An untouched young girl who was ready to trust, to learn, eager to learn anything he might care to teach her. Oh God!

He smoothed his own mouth on hers, moving his head

slightly from side to side, his lips parted a little until he could feel the gradual opening of hers, then her breath which was beginning to quicken. He caught her bottom lip between his own then moved to her long, upper lip, licking it then nipping it gently with his teeth. Soft, soft. He tilted his head and his mouth exerted more pressure, caressing, folding on her own. It became more demanding, opening hers wider and his tongue touched hers and she began to make small mewing sounds deep in her throat. His arms folded about her, holding her strongly against him, one hand at the back of her head as though afraid she might draw away. His lips moved up her cheek to her eyebrow, to each closed and quivering eyelid, the tender bruise about her eye and her breath rasped in her throat, forced out of her mouth and against his own throat, warm and shuddering. He moved down again to her jawline and she threw back her head with a small moan, arching her back and throat strongly. Her hands had gone to his hair, pulling his face down to her and he held her even more tightly, wanting to hurt her a little for she was exciting his flesh against his mind's will. He wanted to savour the warm, womanly smell of her skin and hair, to blend her long limbs to his. She shifted her body, doing her best to get even closer to him and his mouth came down again on hers, but more urgently, more demandingly since, his body told him, he was a man holding a willing woman and by God, what could be better than that? Her cloak, and his, had fallen open and he could feel the firmness, the roundness of her breasts against his chest. It seemed she did not mind what he did to her as he mastered her. His male body rejoiced in it, in his triumphant domination of hers. His hands moved to the soft flesh of her throat, caressing the flaring pulse beneath her chin with his thumbs then one enquiring finger travelled down across her bodice to the hard peak of one full breast.

"Oh God," he moaned in the back of his throat, pleading with her to stop him for he could not do it alone.

"Conal . . . Conal . . ." Her breath fanned his cheek and her moist mouth, as she grew more confident, found the soft and erotic place beneath his ear. Her hands fluttered about him, about his face and neck and chest, pressing their warmth through his shirt, smoothing his nipples which instantly hardened. She was so lovely . . . lovely . . . The hot, sweet smell of her whipped through him . . . lovely . . . her skin . . . what did it smell of? . . . flowers . . . some flowers and it was like satin, creamy . . . rich . . .

She arched her back even further and the line of buttons down the length of her bodice presented themselves to his hands which fell on them eagerly. He would have undone them, every tiny one, feverishly obsessed with having her naked flesh under his touch . . . her full breasts, her nipples, round and hard and sweet in his hands and mouth but when her fingers raced to help his, scarcely able, like him, to wait another moment; when she moaned, like a creature which is injured in some way, he came abruptly, agonisingly, gaspingly . . . oh thank God . . . thank God . . . to his senses. She was trembling, unsteady and when she began to whimper, clawing at him, crying for him to go on, it was all he could do to hold her.

"I love you, Conal . . . love me . . . please love me," she cried, her face anguished for she already knew it was not to be, her hair a rippling, living mass of fire about her contorted face.

"Dear God, girl . . . here?"

"Where then . . . where?"

"For Christ's sake . . . calm down, Jenna . . . stop it . . . stop it, darling."

"Conal, please . . . I love you."

"No . . . no, you don't." He had her in his arms now,

held against the steadying rock of his body though her closeness was agony to him. She continued to writhe, her own awakened unsatisfied woman's body alive with sensations she had not known existed. There were hot tears on her face, tears of frustration, of anger and of love, the love she had been ready to give to him with all the simple, uncomplicated ardour of her young and passionate heart. She was not subtle or artful. All her life she had said exactly what she thought or felt and she could see no reason to be different now. But she was beginning to calm, accepting that this was not the moment, her own intelligence whispering to her, as though to placate her throbbing body, that he was right. This was not the place. Not here in the frozen stillness of the wood. They needed warmth, comfort, seclusion when they gave themselves to one another for the first time, and she would find it. She looked no further then that. Yet! She looked no further than the moment when they would do whatever it was he was to do to her. Whatever it was she was to do to him. His body and hers . . . She loved him and he would love her. She would make him love her!

But true to herself she could not pretend. Tipping back her head so that she could look into his face but keeping his arms tight about her, she smiled.

"I love you, Conal," and he could see she thought it was true.

"And I . . . I find you most . . . agreeable too, Jenna Townley," he said lightly.

"Agreeable? Is that all?" She put her lips against his, moving them softly and sweetly as he had just shown her and he could feel, along with the warmth and moistness of it, the smile that lay beneath it.

"Jenna, you really must stop this, and so must I . . ."

"Why?" she challenged him, her face alive with delight and he could feel the irritation – with himself – mounting in him.

"This must stop, Jenna. No young lady should . . ."

"Don't, Conal, don't spout that nonsense to me. You know I am not a young lady, at least not in the way you mean. I love you. That's the truth of it and I shall keep on saying it until you admit you love me."

"Lassie, you're not to do this."

"Kiss me then. Just once before we go."

"Oh, Christ Jesus . . ." but he could no more resist her as her mouth clung like a ripe peach to his than he could resist her laughing, flaunting, challenging beauty. By God, it was a damn good job he was leaving this afternoon and the sooner he was back in Liverpool and living his own life again the sooner he would forget this whole delightful but mad episode. There was a certain lady, wife to a business acquaintance of his who was well versed in the art of fulfilling the needs of a man and who was pleased with what Conal could do for her since her husband was elderly. It was all very discreet and sophisticated just as he liked it to be, just as she liked it to be, with no mention of the love Jenna imagined she felt.

He kissed her gently now, brushing away with his lips the traces of her tears. He cupped her face with his hard brown hands, hands which still had calluses on the palms put there over ten years ago when he was a youth on his father's ships. He smoothed his thumbs across her silken flesh, looking down into the clear, steady gaze of her eyes. God in heaven, but she would have to learn to hide the emotions, the feelings, the very thoughts in her head which showed so visibly on her face. He hoped he had not hurt her too much with his rejection of all she had been so willing to give him and with the worst rejection he would offer her when she discovered he had left without a word. Perhaps he would leave her a note . . . no, *no*, by God, he musn't . . . but she was so . . . Dear God, but he could find it in his heart to . . . she was sweet, lovely and she had touched him as no other woman had ever done but she was no more than a child, dammit . . . Dammit, it just would not do!

"What are you thinking, Conal?" she urged him to tell her and again he marvelled at her youth, for what mature woman would ask that of a man she had just met?

"That you must go home or there will be a hue and cry," he lied.

"No, you weren't. You were thinking of love. Of me and love."

He wondered at her perception, pulling her hard against him, tenderness flowing through him in overpowering waves. Tenderness and regret and . . . no . . . *no* . . . nothing else, he told himself as he put her from him.

"Go home, Jenna." His face was serious so that for a moment she felt a shaft of terror pierce her heart.

"When will I see you, Conal?" Her fear showed in her mouth which trembled and in her eyes which seemed about to brim with tears.

"Your papa has, I believe, invited us to dine with you tonight," he managed to say calmly. It was no lie, of course, since Laura had told him of it this morning at breakfast. There were innumerable invitations, it appeared, from prominent families in Marfield, those who had heard of Mark Eason's younger brother, a successful man and a bachelor and one who the mamas at least would be eager to have at their table. No doubt word would have got about that he was a prosperous ship owner, a gentleman, grandson of a Scottish laird, for these things took no time at all to spread and would be irresistible to husband-hunting young ladies.

Well, they would be disappointed, at least for now, since he supposed he would return to visit his brother in the future. He would like to get to know him, and his wife Laura who had, strangely, reminded him of his own mother. His niece, Verity, had seemed a sweet-natured child and she was, after all, the only niece he would ever have. But for now, until the girl who rested so quietly, so perfectly against the length of his body, her head beneath his chin, her hair brushing his skin, had got over this attachment she had formed for him and found someone of her own age to love, he must stay away.

He watched her go, striding off with that coltish grace which had not yet quite become the elegance of a woman. Her hair blazed like a bronze chrysanthemum against the sharp and frozen whiteness of the wood and her blue cloak swung about her as she turned.

"I'll see you tonight, Conal," she called, then, her face breaking into a brilliant smile, she blew him a kiss. His heart moved in his chest and he almost called to her, almost called her back to him, almost ran after her, wanting to lift her into his arms, to crush her against him but he did none of these things.

Not wanting to see her go he turned abruptly on his heel and strode off towards his brother's house.

Chapter Five

Simeon Townley glared across the breakfast table at Jenna, the expression on his young face one of complete astonishment, then he turned to the man who sat at its head.

"You can't mean to allow her to come down with us, Sir? Not below ground? I've never heard anything so . . . so preposterous in my life. I appreciate that one day it will all belong to her—" the idea obviously not to his liking— "but to expect to be taken to the pit face where the men will be working is surely not . . . not decent. It's far too dangerous for a woman, not to mention awkward, hampered as she will be by her skirts, and besides which, the men won't like it."

"It's you who are being ridiculous, Simeon Townley, and anyway, it's none of your business." Jenna's face was flushed with indignation. "If Papa says I may go then what has it to do with you? Years ago women worked in the pit . . ."

"Yes, and got themselves killed in it as well."

" . . . and if I am to be hampered by my skirts then I will put on my breeches . . ."

Jenna stopped speaking abruptly and what might be called a shifty expression flitted across her face. Her mama, who was placidly spooning creamy porridge into her mouth, well used, it seemed, to these running battles between Jenna and Simeon, looked up, her eyes questioning, and every smooth and shining head, those of Jenna's sisters and cousin, turned in her direction.

"Breeches, Jenna?" her mama asked hazardously. "What breeches are those?" and all about the table and at the back of the room where the maidservants, Dolly and Tilly waited, ready to serve the family, everyone held their breath. Except Simeon.

"So that's where my breeches went," he exploded. "I might have known it was you. 'Let me help you look for them,' you said when they went missing, pretending to look high and low and what I want to know is why? Though I suppose the reason is pretty obvious." Simeon's face was crimson in his rage. "You've been itching to ride ever since I got my first pony, haven't you, hanging about and begging me for a go when Papa said no to you, sneaking out when the grooms weren't looking and galloping round the paddock with your skirts above your knees. Oh yes, don't pretend with me, my girl. It's Leander, isn't it? You've been riding him while I've been at school, haven't you? Just wait until I get my hands on those bloody lads in the stable . . ."

"Simeon, control yourself," Jonas Townley growled, "and watch your language with the ladies."

"Those bloody lads in the stable, as you so politely put it, had nothing to do with it. I can saddle a horse myself, you know. It doesn't take brains otherwise you wouldn't be able to do it, or even a great deal of strength though men pretend it does so that they can prevent women from doing it."

"So you admit it? You have been taking Leander out behind my back and wearing my bloody breeches to do it! Well, let me tell you this, lady—"

"Simeon, just watch that mouth of yours, Sir," his guardian thundered, "and you, Jenna, let's have an explanation, if you please. What the devil goes on in this house when my back is turned, Nella?" he beseeched his wife to tell him. "Did you know anything about this, and if not, why not? Do you mean to tell me this . . . this child's been roistering about the countryside on Simeon's animal and in Simeon's breeches and you knew nothing about it?" He glared perilously at Nella Townley.

"Of course I didn't, Jonas." His wife, whose own temper was none too steady, answered him as patiently as she could. "If I had, do you think I would have allowed it?" She turned her icy gaze on her daughter and Jenna felt the despair trickle through her veins and clamp about her sinking heart. With one word, one stupid, unthinking slip she had threatened not only the slim hope she had harboured that her father would allow her to accompany him and Simeon into the Townley Colliery but had destroyed the one escape, the one joy left in her sterile life, which was her unfettered – and secret – gallop out at dawn on Simeon's roan, Leander.

For the past four weeks, ever since she had found – and lost – Conal Macrae, it had been her only solace. She sometimes wondered how she had managed to recover, if she could be said to have recovered, from the quite dreadful blow he had dealt her when he had failed to turn up at Bank House for dinner with Mr and Mrs Eason who had apologised on his behalf, saying that urgent business had called him back to Liverpool.

Even in the depth of her own desolation she had been aware of her mother's relief. Her mother had not been pleased with her on the night of the ball, nor with Conal Macrae who should have known better, and if she had been aware of their meeting in Seven Cows Wood the next day she would have been even less pleased.

Jenna had said nothing. In fact she had been mim as a mouse all that evening, hardly eating any of Mrs Blaney's superb veal and half way through the meal had excused herself saying she had a headache.

He had not come again. He was a busy man, Mrs

Eason had told Jenna's mama, unaware of the knot
of tension which had held Jenna in her seat as they
sipped afternoon tea in the Bank House drawing-room.
She had been surprised, Jenna could tell, when Mama
adroitly changed the subject, and no doubt later Mama
would explain to Mrs Eason why she had done so but
in the meanwhile no one, not even Conal Macrae's
sister-in-law, would see Jenna Townley brought low by
Conal Macrae's indifference to her. She had caused her
mother, she knew quite well, some anxious moments.

But it was her freedom to escape from them all, from
her sisters and the restrictions set about her by her mother,
from Miss Hammond and her own upbringing, away on
the smooth muscular back of Simeon's spirited roan
which had pulled her together. She had been constantly
amazed on her wild gallops through Seven Cows Wood,
across Roundhill Pasture, leaping Old Lady Brook, over
the fence which guarded her papa's land and on to the
common, that no one had seen her, or if they had, had
not reported it to her father. Of course, in Simeon's
breeches, a warm jacket and scarf and an old cap she
had filched from a hook on the back of the stable door
and into which she had stuffed her hair, perhaps no one
she met had recognized her. Leander would be known,
naturally, since he was an expensive, well-bred mount but
she supposed those crossing the common, as she streaked
past them, would think she was a young groom exercising
the roan.

It was those early morning rides and her hope, her
vision, her absolute determination to make her father see
that she meant to take up her inheritance, to work at what
would one day be hers and not just leave it to be managed
by Simeon and the viewers in his charge that had got her
through the past weeks. She must have some purpose in
her life, she told herself desperately, some undertaking
with which to fill her tedious days and the only ambition

in her which made any sense, which gave her any joy, was that of running what would one day be hers. She would never marry, she told herself fiercely. Since she had left the schoolroom, put up her hair and been allowed to mingle in society with young bachelors there had been no man to stir her heart. Only Conal Macrae and he did not want her. He had kissed her carelessly, taken her young heart and then walked away. She could not forget him but she would not let him spoil her life, the life she meant to have. She was quite well aware, for hadn't he said so many times, that her father meant to put her cousin Simeon in charge of the collieries when he himself was gone. Perhaps give him a decent percentage of the profit, stock or something, or was it shares in the splendid business he had built up. She also knew that it would be completely unacceptable for a woman to go down into the pit but that was a job Simeon could do for her. With the foremen and viewers to report back to her, he would be in charge underground while she managed the rest. There was talk of Simeon going to university, the same one her father had attended, to gain an engineering degree which, naturally, she could not do but she could certainly sit in her rightful place in Papa's office when the time came. Have it in her charge. Control it, make decisions, have the reins of it in her capable hands, the organisation of it in her clever head.

But she must have some idea of the workings beneath the ground, even if it was only one short visit, one conducted tour, so to speak. A glimpse of what the men did, for goodness sake, if she was to manipulate it all successfully as she knew she was capable of doing.

And now, dear God, now she could see it all slipping away as her dreams of Conal Macrae had slipped away but whereas she could do nothing about Conal, she could fight for this since it was hers. Hers!

She took a deep, controlled breath. "Papa, I'm sorry if I offended you by riding Leander—"

"Offended me! You have *terrified* me. Dear God, girl, have you any idea of the danger you put yourself in by what you do, by what you keep on doing? Apart from the unseemliness of a girl such as yourself going about alone, and in men's breeches . . ."

"I won't do it again, Papa, I promise, if only . . ."

"No, you damn well won't." Simeon crashed his clenched fist on the table and at the back of the room Tilly squeaked in alarm, exchanging glances with the more phlegmatic Dolly. Dolly had been housemaid at Bank House for over twenty years and had been a spectator at many a set-to between Jonas Townley and his father-in-law, Ezra Fielden, and between Mr and Mrs Townley who had often been at each other's throats in the early years of their marriage though it was hard to believe now. She was used to this kind of thing, her rolling eyes told Tilly. Just be patient and it would blow over, her expression said.

"If you so much as put a hand on that roan again, I'll . . . I'll . . ." Simeon was almost speechless with rage, unable to say, to threaten what he longed to threaten.

"Oh yes, and what will you do, may I ask?" sneered Jenna, unable to restrain herself as she had sworn, only seconds ago, to do. "If you don't watch your language I shall—"

"Will you both be quiet at once! Dear God, it seems that no sooner does Simeon come home from school than we are unable to have a peaceful meal . . ."

"It is not my doing, Sir, " Simeon remonstrated hotly.

"It's never your fault, Simeon Townley, never, and I just—"

"Jenna, hold your tongue." Her mother's voice was like the lash of a whip. Nella Townley, who had been watching the exchange between her husband and the two youngsters with increasing anxiety, stood up imperiously. Jonas's cheeks had turned that alarming shade of puce which had coloured the face of her own father when he was in a wild stampede of rage. He had died of a seizure and by the look of him her beloved husband, torn between these two wilful young people, both set on their own way and in direct opposition to one another, might go the same way.

Yet at the same time she could see why they were as they were. Simeon was a boy not yet sixteen but ready to clench his fists and strike out at anyone who stood in his way, even his guardian, Jonas Townley, and certainly his cousin, Jenna Townley, who was female and therefore must be content with her female lot in life. She must not impede his progress and as for riding his fine thoroughbred roan which was the joy of his life, he was ready to clench his jaw and his fists at anyone who had the temerity to chance it. At least without his permission!

And Jenna, what of her? She was bright and intelligent, clever and brave and her mother, who was the same could see no reason why she should not take hold of her own inheritance as she, in her day, had held on to what was her destiny in life, the charitable shelter and school she had begun on Smithy Brow. Why should her daughter not be trained for it, allowed to control what was hers by law, as other enlightened women in the country were doing? Only a handful, of course, but why should Jenna not be among them?

"Mama, please, please, may I not discuss this with Papa?" Jenna pleaded. "I will be . . . circumspect, I promise. If Simeon will . . . please keep quiet for a moment . . . please . . ." throwing the boy a desperate look.

"Why should I? You might have damaged Leander's legs."

"May Leander turn yellow and rot," she hissed, her control gone again.

"That's it, I've had enough." Jonas Townley leaped to his feet, throwing his napkin to the table and overturning his chair with such a crash Tilly dropped several spoons which, in her nervousness, she had begun to polish and the four young girls about the table jumped violently.

"Do sit down, darling, and finish your breakfast," Mrs Townley said soothingly, sitting down herself. "No one is to say another word on the subject, at least not until this evening," when, presumably, everyone would have had a chance to calm down, the expression on her face seemed to say. "See, Dolly," she continued, "pass Mr Townley some of that bacon, oh, and mushrooms. Mrs Blaney's bacon and mushrooms are the best in Marfield, Jonas, you know that. Do sit down, dearest. You and Simeon cannot go underground – be quiet, Jenna" – as her daughter would have interrupted – "without a decent meal inside you. Please, Jonas, for me. Eat just a little."

Gradually the jangling friction eased somewhat. Jonas Townley, his temper calmed by his wife as only she knew how, condescended to address himself to a heaped plate of Mrs Blaney's crisp bacon and mushrooms to which sausage and fried tomatoes had been added and Simeon did the same. The four younger girls bent their smoothly brushed heads over the toast and Mrs Blaney's delicious strawberry jam, only Jenna, still inclined to glare at Simeon, who glared silently back, her hand fiddling with the knife beside her empty plate, refusing to eat.

"Now then, girls," their mama enquired, "have you decided what you are to wear for your party? I know it is not for several weeks yet but these things must be arranged in plenty of time. Miss Compton will be very busy at this time of the year with her spring collection and you must choose your materials soon."

At once, as Nella had intended, the four younger girls were rapturously absorbed with the details of their birthday party which took place on March 21st and Jenna sank back in her chair, thankful for her mother's diplomacy. She listlessly buttered a slice of toast, the heated flush at her cheeks subsiding until her skin was its usual creamy white. Her eyes stared blankly at the toast and her tongue did not taste it when she put it in her mouth. She did her best not to sigh though her heart was heavy with despondency. Her father and Simeon chomped their way through the heaped plates of food Dolly had put before them and she felt the bitterness twist inside her at the unfairness of it. They had both bellowed and displayed their male and arrogant displeasure, not caring what they said for they knew it would make no difference to their lives. No difference to what they would do today, but she had to bite her tongue and grit her teeth and be polite, politic, fight every inch of the bloody way for what was hers, godammit and even then it was not guaranteed. What Simeon was to do this morning with her father should be hers, since one day it would all belong to her and yet she was forced to grind her way slowly, inch by inch, which was against the very heart of her nature, towards her goal, speaking placatingly to Papa, trying to be calm and patient when all she wanted was to leap up when he did and accompany him on his journey into the black and frightening depths of the pit. Oh yes, she was frightened of it, but by God, she'd not let that stop her. She would do it. She would do it but until then she must sit here and listen to the birds twittering, the lunatic sparrow twitterings of Beth and Nancy, of Rose and Bryony as they discussed the merits of saxony or mohair shawls, taffeta or brocade and how many flounces their party dresses were to have. Should they wear silk or gauze or muslin and what colour would suit each one of them best, cream or blue or ivory?

"I'll speak to you in the little parlour, Jenna, if you please," her mama told her as the family rose from the table. Simeon smiled triumphantly for in his youthful opinion a wigging from Aunt Nella was no more than Jenna deserved but her father frowned and was seen to shake his head at his wife as though to beg her not to be too hard on the girl. He was sorry for what had happened, his unhappy glance told his daughter but she must see it would not do. He would have given his right arm to allow her what she wanted but it just would not do!

"Sit down, darling," her mother told her, seating herself in front of the cheerful fire which blazed in the grate. This was the room which no one but the family and servants ever entered, the little parlour, the back parlour tucked away behind the stairs and in which Nella Townley consulted with Mrs Blaney on all household matters. It was here that Jenna, sometimes her mother, sometimes Bryony and her young dog came to be alone for a bit of peace which was often hard to come by at Bank House. Bryony liked her own company, walking for hours in the extensive gardens with her dog, Gilly, or curled up here in a chair with a book when the weather was inclement. Beth and Nancy, both gregarious, liked nothing better than to sew and gossip in one another's company and rarely, if ever, found any use for the room, preferring the cosy nursery or their mama's elegant front drawing-room.

"You really must learn not to argue with your papa, Jenna. Not if you are to achieve what it is you're after," her mama began as soon as Jenna flung herself into her chair, "and do sit up straight, dearest. No lady ever slouches like that. You are almost eighteen, you know."

"Yes, Mama, I do know and I also know I'm not a lady."

"Of course you are, though I know what you mean. I thought the same at your age. I had your aunts to care for though, since my mother was dead and they were so much younger than me."

"I know, Mama."

"I wanted nothing more than to be a man and go about

with my father as you want to do but I knew I couldn't. There was no one else, you see, to attend to Linnet and Dove and I had to wait until they were married before I could, well, not exactly do as I pleased for I was married myself by then but find something which gave me a great deal of . . . satisfaction, fulfilment, I suppose you'd call it. I compromised, that's what I did, when I opened Smithy Brow—"

"Oh God, Mama, it's not the same at all."

Jenna jumped to her feet and flung herself across the room to stare blindly out at the swathe of just opening daffodils which lay as far as the eye could see down the slope at the side of the house. The trees, their leaves only just coming into bud and which in summer hampered the view from this window, allowed her to see right down to the small lake where John and Seth, the gardeners, with their lad Dinty, who had only just recently been taken on, were industriously clearing the weeds which clung to its edge. It was a fine, cold day, blustery by the look of it, the wind ruffling the waters of the lake and causing the family of ducks who lived on it to bob frantically up and down on the small swell.

"Yes it is, Jenna. It is the same and if you'll just be patient you will have what it is you want."

Jenna turned slowly and looked with wonder at her mother. She was sitting in her usual straight-backed posture, as all ladies of her class did, as Jenna had been taught to do, so that her shoulder blades were at least three inches from the chair back, but there was something . . . strange about her. Some tense thing which showed in the dark-shadowed brilliance of her eyes, in the clenching of her hands in her lap and the firm snap of her usually smiling face.

"I don't know what you mean, Mama." Jenna walked carefully back towards her mother, just as though this

somewhat curious turn of events must be treated with
the greatest delicacy.

"There are other ways of achieving your goal than by
the bull at a gate method you employ."

"Mama!"

"Yes, you may well look astounded and sometimes I
must admit I astound myself but . . . well, enough of
that. Now, promise me you will not repeat what I say
to your papa since he would be dreadfully hurt by it."

"Mama, I can't imagine . . ."

"Promise me, Jenna, or I won't help you."

"Help me! Dear Lord, Mama, I can make neither head
nor tail—"

"Will you be still, child, and let me continue."

"Of course, but—"

"No buts. Just promise me that, for the moment, this
is our secret."

Jenna's eyes had begun to glow with excitement. The
room was darkly furnished in the old-fashioned style
favoured by her own grandmother, the wallpaper, the
curtains at the window making it, not dismal, far from
it for it was cosy in the firelight, but shadowed, shrouded
about the walls. In it Jenna's face was a vividly snapping
focus of light, of brightness and vitality and her eyes were
filled with the intoxication of it.

"Oh Lord, Mama, what it it? I can't bear it."

"Promise me."

"Of course I will, darling Mama, but what can
possibly . . .?"

"Jenna, this is serious. If you let me down you could
cause a great deal of damage to my marriage, to my . . .
to your Papa's feelings for me."

"Mama, you're beginning to—"

"Frighten you?"

"Well, yes . . . Heavens, it sounds so . . ."

"Darling, promise me then that this is to be between

you and me. No one else, well perhaps only one or two and they can be trusted, will know of it. Have I your promise?"

Her mother's eyes were almost feverish in their intensity but then so were hers for the excitement, the sheer exhilaration, the powerful energy which burned in her mother was in her too, for was she not Nella Townley's daughter?

"I promise, Mama, on my heart," which belonged to Conal Macrae and always would and was therefore immutable, "I promise to tell not one soul what you are to tell me."

"It is not a question of what I am to tell you, Jenna, but what I am to do to help you . . . get what is rightfully yours."

The two men went down in the cage alone. The banksman touched the peak of his cap respectfully to Mr Eason who was one of the men but he did not recognise the other, a tall, slim lad who kept his head down and his face averted. They both wore sturdy jackets and trousers, hoggets pulled up to their knees and iron-soled clogs, but the second chap had a long woollen scarf twined closely about his chin and neck and his peaked cap was pulled well down over his forehead. The banksman wondered who he was but it was not his place to question Mr Eason. Not on the identity of the lad, nor their reason for going down after the last shift had come up on this Saturday night.

"Them ventilation doors've bin set, Mr Eason," he warned politely, reminding the manager that they must be left closed. Years ago, one Saturday night just like this, before Mr Townley had appointed a man whose job it was to check the trap doors on leaving the pit, a careless collier had left one open. A child, a young hurrier, had closed it when he went down with others on the Monday morning. The closing of it turned the current of air through the workings, drawing gas out in a body to the pit bottom. The candle held by the boy had detonated an explosion which had killed himself and ten others. But Mr Townley was a great one for safety, as much as a pit could be made safe, and the banksman knew he had no need really to remind Mr Eason who was the same.

They were gone a long time, such a long time the banksman was beginning to worry though Mr Eason was a conscientious chap, reliable and trained as a mining engineer so he'd do nowt' daft, not like some who had no respect for the danger below ground. Young colliers who liked nothing better than to show off, to lark about as though they were up on the bloody common, wrestling one another, swaggering with their picks over their naked shoulders, for were they not the "aristocracy" of the colliery? The hewers. The getters of coal and therefore the most important men underground. But there were none down there this Saturday night. They'd all be at the Colliers Arms, drinking and gambling and carrying on like cocks on a dung heap before stumbling home to claim their conjugal rights. Mind you, given the chance he'd do the same!

The two men came up an hour later, the younger one almost running from the cage, gasping and . . . well, if the banksman hadn't known better, ready to faint like a bloody lass. Who in hell was he and what was Mr Eason doing taking some green lad down to't pit bottom, even pit face for all he knew, since they'd been down there near on three hours?

"Aw'reet, Mr Eason?" he asked anxiously as Mr Eason took the lad's arm and led him away. 'Appen he was a young relative of the mine manager's who'd fancied having a look at where the colliers laboured and having done so was overcome by the harshness of it! He wouldn't be the first, nor the last!

"Fine thanks, Kebble. My young friend is unaccustomed to such close confinement but a breath of fresh air will put him right."

"Aye, first time's allus a bit of a facer."

"Indeed, well, good night, Kebble."

"Night, sir."

"Well?"

"Mama, it was appalling." The words, simply said, were all the more compelling because of it.

"I believe so, though I myself have not been down."

"It was . . . well, I know it has been said before but it was like being buried alive. Like being in your own coffin." Jenna shuddered so violently her teeth clicked together. "Mr Eason had a safety lamp but it shone for no more than a yard or two and we just stepped out into . . . into a black space. I had the feeling we were going to tumble into an enormous, bottomless hole. I kept falling on the track and had Mr Eason not held my arm and guided me as though I was blind would have done myself an injury. I was . . . disoriented and . . . Dear heaven, Mama, the smell. The men, they have nowhere to . . . to . . ."

"Relieve themselves?"

"Is that what they call it?"

"That's what I call it though I believe they have a more . . . colourful phrase for it."

"Oh Mama . . ." Jenna subsided into weak laughter.

"So that is one of the reasons why it would not do for you, or any woman of sensibility to go underground. They just relieve themselves wherever there is an abandoned working. Edda Singleton, whose husband was a collier, told me, so of course . . . well, you smelled it so you will know what I mean. And they wear no clothing, did you know that?"

"No . . ." Jenna's voice was faint.

"And years ago, before your father's time, neither did the women who worked there apart from a pair of drawers."

"Mama, how did they manage it?"

"They didn't some of them. They were interfered with . . . you know what I mean, don't you, darling? Men took advantage of them, of their vulnerability. That is one of the reasons I opened the shelter. But I wanted you to see why it would not be acceptable to your papa to have you go down the pit as he does. As Simeon will and so you must stop pestering him to allow it. It is quite possible for you to run the collieries from the pit head. With responsible men, men you can trust to overlook the underground workings I can see no reason why you should not be in full control. You will need to go with Papa and Simeon to the Coal Exchange in Marfield to see how that is run which will cause some consternation, I'm sure, but then, if you are to do this thing you must be prepared for unpleasantness, Jenna."

For a moment her mother's eyes gleamed, twinkled, Jenna would have said. Just as though she was enjoying some enormous joke and her own narrowed in a smile of conspiracy.

"I do believe you are persuading me to . . . to rebellion, Mama."

"No, not that, darling, just a helping hand from one woman to another in this gentlemen's world. The collieries are *yours*, Jenna." The words were spoken with such vehemence, Jenna was surprised since everyone knew that. "But sometimes you have to fight, even for what is yours."

"Like you did, Mama, for Smithy Brow?"

"Well, I suppose so, but Smithy Brow was not my inheritance, as the pits are yours. Smithy Brow was allowed me to . . . placate me, I suppose, since I was a woman determined to do something other than be wife and mother. It was charity work which made it acceptable to a lady such as myself, but you are different. This is different. Now then, one last question before I'm completely satisfied. Would you go underground again if you had to?"

"Of course. I would not like it but I would go."

"I thought so. Very well, let us mount our campaign against Papa."

"She's been down to the pit face, Simeon."

Simeon Townley whirled to face his sister in appalled horror, knowing exactly what she meant, clutching at her arm with a fierceness which almost had her over.

"The pit face? The pit face! Damnation, Bryony, what are you saying, and how the hell d'you know? Even if it's true, which I can't believe since Uncle Jonas would never allow it, how do you know?"

"I overheard her and Aunt Nella talking about it. It was Aunt Nella who arranged it with Mr Eason."

"Bloody hell!"

"But you must say nothing, Simeon, promise me, or they'll want to know how you know and that could be awkward."

"But what does it mean? Surely they don't mean to allow her to run the collieries. Uncle Jonas wouldn't have it and if he did, where would that leave me?"

"Exactly."

"What in hell's name are we to do, Bryony?" Simeon pushed a distracted hand through the thick tumble of his rich ebony curls, disarranging their brushed neatness and they fell at once across his forehead. Though he was not yet sixteen he was tall and exceedingly handsome and was already the focus of a good deal of female admiration. He looked at his sister, begging her to give him an answer and the incongruity of it seemed strange to neither of them. Though Bryony was the younger and would not be fourteen until March she it was who had the ability for quick thinking which her brother lacked. She was clever, he was stubborn. Where he would go at a problem like a carthorse, pushing aside resistance with the brute force of his strong body, she was light, sharp, nimble and cunning. Her brother trusted her and her judgment as he trusted no other person in the world. She had his welfare at heart, as no other person did, not even his guardian, for was he not concerned with his own children? If Bryony advised caution, despite his own impatient need to rush headlong towards a confrontation, then Simeon would proceed cautiously.

"What does it mean, Bryony?" he asked again anxiously. His dog, Blarney, raced beside Gilly through the growing spikes of the wild daffodils which carpeted the grassy slopes of the gardens about Bank House with a trumpet blaze of golden yellow. Both dogs were big, covering the ground so quickly their dark coats were a blur against the green and yellow.

"It means nothing since Uncle Jonas will never allow her to go down, we know that, but we must be careful, Simeon. You must be careful. Make yourself indispensable to Uncle Jonas and, most especially, stay friends with Jenna."

"That won't be easy." His face fell into sullen lines.

"I know, but she is the heir, the eldest girl and cannot be overlooked. You know she has fallen for this Conal Macrae, don't you?"

"No!"

"Yes, and should be encouraged in it."

"Why?"

"Simeon, if she marries him that leaves the field all the more clear for you."

"Bryony, you're a bloody marvel. How in hell d'you know all this?"

Bryony smiled, a smile which lit her already lovely face to a bright incredible beauty.

"Aah, brother mine, it's just a question of knowing where to be at the right moment. And I've had years of practice at that."

Chapter Six

It was the end of February and still he had not come and though for two weeks now she had been allowed to accompany her papa and a somewhat surly Simeon to the coal exchange and the offices at the pit head being patient, or trying to, as Mama had advised, which was hard – it was a bad time for Jenna. She could still not bring herself to believe that he would not simply turn up to claim her. Six weeks since that meeting in Seven Cows Wood. Six weeks since he had kissed her, melted the bones and heart of her, stricken her with this malady of love which was so hard to recover from and though it was her nature to be positive, to be optimistic, she was not a fool and was well aware that a man who is interested in a woman, even if it was no more than the interest of the . . . well . . . purely physical sort with no expectancy of marriage, would not let six weeks go by without seeking her out.

Her entrance into the coal exchange in Marfield, where no woman had ever set foot, caused a sensation, though of course those who had known her mother in her younger days asked what could you expect of Nella Townley's daughter? Freakish, they had called Nella Townley when she had shown such a lively tendency to mix with the wives of her husband's own colliers. Now it seemed Jenna Townley was to be the same. Conforming to no pattern they and their wives approved of, straining against the rules of their society, wilful and uncontrollable, just as her mother had been. Worse, really, for at least Nella had kept her tomfoolery confined to that place of hers on Smithy Brow where she could not offend the susceptibilities of decent people but here was her daughter, accompanied, it was true, by her father, crossing the threshold of the hallowed, male-dominated halls of the coal exchange just as though she had every right to be there!

They blamed Jonas Townley for it, naturally. He was known to be soft on that daft wife of his who had no doubt put him up to this. Knowing her nature to be the sort that actually believed women could do as men did, at least in many respects, and that girl of hers apparently the same, the pair of them would have worked Jonas round to this lunatic scheme and here he was, glaring about him as if to defy any man who tried to bar his daughter's entrance, defying any men to say to his face what they were obviously thinking, which was that he must be mad to allow this girl of his to step out of her place and into theirs; to allow her to wind him round her little finger as his wife did. Who would have believed it? they asked one another, remembering his own first triumphant, arrogant entry into the exchange after the death of his father-in-law many years ago. And what the devil was he up to for everyone knew he meant to put that lad, Simeon Townley, in charge when he himself was gone.

Jenna walked beside her father, Simeon forced to trail at their backs which she knew did not please him but what did it matter to her since she was, at last, in her rightful place. Let them talk behind their hands, the old fools. Let Simeon glower and mutter beneath his breath and throw her looks of barely disguised resentment, it meant nothing, less than nothing to her on this magical day for inside her was a glowing tremble of breathless anticipation at what was to come. She knew that it was here that coal owners sold their coal to merchants, that prices were fixed, that negotiations between merchant and coal owner, or the coal owner's agent, were settled and it was here that she meant to do just what her father and grandfather before him had done.

The building was very fine, a four-storey edifice with an enormous domed window in its roof from which sunlight fell in dancing dust motes and the room they entered was as high and lofty as the building itself. It was round with tiers of balconies encircling its entire circumference, each balcony edged with a delicate wrought-iron balustrade over which, in hushed silence, dozens of top-hatted gentlemen hung, none of them wanting to miss the incredible sight of a woman parading herself in their domain.

She wore grey, a pale, pale grey that was almost white, velvet, banded at wrist, neck and hemline in a darker shade of grey. It was neat and suitable for morning wear with a bodice which curved snugly across her full young breast and a wide, swaying skirt which could barely be got through the doorway. Her bonnet of pale grey watered silk was lined beneath its brim with ruched white muslin and her hands were tucked into a white ermine muff. The outfit was modest, faultless, almost nun-like and on any other female would have appeared so, but Jenna Townley held her graceful back so ramrod straight and her head so high and proud, the posture lifted her breasts and raised her chin so that she looked imperious and at the same time provocative. With that red hair of hers and her curving apricot lips there was not a man amongst them who did not wonder on Jonas Townley's folly in bringing her here. The holder of Jonas Townley's collieries she undoubtedly would one day be, but surely there was no need for her to enter the coal exchange, flaunting herself as their womenfolk would never dream of doing? That cousin of hers, though he was still no more than a lad, could do any bargaining that needed doing when the time came but it seemed she was bent on learning how to do it herself, and the hush, beginning at the door, spread like a ripple on a lake as she moved, calm as though she was in her Mama's drawing-room, her papa beside her, towards the stand which had the name Townley Collieries inscribed upon it.

She did and said nothing that day which could in any way offend a single gentleman there, only her presence doing that, but had her father not been the influential, enormously wealthy man he undoubtedly was they would not have stood for it. She listened and watched, her eyes everywhere at once, bowing her head graciously whenever she caught the eye of any gentleman she knew, demure when her father introduced her to the astonished merchants who had come to buy his coal. She moved when he did, spoke to no one unless he did, her smile shadowed beneath the brim of her bonnet, but it was noticed by more than a few that that lad Townley had taken up years ago did not like it and could you blame him? Only fifteen they said he was and not yet ready to leave school but you could see he thought Townley's lass was taking over what would be *his* concern when the time came and he didn't like having his nose put out of joint by a woman. Well, no man did, or would for that matter, and it would be interesting to see how the pair of them shaped when Jonas Townley let go of the reins. Not that that would be for a long while yet, thank the good God, for it was coming to something when a woman, a lady, was allowed to step where only men had stepped before. It was the same at the pit head offices Jenna found, though it did not unduly concern her since her papa would brook no argument in a contest of wills and besides, the mines, the offices, the pit yard and everything in it belonged to him and his word was law. To Fielden Colliery, Townley colliery and Kenworth she accompanied him and if it was his wish to have his daughter beside him every day and not just on an occasional visit as he had allowed in the past, who were they to deny it? A woman might conceivably be – had in fact proved herself to be – brazen enough to walk into the coal exchange but no woman with the least pretence to gentility and decency would go near a place where colliers, rough men renowned for drunkenness, gambling and foul tongues, jostled elbow to elbow on their way to and from the pit face. Surely he did not mean for her to address these men? decent folk asked one another. It was repugnant, scandalous, unnatural surely, and had Jonas Townely lost his senses, but then he had always been a man with a will of his own, a stubborn streak which would brook no interference and who were they to try?

Jenna had no idea how Mama had managed it, nor did she care really, as she set out each morning with Papa in the carriage either to Fielden, Townley or Kenworth Colliery. Those magical places she had longed to be part of; which she had, contrary to her father's wishes in the past, tried to be part of and which now, at last, he seemed disposed to allow her to be part of! He did not take her underground, of course, and had no idea that she had gone down with Mr Eason who probably, had her father known of it, would have been fired, but she sat at her papa's elbow when he met with his managers, his viewers and all the other men who worked in his mines. Trailed at his heels across pit yards inches deep in muck and mud and coal dust, scarcely noticing the ruination of her boots and the hem of her skirt and if she did, saying nothing about it for she knew Papa was testing her and one, just *one* remark of complaint that would only be made by a woman, would be the end of her bright and hopeful dream.

She accompanied him to the bank and his broker's office where the mysteries of stocks and shares, of investment, interest, profit and loss – though there were not many of these last – were explained to her and woe betide her if she could not repeat it all to Papa later that evening. And not only repeat it but prove to him that she understood it. Simeon who, after the Easter holiday would return to school, would be only too glad to have his belief confirmed, his belief that her papa was mad to allow a female, even if she was his daughter, to be involved in the running of the colliery and she meant to give Papa, and indeed no one, the chance to criticise. While she was with Papa, naturally she would be protected for no one dared speak out against the madness of allowing a woman, his own daughter, to enter a male-dominated world, but one day, as any son of Papa's would have done, she must tackle it alone and she meant to have inside her sharp brain, her stubborn mind and unafraid heart every means at her disposal to stand up to them. Not for years yet, of course, since Papa was in his prime but by the time it was her turn she would be ready. Simeon would leave school at Christmas when he was sixteen, having stated that he had no wish to go on to university but meant to go straight into the colliery, and since he had a head start on her, having done what she now did with Papa for the last two or three years, she must work hard to catch up.

"You must know everything the fellow who works for you knows," Papa had told her again and again and while she could not, as Papa and Mr Eason had done and presumably Simeon did, go underground and actually hew coal, she would learn every other aspect of running a colliery that it was in her female power to do.

It was later in the month that the Townleys were invited to attend a dinner party in honour of Mr and Mrs Jonathan Lockwood's eldest daughter, Prudence. Prudence was seventeen and had just become engaged to be married to a well-connected young gentleman from St Helens.

Quite a catch, Mr Jonathan Lockwood had confided to Nella Townley, since his cousin on his mother's side was a baronet, and the bridegroom himself, his father being a gentleman in the building trade, was very wealthy.

"You must have new gowns, girls. Grand enough to match Prudence's grand fiancé," Nella Townley told her two elder daughters, whisking them off to Miss Compton who was dressmaker to anyone of note in Marfield, though Jenna was of the opinion that Miss Compton was somewhat old-fashioned with her designs. Not stylish, as Miss Sabrina Renshaw, who had had the temerity recently to set up in competition to Miss Compton, was whispered to be. Miss Renshaw had taken a small shop with a bow-fronted window just off Smithy Brow Lane and was considered to be very daring which Miss Compton had not been for years. Miss Renshaw was beginning to make a name for herself with the younger ladies who wanted what was called Paris fashion. *Haute couture*, whatever that stood for, which was undeniably smart, a fact Jenna put to her mama.

"But darling, Miss Compton would be devastated if we were to take our business to Miss Renshaw. I have dealt with her for years . . ."

"Indeed, Mama, and I'm not saying you are unfashionable, not at all, but perhaps if one of us were to give Miss Renshaw an order Miss Compton would not be too offended to do the other one. Two, if you have a new gown as well."

"Well, I suppose . . ."

"And if Miss Renshaw's designs please me . . ."

"I see. *You* are the one who is to patronise Miss Renshaw, is that it?" Her mama smiled wryly and Jenna returned it. They knew one another well, Jenna and Nella Townley, being so alike and Jenna would never be able to demonstrate to her mother the true extent of her heartfelt gratitude, her utter thankfulness and devotion for what her mother had done for her over the past weeks.

"Well, Beth is so . . . conventional . . . is that the word?"

They were sitting companionably, one on either side of the fire, in the drawing-room. Her mother was studying the latest copy of *The Times* in which it was reported that several politicians, amongst them Lord John Russell, were seeking to remedy the defects of the Reform Bill of 1832. The public at large were not greatly interested in parliamentary reform but Nella, with her very real knowledge of poverty and exploitation, was. Still, home affairs must come first, she sighed to herself as she looked into her daughter's face, thankful that it had lost that strained and desperate look of despair the young feel when their emotions have been injured. She herself had suffered it years ago and so she could sympathise with Jenna over the blow, whether to her heart or her pride, she had met with at the hands of Conal Macrae. It had taken many patient hours to persuade Jonas that it would do no harm to their daughter to allow her to oversee the workings of the Townley concerns. She was not as her sisters were and did Jonas want to see her run wildly off the rails, getting up to all sorts of mischief such as riding, unaccompanied, Simeon's roan, and in Simeon's breeches, which would undoubtedly happen if Jenna was not given some satisfactory employment to fill her time until she got married, as women did. No, not needlework or painting nor even helping Nella at the shelter at Smithy Brow since she had no inclination for it and surely she was safer under his eye than left to the guardianship of Miss Hammond or Molly? No, she herself could not drag Jenna forcibly to Smithy Brow, nor would she give it up to sit at home and play gaoler to her eldest daughter, she had told him adamantly. He had given in.

"Oh, you know Bryony. She doesn't care for fashion at

all," Jenna said airily in answer to her mother's question. "And she is so incredibly beautiful with that golden skin and her gorgeous eyes so deep and brown, it wouldn't matter what she wore."

"You think her . . . beautiful?" her mother queried, with a curious expression in her eyes.

"Mmm, don't you?"

"Yes, she's very like her mother . . . very . . ."

"You knew her mother?" Jenna leaned forward, her interest caught.

"Yes, I knew her." Her mother's voice was vague and her eyes gazed into the past, narrowed and unfocused.

"What was she like, Mama? Nobody ever speaks about either of them. How they died and when? Simeon and Bryony have been with us so long I can't remember a time when they were not at Bank House. Was she very lovely, their mother?"

"Yes, a lovely woman, in every way."

"What d'you mean, Mama? In every way?"

"She was kind . . . gentle." Her mother sighed as though at the loss of a friend then she stood up suddenly, crumpling the newspaper and tossing it to the floor, quite unaware that she was doing it, her daughter thought.

"Good heavens, is that the time?" she said sharply tutting, her eyes on the clock on the mantelpiece. "I promised Laura I would call in at the centre and . . . well, she and I have . . . I must go, darling."

"But it's Sunday, Mama."

"Dearest, illness strikes on Sunday just as on any other day of the week. There are several . . . well, I shall be home for lunch, tell Mrs Blaney."

"Yes, Mama, but won't you . . .?"

"I must fly, Jenna, I really must," and with a swift kiss on her daughter's cheek she was gone.

On the evening of the dinner party there was no doubt

Jenna would outshine, despite her lack of "prettiness", every girl and young woman who had been invited. She had style, a style not one of them could copy since she was so utterly different to them, besides which, none of them had the courage even to try. She was tall and made herself look taller – since she could not hide it – with the simple, classical line of her gowns. She wore bold colours, or plain whites and creams with none of the contrasting colours such as trimmings of green on purple, blue on green or alternate stripes of pink and mauve, the plaids in vivid shades of magenta and tangerine which were so coveted by the fashionable lady. She despised fussy bows and ribbons. She wore no clutter, did not aspire to rosebud lips and dimples but the sharp contrast between the rich cream of her complexion, the winging arch of her delicate copper eyebrows, her long, coral-tinted mouth, the rich fire of her hair and the shining blue-green of her eyes was enough to draw every gentleman's glance to her. Cream and bronze and turquoise, vibrant and striking and the dress Sabrina Renshaw had designed and made for her was quite superb. It was of white satin, a vast skirt, a plain bodice with nothing on it but a white silk rose pinned at the waist, another in her hair. Marian had dressed it low on the nape of her neck in one massive coil and the rose was in its centre. Her neck was long and slender, swaying beneath the weight of her hair and was accentuated by the narrow velvet ribbon embroidered with clusters of seed pearls which she had tied around her throat. Her days spent with her father in the serious consideration of what was to be her future had given her a youthful maturity, an almost regal steadiness which astonished those who were in her company that evening since she was known to be giddy, flighty, wilful. Every other young lady in the room where the dancing was later to take place was in girlish sugar pink, primrose yellow or ice blue. Gauzes, muslins, tarlatan with ribbons and bows and downcast eyes, shy and modest as unmarried girls were supposed to be, but Jenna Townley stood beside her parents and her sister, no shrinking miss but a fully fledged young woman of business, her manner said, her head proudly set, her hand firmly clasping every one which was held out to her, as gentlemen do.

Stoneycroft Lodge, the home of the Lockwoods, was as splendid as Helen Lockwood could make it that night since her future son-in-law and his grand connections must not think her provincial. It shimmered in the darkness with a brilliance which could be seen in the sky for at least a mile. It spilled over the greening lawns, still studded with late blooming daffodils and each tree lining the driveway to the house was linked to its neighbour by a string of bobbing lanterns. Carriages took their turn on the gravelled drive, dozens of them, discharging their passengers on to the steps on which were lined pots of vast, hot-house blooms, leading them into the hallway, again a magnificently arranged profusion of flowers amongst which stood Mr and Mrs Jonathan Lockwood, their seventeen-year-old daughter Prudence and her grand fiancé, Alfred Ryegate.

Mr and Mrs Jonas Townley, with their daughters Jenna and Beth only, since it had been decided the others were really too young for such a grand affair, had taken the hands of their host and hostess, their daughter and her future husband, relieved themselves of their wraps and had lingered in the bright hallway for a moment to speak to Mr and Mrs Andrew Hamilton. Jenna was smiling at Angela Hamilton, the false smile she found she used more and more often when in the company of girls her own age, for what possible interest could she, a person of business, find in the small talk they indulged in? New arrivals came by the minute, greeting one another, laughing and exclaiming on the sudden change in the weather, the splendour of the Lockwoods' flowers and when her mama signalled to Jenna that they were about to go into the drawing-room, she half turned, ready to go with them.

He came in behind Mark and Laura Eason, his face smooth and expressionless and for a dreadful moment she could feel the blood drain from her head, or at least that was what it felt like as her senses became dazed with the joy of seeing him again. In front of the Easons were Mr and Mrs Robert Gore and their daughter Victoria and in the flurry of introduction, of Mrs Lockwood's discreet signalling to her housemaids to relieve her guests of their cloaks and wraps, of the smiles and congratulations to the newly affianced couple, their eyes met, met and delivered their own message before either of them had time to conceal it.

It is still the same then?

Oh yes, it is still the same . . .

Gladness, softness, a joyful meeting of their rapturous senses, a smiling, a remembrance, a lilting surge of heart and soul, a sudden trembling. For a brief moment she distinctly saw it in his eyes. They had been a pale, golden brown, like amber in the candlelight, slightly bored but immediately they came alive, snapping, deepening to the colour of treacle as the pupils widened. His face muscles lifted in a delighted grin and his teeth gleamed white between his curving lips then, before she had time to savour it to the full, to rejoice in his obvious pleasure, it was all gone and the courteous, one could almost say weary expression returned. The expression which said, at least to her, that he had been dragged here by his brother and sister-in-law, dragged against his will and the sooner it was over and done with, allowing him to get back to his own world, the better he would like it.

She understood. Oh yes, she understood the message he was doing his best to convey but it was too late! She had seen what was inside him in that first moment and her

A WORLD OF DIFFERENCE

heart raced joyously, thumping its rhythm of happiness beneath the smooth satin bodice of her gown, moving it so rapidly it was plainly visible, beating and beating beneath the rich fabric. Don't look away, her eyes begged his, please don't look away, though her face was smooth and smiling, ready to be greeted by Mr and Mrs Eason.

"Laura," she heard her mother say, "how lovely you look, dear," and for some reason, she didn't know why, her mother's hand found hers, gripping it tightly.

"And so do you, Nella. But then you were always stylish, a gift your daughter seems to share. Jenna, that is a beautiful gown."

Mrs Eason kissed Jenna's cheek and again Jenna had the feeling something was being communicated to her, first by her mother, then by Mrs Eason. Mr Eason shook her father's hand, nodding smilingly at Jenna before turning to draw Conal Macrae forward.

"You remember my brother, Nella? Conal Macrae."

"Indeed. Mr Macrae, it's a pleasure to see you again."

"And you, Mrs Townley. Sir," taking Jonas's outstretched hand, and then it was her turn, their turn, and again, as he took her fingers and bowed over them she was conscious of her mother gripping her other hand.

"And their daughter, Jenna," Mr Eason was saying in that pleasant smiling way he had.

"Miss Townley."

"Mr Macrae." Her voice was steady, her face impassive, her demeanour perfect. A young lady in absolute control of herself, well mannered, not demure of course, but with none of that wilful tendency to do and say whatever came into her head and beside her she felt her mama relax and the strained expression left her face.

Dinner was a formal affair as befitted the importance of the event it celebrated. There had been a polite half-hour before dinner while drinks were served and Mrs Lockwood moved about the room making soft-voiced

109

introductions and Mr Lockwood circulated amongst their guests, conscious of the importance of the evening and the splendour of their future son-in-law, his son-in-law's relatives who, one or two, were of the minor peerage. Sir John and Lady Brown, Lady Brown being cousin to Mrs Algernon Ryegate who was mother to Alfred. Mr Lockwood found it . . . well, almost as though he was taking liberties to address the baronet as Sir John, and his wife as Lady Brown, which was apparently correct, or so his wife informed him according to the book of etiquette she had read for the occasion. After all Jonathan was himself only a coal owner and his own grandfather no more than a hewer! It was Mr Lockwood's task to inform each gentleman the lady he was to take into dinner, which he managed successfully, leading the way with Lady Brown on his arm, his wife with Sir John.

Jenna was with Conal. They had both been brought up in the niceties of dining out, of what was expected of them at their hostess's dinner table, as had every other guest and for several minutes there was the usual polite hubbub as each gentleman made sure his partner was seated comfortably. They waited, each one of them, until all the ladies had removed their gloves before sitting down themselves. Conal helped her with her napkin, never once looking into her face, took her gloves and her fan and put them to one side, then turned politely, prepared to engage her in conversation as each gentleman was supposed to do with his partner.

The table was quite magnificent. Arranged over it was a foamy white lace cloth decorated at each corner with moss, with ferns and tiny pink rosebuds, from the Lockwoods' hot-house. Trails of ivy were twined, again with roses, from candelabra to candelabra. Pale pink tinted candles scented the air, their flames touching the silver and the crystal, and for the space of two hours as they ate their way through salmon and whitebait, through quail and plover and good English roast beef, through mouth-watering delicacies which were a marvel to the tongue and a credit to the Lockwood cook's ingenuity, Jenna Townley and Conal Macrae sat and talked the polite trivialities expected of dinner guests.

The ladies retired to the small drawing-room where coffee was waiting, while the gentleman, Conal included, remained at table to drink port and smoke the cigars which could so offend the susceptibilities of the ladies.

The Lockwoods, having no ballroom, had cleared their drawing-room and after dinner, while the older gentlemen played cards, the bachelors and the young unmarried ladies danced to the music provided by the quartet of musicians the Lockwoods had hired for the evening, chaperoned by the married ladies. There were waltzes and polkas, the Schottische and exuberant country dances and Jenna danced every one, but not with Conal Macrae. She watched him, not appearing to do so, of course, since she was having such a marvellous time flirting with Charlie Graham and Frank Miller, with Thomas Young and even, to Prudence's chagrin, with the bridegroom-to-be, Alfred Ryegate. Conal danced with Susan Finch and Emily Hensall, with Sarah Bradshaw and Louise Davies, with his sister-in-law Mrs Mark Eason and his hostess Mrs Jonathan Lockwood and her daughter Prudence.

Nella Townley, far from being relieved by the total lack of interest shown not only by Conal for her daughter but by her daughter for Conal Macrae, became so worried she went so far as to draw her friend, Mrs Eason, to one side to confide her fears to her.

"Look at them, Laura," she whispered. "Not a word, not a look and yet you can tell they have been aware of one another from the moment he came into the house."

"I know. I had no idea she was so serious."

"What shall I do, Laura?"

"Dearest, I don't know that you can do anything and would it be so bad if they were to . . . well, make a match of it?"

"No, I suppose not but Jenna is so intense and if nothing was to come of it she is likely to . . ."

"I know, I know. She reminds me so much of you when you were younger. Perhaps it will all blow over, Nella." Laura smiled placatingly into her friend's face.

"Do you think so? Oh dear, I do wish Mark had not brought him along," but it was plain from the disbelief in Nella Townley's face that she didn't share her friend's optimism.

Chapter Seven

Nella Townley watched her eldest daughter as she strode about the spring lawn with Verity Eason beside her. Deep in conversation they were, at least Jenna was and what could Jenna Townley, almost eighteen, have to say to Verity Eason who was not yet fourteen? Verity seemed to be denying something for she shook her head vigorously from side to side and the long plait she wore down her back swung with it. She also appeared awkward, Nella thought, embarrassed as though what Jenna was saying to her or asking her was not to her liking. Jenna could be very forthright at times, her mother knew as she watched her daughter pulling at Verity's arm to bring her to a halt. She faced Verity, her hands on her hips in the attitude of someone determined to have their own way but even from here Nella could see the mutinous expression on Verity's face. She was a sweet-natured girl, with a lot of her father in her but she could be stubborn, as stubborn as her mother Laura and whatever Jenna was up to it was clear Verity wanted no part of it.

Verity Eason who, on most days shared the schoolroom and Miss Hammond with Nella's own younger daughters, as she had once shared their nursery, was exactly the same age as Rose and Bryony, for the three of them had been born on the same day in March nearly fourteen years ago, just as spring was breaking. Nella could picture it even now, the days pulling out, morning and evening, the birds beginning to sing and fly about with bits of straw in their beaks. She and Laura had worked at the Smithy Brow Shelter almost up to the week in which their daughters were born, Laura in the schoolroom, Nella in the dispensary and the birth of the babies had brought them even closer together.

So what was Jenna up to now with Laura's daughter and really, could the answer to that question be any other than Verity's new uncle who had sat next to Jenna at the Lockwoods' dinner party? She had watched them and even overheard the platitudes they had mouthed but their eyes had spoken of other things. Afterwards he had taken about as much notice of Jenna as he would her twelve-year-old sister, which was even more worrying and though she could not have explained to Jonas *why* it had worried her, nevertheless she felt a strange sense of foreboding.

Well, whatever it was that Jenna was up to now, probably concerning the next visit of Verity's uncle to Marfield, it would do her no good since Conal Macrae was a busy man, or so Laura said, with no time for trailing about the country visiting relatives.

Nella would not have been quite so complacent if she could have overheard the conversation which was taking place between her daughter and Verity Eason.

"I don't know where he lives, Jenna, so it's no good going on and on about it. I don't know anything about him, only what he told us when he was here."

"Tell me about that then."

"What is there to tell?" Verity's voice had desperation in it. Jenna could be very overbearing, frightening at times, dominating them all, years ago, in the nursery, making them play games of her devising in which she was always the queen, or the captain, the pirate chief or Robin Hood, while they, even Simeon, were subservient to her and must jump to do her bidding. The fights there

114

had been between Jenna and Simeon had often reduced the rest of them to tears.

"Tell me the things he spoke of when he visited you. Surely he must have had something to say on how he spent his time. What he did with himself and with whom. Is he . . . perhaps . . . about to be married?" Verity was surprised by the look of . . . she couldn't say what it was on Jenna's face, only that it seemed very painful.

"He didn't say so."

"Engaged?"

"He didn't say that either."

"What did he say? Surely you must remember some of his conversation. Why he left so suddenly after the January ball, for instance, and again after the Lockwoods' party?"

"What d'you want to know for, Jenna? Why are you asking me these questions? What business is it of yours what Mr Macrae does, or says?"

"Mr Macrae! He's your uncle."

"Yes, I know, but we're not very well acquainted and he's so . . . so . . ."

"What?"

Verity had been about to say fascinating, hypnotising, beautiful even, for like any young girl, like Jenna herself, she had been overwhelmed by her uncle's wit, his charm, his whimsical smile, his male attention to her who was only a schoolgirl, after all.

"Well, he seemed too young to be an uncle. Years younger than Papa."

"I know." Jenna sighed. Her skin still prickled when she thought of him and yet at the same time it glowed and in the centre of her, about six inches below the broad sash about her waist, something stirred painfully. Her lips parted moistly and there was a faraway dreaming expression in her narrowed eyes, turning them from vivid turquoise to the clouded blue-green of a dove's egg. She could hear his voice in her ears, strong and soft and lilting and the longing struck her so fiercely she wanted to clutch at Verity's arm for support. She loved him so much it was a physical pain and she could stand it no longer. He loved her, his actions the other night and last January had proved it and if Verity didn't help her, provide her with an address to which she could write then she must find another method of reaching him. She had been like a soul possessed since the dinner party, when he had, to all intents and purposes, totally ignored her except for his obligations as her dinner partner, then he had run away again, for what else could you call it, and it was only this thought which had kept her steady and silent for only a man afraid, afraid of his own feelings, runs from the woman who loves him. Had he not cared he would have stayed, been firm with her, forced her to recognise he had no feelings for her. Instead he had ignored her and run away.

"But surely you must have an address," she persisted, shaking herself out of her reverie. "Your papa must know where to reach him."

"I suppose so, but I can't see why you want it. If your papa is to do business with him, he will have it and if so why don't you ask him?"

"I . . . he . . . dropped his . . . handkerchief . . . no . . . he lent it to me . . ." Inspiration!

"When?"

"It was at the Lockwoods' dinner party." Verity had not been there so that was safe. "I had a . . . a smut in my eye and he lent it to me. I want to return it to him."

"Then give it to your papa and—"

"I want to thank him, Verity. It's only manners." She was ready to take Verity Eason by the shoulders and shake her. She was a ninny at the best of times but now, just when Jenna needed her to be concise, unquestioning, obedient, she was proving as awkward and prickly as a rose thorn.

"Well, I can't help you, I'm sorry. I don't know—"

"But your papa does. You could get it for me." Jenna's eyes gleamed in triumph. "But you mustn't let him know," she added hastily.

"Why don't you ask him, Jenna? Why should I . . ."

"Because I don't want him to know, that's why for God's sake."

"Why? Why not?"

"Christ Jesus," Jenna hissed through her teeth.

"Jenna! You really shouldn't talk like that." Verity had gone quite pale, the blasphemy on Jenna's lips shocking her and she took a hasty step back, convinced, or so it appeared, that Jenna was about to knock her to the ground. Really, she was quite ferocious, and all over a silly handkerchief, for goodness sake. Well, whatever it was, and she for one could not really believe that that was all there was to it, she wanted nothing to do with it.

"I must go, Jenna, Miss Hammond will wonder where I am. The carriage dropped me off ages ago and I can see your mama at the conservatory window."

Jenna sighed. Her shoulders slumped as she watched Verity run across the lawn, waving to Jenna's mama as she headed for the side door and the stairs which led up to the schoolroom. She took a deep, shuddering breath, doing her best to plaster some expression on to her stiff face which would satisfy Mama. She could sense her, though she did not look, hovering on the other side of the glass, wondering, she was well aware, why her eldest daughter should engage Verity, who was still a child, in such engrossing conversation. She supposed, when she had pulled herself together, she would have to think up some believable reason to appease and lull her mama's curiosity but her brain felt quite numb.

She moved slowly round to the side of the house, not

117

really aware of where she was going. She was certain of nothing but the quite appalling emptiness inside her and when, on opening the gate which led into the stable yard, Dory and Duff pranced about her skirts she could barely bring herself to bend and stroke their heads. They reminded her every time she saw them of him, of his hands on their collars, of that day, the day when he had told her about his life – she wouldn't, she would not think about his kisses, it hurt too much, hurt her so badly she could hardly draw breath – when he told her about his father and his ships, the cargoes, the docks, the . . . the . . . her steps faltered, then slowed to a complete stop and her unfocused eyes became sharp, keen, as thought flowed vigorously to her brain. The docks! He rented offices. Oh God, where? *Where*? Where had he said? Some place from which he could watch his ships enter and leave . . . where was it? Think . . . *Think!*

The dogs jumped up, leaving muddy paw marks on her cloak and she bent to them now as though to get inside their heads with her eager probing fingers. She squatted between them, careless of the hem of her gown on the wet cobbles of the yard. Ted and Arthur had been exercising the horses and small pools of water, wisps of straw, mud and horse manure which Arthur would sweep up before the end of the day clung to her skirt but she didn't care, nor even notice as she strained to find those words, that sentence about the docks, the office, which he had spoken of in January.

"He likes to sit and watch his ships enter and leave . . ." Conal had said . . . leave . . . he likes to . . . ships . . . enter and leave George's Dock. That was it! On the corner of . . . of Chapel Street and New Quay!

She drew in a deep satisfied breath, then let it out again thankfully. It moved the dog's fur as she turned first to one then the other, burying her face in their ruffled necks, lavishing kisses on them so that over the stable door Arthur's face was a picture of astonishment.

"All I have to do is get there, boys," he heard her say softly. "He'll not escape so easily this time."

She left a note. Not saying where she had gone, of course, but telling them she was safe and they were not to worry. She would be back by late afternoon, she said, remembering Conal's remark that Liverpool and St Helens were no more than ten or twelve miles apart. She knew nothing of train times, of railway stations, of all the complex variations of this line and that which carried passengers from this place to the other. She had never travelled alone, not even in her papa's carriage but the exciting prospect of finding her own way from one town to another – if you could call the thriving port of Liverpool a mere town – filled her with exhilaration. She could not take the family carriage to get her to the railway station in St Helens, naturally, but must tackle the difficult problem of hiring a public hansom cab in the main street of Marfield where every soul there would know Miss Jenna Townley but she would manage it, by God, she would.

And then there was the tricky question of what to wear. She wanted to look her best, agonising over her new apple green day dress of Vienna wool, the skirt of which spread out over her crinoline in six flounces, each one edged with the creamiest Honiton lace. The bodice was fine and clinging, emphasising the swell of her full breasts. The material was patterned with uncut velvet in a darker shade of green with a broad sash of the same material. The lace frothed at her wrists and neck and was ruched under the brim of her small green bonnet which shaded the feverish brilliance of her eyes.

Or should she wear her amber velvet walking-out costume with its three-quarter-length coat shaped to her small waist? The sleeves, at the wrist, and about the high neckline were edged with a pale brown fur and her velvet bonnet, the same shade as the costume, had lashings of amber silk rosebuds about the brim. She looked well in both the outfits her mirror told her, twirling before it, first in one then the other. They were stylish and elegant, worn with high-heeled boots of the finest cream kid but were they sensible for travelling? She didn't know, that was the problem, since she had only ridden in a train three times in her life, each time in a private carriage as clean and comfortable as their own horse-drawn carriage, going into Manchester to shop with Mama and Miss Hammond. The city of Liverpool, and the sea, the river, the docks, all the wondrous things she was to see for the first time might have been in New York or . . . or China for all she knew of them and as for the journey, the getting from St Helens to Liverpool, it was as unknown to her as the crossing of the great Atlantic Ocean, but she'd make short work of it, she told herself confidently. She was almost eighteen, wasn't she, with a tongue in her head and if she couldn't travel a matter of ten miles and back again, then her name wasn't Jenna Townley!

She wore the amber velvet but over it she threw her dark blue cloak since it covered her from neck to hem, deciding that she looked less conspicuous and besides she could discard it somewhere, it didn't matter where, when she arrived at Liverpool. Over her dashing bonnet she draped an unbecoming veil, laughing somewhat hysterically at the sight of herself in the mirror. She looked like a widow which was perhaps a good thing for were not widows treated with respect and certainly no one, meaning a gentleman, would try to engage her in conversation and she'd soon put any man in his place who did.

She slipped from the side door the moment she heard Papa's carriage on the gravel driveway as he drove down to the pit. Mama and the girls would still be in their beds and the servants busy at their early morning tasks in the breakfast-room and kitchen, cleaning and lighting fires and certainly with no time to hang about in the side passage. She had pretended she had a cold coming on the previous evening when Papa had told her that Mr Bennett, his head clerk, was to go through the wages book with her the next day so her father was not expecting her to accompany him.

It was just half past seven, not quite full daylight on this spring morning but it made her walk along Moss Bank and Smithy Brow Lane much easier. No one took any notice of the tall, darkly clad woman who summoned the horse-drawn cab which stood at the kerb and her journey to St Helens was uneventful. The driver was cold, half asleep and eager to be off when she asked him how much she owed him and it was only then, as she walked boldly into the railway station, that he became aware of the size of the tip she had given hem. A whole shilling, a whole bloody bob, so where was she from, he pondered, on his trip back to Marfield and, more to the point, where was an unaccompanied lady, for she was that all right, going at this time of the day?

The first hitch occurred when she enquired politely of the man in the ticket office for a first-class ticket to Liverpool. The station was almost deserted and she had wondered why, her heart beating fast as she moved with confidence across the forecourt.

"Nay," the clerk chided her, looking astonished, "theer's no train from 'ere ter Liverpool, lass, on account as theer's no line ter Liverpool, not from 'ere, any road."

He smiled over her shoulder at a passing porter, pleased with his own wit. Trust a woman not to know that, his expression said. All over the country they were being laid, hundreds of miles of track every year but there were still towns which had no direct line to them and St Helens was one of them, at least to Liverpool! Any chap would have known, of course, but women went about, ignorant as bairns and could end up in all sorts of trouble if not watched carefully. Come to that, what was this woman doing here, a respectable widow by the look of her, travelling all on her own? Perhaps having lost her husband she'd no choice. His tone became more sympathetic.

"Now, did tha' want ter get ter Southport I coulda helped yer theer. Line opened only last March but a train to Liverpool from 'ere, that I can't do."

"I don't wish to go to Southport. I want to get to Liverpool," Jenna told him sharply, speaking as though the man was merely being awkward and could be made to produce the very train she needed if made to understand. "I have a . . . a very important meeting."

"Sorry, miss. T'main line from Manchester ter Liverpool runs south o' St Helens. Theer's a station at Collin's Green an' another at Rainhill—"

"But Rainhill is only a mile or so south of Marfield."

"Is that wheer tha' from?"

"Yes."

"Theer tha' go then! Just goes ter show. Tha' shoulda made enquiries first afore tha' set off."

"Yes, yes, I see that." The man's triumphant tone which implied that it was true what they said about the foolishness of the female sex annoyed her intensely. Couldn't find their way across the street without a man to direct them, it seemed to say, but she would not be beaten. Not by this patronising ticket clerk nor by the railway system itself.

"There must be some way to get to Liverpool," she pronounced firmly. "I cannot believe that gentlemen with business there and who live north of St Helens must take a hansom cab all the way to Rainhill

to catch a connecting train. Kindly look at your . . .
er . . ."

"Well, tha' could get on't Runcorn Gap train." He
thumbed through a timetable, his tongue protruding from
between his lips, then smiled jubilantly. "T'Manchester
ter Liverpool stops at St Helens junction which is on't St
Helens ter Runcorn Gap line so if tha' look lively tha'
should just mekk it."

"Thank you, and that will be . . .?"

"First class, tha' said?"

"If you please."

"An' will tha' want single or return?"

"Pardon?"

"Are tha' ter come back, miss, or will tha' stay in
Liverpool?"

"Of course I am to come back." Her tone was sharp.

"Then tha'll want a return an' that'll be one shillin'
an' threepence."

The St Helens and Runcorn Gap Railway was a
leisurely affair, devoid, it seemed to Jenna, of any
connection to such things as timetable departures or
arrivals for no matter who she enquired of no-one
seemed to know anything much about it except that it
definitely arrived and departed at some time. When it
did it was a haphazard arrangement, just a coach or two
added to it for the convenience of passengers, herself only
at that time of the morning, at least in what purported to
be the first-class compartment, the line used mainly for
minerals and merchandise being transported to the dock
at Runcorn Gap.

Lime Street Station in Liverpool was of a different
order altogether, being so busy, so bustling and alive
Jenna was reminded of a beehive in which, years ago,
Simeon had stirred a stick. A clamouring, heaving,
humming mass of humanity all intent on their own
business, on their own departures and destination. She

realised incredulously she could have worn a ball gown with a diamond-studded tiara and little notice would have been taken of her. There was a great coming and going, a rushing to and fro, men whistling, men shouting, doors banging, engines shrieking and all taking place amidst the hiss of steam, the acrid smell and taste of smoke, dim with yellow and grey swirls and as dense as fog. There was great wealth in England and especially in this splendid port of Liverpool. Fortunes being made from merchant adventuring on the high seas, from trade routes forged with continents such as Australia, with China and the Mediterranean. Goods poured from factory, mill and mine to ships at the dockside, ships straining to be away to their destination and it was through here, in the tumultuous maelstrom of the railway station that many of them passed to continue on their journey.

Her cloak was left with a good-natured, incurious little woman who stuck her head out of a window marked "left luggage" and who had a nasal accent so thick and adenoidal Jenna had great difficulty in understanding what she said.

"It'll be orlright 'ere wi' me, queen," she seemed to say, imperturbably stuffing the cloak in some cupboard behind her. "Ah'll give yer a ticket, orlright, an' when yer wanit back again just show it me."

The day was fine, thankfully, and Jenna drew in a deep breath as she stepped out from beneath the magnificent portals of the station. The air contained a dozen smells, some of which she recognised, drifting on the breeze which came from the river and its shipping. Timber, coffee, tobacco and tar were but a few of them and she dragged them right down into her lungs as she hurried across the wide thoroughfare, dodging hansom cabs, carriages, horses' hooves, wanting to shout out loud, wanting to skip and jump like a child it was all so exciting.

She stopped to look back at the magnificent façade of the station, impressed by its grandeur, by the thirty-six Corinthian columns which supported the colonnade. Its vast roof span was all of gleaming glass which seemed to float above it like a bubble, fragile and graceful and before it were a dozen wide steps stretching across the whole of its front, up and down which scrambled hundreds of frantic travellers.

Opposite the entrance to the railway station was the massive structure of St George's Hall in which were to be held, it advertised, concerts and musical entertainments, for it had only recently been opened to the public.

But she had no time to stand about gaping at the sights, she told herself. It was gone ten o'clock and she had to get down to Chapel Street as soon as possible. She could stay no longer than an hour with Conal, her heart turning over at the prospect, for she must get back before dark or Papa would have half the police force of Lancashire out looking for her. Of course she had no need to take the circuitous route she had journeyed this morning when she returned but could travel the eleven and three-quarter miles – as she had found it to be – from Liverpool to St Helens junction in half the time and from there hire a hansom cab to take her directly home. After all, she was an experienced traveller now. She had changed trains at St Helens junction with the panache of a seasoned explorer, nipping smartly from the St Helens and Runcorn Gap "chugger" on to the smart, eager to be on its way, Manchester to Liverpool "dasher", aware, since she was a woman and alone, of many curious male stares. No one approached her though, nor even allowed his gaze to linger, in respect for her widowed state, she supposed, ready to giggle, preening herself on her own cleverness.

Her skirt dipped and swayed as she began the walk down Shaws Brow which a respectful porter had informed her led to the river but before she had taken more than a dozen steps she realised that her wide crinoline, though it looked enchanting, was just not made for walking far, nor were the roadways made for her dainty cream boots. Every pedestrian, mostly staring men, she was alarmed to find, had to make a wide detour to avoid her skirt which took up most of the pavement. The roadways, despite the efforts of the barefoot sweeping boys on every corner, were clogged with horse-droppings and other filth and she began to wish she had taken one of the hansom cabs which had stood outside the station. The porter, eyeing her with the amazement most of the men about her did, had advised her to do so but she could sit still not a moment longer and after the train journey wanted nothing more than to run, swift and sure, fleet as a deer, down the long brow which would lead her to Conal.

"Oh aye, straight down Shaws Brow an' Dale Street, turn right an' past St Nicholas Church," the porter had said, which didn't sound far but she was very aware that she was the object of every astonished male stare and of some female derision. They were all of what Miss Hammond called the "lower orders" for real ladies and gentlemen rode in their own carriages, dozens of which crammed the streets. She looked her best and it was not just the admiration she saw in the men's eyes which told her so but her own reflection in the mirror earlier that day. Her fitted jacket clung to her breast, waist and hips and the colour of it enhanced the flame of her own very noticeable hair. The excitement had put banners of peach in her cheeks and the brilliance of turquoise in her eyes. She was Jenna Townley and going to meet the man she loved but the further down Dale Street she progressed the more she wished she had heeded the porter's advice, but there was nothing she could do about it now but stride on. Those who jostled by her were working girls, many with shawls about their heads and clogs on their feet, girls from factories of which there appeared to be a great many in the narrow side streets leading off Dale Street.

There were enormous waggons heavily laden with barrels and bales, pulled by patient, broad-backed, proudly bedecked Clydesdale horses, all making their way to the docks and the ships that waited for what they carried and she kept pace with them, her head as proudly held as theirs.

The smells of the river became stronger the nearer to it she got and she gritted her teeth, glaring back at any man, or woman, whose eyes she met. She had as much right to be walking these pavements as they did, she told herself, boldly lifting her flower-strewn bonnet, doing her best to look as though this was her usual morning promenade, but she wished, dear God she wished she could see Chapel Street.

Conal Macrae thought he had fallen asleep and was deep in a dream about her. He had been up to the station to unravel some problem with a delivery of coal which had come straight from the coalfields of south Lancashire and which was to have gone directly to the docks for the coaling of his ships. For some bloody reason the waggons had gone astray, landing up at Edge Hill and *Mary Macrae* and *Gem Star*, to sail on the next tide, were sitting at their berths, cargoes already loaded and no coal in their bunkers.

"I'll go and see to it," he had bellowed at his cowering clerks. "Do it your damned self if you want it doing right," he had added, astonishing and offending them for it was not their fault that the coal had gone astray. He was normally a just employer but he had been like a bear with a sore head ever since he came back from Marfield, or wherever it was his relatives lived, finding fault with everything and everybody so they'd be glad to see the back of him for an hour.

He had thought of no one but her since the dinner

party. Ever since he had come back from Mark's she had been in his dreams, hovering on the edge of his subconscious mind even when he was at business, making deals, arranging cargoes, discussing prices and costs and it had alarmed him. It had been bad enough the first time, remembering the feel of her young body in his arms and the soft expression in her glowing eyes. But he had put her firmly from him, helped by Evelyn Armstrong, of course, and had vowed not to return to Marfield again. Fool, God, he was a fool to have accepted Mark's invitation, his repeated invitation to visit them again, and now look where it had landed him! How in hell was he to continue to be the sharp-witted, high-pressured, cunning man of business which was needed in the shipping world, as his father, who had taught him everything he himself knew, had been? As Conal Macrae, after fourteen years in the trade of moving cargoes, was, if he could not rely on his own wits to foresee pitfalls; to recognise a sharp manoeuvre; to exercise his astute brain in the transactions which took place a dozen times a day in his full life? He must be alert, extra vigilant if he was not to let a bit of good business go to another ship owner, of which there were scores in Liverpool, all willing to undercut his prices in their eagerness to take his cargoes. Over one hundred and seventy ships, 26,754 tonnage in all, entered and departed Liverpool each day. Two million annual tons of coasting traffic which was fully one-third the tonnage using the port and all of these coasters without exception would be glad to take his business, see his ships idle about empty and profitless if he did not apply himself constantly, vigilantly to his enterprise and to do that he must put all thoughts of Jenna Townley from his mind.

He'd tried, by God he'd tried, spending two frenzied hours only last night in the arms of his mistress in an attempt to escape the expression in the narrowed, thickly lashed, turquoise eyes of Jenna Townley. But even in the throes of the orgasms Evelyn aroused in him, when her knowing hands smoothed his body and her own body bucked under his, as they did their best to swallow one another whole in what he recognised as greed and lust, at the most inconvenient and unpredictable moments she came to plague him with her wicked yet sweet smile, her steady, clear-eyed gaze, her brave, honest spirit which had shone from her at the Lockwoods' dinner table, her impudence, her arrogance, her stubbornness. Jenna . . .

The hansom cab in which he rode from Lime Street Railway Station back to Chapel Street was held up just in front of the town hall where it stood at the confluence of Castle Street, Dale Street and Water Street. An enormous brewer's dray pulled by two equally enormous Shire horses had lost several barrels of beer, two of which had fallen with such force their sides had stove in and the good ale was gushing freely, to the delight of a dozen or so boys and young men, down the gutter beside the pavement. Joyfully the youths advanced on it, doing their best to catch it in any handy container they had about them, caps, their cupped hands, even their boots and the laughter and revelry were uncontained. Cabs and carriages were forced to swerve, horses rearing nervously as men darted beneath their hooves and Conal found himself and the cab which carried him jammed up against the railings which surrounded the town hall. An imposing building which had replaced the original, burned down in a January of sixty odd years ago when the water pipes had been so frozen they prevented a supply of water being obtained to put out the fire. In two hours the whole of the building had been destroyed including the antiquities which had accumulated over the centuries. In 1802 the present town hall had been completed, Corinthian columns and pilasters, spacious windows, a ballroom so lofty and wide the whole of the Macrae fleet of coasting vessels might have been docked in it, and in the centre of the roof a high and elegant dome was surmounted by a figure of Minerva.

But Conal Macrae saw none of this as he stared, transfixed, at the animated face of the young woman on whom his thoughts had been centred, not only for the past week but since he had met her on the first day of this year 1859. She had not seen him. She stood on the pavement amongst the crowd of onlookers, her face alive with excited laughter, her eyes brilliant beneath the brim of her fetching bonnet. They snapped with joy and her rosy mouth curved over her even white teeth and, amongst the sober, black-suited businessmen who had come to trade at the Royal Exchange which stood at the back of the town hall, amongst the dockies and labourers who thronged the dock areas, the drabs, the flower girls and "Mary-Ellens", the street-sweeping boys, the errand boys, hawkers, street entertainers and tradesmen, she stood out like a bright bird of paradise in an aviary of squabbling sparrows.

She still did not see him, nor was even aware of his presence until she felt his hand under her elbow dragging her away from the mêlée towards the corner of Rumford Street which cut from Water Street into Chapel Street.

She shrank away from him for a moment, her female instinct which had not yet recognised him making her wary, telling her of her vulnerability in this strange city, in this challenging, unfamiliar environment where no one knew she was Miss Jenna Townley, daughter of one of Marfield's leading citizens and therefore inviolate.

"Let go of me, you . . ." she began, prepared to lift her fist to him, then, recognising him, ready to fling herself into his arms, he could see it plainly in her expressive face which could hide no emotion she felt.

"Conal . . . oh Conal, it's you," she gasped, her eyes alight with that brilliant expression he knew so well.

"Aye, lassie, in the flesh and what the bloody hell you

think you're doing here I canna imagine but I suppose you'll tell me soon enough. Until then, and until I can get you home to your father you'll close your mouth and behave yourself."

Chapter Eight

"So you see, sir, until she is eighteen, in April she tells me, I'd be glad if you would keep all I've told you to yourself. Oh, I dinna mean from your wife, of course," the man who sat opposite Jonas Townley added hastily, "for she's Jenna's mother and must, naturally, be made aware of my intentions."

"That's good of you, Macrae," Jonas answered ironically, a small smile playing about his lips, "but I shall decide who, or what shall be told in my own home."

"Of course, forgive me. I dinna mean to advise you on how to go about . . . well, what I had in mind was keeping it from Jenna herself."

Conal Macrae's face hardened and he clamped his lips more firmly about the cigar his host had offered him as though he needed something to keep him from saying far more than he intended, or might be good for his cause. He could not forget the appalling lurch of his heart nor the frightening dryness of his mouth when he had seen Jenna standing boldly on the pavement amongst the rough element of Liverpool's working men and women, her laughing face innocently turned to whoever it was who stood beside her, sharing their laughter, their broad humour, just as though there was nothing unusual in her situation. In her beautiful outfit, her expensive if soiled kid boots, the delightful nonsense of her bonnet, she would be considered tasty pickings by the common, petty criminal who lurked wherever a crowd gathered. The reticule on her arm – the thought was plain in many slyly staring eyes – would be bound to contain more than enough to buy their gin for the next month. Down the next narrow alleyway, which was Covent Garden, they would gladly drag her, taking her reticule and anything else they could easily deprive her of in some secret doorway, and the image had so devastated him it was all he could do not to fetch her a smack across her widely smiling face as he stampeded her back to his office.

"Conal, Conal, you are hurting me," she had cried, doing her best to wrench her arm from his vice-like grip at the same time as they turned into the quieter, narrower thoroughfare of Rumford Street, to get in front of him, her face to his so that they might kiss one another. Oh yes, even there in broad daylight with errand boys and clerks, road sweepers and chestnut sellers cluttering the narrow pavement she was eager to be in his arms, to kiss him, have him kiss her, oblivious of their stares. Shameless, he would have called it had he not been so bloody, incredulously delighted to see her!

"You deserve to be hurt, lassie, and when I get you back to your father there's no doubt, if he's any sense, he'll give you the tanning of your life." He spoke through gritted teeth.

"Conal, please, let me explain though really I don't see why I should have to. The other night at the Lockwoods was a farce, a charade which you put on for the company. Oh yes, you can't deny it" – as he opened his mouth to protest – "and I went along with it. I could hardly ask you in front of the other guests why you had not come back to Marfield, could I, and you gave me no chance to speak in private. I deserve an explanation after . . . after what happened that day in January when . . . for God's sake let go of me and let me finish. I only wanted to see you. Find out . . ."

They had turned into Chapel Street by now, Jenna almost running to keep up with Conal's long stride which became longer and more emphatic with every step he took. Her elbow was almost up to the point of his shoulder as he towed her forcibly along Chapel Street towards the exuberant noise, the sheer energy and vitality of the docks which lay at its end. She could hear men singing and shouting and whistling and the sounds of hammering and sawing, of dogs barking. The heavy clang of chains and the heavier crash of the hooves of the great gentle giants, the majestic horses without whose strength and patience much of the loading and unloading of the ships could not go on. She could hear a strange creaking, a rhythmic to and fro as something moved, a murmuring which sounded like wind whispering through trees and smell the fragrance she had first caught a whiff of up at the railway station. Here it was stronger, strange and exotic and she found her nostrils were flaring as she drew it into her lungs, as she had seen Dory and Duff do when they stood to sniff the air.

They turned again at the church of St Nicholas and the miracle of it all was spread out before her, the splendour and raw virility of the great port, the great river, the great ships which took her breath away and not even Conal's cruel hand on her arm could drag her further. She was entranced by it as she was entranced by the vigour and drive, the masculine force and power of her father's world and she came to a stop, her mouth open in a circle of awe, of rapture, her eyes wide, brilliant with what Conal thought might be tears.

His anger and fear, for a sweet second, ebbed away as he saw in her what he himself felt about this world of ships, of the great shining stretch of water which could change colour as incredibly as Jenna's eyes did. Of the thicket of ships' spars which swayed over their heads until they could barely see the washed pearl of the sky.

Men and women with buckets, bundles, bales upon their heads, the jingle of harness, the pungency of steam and smoke, the hazard of chain and rope to trip the unwary, proud hulls and prouder figureheads, the redolent smells of raw timber and tar. A banquet of frigate and freighter on which to feast, of four-masted barque and two-masted schooner and the squat but practical lines of a steam-ship, a plume of white steam draped about her funnel. On her side was the name *Mary Macrae*.

She turned to him then, her eyes soft and wondering, her face as open as a freshly opened rose in its beauty.

"Yours! Your boat named for your mama."

"Ship," he corrected her automatically but he could not help but smile down into her face.

"Oh Conal, how splendid it all is."

"Yes." He sighed deeply, a great satisfaction, a great peace, a great acceptance and relief settling in him before his rage returned and multiplied threefold. She had come. He had wanted her to come, or at least he had wanted to be with her again, to talk to her about the Lockwoods' party, to explain how it was with him, how he felt about her but this was madness and he must do everything possible to put it right. To mend the damage she had done, not only to her reputation but his own. She was like a child who, having seen what it wants, goes after it with the single-minded purpose that fails to recognise the danger it might encounter. She knew nothing about him, only what she had heard from her mother who had heard it from Laura. Only what he himself had told her, briefly, about his past and though it was unlikely that a man in his position would compromise a young, respectable woman such as herself, not unless he was a reckless fool with no thought for his own future, she had taken a great chance in coming here.

But even as he hauled her up the stairs to his offices, complaining bitterly all the way that she would not be treated like this; that she wanted to stroll across the busy street to George's Dock and drink in the spectacle of the massed sailing ships; that he had no right to drag her forcibly as though she was a disobedient child; that he was crushing her sleeve and who did he damn well think he was handling her like this, he knew she was excited, exhilarated and would not have changed one moment of this wonderful adventure if she could! There was beneath her excitement and exhilaration, a kind of steadiness, a quietness, a stillness deep within her which sounded contrary, even to himself who was beginning to know her, but it was as though she was aware, absolutely, of what she was doing and its inevitable ending. She was young, naive, inexperienced in the way of the world but she knew herself, knew how she felt and she knew instinctively how he felt.

But she must learn, this breathlessly enchanting, this magnificently unique, this intoxicating, bewitching maddening young woman who thought herself to be above the rules and principles of her society, the conventions and barriers which must not be abused nor crossed and, before it was too late, before it became known, became common knowledge in her home town, he must get her back to Marfield and her family. Dammit to hell, he could wring her bloody neck, he told himself treacherously as he swung her about to face him when he reached the privacy of his office, at the same time longing to sweep her into his arms and kiss her until she begged for mercy. Not that she would!

"Good morning," she had cried to the open-mouthed clerks as he flashed her past them, just as though there was nothing exceptional in their employer dragging a young woman into his office.

"Never mind bloody good morning, Jenna," he had hissed, banging the door to behind him and pushing her unceremoniously into a chair. "Just straighten your bonnet and dinna move while I have a word with my head clerk and tell the lad to fetch a cab. There's a train to Rainhall in half an hour and with any luck I can have you back with your mama by mid-afternoon . . ."

"I don't want to go back to my mama, Conal. Not yet. Not until I've seen the boats . . . sorry, ships, and had a walk along—"

"What you want is of no concern to me, lassie, and the sooner you learn that lesson the better. Have you the least notion how damaging your bloody actions will be, not only to you, but to me? Jesus God, you're seventeen years old and I'm thirty . . ."

"Are you really, Conal?" Her face was alive with interest and her delight was a lovely thing to see and though his own face became even more thunderous she appeared not to care. "I had no idea you were so old. You don't look it. When is your birthday?"

"Jenna, dinna try my patience too far. I might be what is called a gentleman but I'm no' averse to lifting my hand to ye if ye dinna sit down and be quiet." His words were spoken with a chilling menace and Jenna noticed that his Scots accent had become more pronounced.

"When you're angry do you always talk in that . . . do you call it a brogue, Conal? because I admit it's very attractive."

"Jenna! I'm warning you." She was irrepressible, seeing no danger, feeling no need to repress her natural joy, her pride in her cleverness as she thought it, for all her life, within the confines of her upbringing, she had been allowed free rein with her wayward spirit and emotions. Mark had told him of her father's madness in allowing her to believe she might take up the running of his business concerns when he himself was ready to retire and he deplored it. Dear God, the idea of a woman treating with men such as himself in the cut-throat world of business was inconceivable. It didn't bear thinking about. Her mother, radical and what in later years would be known as a "free woman", was as bad, it seemed, allowing her daughter far more freedom – at least of speech – than her peers and, providing she was physically safe from danger, saw no reason to curb her defiant spirit. Because of it and her recent entry into the world of commerce, Jenna had grown, blossomed, matured, become confident and self-assured in a way that was unusual in her class. She was still hemmed in, cast about by many of the observances of her day and generation but compared to other girls of her own age she was liberated, free as a bird, or a man!

"Don't be cross, Conal," she smiled, leaning back in the chair, her face radiant.

Cross! God in heaven, *cross*! It was all he could do not to snatch her from the chair, lay her face down across his knee and leather her backside until she couldn't sit down for a week.

He would not forget the train journey back to Rainhill, not if he lived to be a hundred, he told himself fervently. After retrieving her cloak from the Left Luggage, they had the compartment to themselves since he had thought it provident to bribe the guard in order to achieve some privacy. But not for the purpose she evidently had in mind! The moment the train moved off, after railing endlessly and bitterly on her unwillingness to be taken home without even being allowed to go aboard the *Mary Macrae*, Jenna had done everything in her power to get him to put his arms about her, to kiss her, to smile at least, she added tartly and how he restrained himself from tumbling her into his arms, laying her back on the carriage seat and doing all the lovely things her eyes, her mouth, her body invited him to do was something which would ever be a mystery to him.

"Behave yourself, Jenna," he had said coldly, hoping she would not see the clenching of his fists. "This is neither the time nor the place for such . . . such reckless and unseemly behaviour."

"When, then? Where?"

"Lassie, is it your custom to throw yourself into the arms of every man in whose company you happen to be?" He managed to put a modicum of contempt in his voice and he saw that, at last, he had hurt her.

"Conal, you know how much I love you . . ."

"Yes, yes, I believe you said so when first we met," he sighed wearily, his heart wrenching at the shadow which came to her face.

"Conal, please don't . . ."

"Just sit still, Jenna, and behave properly. We shall be there soon. Your parents must be frantic with worry . . ."

"I did leave a note," she interrupted eagerly.

"Oh, and I'm sure that will have eased their distress enormously. Have you any idea what suffering you have caused them with your selfishness?"

He knew he sounded pompous, superior, pretentious, old even but he must keep a tight hold on all these false emotions if he was not to give way to his natural inclination which was to gather her to him and kiss her suddenly tremulous and uncertain mouth, to tell her she was the most delightful and dangerous creature he had ever known, that he . . . yes, that he loved her and wanted her and meant to . . . Dear God, he must force himself to turn indifferently away from her, gaze out of the window as though she was no more than some irritating fellow traveller with whom he was obliged to share his journey.

There was a uniformed police constable on the drive as the cab Conal had hired at Rainhill drove through the gate and all about the garden and the front door to the house there appeared to be figures, gardeners and grooms and housemaids, wandering haphazardly as though they searched for something over ground they had already thoroughly covered.

"Oh dear God," he groaned under his breath and when the tall and threatening figure of Jonas Townley loomed from beneath the porch, his distraught wife at his back, even Jenna, brave-hearted, self-assured Jenna, shrank back against the leather seat of the cab.

"Oh Lord," she whispered, "Papa is home."

"Did ye not think he would be then, lassie? Did you think your mama would simply crumple up your note and say to herself, 'She'll be home soon,' ordering lunch as though . . . Girl, oh girl, have ye no' a bit o' sense at all in that wilful mind of yours?" It was worse than he had imagined. Much worse! He thought Jonas Townley was going to knock him to the ground. In fact he knew Jonas Townley would have knocked him to the ground had his wife not been hanging on to his arm like one of those game little terriers he had seen in a dog-fight. Jonas did his best to shake her off, snarling, white-faced and completely out of control, which was surprising really in a man who was in business and where restraint, coolness and self-discipline were necessary. It was true that Jonas Townley's daughter had been missing for the best part of eight hours, only the good God knew where and into whose company she had fallen but really, Conal was quite bewildered by Townley's . . . what was it . . . terror? Uncontrolled anger, certainly, but there was something else there that was quite indescribable.

"Jonas . . . Jonas, darling, she's all right. She's here, look, with Mr Macrae. She's all right, Jonas, aren't you, Jenna? She's not harmed, my love. Calm yourself . . . hush now, sweetheart . . . hush now, there's no need for . . . Jenna, tell Papa you're not harmed in any way . . ." and it seemed to Conal that Mrs Townley was soothing an animal, a terrified, highly strung, dangerous animal that had been dreadfully frightened, horribly injured and would take a long time to recover.

"What the bloody hell have you done to my girl, you

bastard?" Jonas Townley roared, flecks of spittle spraying from his straining mouth and it had taken the police constable and two of the hovering manservants several minutes of restraining him before he calmed sufficiently to stand alone. Jenna had been led off, weeping and desolate, saying that she had no idea that Papa would be so upset and swearing that she would never do it again, her mama's arms supporting her and it took more than half an hour's pleading before Jonas Townley finally allowed Conal Macrae to sit down opposite him in his study and say what he had come to say.

"I want to marry her, sir," he announced baldly, knowing no other way to break through the snarling menace of Jonas Townley's rage. "Not because of anything that happened today though that brought it more quickly to a head, but because . . . well, sir, you know your own daughter better that I. She is, without meaning to give offence to you and Mrs Townley, the most pig-headed woman – girl – that I have ever come across." He saw the flicker of amusement – was that what it was? – move in Jonas Townley's eyes and a faint relaxation of his stiff figure. "When she wants something she goes after it and . . . it appears she wants me. Yes, sir, she does, and I want her. I willna say I like the way things have turned out today. We met only a few weeks ago. She is seventeen and I am thirty but I've a good business and I can give her everything she's used to and I'm not boasting when I say she willna find it easy to get the better of me."

"You bloody young scoundrel!" Jonas Townley's face had lost that white mask of livid temper and fear, becoming empurpled with his outrage. "You have the bloody nerve to spend the best part of the day alone with my daughter who is little more than a child, then you come back here and inform me that you want to marry her. I've a good mind to call that constable and have you arrested."

"I haven't broken any law, sir."

"Interfering with a minor is breaking the law, you blackguard."

"I havena laid a finger on her . . ." For a second the memory of that bewitching half-hour in Seven Cows Wood slipped into his mind and his body warmed beneath his expensive and immaculately tailored suit. It must have shown in his face, or in the moving depths of his golden-brown eyes for the man he would call "father-in-law" rose to his feet with a furious bellow.

"You bastard . . . you black-hearted . . ."

Conal rose with him, ready to defend himself.

"I kissed her, sir, I admit it. Jesus Christ," he went on desperately, "I meant no disrespect to her . . . God, I'd let no man lay a finger on her . . . but she's the most . . . irresistible . . . the most . . . sir, listen to me, she is today exactly as she was before I met her and you must know what I mean by that! Do you think I would harm her? I love her and I want to marry her . . . but, sir, sit down please, sir . . . please listen to me . . ."

"I'll lock her up for the rest of her life," her father hissed, "before I'd give her to good-for-nothing riff-raff," but Jonas's face had returned to its normal colour and the madness had left his eyes. "She's not for the asking, Macrae. She's not ready for any man yet."

"Oh yes, sir, she is."

"She's seventeen, for Christ's sake," but again Conal recognised the slow return of sense and reason and belief to Jonas Townley.

"A child, no more," Jonas muttered, still fighting.

"In many ways, sir, I agree, and all I ask is that when she's eighteen, which will be . . . what date?"

"April 23rd," Jonas answered irritably.

"All the better. Give her a few weeks to cool her heels and see the error of her ways."

"Oh, she'll do that, you can be sure of it," her father added perilously.

"In April, then, on the day of her birthday and with your permission I shall call on you and ask to pay her court."

"Pay her court? What in hell's name does that mean?"

"Well, I don't know, never having done it before, but whatever a man does who has marriage on his mind."

"Over my dead body." Jonas's voice was obdurate but there was a look in his blue eyes, so like that of his daughter, that said the idea had a certain merit to it. Not that he had given permission for this scoundrel to call on his daughter, far from it, but the notion of making Jenna toe the line, sit at home and repent in the belief that Conal Macrae had no time for her and that he, her father, had no time for Conal Macrae was very tempting. And she'd seen the last of the damned colliery as well, he told himself implacably, glad of the excuse it gave him to keep her safe at home with her mother. Marriage, to a strong-willed suitable gentleman was just what she needed, by God. He had no doubt in his mind, now that she was safe and he could think straight, that she imagined she felt a great deal for this man who sat carefully opposite him. She had shown no interest in any man before this, calling them fools and dolts, declaring in that strong-headed, wrong-headed way of hers that she would never marry but would follow in his footsteps and become a coal owner. Proud he was of her, loving her, wishing to God she'd been a boy, wondering how in hell's name he was going to break it to her that she must give up all idea of it but now, within his grasp, was the answer. A well-to-do, older man to settle her down, to show her who was the master, not break her, of course, for there was not a man in the world who could do that and if he tried Jonas would break him, but gentle her, mould her into a woman such as her mother had become. Mark Eason's half-brother must surely have some of the fine qualities of Mark in him and naturally, before he even came half way to considering marriage, Jonas Townley would make some enquiries, find out exactly what and who this chap was. Before April came along, in fact, Jonas would know more about Conal Macrae than he knew himself. If, *if* he passed muster, then he might, might allow it. Anyway, before then Jenna, in the way of young women, could have changed her mind and if so then this fellow-me-lad could go and walk in the river on which his ships sailed until his hat floated!

"As I said, sir, I trust you will keep all this from Jenna herself. Her recklessness today could have led her into grave danger. I suggest she is never left alone for I wouldn't put it past her to creep out and find her way to Liverpool again."

"Now see here, Macrae, if you are insinuating that my girl would demean herself by chasing after you—"

"She did today, sir," Conal interrupted calmly, "I don't think you have any idea, even now, of her feelings."

"And you have?" Jonas asked ominously.

"Oh yes, sir, you see I share them."

"And yet you still insist that she be hurt, caused grief if you are right, by letting her believe you have no interest in her."

"Yes, I do. It will give her time to . . . to find out the true strength of her feelings for me and prove to you that she has them and also to realise and regret the monstrous worry she has caused you and her mother."

"What if she changes her mind? Snaps her fingers at you."

Conal grinned and Jonas could not help but return it.

"She won't, sir."

"Do you mean to say he just delivered me to the door and then left?" Jenna's voice was incredulous. "That he just tipped his hat, climbed into the cab and left?"

145

"Well no, darling. He and Papa – you saw how Papa was – had a few words. He had to explain to Papa what had happened. How he had found you in Liverpool and for your own sake felt it incumbent upon himself to bring you back as any gentleman would. Though he is not related to us, nor is even a friend really, knowing that Mark, Mr Eason, is employed by your father, he seemed to feel a certain responsibility."

"Responsibility! Stuff and nonsense! He loves me, Mama and I demand to . . . well, that you and Papa and I, since I can't go alone after the way Papa . . . well, that we go to Liverpool and ask him his intention towards me."

Jenna's face was unnaturally flushed and her eyes were bright and feverish. She had wept for a full hour, not for herself, nor in repentance for what she had done today, but in fear for her papa's reason. This was not the first time her papa had been angry with her when he thought she had, with her foolish need for a small degree of physical freedom, put herself in what he thought of as danger. He saw it everywhere, not just for her of course, but for Nancy and Rose, for Beth and Bryony, but they never wandered as she did, never did anything that was reckless and chancy or even the least bit exciting and so Papa never saw danger to them. What kind of peril he envisaged for her she couldn't imagine but there it was. He was over protective, at least she thought so and today, she supposed, all the fears he had had for his girls had been realised. Not in the true sense of the words but in his frantic mind and she had wept for upsetting him so. And while she wept in Mama's comforting and sensible arms, Conal had simply gone away.

"Did he leave a message, then?" she demanded to know.

"A message, dearest? What kind of message?"

"To say when he meant to call again."

"No, Papa mentioned no message. I believe he offered Mr Macrae some refereshments but Mr Macrae said he must get right back. Something to do with some coal not being delivered to his ships," Mama finished vaguely, moving to the window of Jenna's bedroom and drawing the curtains against the sudden chill of the March afternoon. It was no more than four thirty but already the sky was darkening, threatening rain or so old Absalom foretold it. The gardener was pensioned off now but he was still intent on what Seth, who had taken his place, called "interfering".

Nella turned to see her daughter tugging at the door handle and as it had when she was a toddling child, it seemed the flowered porcelain doorknob was beyond her fumbling fingers.

"Jenna," her mother called anxiously, for Jenna was dressed only in her robe, the one she wore in the seclusion of her bedroom. A robe not meant to be seen, even by her papa, nor by the servants who might still be about.

She was down the stairs and half way across the hall, her fingers reaching for the handle of her father's study door when her mother reached the top of the stairs and before she could call out to her Jenna was inside the room, the courtesy of a knock far from her mind.

"Where is he?" she heard her daughter ask, her voice loud and frightened, the voice of a child again who does not really believe that what it longs for is beyond its reach. How were they to keep up the pretence, as Conal Macrae had asked them to do, cruelly in Nella's opinion, that he had no feeling, no interest, no concern for Jenna Townley? she agonised as she sped down the stairs.

"Who?" she heard her husband say, foolishly she thought, for who else would Jenna be asking for but the man she had travelled to Liverpool to see and surely Jonas's feigned ignorance would give it away.

"Conal. Where is he?"

"He's gone back to Liverpool, my girl, where he belongs. Business to attend to . . ."

"What did he say about me? About when he would be back to fetch me?" Jenna's eyes were frantic in her suddenly yellow-pale face.

"Fetch you? What the hell's that supposed to mean?" Jonas rose to his feet and even though he had agreed to Conal Macrae's scheme his daughter's manner alarmed him.

"When will he be back, Papa? He must have said something to you about me . . . about us?" She gulped, her distress so plain her father moved round his desk towards her but he must not give way, he told himself. He must be sure, he must find out about Macrae, convince himself that not only did Macrae want her but that she wanted him. That this was no girlish fancy which, next week, next month would be forgotten. It did not seem likely knowing his daughter as he did but he could not easily forget the furore she had caused, the horror of today, the appalling nightmare of fear he had lived in for so many long hours and Jenna must be made aware that she could not, and never would be, despite the hours she had spent with him at the coal exchange and the pit head offices, allowed to do exactly as she liked with her own life, nor with other people's feelings.

"I don't know what you mean, Jenna," he said coolly. "Mr Macrae needed to get back to Liverpool urgently, he said. He explained to me that he found you wandering in Liverpool and he felt compelled to bring you safely home, for which I thanked him. Have you any idea of what your mother and I have gone through today? Have you? We were out of our minds . . ."

"I'm sorry, Papa. I told you I would be all right but—"

"I don't think you are sorry, Jenna, at least only because *your* plans have been—"

"Papa." Her voice was high and terrified. "Don't do this to me, Papa. Tell me he is coming back to me. For me, please . . ."

"Get a hold of yourself, child, for that is what you are to Conal Macrae. A child. Go with your mother and we will forget all this."

"Please, Papa, did he not give you a message for me?" She implored him, startling him with the wash of tears which flowed across her cheeks and dripped off her chin and he faltered in his resolution, then, remembering his own terrified anguish and Macrae's promise to return on her eighteenth birthday, he hardened himself again.

"No, he did not." It was not a lie, he told himself as he watched her stumble blindly into her mother's compassionate arms.

I hope you know what you are doing, you men, his wife's eyes signalled to him over his daughter's bowed head.

Chapter Nine

"Well, a week or two ago I must admit I had my doubts, Nella. She seemed so set on him but would you look at her now? Romping about as though Conal Macrae had never existed. It seems our daughter has a fickle heart, dearest, and I'm sorry, for that Scotsman would have made her a good husband. A thriving business with a growing fleet of ships, five now, did I tell you? . . . yes, I did . . . a fine house on Everton Brow and very well thought of in Liverpool, so my sources tell me."

Jonas Townley sighed regretfully and leaned back in his chair, drawing deeply on his cigar, watching with a keen and somewhat disapproving eye the vigorous cotillion which was taking place in his drawing-room. The occasion was the birthday party for his girls. A joint birthday party for not only Beth, but Nancy, Bryony, Rose and Mark Eason's daughter, Verity, had all been born by some quirk of circumstance in the month of March, Bryony, Rose and Verity on the very same day. Always on this date, March 21st and the first day of spring, ever since the girls were tiny a party had been held for them. Jenna, whose birthday was in April, and Simeon, born at Christmas, had their own separate celebrations, but this annual "get-together", as Jonas called it, was quite the high note of the year as far as birthdays were concerned, at least in the eyes of his youngest daughters. Friends and family from far and near came to share the special day. Mark and Laura Eason, of course, with Verity. The Lockwoods, James, his brother Jonathan and Jonathan's wife Helen and their two young daughters, Prudence who was to be married in June, and Frances, who was the same age as the young Townley girls. The Hamiltons, Lucy and Andrew with their daughter, Angela. Roger and Katherine Ellis who had four children, all much the same age as Jonas and Nella's and named Jane, James, Anne and Grace, though young James made it quite plain he would rather be anywhere than here with his mama, papa and three sisters. Robert and Hope Gore with Victoria, Albert and Alice, Hope being a great admirer of the royal family. There were Thomas Young, Frank Miller and Charlie Graham, all three that most coveted thing, an eligible bachelor, and accompanied by their hovering and hopeful mama's, Susan Finch, Emily Hensall, Sarah Bradshaw and Louise Davies, who all hoped most fervently to alter their own single status with any of the three.

But by far the most important guests, at least in their own eyes, were Nella Townley's sisters, Linnet, Lady Spencer and Dove, Lady Faulkner. Lady Spencer, a widow at thirty-three, whose husband, the dashing Sir Julian, had been killed only last year in an accident on the hunting field, was accompanied by her children, twins of seventeen years, Amy and Timothy, the boy having inherited his father's baronetcy on his death. Lady Faulkner, her husband, Sir Edward, reluctantly in tow and there only because Townley was known to have the best claret in Lancashire, kept a close watch on her three children, Blake sixteen, Christopher fourteen and Caroline, Caro as she was called, just eleven, since it was not Lady Faulkner's intention to waste her progeny on some hobble-de-hoy colliery owner when something much more splendid was surely round the corner for all three? She moved in illustrious circles, mingling with the gentry, the minor aristocracy and Blake, who would one day be Sir Blake, was meant for some great heiress, Chris the same and Caro a title of *any* sort.

Only Simeon, Jonas Townley's ward, was not present and if anyone thought it strange they did not remark on it. He was at school after all, everyone knew that and would apparently not be home until Easter. Tim Spencer, Blake and Christopher Faulkner, who all attended a well-known public school, were home a week earlier than Simeon but again the fact was not mentioned.

So, around fifty in all Nella had told her husband, bigger than usual but then the girls were growing up. Beth was sixteen and Nancy only a year younger, both of them old enough now to be considered in the marriage mart and so this year the format of the party had changed somewhat. A grown-up party, Beth and Nancy told one another excitedly, with real dancing and young men to dance with. There would be games, of course, for the younger ones must be considered, singing accompanied by Miss Hammond, an accomplished pianist, and a splendid buffet supper in which, Nella had confided to Jonas, Mrs Blaney had surpassed herself. There was the most magnificent lobster, tongue, ribs of lamb, mayonnaise of salmon, pigeon pie, raised pies of every sort and mayonnaise of trout followed by Macedoine of fruits, jelly with whipped cream, ice pudding, charlotte of pommes, melon and green figs, candied oranges, Chantilly basket, ribbon jelly, Neapolitan cake, the whole arranged most tastefully by Dolly, the head housemaid, who had a way with such things. A lovely contrivance of flowers and fruit, pretty ribbons and draped ivy with a magnificent display of spring flowers formed the centrepiece. The dining-room had been set out with a dozen small tables surrounded by chairs in order that the older guests might eat in comfort but the large drawing-room had been cleared, even the carpet taken up to facilitate the dancers. Candles glowed, hundreds of them. In the conservatory birds sang above the heads of those who rested between dances and the quartet of musicians were arranged in the hallway just outside the wide double doors which led into the drawing-room. They played lively polkas and quadrilles, the Schottische, the Gay Gordons, dreamy waltzes, the young dancers watched by hawk-eyed chaperones, and just at this moment it was the turn of the cotillion.

The ladies were like bright birds of paradise in their expensive evening gowns. There were some who were inclined to such colours as garnet red, apricot, primrose yellow, turquoise, emerald green and prussian blue, though there were, naturally, ladies like Mrs Mark Eason who did not care for such vividness and was in an attractive shade of chocolate brown. The younger girls, Bryony Townley, Verity Eason, Frances Lockwood, Caro Faulkner and those of a similar age were in white. Pretty muslins or gauze, demure, with a broad taffeta sash in pink or blue or lemon with little slippers to match, and shining, well-brushed hair tied with bright ribbons hanging down their straight young backs.

It was Jenna who was the centre of attraction though, much to Beth's chagrin since this was *her* day, hers and the others and Jenna was mean and spiteful to steal it from her. Her own dress was of the palest pink gauze, its flounced skirt strewn with knots of silver ribbon and tiny sprays of pink flowers but somehow Jenna managed to overshadow her in a gown of pale, gold shot silk with a low, tight-cut bodice and a vast skirt with nothing but a pair of long gold earrings as adornment. Her hair was piled high in a tumble of curls in which a gold satin ribbon was carelessly tied. The style emphasised her long slender neck, the creamy whiteness of her skin and the incredible turquoise of her narrow eyes. The gown was simple, elegant, cool and unruffled which could not be said of Jenna herself who snapped and glowed like a firecracker, her eyes promising all they had ever dreamed of to each gentleman with whom she danced. Her laughter could be heard even above the sound of the music and Beth wanted to stamp her foot and burst into tears. She looked well herself, she knew she did. The pale and pretty pink was a prefect foil for her own dark good looks, the shining ebony of her smooth chignon, put up for the first time only yesterday, the glowing cream of her skin and the vivid green of her eyes but somehow Jenna exploded, fizzed and snapped with such energy she put every other female in the shade and gentlemen's eyes were drawn to her quite openly.

The gentlemen themselves were sober in the black and white of their evening dress but as the cotillion was announced the ladies were invited to pin knots of gaily coloured ribbon to their partner's shoulder. It would add dash to their coat-tails, Nella Townley announced, smiling. The gentlemen wore white kid gloves to avoid leaving finger marks on the ladies' expensive evening gowns and as the music struck up they formed into groups of four, two ladies and two gentlemen to each group, weaving and bobbing, the ladies light and graceful, the gentlemen smart and steady as they followed the intricate pattern of the dance.

Feet began to tap as those who were not dancing beat time to the music and it was noticed by more than one lady that already Jenna Townley's vivid hair was drifting in long corkscrews of tight curls down her smooth neck. She lifted her skirts to reveal her fine ankles, tossing her head and laughing over her shoulder, not only at her partner, the bemused Frank Miller, but at every other lady's partner as well.

There were whist and loo, piquet and Pope Joan in the library and study for those who did not care for dancing, poker for the more elderly gentlemen friends of Jonas Townley. A spirited game of blind man's buff was going on in Nella's back parlour, with Molly in attendance to see that it did not become too unruly and, when the company collapsed exhausted, should such a phenomenon occur, there would be singing and recitations, champagne for the older guests and a reluctant bedtime for the younger.

Jenna danced with every gentleman in the company from her own papa and the papas of the young ladies who were her own contemporaries right down to thirteen-year-old Albert Gore who ruined her new satin slippers with his clumsy, only half-learned waltz. She smiled and flirted with them all, even papa a little, ignoring the disapproving glances of the married ladies who grouped together the better to gossip and criticise the bright-eyed gaiety of the young girls. And there was none more bright-eyed, none more gay, witty, dashing than Jenna Townley whose heart moved heavily and painfully beneath the gold silk bodice of her lovely gown. She made her partners laugh out loud, laughing herself, teasing, tossing her head at their compliments until her gold earrings danced as lively a jig as she did.

They all hated her, she knew they did, all the other young ladies whom the gentlemen, when she was not available, steered round the floor and Mama was cross with her, she knew that, too. Frank Miller, he of the thriving undertaking business, had begun to show a marked interest in her sister Beth and on several occasions over the past month had begged to be allowed to walk her home from church. Frank Miller needed to marry where there was money and none blamed him for it. Had not Jonas Townley done the very same thing when he wed Ezra Fielden's Nella, and with Beth's dowry behind him Frank could afford to buy up a rival firm of undertakers and put money into it. It was perfectly acceptable for a man to marry where there was wealth, the hard-headed men of business believed, and so did their equally sensible wives. Tonight, despite the impropriety of it, Frank had danced attendance on Jenna, almost ignoring poor Beth and tomorrow Jenna herself knew she would be sorry about it, but tonight it didn't seem to matter. Nothing mattered but the ache in her heart, the hollow, empty ache which had been left by Conal Macrae's complete lack of interest in her.

Three whole weeks and now it was March 21st and he had not come. At first, after that disastrous trip to Liverpool, she had convinced herself, remembering his kisses in Seven Cows Wood, and his ardour, instantly suppressed, at the Lockwoods' dinner party, that he would. That he was punishing her for making him look what he apparently chose to believe as foolish, perhaps a scoundrel in her father's eyes, but as the days and then the long anguished weeks dragged by she had begun to realise that he had meant what he said. That she was a child, no more. That what she wanted was no concern of his. That at thirty years of age he did not care to contemplate a relationship with a seventeen-year-old, well, almost eighteen-year-old girl. That her behaviour was reckless and unseemly and he wanted nothing to do with her. She had considered getting on the train again – to hell with Mama and Papa, this was her life – now that she knew how to go about it and confronting him on the matter of those kisses in the wood. If he had no interest nor regard for her why had he done it, she would ask? Why had he kissed her so . . . so ardently, she wanted to know, or perhaps, she had considered forlornly, any male, presented with a female as willing and . . . and gullible as herself could not fail to take advantage of what she had been so eager to give him? She had been what Mama would consider forward so perhaps Mama was right. Perhaps she should be sober, self-possessed and then when . . . Oh God, *if* he came again and she was more circumspect might he not . . .?

At this stage in her laboured, tortuous, careful consideration of every word of the conversation they had shared, of every moment they had shared in the short time they had known one another, she would throw back her head in despair or bury her face in her hands. She was determined she would not weep again, she told herself, determined not to give him one more thought, but then, in the dark of her bedroom she would see the pure, golden brown of his eyes, the dark flecks in them swimming like fish beneath the surface of a pool, the thick fan of his dark lashes, the flat planes of his brown cheeks, his mouth – oh dear God in heaven – his wide, smiling mouth as he bent his head to kiss her and she hurt so savagely in the region of her heart it was all she could do not to cry out. Was it always like this? Did all women love a man, some man at one time in their lives and did they feel as she did? Did this pain go deeply, jaggedly into the centre of them, hurting them as it hurt her? It was just as if she had been stabbed with the saw-edged bread knife Mrs Blaney wielded in the kitchen. Had Mama loved Papa as Jenna loved Conal Macrae, and Mrs Eason, what about her and Mr Eason? It was savage, savage. She felt torn apart by it, appalled by it, wondering when it would stop, praying for it to stop and in the meantime these men, these cut-out, cardboard men whose eyes devoured her, whose eyes told her she was desirable, to them if not to him, that she was worthwhile, and that given the chance they would not treat her as an irritating child, must give her what she needed, though God alone knew what that was if it was not to be with Conal.

The party was an enormous success they were all telling one another. The back parlour was empty now of everything but a deflated balloon or two and several plates on which melting ice-cream and strawberries floated. Molly and those she had watched over were in their beds at this midnight hour. Lady Faulkner, Sir Edward, and Caro with Christopher accompanied by Lady Spencer, had left earlier in Lady Faulkner's carriage, though the older children Amy, Tim and Blake, had been allowed to stay on to be sent home in their Aunt Nella's carriage. The crowd was thinning in the hall, the music still playing, servants bustling about and glad it was almost over. There was a general air of departure, of searching for cloaks and shouting for carriages and no one missed Jenna Townley. Nella was deep in conversation with her friend Laura Eason, no doubt about that women's shelter of hers on Smithy Brow which, in the eighteen years or so since it was opened, had doubled in size. Tim Spencer, Sir Timothy, was teaching Bryony Townley, who really should have been in bed those matrons who noticed her were inclined to think, the intricacies of the Schottische, making her ebony curls bounce, her golden skin flush and her golden eyes sparkle.

When the pair of them vanished, disappeared suddenly from the ballroom, it was assumed that Nella Townley had whisked the child off, as was proper, to her bed and that Sir Timothy had found entertainment elsewhere. Jonas Townley and Fred Lockwood were laughing together, Jonas having allowed his guest to win a small sum of money from him at cards since it did no harm to keep in with old Fred who had a certain amount of influence in the township. A man never knew when he might need another these days and the sum was a paltry one. Everyone was absorbed in their own affairs, taking no interest in what went on behind the scenes at Bank House, unaware that anything did. Jane Ellis, plain, patient, good-natured, dignified beyond her sixteen years, sat and waited for her mother who was engrossed in something Helen Lockwood whispered in her ear and when Frank Miller approached Jonas Townley, hand in hand with Jonas Townley's daughter Beth the company could scarce believe their eyes for the undertaker had been carrying on with Beth Townley's sister all evening. And where was Jenna Townley, everyone asked, when

Jonas, considerably put out, whisked Frank Miller off to his study and sent his daughter in a state of collapse and weeping desolately that no one took any notice of her, to her bed.

They found Jenna in the small back parlour situated at the end of the passage behind the stairs. She was in the arms of Charlie Graham, known for his reputation with women, of a certain kind, of course. He had removed the ribbons from her hair which swept in glorious rippling turbulence over her shoulders. Charlie had his hands in it, pulling her head back, arching her throat down which his mouth travelled. Jenna's eyes were blue-green slits, narrowed and unfocused and Nella, with Laura beside her, passionately thanked the gods who had put Jonas and Frank Miller safely in Jonas's study, and the rest of the company, except Laura and Mark Eason, on their way to their own homes.

Nella was instantly aware that her daughter was drunk. Her arms were about Charlie Graham's neck, the movement lifting her breasts, which were completely exposed, above the low neckline of her gown. Charlie Graham's hands moved down to them; his thumbs smoothed the hard nipples and Jenna groaned deep in her throat, twisting her body to get closer to him. Charlie, and could he be blamed? Nella had time to think hysterically, needed no urging. He was doing his best to undress Jenna, his senses exploding, sense gone, his hands all over whatever naked bit of her body they could find, the area increasing with every movement. Surely he must be mad, again Nella had time to think as she and Laura stood, open-mouthed, white-faced, paralysed for no more than ten seconds, she realised later, though it seemed an hour.

Charlie became aware of them then though Jenna was still moaning, clutching at him, ready to fall, speaking his name in a slurred voice, at least it was some man's name. She was so impossibly inebriated it was difficult to decipher and Nella wondered how she and Laura were to get her up to her bed. It must be done without anyone knowing, of course, or Jenna would be ruined, her reputation, her prospects for a decent life gone for ever.

Charlie jumped back in horror when he saw them, at the same time – which would have made Nella smile had it not been her girl involved – putting a polite hand to Jenna's elbow to steady her just as though she had stumbled on a stone in the garden. His face was sweated, his eyes were glassy and when he realised what he was doing his hand returned to burrow deep in his trouser pocket, just like a schoolboy caught with the biscuit barrel. No, not me, his manner said, hopelessly, he knew.

But at that moment Nella was not concerned with him. She would deal with him later, make no mistake about that and without Jenna knowing, naturally. She and Laura, who was discretion itself and with whom Nella would trust her life, her children, indeed everything she held most dear, would see to Jenna providing, please God . . . PLEASE PLEASE GOD . . . they could get her to her bed unseen.

They did it. She cried and moaned and Nella again wondered hysterically on the state of this evening. Two of her daughters put to bed in tears and there would, no doubt, be more tomorrow but at last she and Laura had Jenna in her own bed, out to the world it appeared in her drunken state, her disordered hair lying about her pillow and hanging in lively disarray over the side of the bed. Laura would have tidied up the garments they had stripped from her but Nella stopped her brusquely.

"Leave it, Laura. Marion will see to it in the morning. I must go and have a private word with Charlie Graham." Her voice was ominous. "That's if he hasn't already fled."

*　　　*　　　*

Conal Macrae was in his shirt sleeves, his cravat thrown carelessly to the chair, his good tweed jacket beside it. It was Sunday and he was casually dressed in well-fitting doeskin breeches, knee-length, highly polished riding boots and a fine cambric shirt. He had ridden down from Beechfield Lodge and his tall bay was stabled for the moment in Lancelot Hey which ran at the back of Chapel Street. When he had finished what he had come for in his office he intended riding, as he did most Sundays, out towards Bootle and Crosby sands, giving MacBrodie his head along the wide, flat beach which ran from Canada Dock Basin all the way up to the Ribble estuary. With the Crosby Channel, the great sweep of Liverpool Bay, the Formby and Crosby Lightships on his left and the Crosby by Southport railway on his right it was possible to gallop for mile after exhilarating mile, providing the tides were right. He loved the coastline, the varied patterns of the land on one hand, the wide expanse of ever-changing water bounded by the sharp horizon on the other. It was said the bluest of seawater was the most lifeless, the richness of its colour an indication of the depth to which the light penetrated and in that case the gliding, murky waters of the Mersey estuary must positively teem with sea life. There was seaweed rising and falling on the swell of the low tide, leaving its fringed ribbons of green and brown as a marker along which he and MacBrodie flew, both light as birds, free as birds, those that made their home on the seashore. As horse and rider went by they scattered them, coastal colonies of the Brent goose which frequented the muddy flats; the Shelduck nesting in the sand dunes and the rough grazing near the shore; the bold gull, its beady black eye set in the gentle expression of its face.

Sometimes he went as far as Southport or even beyond to where the River Ribble swept into the bustling port of Preston where his own ships went and where he and

MacBrodie would stand and rest, recovering their breath as he let his eye wander down the coastline across the estuary from the tiny fishing hamlet of Lytham and the marshes to Preston.

But first he must address himself to the bills of entry intended for the Customs and which must be completed before the month's end. There were other papers, dozens of them, scattered about his desk top pertaining to cargoes, consignments of which entered and departed the port daily, the record of their destination and content and quantity. His coasters travelled a distance of two hundred and forty miles to the north of Liverpool, three hundred to the south and two hundred miles across the Irish Sea and though, at this moment he had only five, later in the year he would have his sixth for which he already had a name though he had revealed it to no one. The *Jenna Macrae* she was to be, he had decided, smiling somewhat foolishly to himself for he could picture her delight when he told her. He leaned back in his chair, the pen with which he was making notes idly tapping the desk top, his eyes, soft and bemused, staring beyond the large bow window of his office to the forest of ships' masts, the cobweb tracery of rigging, the thicket of spars which clustered, so close he could almost touch them from the window. They were berthed on the far side of New Quay and if he stood up and moved into the half-circle of the window he could look north beyond Princes Dock to Waterloo, Victoria and Clarence Docks and even further, for the day was fine and bright. To the south were the vast warehouses of Albert Dock, King's Dock, Queen's Basin and as far as the eyes could see were ships rocking gently at their moorings and about them, like ants round a spilled jar of syrup, were the men who worked on them for not even on the Lord's day did the business of loading and unloading slow down. Conal could see his *Sea Serpent* and *Gem Star* both being loaded. *Serpent* with salt for the fishing grounds up north and *Star* with tobacco and hemp for Dublin; within the week they would have berthed, unloaded their cargo, loaded up again and set steam for their home port of Liverpool. His three other ships were *Mary Macrae*, *Bonny Rose*, and *Thistle* and soon there would be another, for already the keel of the *Jenna Macrae* had been laid.

It was as though his thoughts, soft, tender, bewitched, amused, had conjured her up and for ten seconds he could not move, nor speak. His mouth hung open, foolishly he knew, like any half-witted dolt gawping at a pretty girl, then his whirling senses began to steady and Conal Macrae got slowly to his feet.

"What the bloody hell are you doing here again?" he snarled, his jaw clenching dangerously.

She had been ready to smile, willing him to do the same and he watched as her hope and confidence ebbed from her, leaving her no more than a child who has been naughty and expects to be punished for it.

"Conal, please, I had to . . . to talk to you," she stammered. "I had to know for myself how you felt about me." She gained a small amount of composure, pushing her unbound hair back from her forehead with both gloved hands. The movement parted her cloak and he was further astounded to see she wore beneath it a pair of tight breeches and riding boots with a silk shirt tied in a loose knot at her waist. Her breasts rose, two perfect orbs in which the circle of her nipples could clearly be seen and he found himself considering whether she wore much, or indeed anything, beneath the shirt. His breath caught in his throat and his own breeches became uncomfortably tight.

"Jesus Christ, girl, what in hell's name have you got on?" he hissed, his eyes unable to leave the magnificence of her slim body, the fine length of her shapely thigh and leg. "Do you mean to tell me you've come from

Marfield dressed like that?" He had pictures, appalling pictures of men, porters and stationmasters, labourers and cabbies, street sweepers and vendors all privy to the exciting curves of this maddening, adorable, bloody-minded woman and his male jealousy and possessiveness could not bear it. She was *his*! His woman. He was the only man who would be allowed to inspect, wonderingly and at length, the beautiful and abundantly ripe body of Jenna Townley. To linger over and touch every inch of her, to . . . to . . . Oh God, he must get her back to her mother and father before . . . God blast it, she was the most . . . the most glorious, impossibly aggravating creature he had ever known. She was no more than a girl, innocent and unthinking and it was up to him to protect her, from herself and from *him* who would, if he allowed himself to be swayed by the tears welling in her eyes and the trembling of her soft lower lip, be able to do nothing beyond drag her into his arms. And yet she seemed to have changed, gained something since he had delivered her back to her father three weeks ago, an indefinable something, an illusion perhaps, of maturity, of a certain . . . sorrow – was that it? – which seemed to tell him that she was not quite the wilful girl she had been then. What was it? What made her look away from him suddenly, tears still glistening on her cheeks? She was soft, anguished, troubled, and yet, when she turned back to him he could not fail to recognise the emotion which glowed in her eyes.

"I came on Leander, not the train." Her voice was apologetic and at the same time reassuring, just as though she could read his thoughts.

"Leander? What the hell's Leander?" His voice was heavy with peril, letting her know she'd not get round him in a hurry.

"He's Simeon's roan. He's strong and brave. I've left him tied to the door downstairs. Will he be safe there, d'you think?" Her eyes beseeched him to forgive her.

"You've come all the way from Marfield on bloody horseback?" His face was again a picture of confoundment and she took a step towards him, putting out a placatory hand. The cloak fell back from her shoulders and he drew away from her hand as though it was a live cobra, dragging his eyes from the full swell of her unconfined breasts. The cloak was too long for her and she was forced to hitch it up at frequent intervals, the movement giving her the appearance of a comical child dressing up in an adult's clothes and the trouble was, he wanted to laugh, to laugh and to cry at the same time. She was the bravest, the most . . . the most . . . God, what words could he find to describe her, but at the same time he wanted to beat her as one beats an unruly child, for how else were you to teach it care and judgment?

"Dear God, lassie, have ye no the sense ye were born with?" His voice, thickening with the brogue of his birth, was aghast with horror. Nearly twelve miles across open countryside and villages, then through the streets of Liverpool, a girl dressed like a lad on a thoroughbred roan, since he was certain Leander would be the best horseflesh Jonas Townley could buy. Sweet Jesus, she could have been stopped in any number of uninhabited places, dragged from the animal, for it alone would be worth stealing, her indecent breeches dragged down . . . Oh God, Oh God . . . he could barely get his breath, the pictures which swam into his mind dazing him, terrifying him, infuriating him.

"I wore Simeon's cap, Conal," she said, her voice almost a whisper, holding out a schoolboy thing of grey corduroy with a large peak and a button on top. "It was too big for me but it allowed me to tuck all my hair inside it so that no one would know I was not a boy. Would you like me to show you?"

"No, I wouldn't," he roared, "and being a boy isn't always an advantage with certain kinds of men."

"Pardon?"

"And I'd be obliged if you would draw that cloak about you, woman. Have you no shame? Flaunting yourself like some whore at a street corner."

"Is this what whores wear, Conal? I didn't know or I would certainly not have worn—"

"Dinna ye talk to me like that, Jenna Townley, else ye want to feel the flat of my hand on your backside."

"I think I deserve it, Conal, really I do." She lowered her eyes but he could see the corner of her mouth lift, so slightly it was barely noticeable.

"You're no' fit to be out on your own, d'ye ken that, woman?" but in his own chest a great bubble of joyful laughter rose and could no longer be contained. "You're a witch, a damned witch and should be . . ."

"Kissed?"

"Dinna play games wi' me, girl."

"I'm no' playing games, man," apeing his brogue.

"Jenna, I'm warning you . . ."

"I know, but I love you just the same, and you love me, don't you?"

He gave in. How could he do anything else? He opened his arms and she flew into them like a homing pigeon, content to sit on his hand, as a pigeon does on the hand of its master, at least until it suited her to do otherwise.

"I love you, my bonnie lassie," he murmured into her hair, "but you'd no' wait at home until I told you so, would you? And you'd best learn to mind your manners when you marry me."

She smiled against his chest, restraining her natural inclination to offer him her eagerly parted lips, at least for now.

Chapter Ten

They rode back to his home together, she on Leander and he on MacBrodie. They were to pick up the carriage there, he said, and then he would take her straight back to her parents.

"Yes, Conal," she agreed, her eyes cast down in that new and modest way he approved of. He still had not got the true measure of Jenna Townley's wilful nature.

"I'll have words with your father when I get you home, and this time, by God, he'd best keep you by his side as he promised," he growled as he helped her down from her horse. The implication of the words passed Jenna by in a daze of happiness. "And keep that damned cloak about you or my housekeeper will have a fit. No, you've no need to wear the cap. A body'd need to be blind to see you're no laddie but try and keep the breeches hidden, there's a good girl."

"Yes, Conal," she said again, wrapping the cloak about her so that she was covered from chin to ankle in its voluminous folds.

The door to the front of the house opened and a pretty young housemaid peeped out, her face rosy and keen with interest. She dropped a curtsey, holding the door wide, her eyes even wider as they surveyed the incredible young woman her master had brought home.

"Good morning, sir," she piped, her glance barely touching him as it raced back to the young lady. "We wasn't expecting you back so soon," and certainly not with this strange creature, her amazed expression seemed to say.

"No, I don't suppose you were." Conal's voice was irritable as he led Jenna past the goggle-eyed maid. He held her arm with a hand of iron just as though he wouldn't put it past her to do some damn fool thing like darting about the hall and inspecting the fine pieces of furniture in it, throwing her cloak back as she did so for the edification of the already fascinated maidservant.

"Ask Mrs Garnett to come and see me, will you, and fetch some tea or coffee or something. We'll be in my study. Oh, and ask Percy to see to the horses."

"Yes, sir." The maid, whose name was Dora though she did not expect her master to remember it, sketched another curtsey before hurrying off as fast as her young legs could carry her back to the kitchen before she forgot one last detail of the visitor's strange garb, her green – or were they blue? – snapping eyes, the incredible hair, and the way she had looked at the master! Who was she and what was she doing here and, more to the point, what did the master intend doing with her?

"The master wants you, Mrs Garnett," she gasped holding her hand to her heaving bosom just as though she had run all the way from the front gate. "An' there's a . . . a . . . lady with him." Dora was not awfully sure of the truth of this last. Oh, she was female right enough, but would a lady look as Mr Macrae's visitor did?

Every head in the kitchen turned to look at her and Mrs Garnett, who had been just about to settle herself comfortably before the kitchen fire with her mid-morning cup of tea, hot, sweet and black as ink as she liked it, secure in the knowledge that Mr Marcrae would be out of the house for the best part of the day, heaved herself to her already aching feet. Tried to keep off them as much as she could, so she did, leaving the "running around" to the more lively maidservants who were under her command, supervising them and their every move from the comfort of her vast rocking chair but naturally, when Mr Macrae asked for her, which was not often, she had to go. Most of the time he left everything to her, relying on her strict management of the servants, on her scrupulous honesty, her stern moral code with her "girls" and her own talent for producing his meals, well cooked and served whenever it was required of her. He didn't entertain much, having no hostess to do it for him but when he did, gentlemen mostly, who got up to all sorts of daft tricks in their cups, she could rise to the occasion with no trouble at all.

"You should see 'er," Dora continued excitedly, her head snapping round from one interested face to another. "She's gorron this long cloak . . ."

"What's wrong wi' that?" Sarah, who was kitchen maid, asked scathingly.

"You might well ask an' if you saw 'er you'd know what I mean. Hair hangin' past 'er waist, all of a tangle like she bin on the sea front. No bonnet, mind, an' ridin' a horse as big as a barn—"

"That will do, Dora," Mrs Garnett interrupted sternly. "You've things to do besides chatter, I presume?"

"Oh aye, tea he wants, or coffee. Which shall I take, Cook?" she added anxiously.

"Coffee, I'd say. The master likes coffee and look sharp about it. Where is . . . where are the master and his guest?"

"The study, he said." Dora began to dash about as Mrs Garnett moved majestically through the kitchen door and into the hall. She always moved thus, not because it was her nature but because it was easier on her poor old feet. As the door closed behind her, Dora crashed a tray on to the large, well-scrubbed table in the centre of the kitchen then reached for the good china, eager to get back to the excitement in the study, reflecting out loud to the rest of the wide-eyed servants on who the visitor was and what she had to do with the master.

Mrs Garnett could have told her. It was a full thirty seconds before her master and his guest noticed her and had she not been a wise and somewhat worldly woman, tolerant of the peccadilloes of those she served, though not those who served *her*, she might have been badly shocked. The young lady was in her master's arms. Well, that was putting it mildly but Mrs Garnett, who, despite the customary Mrs before her name was an unmarried virgin, knew of no other way to describe the desperate clinging to one another Mr Macrae and his guest were engaged in. Mr Macrae had never in all the years she had been in the family's service brought a young woman to the house. Not that Mr Macrae was a gentleman uninterested in young women, of that Mrs Garnett was sure, often spending nights away from Beechfield Lodge, in their company, she presumed, but this one was really no more than a child, years younger than him though you'd not think so the way she was returning his kisses. They might have been bound together by bands of steel, their straining bodies so close she'd have been hard pressed to ease a sheet of tissue paper between them. The young woman's cloak was flung back and her trousered legs, yes, *trousers*, God help her, were clamped against his, her arms about his neck, her silk shirt stuck to her back and from what Mrs Garnett could see of them which was not much since they were pressed tight to the master's chest, to her breasts!

"Jesus, Jenna . . . oh Jesus, we'll have to stop this," Mrs Garnett heard her master gasp, and she could not help but agree with him.

"Why . . . why, Conal?" the lady – *lady* – murmured against his mouth, wriggling even closer, if such a thing was possible and it was then that her master saw her.

At once he stepped away, his hands reaching to the back of his neck and unclasping the young woman's, holding them with both of his against his chest. She still did her best to get at him, the hussy, reaching to place kisses on his chin, his cheek, his bare throat, anywhere she could manage and when, at last, Mr Macrae drew her attention to Mrs Garnett's disapproving presence she turned to stare in a high-nosed fashion Mrs Garnett didn't care for.

"Yes?" she demanded, raising her well-shaped coppery eyebrows, flinging back the most magnificent hair Mrs Garnett had ever seen with a gesture of such hauteur she might have been the mistress of this house, and Mrs Garnett her servant.

"You asked to see me, sir?" Mrs Garnett said, completely ignoring the hussy and at once Mr Macrae was himself again. Oh, he still had a sort of heat about him, a glowing fire in his lovely brown eyes, a certain maleness which Mrs Garnett, despite her unmarried state, had seen a time or two when she was younger. The ardour of a man who is about to dominate a woman, to tilt triumphantly in the lists of love but he was calm now, in control, of himself and his guest.

"Sit down, Jenna, if you please, and damn well behave yourself," he ordered her sharply, which was rich coming from a man who had been as eager as this Jenna, whoever she was, to misbehave!

Jenna flung off her cloak and did as she was told, ready to glare, ready to glower at Eliza Garnett who was, after all, no more than cook-housekeeper in Mr Macrae's house but suddenly she smiled, a smile of such humour and sweetness Mrs Garnett, to her own surprise, found herself smiling back.

"You must excuse my outfit, Mrs Garnett," she drawled, still smiling, "but I rode over from Marfield on my brother's horse. You know Marfield, do you? It's

173

quite near St Helens so you see I could not wear my usual clothing."

"No indeed, miss . . . miss . . . ?"

"Jenna Townley, Mrs Garnett. Soon to be Jenna Macrae. Yes, Mr Macrae and I have just become engaged so you see we were . . . well . . ." She didn't even blush. "Do forgive us if we embarrassed you." She stood up and strode across the room with a young man's stride and taking Mrs Garnett's flaccid hand in both of hers shook it gently, still smiling, and never, in all her born days, had Eliza Garnett seen such joy in anyone's eyes, nor such an expression of sheer bliss on anyone's face. And he was the same. Fatuously grinning away there like some daft fool and yet there was something special there, something glowing and shimmering, not that you could see it but it was there between them just the same.

Miss Townley still held her hand. Her imperiousness – which Mrs Garnett now recognised as a certain frustration at being interrupted in her kissing of Mrs Garnett's master – was completely gone and she reminded Mrs Garnett of a child who has just been told she had free run in a toy shop. "I'm not much of a one for housekeeping, Mrs Garnett, as my mama will tell you when you meet but then neither is she and they say we are alike, so I hope you and I will fit well together. I'm sure we will."

"Yes, Miss Townley, thank you, miss," ready to bob a damn curtsey, just like a young housemaid, she was, the fresh, spontaneous warmth of this young woman quite taking her breath away.

There was a tap at the door and as it opened, carrying a two-handled tray before her, Dora appeared, smiling and flushed, her bright blue eyes pinning themselves on her master's guest, her mouth popping open in astonishment as they ran down to her trousered legs. They rose again to the perky, bouncing breasts which pressed against the silk of the visitor's shirt, then averted themselves hastily in the less dangerous direction of Mrs Garnett's face where they clung as though begging the housekeeper to tell her where to look next.

"Put the tray down, Dora. I will serve Mr Macrae and his guest," Mrs Garnett said firmly. "You may go," for Dora seemed inclined to linger and stare, her mouth still agape.

While Mr Macrae and Miss Townley sipped their coffee Mrs Garnett was given her orders. A room to be put at the disposal of Miss Townley, one with a fire. And she would need . . . something . . . some clothing suitable . . . yes, Mrs Garnett understood only too well, and the carriage to be ready in an hour.

"Make that two, would you, Mrs Garnett," Miss Townley interrupted smoothly. "I find I am somewhat tired."

"Yes, miss, of course. The room will be ready when you are."

"When I've finished this cup of coffee, I think. And Conal, could you help me with my boots? Thank you, Mrs Garnett, you have been most kind," turning for no longer than it took to blink her long eyelashes at the housekeeper, the dismissal in her voice quite plain.

Beechfield Lodge was what was known as a gentleman's country residence lying to the east of Liverpool in the open fields and pastureland of old Everton. It stood on North Beechfield Road which lay about two miles from the river itself. The rich, verdant crown of Everton Hill and its western slopes had been built on over the years but there was still scattered about it the foliage of large gardens, of pleasure grounds in which mansions were set, all looking out at the splendid panoramic landscape which flowed down to the Mersey. From the hill could be seen the town stretching out, carpet-like, the land green and gold, russet and brown to where the river flowed, the bay a shining pewter and across it on a fine day could be glimpsed the Welsh mountains and the Cheshire heights. There were pretty villages, an irregular common covered with furze bushes and heath on what had once been known as 'Highertown', bastardised to 'Yertun' which, through the generations had become Everton.

There were still farms and meadow, ploughed fields and grazing land swaying with tall grasses and wild flowers, small wooded areas, common land and bridle paths and meandering streams. There were rows of farm cottages which had once housed farm labourers and their families, several old churches and what had been coaching inns before the advent of the railway.

But the sprawl of Liverpool, the rows and rows of back-to-back houses and tenement buildings which had been thrown up to accommodate those who were employed in the working areas of the docks, the families of seafaring men, factory workers and all the vast army of men and women who kept the city alive, had encroached further and further eastwards. Beechfield Lodge still stood in an acre of pleasant gardens, with beyond it to the rear a paddock in which Conal Macrae's horses grazed, a bit of woodland and a tiny lake. There were very few homes near his and those that were housed the families of merchants and small ship owners like himself. His was a foursquare, solid house with a pleasing symmetry in its rough grey stone walls, its pale, red slated roof, its sturdy chimneys. There were half a dozen bedrooms above which, with dormer windows let into the roof, were the women servants' rooms. On the ground floor were a fine library, a study, drawing-room, parlour, breakfast- and dining-rooms, vast kitchens and pantries and at the back of the house an enormous conservatory which looked out over neat and rolling lawns, all set about with flowerbeds. To the left of the house were the stables and coach house, above which were the male servants' quarters. Five women then and four men and all to look after one bachelor but Conal Macrae never questioned it since it had been his mother's house and the older servants had been his mother's servants and he left it all to Mrs Garnett since he liked comfort without fuss.

The room to which Mrs Garnett led Jenna was large, sunny and luxurious. Though it was richly carpeted and furnished, glowing with beeswax and the daily polishing Mrs Garnett insisted on, it was a guest room, impersonal, with none of the touches the mistress of a house would put on it. The wide window looked out over the pointed roof of the conservatory against which stood a magnificent mulberry tree, its heart-shaped leaves almost reaching the top of the conservatory roof and half concealing the view of the garden from the bedroom window.

Jenna cared nothing for the view!

"Oh, I've forgotten to ask Mr Macrae something, Mrs Garnett. Would you mind telling him to come up for a moment?" She smiled at the housekeeper, her eyes as clear and as innocent as a babe's.

"Perhaps I can carry a message to him, Miss Townley?" Mrs Garnett's eyes were narrowed suspiciously.

"Thank you, but no."

"Very well, Miss Townley."

She was sitting by the fire when Conal tapped at the door. It was a hesitant tap for Conal Macrae was a full-blooded, experienced male who knew his own appetite, his own needs and was also very aware of Jenna's desirability and, more to the point, her cunning. He did not trust her, of course, nor his own ability to withstand her but his masculine curiosity, his masculine excitement had overcome his gentlemanly determination to lead his bride to the altar in the virginal state in which she was born. It was a foolish whim, he knew that, for what did it matter? He loved her, he could no longer deny that, despite the aggravation she had caused him, and she loved him. She was young and passionate, bullheaded in her determination to have exactly what she wanted from life and he was her first goal. Oh yes, he knew just what life with Jenna Townley would be like and his heart quailed at the thought of it but at the same time it lifted joyfully in anticipation for there was one thing that was absolutely certain and that was that he would never be bored.

But he'd not be twisted round her little finger, either, he told himself as he advanced across the carpet, frowning a little to show her he did not care for this nonsense. Mrs Garnett was to fetch some suitable attire, God knew from where, in which he could take Jenna decently home to her parents and until then she would rest and compose herself for the coming battle with Jonas Townley.

"Don't frown like that, Conal," she smiled from the depth of her chair. "I shan't ravish you, I promise. I only want you to help me with my boots. You forgot when we were downstairs."

"Very well." His voice was stern, almost cold but the brusqueness in it told her, inexperienced as she was, exactly how he felt. He turned his back on her, taking one booted foot in his hand. "Put your other boot against my . . . er . . ."

"Yes, I know where you mean, Conal. I have done it for Simeon before now."

"Indeed." His voice was stiff with unease.

"Oh yes. I am not the maidenly girl you seem to think I am."

"I can believe that, Jenna. Now then, your boots are off so why don't you rest for a while?"

He turned to smile down at her, lofty in his belief that Jenna Townley, no matter how provocative, no matter how much he loved her, no matter how much his male body demanded to subjugate hers, was no match for the new and surprising gentlemanliness of Conal Macrae, but, even as he sank to his knees before her he knew it was no good, that he was fooling no one but himself. That from the moment she had walked into his office in Chapel Street, this was what she had in mind. She meant it to happen and with the wisdom of a woman in love knew exactly how to go about it. Not indecently, not hastily, not crudely but with the delicacy of a lover, simply sitting there, her glorious hair about her so that no part of her silk-clad upper body was revealed to him.

"Sweet Christ, why am I letting you do this to me?" he groaned, putting his hands one on either side of her head. "You need a good thrashing . . ."

"I know." Her voice was husky as she sat up slowly, but still not touching him. He knew she was only a girl, a girl who really had no idea how it could be between a man and a woman, a mature, experienced woman but, by God, he longed to show her, and would, when they were married. His hands smoothed her hair away from her face, big and gentle but wanting to be harsh for she was so damned lovely, so damned impossible, impossible to resist. He wanted to hurt her and kiss her, handle her roughly and yet caress her gently, to explore with his tongue that pulse beat just beneath her chin, to feel the warmth of her under his hands, draw the smell of her into his lungs, the smell of her skin and her blinding hair which was falling like a curtain about them.

"Kiss me, Conal, kiss me . . ." she breathed, her young face lifting to his, her eyes unseeing. He took her lips gently – just this one, just one, he promised himself, surely – separating them, working them with his own and his hands slipped down her long throat to her shoulders then to the buttons of her shirt. He could feel the fire of her skin burn his hands which fumbled with the fastenings of the shirt and with a violent gesture he wrenched the garment apart and beneath it, as he had thought – hoped, let's be honest, his mind whispered – she was naked. His hands took each thrusting breast, his thumbs hardening the nipples to instant pleasure and they both groaned deep, deep in their throats.

At the open door at which she had tapped with no response Mrs Garnett stood transfixed then she jerked her stout body back on to the landing as though someone had pulled her from behind. She closed the door again quietly, though the thought occurred to her that the Everton Brass Band could have marched through the bedroom and them two'd not notice.

Conal lifted Jenna from the chair. Her shirt fell away and in the flickering firelight the creamy skin of her breasts and shoulders, the proud, honey-tinted buds of her nipples were dappled with rosy flame. His mouth and hands moved slowly over her smooth skin and she threw back her head so that her hair flowed down to her buttocks in a living curtain of fire. He knelt to strip away her breeches, then picked her up to lay her on the white bedspread.

"Dear God," he whispered deep in his throat, pleading with someone, anyone, her, to stop him for surely he should not do this. She was not yet eighteen and though he meant to marry her he was almost twice her age and should know better. But would you look at her, cream on white, almond-tipped, the copper red flowering centre between her legs the exact colour of her hair, moaning as painfully as he was himself, her arms held out to him, her legs instinctively opening to receive him. Ready she was, one of those rare women who are ready for loving without really knowing how it was done.

When he entered her her naked body surged upwards, wrapping itself about his naked body, her legs gripping him fiercely – he scarce remembered removing his own clothes – she was like a flowering plant twining itself about a tree, shuddering, rippling in immediate orgasm, then she cried out in what he knew to be absolute joy.

"Conal . . ."

"My little love . . . my love . . . Jenna . . . Jenna . . ." He flung back his head, his body nailed to hers, the beginning of his own savage climax overlapping the end of hers and when, at last, it was over, falling to her breast where his mouth smiled against her warm skin.

"By Christ," he said huskily several minutes later when he had recovered his breath, "you're a magnificent woman, Jenna Townley and the sooner we're wed the better I'll like it, I'm thinking."

"Oh yes, Conal please. Is it always like that?" She was smiling with the enchanted delight of a child, one who has come across the most wondrous toy.

He laughed with the same joy, "No, my darling, it's not. But I somehow think you and I will find it mostly . . . pleasurable. You are an unusual woman, my Jenna."

"Am I? Don't all women find it as lovely as I did?"

"I . . . believe not."

"Well, just to make absolutely sure, can we do it again?"

It was in the carriage, dressed in what had once been Mary Macrae's gown and bonnet, the gown too short, the bonnet too big, sighing sensuously as she leaned against Conal's shoulder, that the words suddenly came back to her. She didn't know why, or from where since it was several rapturous hours since he had spoken them but there they were, clear and understood by her sharp mind which had missed them before.

I'll have words with your father when I get you home and this time, by God, he'd best keep you by his side as he promised.

She could feel the jump of her heart, that jerk of something which quickens the blood and sets the pulses racing. It could happen with many things. When you are afraid, or excited, that leap of alarm, or anticipation, that flutter of tension. What had just happened – twice

– between her and Conal had been more thrilling than anything she had known and far more pleasurable than she had ever, in her girlish dreams, imagined it would be. She felt like stretching and sighing, drowsy as a cat, arching her back and turning her head on her neck. She felt like kissing him and touching him and starting the whole delightful process all over again but those words which had just slipped, clear and sharp into her unfocused mind had the effect of plunging her into ice-cold water. She could not, in that first unsteady moment, get the hang of them but she must for they meant something important and she knew she must consider what it was. Consider what he had meant about her father, for that flutter of tension was crawling inside her, and outside her across her skin and she didn't like it.

She spoke abruptly and Conal, who was holding her hand, still dwelling in the delightful aftermath of their amazingly exciting love making, turned to her in surprise.

"What did you mean about Papa promising to keep me at his side?" she asked carefully.

His own sudden tension which was revealed by the added pressure of his hand on hers, warned her.

"What are you talking about, lassie?" Conal did not like deceit himself but he did not wish to hurt her. Not again. He had not known, not really, of the true depth of her feelings, the strength and yet the fineness of her, her own honesty which made her trust unwisely. She trusted him, now that they were truly lovers. She had trusted her father and though no harm had come of the deception he and Jonas Townley had devised, since he and Jenna would be married as soon as it could be arranged, he was ashamed that he had connived at it. It belittled her and her love for him. It had not, as he had meant it to, kept her safe at home from where he would fetch her on her eighteenth birthday, since she had come again in her desperate search for truth between them. But could he admit to it? To being so bloody wrong.

"You heard what I said, Conal. Why should my father promise *you* to keep me at his side? What concern was it of yours? You brought me back from Liverpool, returned me to my father then vanished without a word. As far as I was concerned, as far as you were concerned, I thought, that was the end of it. There was to be nothing else. For you and me. No message, nothing. Weeks ago . . . when you kissed me in Seven Cows Wood I was convinced you . . . felt something for me . . ."

"I did, my darling," falling into his own trap.

"Then why did you pretend not to care, Conal?"

"There was no pretence, Jenna. We didn't see one another again."

"Which was your doing, not mine. I wanted to know, with honesty and truth between us, how you felt about me. I cannot abide duplicity, Conal."

"I'd noticed it, lassie." He smiled wryly.

"And I'm not joking. There's something here I don't quite understand. Something between you and my father and I demand to know what it is."

"Leave it, Jenna. It doesn't matter now."

"It damn well does to me, Conal Macrae."

Campbell, who was Conal Macrae's coachman, could hear the rising of their voices from his seat at the front of the brougham, even though the windows were closed. Conal had considered driving down to the station and taking the train to St Helens junction, then a cab from there but the strangeness of Jenna's outfit, which did not fit her and was years out of fashion, decided him against it. Leander was to be ridden back the following day by the groom, Percy, who would then return to Everton by train. Conal was glad of the arrangement now as Jenna pulled away from him, her face closed and suspicious, her eyes beginning to glitter as understanding ran through her.

"You knew, didn't you?" she hissed.

"Christ in heaven, knew what?" he snapped back at her, his patience slipping away for no woman would speak to Conal Macrae as she was doing.

"I . . . I'm not sure . . ." She put her hand to her brow, dragging her thoughts about her.

"Well then," smiling, "let's forget the whole blasted thing, shall we? Come and lean against me, sweetheart," soft again with his love, "you must be tired after . . ." He bent to whisper something in her ear, the love whispers which mean so much to those in love, shared laughter, stolen kisses, all the delights which are so dear to new lovers but she pulled away indignantly.

"Don't do that, Conal. I'm not some simpering ninny who can be coaxed."

"More's the pity, I'd say. I dinna ken what the hell you are at times, nor what the hell you're getting at now."

She was silent for several minutes, sitting apart from him, both of them staring out of their separate windows.

"You meant to come back for me, didn't you?" she said at last, turning towards him. "You meant to have me but you thought you'd let me suffer a little. I had been . . . forward, acting as no well-brought-up young lady should act and I suppose that's true, so you and Papa thought I should be punished, but have either of you any idea how devastated I have been these last few weeks? At the girls' birthday party I almost—" She stopped as though suddenly aware of how devastated Conal would be should she reveal to him the incident with Charlie Graham. She looked down into her lap to hide her expression. "I . . . I drank champagne and . . . well . . . I flirted with . . ." She turned again to him. "You had no right to treat me as though I were a child, Conal, teaching me a lesson, putting me in my place. It might have led to—"

"Sweetheart, listen to me," he interrupted her, reaching for her hand. "That first time we met . . . well—" he grinned ruefully – "I was quite bowled over. Oh aye, I wouldna admit it then, after all I was no wee laddie to be swept off my feet by a lassie. I was . . . Jesus, you were sweet, sweet and funny and bloody-minded and I'd never met anyone like ye, ye ken, but I thought you were no more than a girl and I was . . ."

"Thirty years old, I know," she said impatiently, but Conal could see the softness smoothing and lifting the corners of her mouth which was still swollen with his kisses.

"Aye, and a man, a man who . . . Jenna, will you believe me when I tell you I've never before loved a woman? Oh, dinna look so disbelieving. There've been women, I'll no' deny it but I loved none of them."

"Conal . . . oh Conal . . ." She sighed deeply, then her eyes became fierce again and her mouth hardened, "But that's no excuse to treat me as you did."

"I ken that, lassie but I was afraid . . . oh aye, afraid of my own feelings, and of you. I didna want it, ye ken, this . . . this complication in my well-ordered life but" – he laughed and, chancing a rebuff, lifted the back of her hand to his lips – "you were too much for me, sweetheart, and I ran away. I told myself it was a passing thing. I'd forget you but just in case I'd best stay away. Then I had to see Mark about some things of my mother's and he arranged it with Mrs Lockwood that I should join them for dinner. I'd no idea you would be there . . . and well," he grinned and she leaned towards him, her eyes glowing with the strength of her love for him which she couldn't hide. Always he was to know what emotion she felt, her love, her joy, her anger, her sadness for it was not in her to pretend. Everything she thought or felt would always show plainly on her face as it did now. His revelation about his love for her, how he had done his best to escape it, and failed, thrilled her, delighted her, touched her heart and she forgave him at once though she was not about to release him immediately for she was a woman.

"Why did you ignore me? You talked nonsense at dinner."

"I know, I know. I think, even then, I was still trying to tell myself it was only . . ."

"Lust?" she enquired gravely, her eyes looking candidly into his as though lust was something with which she was well acquainted.

He shouted with laughter, throwing back his head joyfully, then reached for her. He removed her ugly bonnet, drawing her against his chest and putting his cheek on the tumbled warmth of her hair.

"Never change, my little love, promise me you'll never change."

"If you'll promise me you'll never, ever deceive me again, Conal Macrae," she answered, her voice muffled against his shirt front, "or I won't answer for the consequences."

Chapter Eleven

They were married on a mild May morning when the sun shone from a pearly blue sky, when birds sang and swooped deliriously from greening tree to greening tree and wild hyacinths laid a carpet of hazed blue from the church gate to the porch. Within hours of becoming his wife Mrs Conal Macrae was arguing with her husband.

It was strange really that not once in the six weeks before their marriage – why so precipitous those in Marfield whispered? – had the question of Jenna's involvement with her father's mining business been mentioned. Jenna had continued to travel about with her father – and Simeon when he came home from school – spending time at his three collieries, Kenworth, Fielden and Townley, sitting at what she called her desk, poring over engineers' reports, costing reports, the selling price of slack, which was small coal, of coking coal, house coal, studying delivery notes, wage sheets, plans of the three collieries and any new workings, coal mining regulations, accident reports and every minute detail of the running of the pits. She visited the coal exchange on market days and in the evening engaged her papa in long, earnest conversations on the current state of the business investments he had made in the growing industries of Lancashire. In railways and shipping, in salt mines and chemical factories and a dozen others and Jonas allowed it, for was she not to be married to a man of whom he approved, a man who appeared to be the perfect husband for his headstrong daughter and though he would be sad to lose her for she was dear to him he was pleased to be putting her in good hands.

So, let her have her last few weeks playing at being a coal owner for there was nothing more inevitable in this life than the absolute certainty that Conal Macrae would allow no wife of his to be in business.

Jonas was right.

It was a splendid wedding, the bride quite glorious in her new-found happiness, cheeks flushed, eyes brilliant, her mouth rich like a luscious peach as her new husband raised her veil to kiss her. Though her maid had fixed her hair with a vast array of combs and pins so that it might, on this one important occasion, be as circumspect and well behaved as the bride herself, it could clearly be seen that several coppery-gold strands drifted from her simple cap of lace and orange blossom as she floated back up the aisle on her husband's arm. At the church porch he stopped her, turning her to face him and in full view of the delighted onlookers, those who could not get into the crammed church, he tenderly tucked a wayward curl behind her ear then kissed her again to which she responded most eagerly, just as though she was well used to it. They were not to know, and neither did she, that she was already carrying Conal Macrae's child.

Crowding at the bride and groom's backs were the bride's pretty sisters and their equally pretty cousin, dressed, as bridesmaids should be, in a tender shade of peach gauze which was almost colourless. Beth, who was now engaged to marry Frank Miller as soon as Jenna had had her turn, struck a pose, no doubt dreaming of the day when she would be not merely bridesmaid, but bride.

Present were the Faulkners and Spencers and other minor titled personages who were their friends. There were Lockwoods, Ellises, Hamiltons and Youngs, and, of course, the bridegroom's half-brother and his wife and daughter but none of them were as grand or as dashing as Conal Macrae's relatives from over the border, among them a laird. Macrae of Glencairn, no less, those who had already been introduced to him told those who had not, awed by the wonder of it and he certainly put Lady Spencer and her hoity-toity sister Lady Faulkner in the shade. The men, including the bridegroom, wore the Scotsman's full ceremonial dress, the Macrae tartan draped across their shoulders, brilliant in the pale sunlight. Fine lawn shirts, tucked at the front and lace-trimmed at the wrist. Kilts that swung gracefully as they walked and velvet jackets of every jewel colour from golden yellow to clear scarlet, with neat hose and silver-buckled shoes. In each stocking top was a dirk and below each stomach, some rounder than others, hung a sporran. An impressive sight indeed, one which drew a gasp from the congregation before silencing them so that even a pin dropping might have been heard. They followed their kinsman into the church, having stayed at his home in Everton the night before, and at the reception afterwards drank Jonas Townley's splendid Scotch whisky as though it was water but you could see they had all taken a shine to Jenna Townley, the men at least, Jenna Macrae now, calling her Jenny which they agreed was a good Scottish name.

Jenna Macrae had changed into her travelling outfit and was bidding her family farewell when the argument flared up. They were to spend a few weeks, which was all Conal could spare from his business, travelling about Italy, seeing Florence, Naples and Rome where it was said spring was heaven, then back to Liverpool and the house in Everton.

"And I'll get over the following day, Papa, so don't allow anyone to clear my desk, will you? I know it is inconvenient but I'm sure you will understand how important it is that Conal and I have this journey together. I'm sorry that I had to spend so much time with the wedding preparations too, but these things are time-consuming . . ."

Which was precisely why women had no place in business, most of the gentlemen who overheard the remark were thinking. Could you imagine a man about to be married taking days off here and there whenever there was a fitting, or a new consignment of shawls or fans or bonnets to be seen at the milliner's? Boots and dancing slippers and undergarments to be measured for, fabrics by the hundreds of yards to be chosen and ordered, and all the dozens of preparations a young lady of position and wealth, and her mama, must see to.

It was noticed that Conal Macrae, who was shrugging his shoulders and grinning ruefully at his bride, stiffened, and his face lost its smiling patience. He was waiting to climb into the carriage which was to take them to Warrington where they would pick up the Liverpool to London train on its two-hundred-mile journey to the capital. It was not yet the day of what would be called the sleeping-car, though they would come soon, Conal had told his wife, but he had reserved the whole of a first-class compartment where the blinds might be drawn and he and his bride would have a degree of comfort and privacy. Jenna could lie down and rest and then tomorrow night they were to stay in London before travelling on across the Channel.

"What desk is this, my love?" he asked her pleasantly enough, and those who watched, and wondered, saw Jonas Townley take his wife's hand for some reason as Jenna turned to Conal.

"My desk at Townley, Conal. You know I am to help Papa."

Help papa, indeed! Fred Lockwood and Jack Ellis exchanged glances and smirked at the very idea of Jonas

Townley needing anyone's help, let alone some damned flibbertigibbet girl.

"He is teaching me how to run it," she continued innocently, "so that . . ." She turned her brilliant and lovely smile trustingly on Jonas and Conal felt his heart move for her but she must be told, especially here and now when his family were intently watching. They growled under their breath for they'd let no lassie of theirs speak freely with other men, men they didn't know and Conal was only too well aware that they expected him to make it plain from the start. He intended to do just that.

". . . well, it will be years yet, won't it, Papa," she was saying, "but I must know how it is done if I am to—"

"Get into the carriage, darling," her husband said, "we can talk about this as we travel."

"Just a moment, Conal, I must make some arrangements with Papa to—"

"Get into the carriage, Jenna."

"Conal, there is no need to be so brusque." There was a hiss of outrage from the Scots contingent. "We have plenty of time for the train and I'm sure our guests will not mind if I—"

"Best do as your husband says, Jenna." Jonas was almost apologetic as he spoke gently to his daughter. She was no longer his to command, no matter how benignly. He should have warned her, he knew he should, made her aware of the nature of the man she had married, indeed any man in this age of male-dominated society. Conal was no different from them all and would certainly expect, demand, that his wife stay at home where she belonged.

"Papa, I wanted to have a last word about those new workings in—"

"Get into the carriage, Jenna. This is no time to be talking about new workings. We are about to make our wedding journey and our guests wish to give us a send-off so will you get into the carriage and let them do it."

You could see it coming and from behind Jonas and Nella Townley, Simeon bent his head, his hand over his mouth, his eyes turning gleefully to those of his sister, both of them ready to burst out laughing, ready to double over with laughter for there was nothing they liked better than to see Jenna getting her just deserts. She was so bloody high-handed, treating Simeon at the colliery as though he was no more than a damned under-viewer, strutting about the place as though she already owned it, but it seemed this husband of hers had the good sense to let her see it was all for nothing. Stay at home and play hostess, have babies and do charity work, that was women's role in life and thank God Conal Macrae was the sort of chap who could make her do it. He winked slyly at Bryony.

"Conal, I beg your pardon, but I was under the impression—"

"Well, you were wrong, dammit. Now get in the carriage or we'll miss the train."

"To hell with the train, Conal Macrae, and to hell with you." Her eyes glittered in that fierce, cat-like anger her mother had seen in her a hundred times over the years, and ordering her to do as she was told would do no good. Conal Macrae had a lot of heartache ahead of him, and so had Jenna, if Conal didn't learn that coaxing, laughter, an appeal to her better nature would get him everything he needed from his new young wife.

"I won't have this, Jenna, nor will I have our guests, your family and mine offended in this way." Without another word he took her by the arm and began to draw her across the gravelled drive towards the waiting carriage.

"Conal, I'd be obliged if you'd . . ." Jonas had begun to growl quite ominously, ready to leap forward and protect his child but his wife's hand on his arm stopped him, though it could be seen it took a great deal of effort on his part.

"She's Conal's wife now, darling," the highly diverted company heard her say.

"Take your hand off me, you . . . you . . ." Jenna Macrae shrieked, and all about her and her husband, their wedding guests, according to their gender and place in life felt a great deal of satisfaction, or distress. She was tumbled into the carriage, her brand-new bonnet of stiffened ivory silk and its profusion of ivory silk roses falling in a quite comical way over her nose. She looked ridiculous and it tore at Conal's heart to treat her like this, today of all days and in front of these people but she must learn who was master. His grandfather, his uncles, his cousins, all witnessing this disgraceful defiance and himself her husband no more than a few hours. There would be tears and coldness which was a bad start to any relationship but let him get her into that train and in his arms and he'd soon put it right.

How wrong he was! How woefully wrong he was, for Jenna had been indulged for most of her life and it was not until they reached Paris and the luxurious suite he had booked for them in the lovely city's most magnificent hotel that he claimed his bride for the second time. Their wedding night in London had passed in cold and painful segregation, she on her side of the wide bed, he on his, both of their strong-willed natures longing to be one but neither willing to be mediator. Their faces were white and strained on the Channel crossing and what would have been the shared excitement of Jenna's first trip abroad passed in averted faces and unsmiling silence. They took tea on the hotel's terrace, the warm spring sunshine setting fire to Jenna's uncovered hair. They had exchanged a word or two in that polite fashion which exists between strangers and he had been amazed at

193

her restraint since her passion for outspokenness was something with which he was all too familiar. They spoke of changing for dinner and perhaps she might like to rest, he had added courteously but when, reaching their suite she had turned to him, blind with her tears, like a child who cannot bear another second of such terrible punishment, he pulled her, gabbling as wildly as she, into his arms.

"Dear Christ in Heaven, I'm sorry . . . I'm sorry . . . It broke my heart to see you so cold . . ."

"No . . . no . . . it was my fault . . . I should not have mentioned the new workings on our wedding day. I don't know what I was thinking of."

Though the new workings in the pit had not been the reason for the damage to the first fragile threads of their marriage he let it go, glad only to have her in his arms.

"Sweetheart, forgive me . . . to treat you as I did on our wedding day . . ."

"No, no, Conal . . . oh please . . . do help me to remove this gown . . . yes, oh yes . . . I need . . . I have been your wife for two days and we have not . . . please, darling, hurry . . ."

"And to drag you into the carriage . . . God, these bloody buttons . . ."

"I know . . . let me help . . . there. It's been so long since . . . and you must not take any notice of my . . . well, I suppose Mama would call them my tantrums. Oh yes . . . yes, that's lovely . . . yes . . . now the other one and then . . . there . . . no, lower down . . . oh, Conal . . ."

"Tantrums, you! . . . never. I was at fault . . . yes, yes . . . lift that arm and then let me just have this thing off whatever it is . . . a chemise . . . and then perhaps these . . . God, what are they?"

"Pantaloons . . . and now put your hand just there . . . Dear God . . . kiss me . . . kiss me in the same place that

you did last time. Conal, that's heaven . . . heaven . . .
Lord, I'd no idea it was allowed . . . yes . . . yes, I see
and now let me do the same to you . . ."

They slept in one another's arms, waking to begin
again because as Jenna repeated solemnly they had two
whole days to catch up on and she meant him to do this
to her every single day, and night as well, until one of
them died.

"Dear lord, I'd best send for sustenance then," her
husband exclaimed, ringing the bell for the chambermaid,
"and perhaps it might be wise if we put some clothes on
until she arrives."

"Why? We are husband and wife."

"That's true, my darling, but we don't want to embarrass the poor girl with our . . . display of affection."

"You promise we can disrobe as soon as we're alone
again? I must say eating a meal naked, only with my
husband, of course, has a great deal of appeal."

"And perhaps in bed would be even better. I have a
fancy to be treated like some Roman emperor and you
could be my slave girl."

"Conal, you have the most splendid ideas."

"Don't I though, and if that bloody meal doesn't arrive
soon I swear I shall strip you again and damn the maid's
embarrassment."

It was three days later, and only because they were due
to move on to Italy, when they emerged from their rooms
and, as Conal said when they arrived in Milan, throwing
themselves immediately into one another's arms and on to
the bed, they could have done all this in their bedroom at
Beechfield Lodge and saved him a great deal of money.

It was June, a cold, wet and windy day when they
stepped down from the carriage at the wide front door
of Beechfield Lodge.

"Hang on, lassie. Let's observe the traditions, if you

please," Conal grinned, sweeping her from her feet and into his arms. "Is the groom no' supposed to carry his bride over the threshold?"

He was kissing her, his mouth warm and moist on hers when Mrs Garnett, who had lined the servants up in the hall to greet their new mistress, cleared her throat. They were all there. Dora, whose face was a rosy red beam of delight since she had a proprietorial interest in this new Mrs Macrae, for she had been the first to see her in March. Of course, their new young mistress, with her mama and one of her sisters, had been over to Beechfield Lodge on several occasions to inspect what was to be her new home, the three of them traipsing from room to room, telling one another, or so Mrs Garnett said, what should be done with this and that. Redecorated, most of it apparently, though the future Mrs Macrae approved of the old Mrs Macrae's furniture. But there would be new carpets and of course a new bathroom to be fitted in the dressing-room which adjoined the main bedroom.

"And the master's bedroom, Miss Townley?" Mrs Garnett had asked delicately.

"Pardon?"

"Which is to be the master's bedroom, Miss Townley?"

Miss Townley was clearly astonished and said so, even when her mama explained to her that it was customary for husbands and wives of the middle and upper middle classes to have separate sleeping quarters.

"Oh no, Conal and I will share a room, Mama," Miss Townley said very emphatically in Mrs Garnett's presence. "The bathroom will adjoin *our* bedroom, naturally. Really, Mama, I cannot understand why you should imagine we would sleep apart. You and Papa don't."

"Jenna darling, this is not the sort of conversation a young unmarried woman should be having, even with her mother," casting a glance at her other daughter, Miss Beth Townley who appeared, as young ladies of breeding should, not to have heard. Even so, Mrs Garnett could see Mrs Townley was amused.

"Oh pooh, Mama! When did you and I ever indulge in such foolishness, and Beth doesn't mind, do you, Beth? You both know how much I love Conal. You have from the start and it will be my greatest joy to sleep in his arms."

"Jenna! Mrs Garnett, I do apologise for my daughter's outspokenness. I'm afraid, though, that you must get used to it. My husband and I . . . we have not curbed her tongue as perhaps we should."

Nor her behaviour, Mrs Garnett said to herself, remembering the scene to which she had been privy several weeks ago, and now would you look at her, her arms wrapped about her husband's neck, kissing him with an abandon which surely should be kept to the privacy of their bedroom, and in front of the blushing maids and grinning manservants too. Mind you, the master was just as bad, ready to carry her straight up the stairs past the line of servants without even giving his new young wife time to be introduced to them – since they would be hers – as was proper.

"You'd best put me down, darling," madam said breathlessly. "My bonnet is coming off and you know what my hair is like."

"Indeed I do," the master answered in a manner which Mrs Garnett could only describe as meaningful, but he set her on her feet and led her to the line of waiting servants. "You do the honours, Mrs Garnett. I swear I can never remember which is Dora and which is Maisie. Aah, I see a new face."

"Indeed, Sir."

"It's Marian, darling, my own maid come from Bank House, so you see I shall no longer need your services with the hairbrush," and again there was that breathless suggestion of some secret thing between them, which was, Mrs Garnett supposed, natural in newly-weds but surely it was best kept to the bedroom.

"This is Dora, ma'am."

"Indeed, Dora and I have met." She grinned, actually grinned at Dora as she did at all of them.

"Sarah, who is kitchen maid."

"Sarah."

"Maisie, chambermaid."

"Maisie."

"Margaret, scullery maid."

"Margaret, what a pretty colour your hair is."

Dear God in heaven, would you listen to her? Margaret, or Mags as she was known in the kitchen, would never be the same again though you could see she thought the new Mrs Macrae was second only to the Queen herself.

"Percy."

"Percy and I have also met, Mrs Garnett."

"Mr Campbell, coachman."

"Yes, Mr Campbell I know."

"George and Eppie . . . Ephraim, from the garden."

She twinkled – Mrs Garnett could think of no other word to describe it – at them all before turning to her husband, taking him by the arm and drawing him towards the bottom of the stairs.

"It was lovely to meet you all and I'm sure we will get along famously. Thank you, Mrs Garnett. We'll ring when we want something, won't we, Mr Macrae?" and the open-mouthed servants were treated to the sight of their new mistress leaning heavily and – though they did not, of course, know the word – sensuously against her husband's shoulder, leaving none of them in doubt as to what they were about to be engaged in!

They did not come down to dinner, asking for their meal to be served in the new and elegant sitting-room which led from their bedroom. It had once been a bedroom but Miss Townley, as she was then, had professed a desire for a private sitting-room where she and her husband might to alone when they needed to be, though she did not voice this last to Mrs Garnett. While they had been abroad an army of builders and decorators had moved in, ripping out walls and doors, blocking up others, stripping rooms and putting them together again so that the sitting-room, the bedroom she and the master were to share, and the bathroom ran across the whole of the front of the house on the upstairs floor. She had ordered cool colours of dove grey, pale blue, cobalt blue, white and caramel in all three rooms, rich carpets and curtains, delicate flowing furniture, except for the bed which was huge and sturdy and would last a lifetime. There were fires in each room, even the bathroom, fragrant candles, drifting white muslin drapes, softness and beauty in which Conal and Jenna Macrae loved one another within half an hour of the bride entering her new home. It was home now, she murmured drowsily against her husband's shoulder in their bed, and yes, she thought she might try some of Mrs Garnett's delicious chicken and mushroom which must be cold by now, since she was ravenously hungry.

"Marriage suits you, my bonny lassie," her husband told her adoringly as he fondled her breast. In his other hand he held a glass of dry white wine, chilled just as he liked it. He sipped it, sharing it with her, his thumb and forefinger gently rolling her pink nipple, watching with narrow-eyed delight as she began to arch her back. "You like that, don't you, you witch, you lovely, lovely witch? You get more beautiful every day and I swear your breasts are rounder and fuller then they were that last time you seduced me, remember, in March?"

"Seduced you! What I do remember is that you didn't struggle much."

"I was afraid to scream in case the servants were

alarmed so I gave in gracefully and let you have your way with me."

"I noticed how reluctant you were."

"You were so forceful. God, I love you, Jenna."

"Show me."

"Hell's teeth, are you never satisfied, woman?" but he obliged her just the same, pulling her down in the bed, spreading her arms and legs, kissing the length of her, tasting the smoothness and richness of her skin, licking and sucking and biting until she moaned in a devastated mixture of pain and rapture.

"Let me . . ." she gasped, wanting to pleasure him with the same exquisite joy he had given her.

"NO," he growled huskily, turning her over, giving the same detailed attention to every inch of her long, graceful back, her sweetly rounded buttocks, her elegantly turned legs and ankles, the soft soles of her fine-boned feet. He wrapped her and himself in the curtain of her lustrous hair, then he took her, bringing her to a shuddering climax which shook even the solid marriage bed.

"Now it's your turn," she told him when she could speak. "Lie down and be still."

"Be still, hell and damnation, how can I be still when you are driving me mad with . . . aahh . . . Jenna, my sweet, sweet Jenna Macrae," arching his lean body, throwing back his head in exquisite agony until at last . . . at last it was done and they were both complete, both still.

It was later, his hand again at her breast, when he repeated what he had told her before.

"Your breasts are definitely bigger, my love," he murmured, then he sat up and looked into her drowsing face, pushing aside the heavy tangle of her hair to study the lines of her languid body.

"Jenna."

"Mmmm?"

"Have you . . .?"

"What?" She was almost asleep. She raised a limp arm to pull him close to her again, sighing when he resisted.

"When was your last . . .?"

"What? For goodness sake. Do lie down, Conal. Put your arms around me. You know I can't sleep now unless I have your arms around me."

"My darling, I'm not awfully sure what well-brought-up young ladies call it. A curse, or a blessing, depending on the circumstances, I suppose, but it arrives once a month. When was the last time?"

Jenna opened one eye and peeped at him, then the other. Comprehension had begun to dawn and she sat up slowly. Her breasts, heavy, full-nippled and infinitely womanly, fell forward into her husband's hands.

"Oh my God," she gasped.

"Oh my God indeed."

"Conal, you don't mean . . .?"

"I think I do, my bonnie wee lass." His eyes began to snap with joy, dancing golden lights blazing from them into hers. His teeth gleamed in his widely grinning amber-tinted face and he pushed one trembling hand through the thick dark tumble of his hair. He had one knee bent, the foot flat on the bed and he rested one arm on his knee, raising his face to the ceiling, scarcely able to contain his delight. He looked beautiful, a fiercely masculine beauty, his body lean and symmetrical in direct contrast to the full loveliness of his wife, his legs long and hard, his stomach flat. Dark, fine hairs lay smoothly on his chest, fanning lightly down his belly to the dense black bush between his legs where the flower of his masculinity bloomed, proven now with his seed already planted in his woman's body.

She was quiet, with none of the elation of her husband, though at that moment of male joy, of male triumph, male fulfilment, he did not notice. She lay back slowly on her pillow, her clouded eyes never leaving his and it was several moments before she had his attention.

"Jenna?" He lowered his head slowly, looking deeply into her face.

"Jenna?" he repeated. "Ye ken what this means, don't you, lassie?"

"Oh yes, I ken what it means."

"And?" He was ready to laugh and shout, to pull her into his eager arms but something in her manner, he couldn't say what it was, stopped him.

"It means I am to have a child, doesn't it?"

"Aye, it does, and . . .?"

"It means I cannot go over to Marfield and continue my training with Papa in the running of the collieries."

He sat back, his body losing, very slowly, that high pressure of joy. It ran from him like liquid running from a jug. It seeped away, drained away, leaving him empty, taut, devastated and because he could not remain upright without something to stiffen his frame he filled his body up again with the only emotion at his disposal.

Rage! Rage and savage disappointment.

"My love, even had you not been with child there is not the slightest chance of your doing that." His voice was stiff, offended, contemptuous and very, very cold.

"Oh yes, oh yes, Conal. That is just what I meant to do whenever I could. Every day if possible. I meant to be fair and give as much time as was neccesary to my duties as your wife, but the pits are my responsibility."

"Don't be so bloody ridiculous, Jenna." His tone was flat. He rose and moved away from the bed, picking up a robe and shrugging into it as if their lovely and natural nakedness no longer belonged here. He took a cigar from the box on the mantelshelf, lit it with a taper from the fire and dragged the smoke deeply into his lungs. "Your father has managed for over twenty years without you by his side and can certainly manage another twenty at least. And he has that lad to help him."

"Simeon! He has nothing to do with our family."

"I was led to believe he was related. A cousin or something. Anyway, that is not the point. You are! You are my wife and by Christmas will be the mother of our child. That is your job, Jenna. We havena discussed this ridiculous notion you have in your head because I thought . . . hoped that you would have forgotten it, or at least realised, here with me, in our home, that this was where you belonged but I see I must set you straight. You may do as you wish, Jenna, providing you do nothing to harm the child, like riding that mare I have in the stables for you. Oh yes, it was to be . . . Well, no matter, she will still be there after the child is born so take the carriage to Liverpool, spend my money, visit your mother and sister as often as you please, entertain, do whatever you like as long as you stay away from your father's collieries. I am no captor, Jenna and providing you are . . . circumspect, you may go where you please."

He softened then, his love for her, which amazed him with its fierceness, fighting the offence she had given him with her obvious reluctance to bear his child. "I shall be with you as much as I can. I thought you might like to sail up the coast on one of my ships to visit our Scottish relatives. Tis a bonny place, Jenna, and they will want to welcome my bride."

He was pleading with her now. Pleading with her to share his own happiness, pleading with her not to spoil it for him. A man who has a son has the world's richest treasure and this was to be his, son or daughter, but he wanted her to feel the same.

"But I'm not ready for it, Conal," she wailed, lifting and crossing her arms over her face with such desolation that for a moment he was sorry. Sorry that he had burdened her with it. With a child when she was really no more than a child herself. A couple of months over eighteen and she was expected to settle down to motherhood and all the hedged-about restrictions that entailed. Then his face hardened again and he turned away.

"Whether ye are or no, tis a fact, lassie," he said harshly, "and you must settle down to it. Now then, you'd best sleep for you'll need your rest. I'll take myself off to another room so that—"

"Conal, please, please, you can't mean to . . .?" She was distraught now, not with the painfulness of their quarrel or his anger but with the shock of realising that her husband, on their first night in their home, should contemplate leaving her alone. "Conal . . ."

"Jenna?"

"Please . . ."

"What is it?"

"Don't go, Conal. Don't leave me alone. I cannot bear it if we . . ."

He was beside her in a second, lifting her from the bed, cradling her against him with passionate arms, kissing her wet face, murmuring her name, murmuring of his love, his deep, deep love, his remorse, his pain and guilt at making her weep.

"Hush now, lassie, hush, I'm here," he whispered, wrapping her in the strength of his love, dominating her vulnerability, bending her to his will, triumphant but loving her as he had loved no woman. In his passion he did not notice that she had made no promise to do as he demanded of her.

Chapter Twelve

Bryony put both hands to the large sun hat she wore, the movement lifting the swell of her breasts and at once the eyes of the young man who lounged indolently beside her under the shade of the wide branches of the oak tree were drawn to them and he flushed painfully.

Her hat, much worn in the country which was where the Townleys considered they lived, was called a round hat. It had a wide, flexible brim and a low, flat crown, shaped somewhat like a mushroom and was trimmed with ribbons which were fastened beneath its brim and tied in a large bow at the chin. It was worn flat on the head, perhaps tipped a little to the front to shade the eyes and face in the bright sunshine which was anathema to the fine skins of fashionable young ladies. Bryony's hat was of pale cream straw, the ribbons a silvery blue to match the broad sash she wore about her waist. Her white muslin dress, a young girl's dress since she was only fourteen, was simple. The puffed sleeves finished above her elbow, the bodice was high-necked and tucked, the skirt gathered and almost touching the toe of her cream laced kidskin boots.

She was sitting in the swing, her foot brushing the grass which had worn away with the dozens of pairs of feet which had scraped there over the years. Her arms were wrapped around the ropes which held the swing to the stout branch of the tree and her hands were to the brim of her hat. No sunlight touched her, or Tim Spencer who watched her with fascinated concentration, but the young man could see the faint round shading beneath the bodice of her dress where her nipples were and the peaks, like two small marbles which were the nipples themselves. Her face was dark, the shadow of the branches and their full weight of high summer leaves toning the pale golden honey of her skin to amber. In it, her eyes, half closed, the lashes thick and ready to mesh together, were a deep burnished gold, like those of a panther young Tim Spencer had once seen in a London zoo.

She licked her lips, her little pink tongue like that of a kitten lapping cream, her lips not pink nor peach as other young girls' were but the rich, red ripeness of a hedge-berry. She gripped the ropes of the swing and began idly to push herself backwards and forwards and, after glancing casually over her shoulder to make sure she was unobserved by the chattering group at the lake side, lifted her feet in the air then back under the seat until she had gained considerable momentum.

"D'you want a push, Bryony?" the young man asked somewhat thickly, his eyes on the calves of her legs, just above where her boots ended. She wore fine white stockings and about them cascaded a froth of fine lace.

"No, thanks, Tim. You stay where you are."

He needed no second telling. The swing went up and up and at each forward movement, as she lifted and pointed her toes, Tim Spencer could see high into her skirt and petticoat. It was a warm day. Tim had read somewhere that years ago, before the reign of their puritanical little Queen, ladies had not considered it necessary to wear drawers, since their skirts brushed the ground. He could not have sworn to it since she moved so quickly but for one tantalising moment he thought he caught a glimpse of white, naked thigh and the mound of thick, dark hair which grew between Bryony Townley's legs.

"Oh dear, I think I've gone too high. Would you come

behind and slow me down, Tim? Really, I think I'm going to fall, please Tim, can you help me?"

Slowly dragged from the hypnotic state the sight of Bryony Townley's, well . . . he didn't really know what young girls called that very private part of their bodies which young men like himself and his cronies had their own coarse word for. He wasn't even certain he had actually seen it but he did know that Bryony Townley had cast him in a spell he was finding it very difficult to resist. Ever since the night of her and her cousins' birthday party in March when he had danced with her, delighted with her shyness, her sweetness, her innocence which had somehow, though he was positive she was not aware of it, promised so much, he found he could not get her out of his thoughts. After those dances they had shared, while the Townley family seemed to be involved in some family crisis, the exact nature of which he was not sure of, nor interested in, he and Bryony had run hand in hand down to the lake beside which at this moment, his mama, his Aunt Dove, Aunt Jenna and all his cousins were reclining and almost, almost, he had kissed her. Had she not been some sort of relative, a cousin of his cousins, he was not sure exactly, he might have done so but then, at the last moment, since it was her birthday and she only fourteen he had drawn back. She had not been aware of it, naturally, a young girl gently reared as she was, but her eyes had been a deep chocolate brown in the moonlight, her lips parted, her breasts lifting as she clasped her hands behind her where she leaned against a tree.

There had been several occasions since, when, somehow or other, he was never quite sure how, they had found themselves alone and each time it had become harder to be the gentleman he had been brought up to be. He was seventeen, eighteen at Christmas and he and Amy, his twin sister, would be expected to marry well, Amy soon, himself eventually, for a man did not take a bride until well into his twenties, or even thirties. Mama would have a fit if she knew of his infatuation for Bryony Townley, who was no match for a baronet, but dear Lord, she was very sweet.

His hands at her waist slowed her down and the swing came to a halt. She looked back over her shoulder, laughing into his face, her breath sweet, her rosy mouth no more than an inch from his and he felt his already swelling manhood press painfully against the crotch of his well-fitting trousers.

"Thank you, Tim. I really must behave myself and stop taking the swing so high. As Aunt Nella is constantly reminding me, I am no longer a child. Perhaps we had better join the others. Jenna and her husband have just arrived and tea is being brought out. Do I look all right after that mad flight up into the branches?"

She held up her face to him, her lips curving over her even white teeth, her eyes mysterious with some message she was sending which for the life of him he could not decipher.

"You're the most beautiful thing I ever saw," he said hoarsely, almost reaching for her, his own soft brown eyes, inherited from his papa and which looked to Bryony exactly like those of her faithful dog, Gilly, becoming almost glazed. He was not handsome, as his papa had not been handsome which had not stopped his exquisitely beautiful mama from marrying him, but his unremarkable face was kind, gentle, good-natured and he *was* a baronet!

"Timothy, you must not say such things to me," Bryony admonished him smilingly, feeling at least ten years older than he was instead of three years younger but then it was well known that girls were much older than men, if not in years then in maturity, more adult and were certainly ready for marriage years before a gentleman was. A gentleman could marry when he pleased, but a woman, having only so many years in which to breed the children her husband expected of her, must start early. Fifteen was quite usual and in nine months' time Bryony Townley would be fifteen.

Basket chairs heaped with cushions had been set out on the lawn by the servants, grouped about half a dozen tables, each one covered with a snowy white lace cloth, dainty china and silver cutlery, napkins and tastefully arranged bowls of flowers. At one of them sat Nella Townley pouring tea which Dolly, Tilly and Betsy handed to the guests. There were wafer-thin cucumber sandwiches, cheese cakes, honey cakes, snowcakes – a Scottish recipe looked out by Mrs Blaney and baked in honour of Miss Jenna's new husband – pound cake, sponge cake, strawberries from the strawberry cloche in Seth's vegetable garden, with generous portions of richly whipped cream, and this was merely afternoon tea to be taken and digested before the real meal which was dinner in approximately three hours.

It was a family party arranged to welcome home the new Mrs Macrae and her splendid husband though it occurred to several of the guests that the recently married couple were not completely at their ease. Five weeks they had been married and home no more than a week or so from their wedding journey and should they be so polite with one another, those about them asked themselves, at least Jenna Macrae's mama did. Jenna looked well, very well. If anyone with Jenna's unusual colouring which was the same as her own could be said to be rosy, Jenna certainly did, her skin glowing beneath its surface with a translucency that was almost pink, her eyes bright, the whites as white as fresh fallen snow. Her hair was vibrant, flauntingly red with gold and copper streaks set in it by the sunlight but why, oh why had not her husband insisted that she control it properly instead of allowing her to bundle it carelessly to the crown of her head with no more than a knot of white ribbons? Her gown, also white, was simple, girlish almost in the purest leno, a transparent, muslin-like material under which was a fine lining of the palest, honey-coloured silk. Very suitable for the occasion, being light and modest, if only she'd worn a hat or at least arranged her hair suitably, her mama thought, as befitted a young matron. As it was it tumbled in wild disarray, long corkscrew curls drifting across her ears and down her back, several loose tendrils over her eyes which she kept blowing impatiently upwards.

"Would you like to borrow a round hat, darling?" her mama asked her. "The sun must be in your eyes," but Jenna refused despite her husband's warning glance.

They were all there. Lady Faulkner with her husband Sir Edward and their three children, Blake, Christopher and Caroline. Lady Spencer, Sir Timothy, her son, and his twin sister, Amy. Nella Townley and her husband Jonas, naturally, with their daughters Beth, Nancy and Rose, and the Townley cousins, the poor orphaned Simeon and Bryony whom Jonas and Nella had taken under their wing at a very early age. The Easons, of course since, as Nella said, they were family now in the true sense of the word for had not Mark's brother married Jonas and Nella's daughter? To make up the numbers amongst the predominantly female company, Nella had invited Frank Miller, Ben Parker, who was a childhood friend of Simeon's, and Thomas Young. Charlie Graham had not been included!

"And how was Italy, Jenna?" Lady Spencer asked. "What did you think to Rome? Was not St Peter's magnificent?" Lady Spencer, having spent her wedding journey in Italy over eighteen years ago though she had not been abroad since, liked to remind those in whose company she found herself that she was not the country mouse she might once have been. Her father had been an enormously rich man, a man of his time, making his money in the mighty industry which had grown in Queen Victoria's reign. He had allowed her and her sisters to spend his money as they wished but he could see no point in travel, in what was known as culture and her journeying to Italy had been a mystery to him when there were so many wonders to be seen in their own fair land.

"It was hot, Aunt Linnet," Jenna answered briefly. "Did we visit St Peter's, Conal?" she threw at her husband. "One saw so many buildings it was easy to forget."

"We did, Jenna," her husband answered, declining with great courtesy to choose something from the vast array of confectionery which was offered to him. Indeed he seemed to shudder and Nella had to hide her smile. She did like Jenna's husband who was no fool. He was being very patient with Jenna's petulance, you could only call it that, when really, what she needed was a good spanking, then a good loving, again doing her best to conceal her amusement at the thought.

"What are you snickering about?" her own husband whispered.

"I'll tell you later, my love," she answered, taking his hand in hers, unabashed by the inclination of her sisters to look at her as though she was quite mad.

"And the David? Lady Spencer continued, looking round the circle of faces to judge exactly their reaction to her remark.

"The David? Now that I really cannot recall," Jenna answered shortly.

"It's a statue in—" her husband began, but she jumped up, interrupting him.

"Oh, one of those. Dear God, I saw so many and all naked." Lady Spencer and Lady Faulkner both gasped and Sir Edward, at the mention of the last word, looked up from his glazed contemplation of the slice of pound cake on his plate.

"Anyway, I'm off for a walk. I've done nothing for

weeks but sit on my . . . sit about and . . . well, it doesn't suit me. Duff and Dory will be glad to see me, I'm sure," clearly indicating that she was of the opinion that no one else was. "I want to tell Ted to get them ready for me to take back to Everton."

"I'll come with you," her husband grated. "If you will excuse us, ladies, gentlemen . . ." striding off after his wife and when he caught her gripping her fiercely by the arm so that she was forced to abandon her headlong flight and march to the rhythm he set.

"Oh dear," said Lady Spencer, eyeing her own perfectly behaved daughter with a great deal of complacency, "what was all that about, one wonders?"

"What?" her brother-in-law asked, wondering himself why he allowed Dove to drag him along to these infernal family affairs the industrial classes seemed to go in for, telling himself – not for the first time – that this would be the last. Of course he did want to get that hunter for Chris. Blake had his, courtesy of Jonas Townley, who else, but a loan, at least that's what he called it, would be very welcome if he was to get one for his younger son as well.

"Oh, you know what newly-weds are, Dove," Nella said smoothly. "Now then, why don't you youngsters get up a game of croquet? And the gentlemen may want to smoke their cigars. Jonas, yes darling, you and Mark and Edward should go and take a look . . . at . . . at . . . well, whatever you care to. Now then, Laura, come and tell me what happened at Smithy Brow yesterday afternoon. I heard Edda and Janie had a bit of a set-to. And Anna Stern called round this morning to tell me that Dorcas Gates's eldest girl is to take up teaching. What do you think of that?"

Lady Faulkner and Lady Spencer exchanged glances. From the lawn where a vigorous game of croquet had begun, one in which all the young people with the exception of Thomas Young who considered he was, at twenty-eight, a bit too old for this kind of tomfoolery, took turns to hit the croquet balls, great gales of hysterical laughter drifted towards the two ladies and they stood up at once.

"Perhaps it might be wise if we . . . supervised, Dove," her sister said since Nella, deep in dreadful conversation in which such things as black spit and ulcers seemed to take a prominent part was clearly oblivious to the goings-on in the croquet game. It was so hilarious, so fast and furious and downright confusing neither of them noticed that Tim Spencer and Bryony Townley were missing.

He was about to kiss her. She could see the glow of it change his eyes to a darker brown and the question was, should she let him? She walked a very fragile line with Tim, gently urging him on towards the goal she was determined to achieve, whipping up his male desires with all the considerable female tricks at her disposal, but at the same time being as shyly innocent and gentle as a dove. She wanted him to want her, which he did, but it must not be the wanting young gentlemen feel for a pretty housemaid. The trouble was, they were both so young and it would be years before they could marry, at least it was years before he would consider marriage and could she keep him dangling that long? He must be allowed some small . . . liberty in order to keep him burning for her, but not too much or he would think her fast, fair game and certainly not a girl to marry!

She was holding her breath, not particularly wanting to be kissed really, not particularly sure she should allow it when Jenna and Conal stormed round the corner of the stable and into the yard. Tim hissed behind his teeth, drawing her further into the shadow of the tack-room, quite petrified, she was well aware, and who could blame him, that they might be seen. Should it get back to his mama that he had been caught kissing Bryony Townley behind the tack-room door, there would be hell to pay, not only for who she was, in their opinion, meaning Aunt Nella and Uncle Jonas, no more than a schoolgirl, but for him who was a baronet and certainly not for the likes of Bryony Townley who was a nobody in the eyes of Lady Spencer.

"There is no need to treat me like a bloody child, Conal," Jenna was saying. Bryony leaned, in apparent terror, against Tim's chest, putting her arms about his waist, telling herself she might as well take every small advantage that was available.

"Then perhaps you shouldna act like one, lassie. You were damned rude to your aunt who was—"

"A stupid bragging fool. Just because she's been to Italy once she fancies she's a world traveller," Jenna sneered. "'Have you seen the David?' Just as though she's seen everything . . ."

"Stop it, Jenna. Can you not hear yourself? And it's nothing to do with your aunt, it it? She just happened to get in the way of that damned wilfulness of yours which is suddenly, no matter how you jib at it, going to be curtailed. You must face it. You are to have a child . . ."

Bryony turned her face into Tim's shirt to stifle her gasp, pressing up closer to him and his arms tightened about her.

". . . And can do nothing about it. Christmas is only six months away and when the baby comes . . ."

Christmas! And Jenna married only five weeks! Bryony's cool brain, despite the growing heat of Tim Spencer's straining body which was doing its best to remain gentlemanly under the most trying circumstances, made some rapid calculations and she drew in her breath then expelled it sharply against Tim's shirt front.

". . . I shall make sure you have no more for a while, I promise you."

"Conal, really, can one do that? I didn't realise." Jenna's ragged thoughts which had ducked and weaved for the past weeks, straining against the bonds which were to bind her, suddenly became engaged and she turned to her husband, leaning her back against the sun-warmed tack-room wall. "I thought babies just came, whether you wanted them or not."

Conal laughed, then leaned forward to kiss her. She had been a hellion this last week, railing against the enforced confinement that he was to impose on her, knowing she could do nothing about it but kicking against it just the same. She *would* go to Marfield, she shrieked. She *would* go the colliery and make sure that that nincompoop – yes, that was what Simeon Townley was, a bloody nincompoop – didn't ruin her chances of becoming a thriving coal owner. He couldn't run a church garden party and if it was left to him the mines would be bankrupt by the year's end. Yes, she was well aware, if she listened to reason which she wouldn't that her papa would not allow it to happen, that her inheritance was in good hands. That Papa would guard it all for her until it was her turn to take it over but how was she to learn to take it over if she was prevented from accompanying him in his daily work? Simeon would be sixteen at Christmas and would be with Papa all day and every day and she must be there too in order to see that he did not trick her out of what was rightfully hers.

"How can he do that, Jenna?" Conal did his best to be patient. "You are your father's daughter. The eldest child and Simeon is no more than a cousin twice removed or whatever the relationship is."

The only way he could divert her raging thoughts was to make love to her which he did enthusiastically, tirelessly, endlessly and their first week at Beechfield Lodge had passed in a frenzy of quarrelling and lovemaking which, as he had known it would be, was maddening

215

but highly diverting. No, he would never be bored with Jenna Macrae!

"My sweet, there are ways to prevent pregnancy, which every man knows and many women too, but a husband will not often use them since he wants nothing but to keep his wife at home bearing his children. The more she has the better. At least in the home of a man of substance. He needs sons to carry on his name, particularly if he is from the upper classes, and to continue in whatever he may have built for himself. My son" – smiling into her absorbed face – "will carry on the shipping line I mean to build. Which I am already building, but lassie, I don't intend to burden you with a child every year as many men would. I love you too much, Jenna Macrae, to put you in bondage, no matter how sweet that bondage might be. You are my wife and I shall expect loyalty and respect for my position but you are not to be a captive. I want children, lots of children for a home needs them and that is what you and I will have, a home, but you must be given space to grow into the magnificent woman you will become as you mature. So, this child at Christmas, my little love, and then some freedom. In the meanwhile, there is always this."

He leaned forward, placing his long, hard body against hers, laying his lips against hers and proceeded to kiss her with a slow, growing warmth, a lingering, smoothing intensity she was beginning to know so well. There was no one about. Walters and Daniels, who were getting old now and were allowed to "tekk it a bit easy" as Walters put it, were sitting amiably, smoking their pipes together on the wooden bench to the side of the vegetable garden, watching as Seth and Dinty, his lad, did a bit of weeding. Jenna's dogs lay panting at their feet in the somnolent sunshine. Arthur had ridden over to Primrose Bank where his old mam still lived and it was Ted's afternoon off. Leander and the carriage horses had been put into the paddock beyond the stable gate where they stood, heads down, dozing in the summer heat beneath the wide shade of the trees which grew around its perimeter.

"Jenna, sweet Jenna . . . I could love you right here . . ." Conal's mouth nuzzled the satin flesh beneath the firm line of her chin.

"Then why don't you?"

"Sweetheart, you're incorrigible and I adore you but where do you suggest we . . ."

"The tack-room . . . there's hay in the loft above it."

"You're a wicked woman, my darling."

"A tumble in the hay . . ." She began to giggle with delight.

"Where did you hear that expression? You know too much for your own good."

Conal's breath was ragged in his throat and his grin a slash of white in his brown face as he darted, hand in hand, with his wife into the shadowed stillness of the tack-room. It had been swept out and washed down that day, as it was every morning, but there was a smell of damp straw overlaid with horse manure from the stable next door, a dank but familiar odour which offended neither of them. The place was deserted and Conal followed his wife up the ladder to the loft above, his hand already reaching for the secret divide between her legs. Their soft laughter went with them and then there was only the rustling of the hay, murmurs and sighs and whispers.

Bryony Townley stood rigidly in Tim Spencer's arms. Her breath, which she had not realised she was holding escaped slowly from between her parted lips and as it did so she raised her head and looked up into his face. She was, for the first time since her childhood, at a complete loss as to what to do next. She had been a composed baby and child, seeming to be aware very early in life that she was not as her cousins were though she had known nothing but kindness from her aunt and uncle.

She had watched them all, her cousins, as they grew
through their protected childhood and girlhood and had
come to realise that life would not be as easily managed
for Bryony Townley or Simeon Townley, the brother she
loved as she loved no other person in the world. Simeon,
though older than she was, was not as farseeing, nor as
patient. He was not content, as she begged him to be, to
play the role it seemed he was destined for and that was
Jenna Townley's manager in Jenna Townley's collieries.
At least for now. He and Jenna had fought all their lives
since Simeon was basically very like her in his passion
to be the best. He was still young and inclined to put
great emphasis on such things as a good horse, a well-cut
jacket, splendid boots and money in his pocket but mining
was as much in his blood as it was in Jenna's, it seemed,
and when he grew from boyish things to those of a man
there was nothing surer than the certainty that he would
not bow his head to Jenna Macrae's leadership. He was
very handsome and the ladies loved him, young as he
was and, with a good marriage, as Bryony meant them
both to have, and with her to steady him, the two of
them would leave behind that faint, unintentional, she
knew that, but there all the same, stigma of poor relation.
Jonas Townley would never, never allow Jenna to run
his business when he was gone, and neither would her
husband, Conal Macrae, or so it appeared and who else
was there to do it in her stead but her cousin Simeon?
Bryony and Simeon Townley would have their rightful
place in the society of Marfield. She meant to fight for
it, for her and Simeon, but at the same time she must
remain on good terms with those around her and that
meant this man, this boy who was pressing his body
against hers – she could feel him, feel something hard
against her stomach – and how was she to extract herself
from this devastating situation her own aspirations had led
her into? How could she turn it to her advantage? Jenna

and her husband had ruined it, ruined the act of sweet, shy innocence she had meant to put on for Tim and she could not stir her normally sharp brain for some way out of it. Some way which would benefit Bryony Townley's cause. Damn Jenna Macrae and damn her handsome husband. Even now they were directly above her and Tim's heads, making the most embarrassingly strange noises and she must get away from them. She must get herself and Tim away, for this was not the atmosphere, this lusty, earthy thing Jenna and Conal had created, with which she meant to bind Tim Spencer to her.

Tim pressed his hot, moist lips to hers and that instinct that had never yet failed her leaped at once to her defence. She did not resist him. That would never do for she did not want to offend him. Instead she simply started to weep, silently, distressingly, abundantly, great fat tears spilling over her long lashes and gliding across her cheeks so that he could not fail to notice them as they washed against his eager mouth. He raised it, looking into her face, a boy who at that moment was about to take the first step towards becoming a man. A gentleman, which he undoubtedly was. Putting a finger to his lips he led her from the tack-room, stepping delicately, silently, leading her by the hand across the cobble yard to the gate. It needed oiling and as he opened it squealed lustily and in the loft Conal Macrae raised his head from between his wife's thighs.

"What . . .?"

"Conal, please . . ."

His wife pulled his head down again and beyond the gate Tim Spencer and Bryony Townley ran, hand in hand, down the length of the paddock. The horses tossed startled heads in their direction and Bryony continued to weep with the desolation of a child.

When they reached the wall which encircled the grounds of Bank House Tim stopped running. He still held her hand though and she continued to sob wordlessly. When they came to the gate he opened it and led her through it, closing it behind them, then across a small field and into Seven Cows Wood. The sun shone through the full panoply of summer leaves creating tiny stars of moving light, hazed shafts of sunshine and fingers of shadows which lay across the mossy floor of the wood.

Tim Spencer had known exactly what Jenna Townley, Jenna Macrae now, and her new husband had been up to in the tack-room loft and it had excited him so much that had Bryony given him the slightest encouragement he would have laid her down, drawn her skirts up to her waist and directed his attentions to that delicious part of her he was almost sure he had seen on the swing. He hadn't seen it, of course, he knew that now and Bryony had done exactly as any young girl of gentle upbringing would do and that was to be afraid. She was so sweet, so trusting, so ignorant she had been bewildered by it all and being bewildered and ignorant of man's lust, she had been afraid. Like a child she had wept in her fear, turning to him for protection. She had not meant him to kiss her and he was ashamed to have taken advantage of her. Look at her now, her incredible golden eyes brimming with tears, quite desolate but so beautiful. So very beautiful. Her lovely poppy mouth trembled and her hair had somehow become free of its ribbon and her hat. Her long ebony curls fell across her shoulders and breasts. Shining they were, and soft and he longed to take them in his hands and lift a dark strand to his lips, to touch her flushed skin, to reach out and cup her breasts . . . Dear God, he longed to put his hands on her – anywhere – but how could he be so crass when she was gazing at him with the trust and belief of a child who waits to be told, to have explained to her what had taken place.

"Bryony, you must not be upset by . . . by what Jenna and her husband did. They are married, you see . . ." He felt himself begin to stammer. Drawing a deep breath he started again and Bryony thought he looked like an owl, blinking and pompous. "There is nothing to be afraid of, you know. Not when two people . . . well . . ."

"Yes, Tim?" she said, her eyes wide and still tearful.

"When a man and a woman love one another they . . . perhaps Aunt Jenna has told you . . .?"

"Told me what, Tim?"

"There are certain things . . ."

"Things?"

He could not help himself. "God, but you're lovely, Bryony. I've never seen a girl more lovely. I'd . . . I know you were afraid but if you'd let me . . . I wouldn't hurt you, really I wouldn't. I love you, you see . . ."

"Let you what, Tim?" Good God above, using one of Uncle Jonas's oaths, would the fool never get to the bloody point? Her eyes were still somewhat alarmed as they looked up into his.

"Would you let me . . . kiss you a little? Just for a moment. I promise I'd stop whenever you said so. I'm . . . do you like me a little, Bryony?"

"Oh yes, Tim, more than a little. I always have," she went on artlessly.

"Then, may I?"

"It won't . . . be like Jenna and Conal, will it?"

"Oh no, my little love . . . I may call you that, mayn't I?"

"If you want to, Tim."

"Then . . .?"

He laid his lips gently on hers, this time aware of them, of her, not distracted by excitement as he had been by the passionate exchange which had gone on above his head earlier. He was surprised and delighted by their fullness, their warmth, their moistness. He had kissed more than one girl before today and had already had several fumbling encounters with a girl from one of the estate farms who had, for a couple of shillings, obligingly allowed him to strip her, then showed him what she had called "the way of things". He would dearly love to pass on and share "the way of things" with Bryony but her shoulders trembled beneath his hands and when he raised his head her eyes were full of tears again.

"Oh, my little love," he whispered huskily, filled with remorse by his own male desires. "Don't cry. I'm sorry. There, let me wipe your tears. Don't cry, it will be better next time, really it will, when you are more used to me." His heart swelled with protective love and though he longed to go on he was not displeased by Bryony Townley's touching innocence and fragility.

"Oh Tim, you are so wonderfully kind," she breathed against his chest where he had drawn her. She smiled since he could not see her face nor the triumph in her eyes.

Chapter Thirteen

"Has my husband left yet, Marian?" Jenna asked her maid who had just left her breakfast tray on the small table beside the upstairs sitting-room window. Conal had insisted with what Jenna had thought tedious firmness, since she had months to go yet, that she stay in bed after he left for the shipping office or at least have her breakfast in her sitting-room and for the past few weeks she had given in. It was so heavenly being married to Conal, so rapturous, so enchanting, she would have agreed to anything in the weeks since they had returned from Italy and especially since that delicious afternoon they had spent in the hayloft at Bank House.

She often smiled, sometimes when they were in company, at the remembrance of that afternoon and she had only to look across at Conal who could be chatting with a business acquaintance, and narrow her eyes and he would know exactly what she was thinking and try hard not to smile in return. She remembered the sun spilling through cracks in the wood across their naked bodies, the stifling heat which coated them both in sweat to which wisps of hay stuck; the scratches on her back and splayed legs, the dust, the raw, earthy energy of their lovemaking away from the silks and fragrance of their bedroom and that moment when, their bodies languid and satisfied from their shared passion, they had walked arm in arm across the lawn back to her mother's guests. Her mother had looked at her intently, then smiled and reached for her father's hand and somehow Jenna was aware that her mother knew, and she did not mind.

It was not just the hayloft, though, which had softened her attitude towards Conal but what he had said to her. This baby and then no more for two or three years he had promised her, providing she stayed at home, or at least did not seek her father out at the colliery. She could summon the carriage whenever she cared to and Campbell would drive her to Bank House to visit her mother though Conal was not too happy about this at the moment since the roads between Liverpool and St Helens, winding lanes which led through West Derby and Prescot, could be rough in parts. In her condition might it not be best if she stayed at home and perhaps her mama could visit her. And then there were the shops in Liverpool itself, the art galleries, the library, strolls on the marine parade, she was free to do as she pleased, within reason, naturally, providing she took no foolish risks with the health of both herself and their child. He wanted her to have freedom, to be happy, but not in the vicinity of the Townley collieries!

Marian paused in the doorway as she answered her mistress. "Yes, madam. He was just leaving as I came upstairs but I could probably catch him. He said . . ." Marian stopped speaking and bent her head, smiling.

"What? What did he say?"

"Well, I hardly like to repeat it, ma'am." Mr Macrae was very forthright sometimes and could apparently see no wrong in allowing the servants to know of his deep feelings for his wife.

"Oh go on, Marian, tell me." Jenna began to smile, knowing Conal's humour by now, and how he liked to shock a little, especially the housemaids.

"He said to tell you it was a lovely day and if you weren't up yet he'd . . ."

"What, Marian, do go on."

". . . that he'd come and . . . Oh, I can't, ma'am, really."

Jenna relented, still smiling. "Oh all right, Marian. I can guess what he said, the rogue." She shook her head, her rich and growing love moving her to a sweet silence in joyful contemplation of it, then she reached for her cup and began to sip her coffee.

"You may lay out my blue tarlatan day dress, Marian. I haven't worn it yet and I'm going over to Bank House."

"Yes, madam."

"And run and tell Campbell to bring the carriage round in an hour."

"Yes, madam."

"And I shall want water for a bath."

"Yes, madam."

"And ask Mrs Garnett for some more toast. I really am starving."

"Yes, madam."

"Well, off you go then, oh, but before you do will you have a look at the hem of my gold silk. I think I stepped on it and I shall need it for tonight."

"I've done it, madam."

"Good girl, now don't forget the toast, and there's no need to tell my husband where I've been today tell Campbell."

It was the blue tarlatan that did it. It had been made up for her just before her wedding and though it had gone with her to Italy there had been no occasion on which to wear it. It was a lovely pale blue, almost grey, almost silver, a tiny jacket bodice shaped to her waist and flaring out over her hips in a basque. It had a V neckline, revealing the deep, shadowed cleft between her creamy breasts with a narrow turn-down collar edged with white. It was fastened down the front with a row of tiny pearl buttons. The sleeves were close gathered at the armhole then tight fitted to the wrist cuff which again was edged in white. The skirt, supported by a crinoline, was fifteen feet around the hem and down its front, following the line of the jacket buttons, was a row in the same pearl. It was very fetching, as was her small straw bonnet to be worn at the back of her head and lined under the brim with white ruched tulle. She had a parasol, a froth of blue-grey lace the same colour as her gown and had looked very dashing on the day of the fitting.

She was quite appalled. The jacket would not even meet across her breasts, let alone do up and the skirt merely hung out at the front, following the quite obvious curve of her belly.

"Oh madam," Marian gasped. She had been aware, since she was madam's personal maid, that her mistress was putting on weight. Mrs Macrae did most of her bathing in the evening with . . . well, when her husband was home and when she did bathe in the morning she liked to do it alone. When the maidservants had filled the bath to her satisfaction she shooed them out, even Marian, spending sometimes an hour soaking in the fragrant water and so Marian had never seen her absolutely naked. The weight gain was, of course, due to her condition, since Marian and the rest of the servants could not fail to notice that she was with child, and so she should be, the way she and the master were with one another but she must be five or six months along, or at least that was what the blue tarlatan told Marian, and what was she to make of that since Mr and Mrs Macrae had been married only three!

Mrs Garnett could have told her!

"Hell and damnation," Mrs Macrae said through gritted teeth as Marian hovered about her, twitching this and pulling that, as though a bit of determination would soon put it right, her expression of dismay quite comical. "Don't do that, Marian, for God's sake. Anyone can see it doesn't fit me and never will now. Oh Lord, what a size I am and still a long way to go. What am I to wear? Marian, tell me, what do women wear when they are in my state?"

"Well, madam, if you were to hitch the hoop of your crinoline over . . . over the . . ."

"The bump?"

"Yes, and then perhaps a piece let in under each arm of the jacket . . ."

"But that would ruin it, Marian, and I shan't be able to wear it afterwards. Not that I'd want to. The style will be out of date by next summer. Oh, damn it to hell and damn this baby and damn my husband for getting me in this state . . ."

"Oh madam!" Marian's eyes widened and she put her hand to her mouth, shocked. They were all aware by now, the servants at Beechfield Lodge, that their new young mistress, who had been so engaging on the day she had returned with their master from their wedding journey, could be a firebrand. Smiling she'd been then, treating them as though they were her friends, and she still smiled and engaged them in conversation when she came across them. George in the garden, Eppy open-mouthed beside him, reported that she had chatted for quite ten minutes, asking him had he any children and when he said he had, ten of the little blighters and all crammed into the cottage at the back of the vegetable garden, she had been most interested. She'd had her dogs with her that day, those she'd brought over from her old home and she'd asked Eppy most politely if he would mind returning them to the stables for her, just as though he would be doing her a great favour. And her the mistress!

Dora said the same. She and Maisie, caught unexpected like, them thinking her still in her bed, polishing the banisters on the stairs, had been quite overcome by her pleasant enquiries into their activities and she was not at all put out by their polishing which should, by rights, have been finished by the time she came downstairs. Even Mrs Garnett, who was still to do exactly as she pleased about the menus, Mrs Macrae had told her, could find no fault with her gracious manner.

But let something displease her, or a servant take a liberty, as she had considered Percy had done when he refused to saddle the pretty little golden mare her husband had bought her, telling her that it was at her husband's command, she became as cold as a pillar of frozen ice. Haughty she was, lifting her head and giving Percy a look that could have struck him dead, he said, regal as a queen with her "we shall see about that when my husband gets home". And when her husband did get home it had come to nothing except her ranting and raving all over the house about being kept prisoner when he had promised, promised . . .!

What it was he had promised they never knew but it had ended as it always did with the bedroom door firmly shut behind the pair of them and silence beyond it and they all knew what that meant!

Next day she'd be all sweetness and light again, humming about the house, a sort of rosy look about her, a soft kind of sighing look which quite embarrassed them all until they got used to it, and her. She was good-hearted and never, never kept up the sulks. Once she'd told you where you were wrong, in her opinion, she was all smiles again, running over to the cottage where George, his wife and their brood lived, taking the children sweets and biscuits she ordered from Mrs Garnett and could you be anything but fond of her? She was busy all day long taking those mad dogs of hers for long walks across the fields towards Walton on the Hill, on up to Walton Nursery where she ordered dozens of completely unsuitable plants to be picked up by George in the pony cart and which were to be planted at her direction. Campbell took her into Liverpool, waiting for her outside Ireland's in Bold Street where there was always a splendid stock of the very best furs; at Mrs Dawson's where French corsets and woven stays were sold though what Mrs Macrae in her condition wanted with those was a mystery. She spent some time at Anne Hillyard's Millinery and Baby Linen Warehouse which was only to be expected, Campbell being called to carry dozens of packages to the carriage, and had begun to patronise the Misses Yeoland, also of Bold Street, where the most discerning and fashion-conscious of Liverpool's ladies were fitted for their gowns and bonnets and mantles, including the most fashionable and infamous of them all, Miss Lacy Hemingway whom, Mrs Garnett had heard her mistress say, she would dearly love to meet. Not that Miss Hemingway was received by decent folk since she had committed the most heinous crime a woman could commit. She had left the protection of her father's home and gone out on her own which Mrs Macrae seemed to think quite admirable. There had been some scandal attached to her name and so Miss Hemingway had left home, thrown out most likely, those who blackened her name said. She had built up her own business, in shipping as Mr Macrae had done, but, worst of all, she had been successful in it.

"Have you met her?" Mrs Garnett had heard Mrs Macrae ask her husband breathlessly.

"No, I have not, and neither will you," her husband answered.

"Why not?"

"Because she is not received in what is known as 'good' society."

"Stuff and nonsense. That wouldn't stop me. Mama has always said—"

"What your mama says has no bearing in *my* house, Jenna."

"Has it not? Then let me tell you I am what my mama made me. Had she not brought me up as she did I would have been as stuffy and mim-faced as the daughters of Mr What's-his-name who came to dinner the other night."

"Mr What's-his-name, as you call him, is a business associate of mine and can put a fair bit of cargo my way, which is, in case you have forgotten, how I make my money."

"In that case, *you* entertain him since he, his wife, his daughters and the horse that pulled their carriage are as tedious and . . ."

He began to laugh then and honestly, Dora reported to them after she had finished serving dinner, you couldn't blame him, and the mistress saw the funny side too, standing up and running to him, sitting down in his lap and kissing him before Dora could get out through the door. Doted on each other, they did, and it could be very embarrassing at times.

"Well, it's no good, Marian," Jenna said now, sighing resignedly. "We'll just have to ride hell for leather over to Mama's and see if Miss Renshaw can make me something for tonight. She has a dozen seamstresses in her workshop, Mama told me, and we are valued customers. Quickly, stuff me into that thing I had on yesterday unless I've grown since then. It's loose enough, and then we'll put on our bonnets. I must have something stunning for tonight since we are to dine with a Mr and Mrs Edward Lucas who are related in some way to Miss Lacy Hemingway and I am dying to know more about her."

"Indeed, madam." Marian was doing her best to "stuff" her mistress into the silk moifé which had a little jacket falling loosely from the shoulders at the front to just below her waist. It was pretty and light and though the skirt was tight about the waist Marian managed to fasten it.

"Perhaps I should try wearing a corset," Jenna said gloomily, eyeing herself in the mirror.

"Oh no, madam, I've heard such things can harm the

baby." It came to Marian then that Campbell had told them that Mrs Macrae had called in at Mrs Dawson's Corset Shop in Bold Street, where all the smart shops were situated and she straightened up, looking accusingly into her mistress's rebellious face.

"You don't mean to tell me you're thinking of wearing corsets? Do you want this baby to be born deformed? Really, Miss Jenna, I've never heard of anything so shameful and if your dear mama was to hear of it she'd take a stick to you. Have you any idea of the damage that could be done? Really, and you with a husband who—"

Marian stopped speaking abruptly, suddenly remembering who she was and, more to the point, who she was talking to, but though her face was flushed with outrage and her eyes narrowed suspiciously, it was plain she was not at all remorseful. She had been Mrs Macrae's personal maid for almost two years now though it had also been her job to help Miss Beth and Miss Nancy. She liked Miss Jenna, which she still sometimes called her, despite her married status, even if her wilfulness had often set the house on its ears but she had always walked carefully around her, knowing her place, safeguarding her position though there had been many times when she had felt like giving her mistress a piece of her mind. She was only two years older than Miss Jenna, for a start. She had worked her way up from kitchen maid to housemaid, since she was quick, resourceful, intelligent and determined to get on. She had spent months learning her trade, picking the brains of Mrs Blaney at Bank House who had worked in big houses before she came to work for the Townleys, and from Mrs Blaney's friend, a certain Miss Walden who had herself been a ladies maid for twenty years. Marian had soon become familiar with the intricacies of dressing a lady's hair, practising on the girls in the kitchen; on how to look after a lady's wardrobe, keeping the contents always in an immaculate condition. Tweeds

and woollens must be laid out on a table after every
wearing and brushed all over with a clean brush, or, if
the material was fine, beaten lightly with a soft cloth. Silk
dresses should be rubbed with a piece of merino and any
repairs needed to be done immediately; bonnets dusted
with a light feather plume, the flowers on them raised and
readjusted by means of flower pliers. Footwear and fans,
parasols and muffs, Marian knew everything there was to
know about their care, for Miss Walden had served the
best families in Lancashire. Furs and jewellery and lace
collars, how to clean brushes and combs, the secret of
putting a shine in a lady's hair though Miss Jenna had no
need of that, nor Marian's recipe, come again from Miss
Walden, on how to promote hair growth. How to arrange
flowers and how to remove candle wax from a shawl; how
to be discreet; how to pack and unpack her lady's luggage,
should Marian ever be called upon to accompany her on
a visit to friends. She had learned when to offer advice
and when to keep her trap shut, or at least she thought
she had and now she'd opened it wide and shoved her
well-polished black boot in it in no uncertain manner.

For a moment she was convinced Miss Jenna was
going to go into one of her narrow-eyed, sharp-tongued
tempers and tell Marian to mind her own damn business
but, give her her due, she really did seem concerned with
the well-being of this baby of hers, despite her remarks
to the contrary, and instead she put her hand to her belly,
drawing back a little.

"What do you mean, Marian? Deformed?" Her tone
was fearful and Marian, again abandoning their separate
places in life, smiled and put a hand out to her. Her
mistress seemed so young sometimes, too young to be
wife to a prosperous businessman and too young to be
a mother.

"Nay, don't you fret, Miss Jenna. I'd not let you do it,
but you see inside there" – pointing to the bulge of her

mistress's normally flat stomach – "there's not a lot of space . . ."

"Really, Oh Marian, what if that space is not enough?"

"Give over, Miss Jenna, there's enough, never fear, but if you go strapping a corset round you, which I've heard some society ladies do," her face aflame at the horror of it, "you could crush that baby of yours and it could be born with . . . well . . ." Marian turned briskly to the question of her mistress's bonnet, not wanting to frighten her. "We'll say no more . . ."

"Marian, please, I could not bear it if Conal's son . . ."

Conal's son, indeed! Would you listen to her, just as though the master had put in an order which would arrive, on time of course, since he was a man who did not take kindly to unpunctuality.

"Now, Miss Jenna, I'm sorry I spoke if I've frightened you but I'd never forgive myself if I let you, through you not knowing what could happen, harm that babby."

"Of course not, Marian and if there's anything else you can think of, or that you see me doing which I shouldn't please tell me, won't you?"

"I will, Miss Jenna. Now I think that's the carriage on the drive, if you're ready."

Marian was surprised and pleased with the docility of her young mistress and her acceptance of Marian's advice. Marian was the eldest of a round dozen and, until she went as kitchen maid at Bank House, had gained experience in midwifery to her mother and in the rearing of her own brothers and sisters. She helped Miss Jenna into the carriage smiling at her own doubts for her mistress had shown a surprising responsibility towards the coming child, really she had, and Marian was pleased about that. Perhaps she was growing up at last, facing the truth of what her life was to be, since none of them, at least at Bank House, had missed the commotion about Miss Jenna working with her papa!

Marian would have been mortified had she been able to read her young mistress's mind. Jenna Macrae, though naturally she wished to bear a healthy child, preferably a son, was concerned only with its prompt arrival, all in one piece and acceptable to Conal who had promised her she could shape her own life once it was here. When that day came she would go over to the colliery, just as he went to his office by the docks. She would work at Papa's side, attend meetings, visit the Coal Exchange and, as Conal did, come home at the end of the day to a bath, to change, to conversation, perhaps a glass of madeira by the drawing-room fire, to a fine dinner and then to bed where she and her husband would love one another vigorously, tenderly, passionately until they fell asleep. No more babies for a couple of years he had said but this one must be healthy or it would have to be done all over again, and at once. She meant to have children, three or four of them, but not yet. Not until she had a good grasp on the collieries.

Mama was pleased to see her and even Bryony hugged her, her face smiling its approval, her golden eyes soft and knowing though Beth, Nancy and Rose appeared to notice nothing amiss in her appearance. They drew her into the garden where, it still being warm and sunny as it had for most of the summer, chairs had been set out. Coffee was called for, or would she prefer some of Mrs Blaney's iced lemonade? Dolly bobbed a curtsey and told her she looked "champion", her eyes as wise as Bryony's and after a long draught of the lemonade Jenna sighed, placing the glass on the white-painted wrought-iron table.

"I'll have to take off my jacket, Mama, if you don't mind. It is so warm."

"Of course, darling, why should I mind?"

"Perhaps the girls should be sent inside since I'm told this sort of thing is not suitable for them."

All the girls, apart from Bryony, looked at one another in mystification.

"If you mean because you are going to have a baby, my dear, it's a perfectly natural state for a young married woman to be in. I can't think why you've not mentioned it before." Her mother's matter-of-fact tone, which she had expected, did nothing to allay her . . . well, she wouldn't call it apprehension since she really did not care about such silly things but she did know that a child born seven months after a wedding was not something a mother would want for her daughter. Of course her mother had known she was pregnant. Didn't she work in that shelter of hers with women, married and unmarried, who bore children with monotonous regularity and so would she not easily recognise her daughter's condition? But did she know? Ah well, in for a penny, in for a pound, as they said.

She stood up, took off her jacket and tossed it to the grass, allowing them to take a good look at her before she sat down again. She turned her head airily, studying each face in turn, assessing their reactions and was momentarily surprised by the strange look of – what was it? – triumph? on Bryony's. The rest ranged from stunned to resigned, the first on the faces of her sisters, the last her Mama.

"Well, darling," Mama said at last, "though I had my suspicions when last we saw you I had no idea you were so . . ."

"Far gone, I believe the expression is, Mama."

"That's enough, Jenna. Remember your sisters and cousin are unmarried girls."

"I did suggest you sent them indoors, Mama." Jenna did her best to be unconcerned but she could see that Mama, despite being the most tolerant, the most forgiving woman Jenna had ever known, was not pleased.

"Well, I am not shocked, Aunt Nella, even if the others

are," Bryony announced firmly. "Surely to have a baby is nothing to be ashamed of."

"Exactly, thank you, Bryony." If Jenna was surprised at her cousin's defence of her she did her best not to let it show, though the expression on her mother's face, which was directed for a second or two at Bryony, confused her. But before she could interpret it her mother rose to her feet.

"Perhaps you and I had better go indoors, Jenna. We need to have a little talk, I think."

"Of course, Mama, but I must leave shortly. I need to get to Miss Renshaw's before lunch. We are to dine at the Lucas's this evening and I have nothing to wear. Well, nothing that will fit me."

"Jenna, you are incorrigible. Have you no sense of propriety at all? To dine out when you are clearly . . . and how can poor Sabrina Renshaw make you a gown and have it ready for this evening? It is already eleven thirty."

"I know, Mama, that's why I must rush. And I'm sure she will manage it, you know how clever she is. I thought something in a pale shade of coffee. Subtle, you know, and draped so that . . ."

"Jenna!"

"I am sorry, Mama, what shall you do with me? That's what Conal says but I must admit I find it quite easy to get round him."

She beamed about the circle of open-mouthed, wide-eyed young girls, three of whom could not seem able to tear their eyes away from the pronounced swell of her stomach. It lifted the hem of her skirt a good three inches from the ground at the front, showing her ankles and she looked down at them, laughing.

"Isn't it awful, girls? Just wait until it's your turn," and Beth, who was to marry Frank Miller in the spring, turned quite pale.

"Jenna, will you please come into the house." Nella Townley was furious with her daughter, not only because she had obviously anticipated her wedding night by several weeks and would be the subject of much gossip and speculation, but by her utter lack of delicacy in flaunting her condition before her sisters and cousin. Completely unrepentant she was, ready to joke about it, for God's sake and when Jonas heard about it he'd no doubt take his horsewhip to Conal Macrae, though it was a bit late for that!

And yet could you help but smile at the girl, so full of life and . . . and yes, enchantment, happy as a lark, unburdened by any sense of shame in her love for her husband and what they had done before their wedding night? It sat about her like a golden dazzle of sunshine, no shadows nor clouds to mar her miraculous delight in what life had brought Jenna Macrae. It seemed the coming child was a joy to her, eagerly awaited, loved already and what had become of that snapping fierceness in Jenna Townley which had told all about her, her father included, that she would have her inheritance, and run it, as a son would when it was her turn?

Miss Renshaw had declared herself to be delighted to "run up", her words, a simple, stylish, suitable gown for Mrs Macrae, *and* by late afternoon, thinking no doubt of future orders since Mrs Townley had four more girls at home, one of whom was to be married in the new year. She showed not the slightest concern at the lateness of the morning, nor the fact that she had only four hours to show what she and her infant business were capable of. She had just the fabric, she said, a guipure lace in a shade somewhere between coffee and cream, lined with silk, the bodice of the gown cut low over the bosom since it was for evening and Mrs Macrae had no need to hide the magnificence of hers. A drape here, artfully done, of course, no definite waist-line to speak of and a wide skirt, perfectly plain?

Mrs Macrae was enraptured and ordered several more gowns for day wear and a very full mantle the colour of burnt copper leaves, with a hood, known as a Highland cloak which measured sixteen yards round the hem and fell in graceful folds to her feet. She promised to come again around Christmas time for what she called her "party gowns". If Miss Renshaw was surprised that a lady so far advanced in pregnancy should be thinking of party gowns she did not show it though she did notice Mrs Townley's grim smile of amusement.

The evening gown was cut out and tacked together for a fitting even before Mrs Macrae and Mrs Townley left the shop for Bank House, Miss Renshaw assuring them that she would put every one of her girls on it and that she herself would deliver it and make the final fitting at four o'clock.

Conal was pleased with her that evening, she could tell that by the soft glow in his eyes. She did not, inexperienced as she still was, recognise the true depth of this new husband of hers, nor the fierce yet tender look of a man who is sometimes confused by the sudden clamouring force of his own newly awakened feelings. She loved without thought, without fear, without doubt, without the slightest need to question or take apart this miraculous gift she had been given. As a child finds no cause to marvel at its great good fortune in receiving the love of its parents so she accepted Conal's love. But her husband was a complex man, a clever man, a many-layered man of sophistication who on the surface was charming, amusing, cool-headed. A man with taste, with a liking for luxury, who enjoyed pleasure, things of the flesh, things his growing wealth brought him but beneath this layer which the world saw lay many others, many facets to his nature which no one, not even his wife, had seen. Not yet. He had a wealth of kindness hidden in him, a tenderness for the small and vulnerable, a sensitivity to others' suffering which often irritated him and which he did his best to hide. On another level he had an inclination to be fair, to see the other fellow's side though he never allowed the other fellow to know it. He was generous though his generosity was played out in secret. He was also impatient, short-tempered, stubborn and proud, characteristics which often warred with his desire to understand, to protect and to cherish.

With all these emotions churning inside him it was no wonder that the love, the deep and unasked-for love he felt for his eighteen-year-old wife constantly surprised him. She was so carefree, so unquestioning, so sure that life was splendid, that it would always be splendid and it made him love her more, a protective love, a possessive love, a love that desired nothing other than that she should never change but at the same time understood that he needed a mature partner to share his life. Time would give him that for she was no delicate, gossamer thing, as her two beautiful aunts had been, with no thought in her head but fashion and calling cards. She would grow, blossom, develop as her own mother had done into a complete woman. The loving friend and ally, the other half of himself, as he would become the other half of her in their marriage but he would be sorry, though he knew it was inevitable, to see her lose this joyous belief which was in her, a belief in him and in the world he had made for her. A belief which shone brightly from her and which she was convinced, as the young are, would last forever. She was still a girl, a passionate girl whom he loved passionately, as he would love the woman and it was this which softened the expression on his face, warmed his brown eyes and made his arms gentle as he drew her to him.

"You are very beautiful, lassie." His voice was husky.

"And though I suppose I shouldna be taking you out in company when you are five months pregnant, and let me tell you, every one of the ladies there will know exactly how far along you are, I find I dinna give a damn. I want to show you off to all the gentlemen whose wives could never shine as vividly as mine does. But there will be talk, my sweet, you know that, don't you? Even though we're married, there's bound to be talk. Can you manage it?"

She lifted her head and smiled into his face, a smile of dazzling good humour, of joy, of love for him, of defiance for the rest of the world.

"Need you ask, Conal Macrae? You ought to know me better than that."

"Aye, that's true, and I suppose it will all blow over. A seven month baby is not uncommon. Now let me have another look at you." His smile widened into a grin, his approval of her, his pride in her, his love for her bringing an answering delight to her own face. Her full breasts were like rich cream, the swell of them showing above the neck of the low-cut bodice. He put his lips to it, smoothing them across her satin flesh, feeling the instant response in her. His fingers pushed down the fabric to reveal one eager, hardened nipple and his lips moved to take it for a moment.

"Dammit, my lovely girl, I've half a mind to . . ."

"Mmmm, me too . . ." sighing against him, but he covered her breast and his hand rose to caress her shoulders which were strong and flawless. The curve of her belly was cleverly disguised by the cut of the gown and he put a hand on it for a tender moment. She looked quite, quite magnificent, her happiness so evident, so spontaneous, so abundant Conal felt a sudden twinge of unease at the thought of what was to come when their child was born, then it disappeared. She would be reconciled, he knew she would. She would settle to motherhood, to being his wife, hostess at his table, the perfect partner and the question of her father's mines would vanish like mist in the sunshine.

Chapter Fourteen

Tim Spencer kissed Bryony Townley with a reverence which was almost holy, like a worshipper paying homage at the hem of the robe of the representative of God, ready to kneel and press his forehead to the ground if it would only convey to her his absolute adoration.

It was the first week of December and he had been treating her thus for almost six months. Whenever he could, that is, for opportunities to be alone together did not happen very often and it had occurred to him during these past six months that there was a certain inconsistency in the structure of the social visits, an imbalance if you like, between his mother, his Aunt Dove and his Aunt Nella. Of course his mother and his Aunt Dove had been married to baronets and Aunt Nella's husband, though enormously wealthy was no more than a coal owner. One of the industrial class, the manufacturing class which had sprung up during the first half of the century so perhaps this was why, although his mother and Aunt Dove were invited on a fairly regular basis to Bank House, and his Aunt Nella and Uncle Jonas dined – a lot less often – at Daresbury Park, his home, and Faulkner Hall, his cousins and their cousins had never once been guests of the Spencers and Faulkners. Perhaps, he had at first thought, his mama and Aunt Dove did not care to associate with the offspring of a class that was not as privileged, as well bred as the

Spencers and Faulkners undoubtedly were, both families going back over two hundred years to the unhappy times of Cromwell and Charles I and the happier times of the restoration when their loyalty to their Monarch had earned them land and titles. But his mama and Aunt Dove had themselves come from the manufacturing class which, one would have thought, would have made both of them more tolerant towards it and yet his own insight told him that the two sisters were even less disposed to mix with those from the class from which they themselves had come and only a sense of family duty and his Uncle Jonas's wealth kept them in touch with his Aunt Nella.

There had been several functions at Bank House over the past six months. A musical soirée, an entertainment of which his Aunt Nella was very fond though Uncle Jonas and many of the gentlemen found them tedious. Because of this Aunt Nella provided cards in her smaller drawing-room so that gentlemen who cared to might escape Mendelssohn and Mozart. Under cover of the general to-ing and fro-ing, as chairs were arranged, as the gentlemen strolled away together, as his Uncle Jonas played host in one room and Aunt Nella hostess in another, he and Bryony had managed almost half an hour of shy overtures – on his part – and shy response on hers, a modest kiss or two, a whispered exchange of growing regard – on her part – a declaration of love on his and though it had made his young male body ache with need he had attempted no more than this since she was his "fair damozel", pure and untouched and until he took her to bed on their wedding night, which he meant to do, this was how she would remain.

There had been a party to celebrate his uncle's birthday, a very informal affair which his mama and Aunt Dove had deplored, where every guest was more or less allowed to do as she or he pleased which was probably the reason why they did not care for it. There were games, singing and dancing, cards, naturally, for the gentlemen and even a new phenomenon, at least in provincial Marfield, which his Aunt Nella had introduced and which was a card game called whist for anyone who could play. She and her friend Mrs Eason adored it, they said, and yes, it was perfectly proper for ladies to take it up since the nobility, even royalty, had been known to play. How easy it had been for him and Bryony simply to slip away to an unused pantry below the servants stairs which Bryony knew about. With the door pulled to and among the walking sticks, the old boots and cricket bats which belonged to Simeon, the croquet set and badminton racquets and several old garden rugs, they had clung together, kissing with as much restraint as he himself could manage since it was very enclosed and they were forced to stand very close together. He was burning for her by now but absolutely determined to curb his frenzy of longing, his hungering and thirsting, her trusting innocence, her ignorance of what her body did to his, a barrier between them he was doing his best to keep strong and unbroken.

There had been a dance to celebrate some political triumph in the township of Marfield, what it was Tim neither knew nor cared since politics did not interest him, but it was important enough to his Uncle Jonas to spur Aunt Nella into inviting her friends and relatives to mark the occasion with them. Again he and Bryony managed half an hour alone but by now these stolen moments were not enough for him and he had pleaded with her to meet him in secret in the little spinney beyond the walls of Bank House. It had a funny name, Seven Cows Wood, but on the pretext of walking her dog it was easy enough for Bryony to manage it. He had ridden over from Daresbury Park and all it needed was for him to tie the animal to a handy branch while he and Bryony walked hand in hand, deeper and deeper into the wood where no one came.

It was autumn by then, the leaves on the trees quite glorious in their gold and copper, their lovely vivid shades from the palest pink and orange to slashing scarlet, the carpet they laid on the ground a magical swirl of the year's dying beauty. It was dry and the carpet crunched beneath their boots and when he leaned her against a broad tree trunk their feet in its roots were ankle deep in their crispness.

She put her arms about his neck that day, pressing her long slender body trustingly against his. She was tall, almost as tall as he was. He held her beneath her arm-pits and the ripe swell of her breasts burned against the inside of his wrists and then, for a feverish moment he lost control. His hand moved to cup one breast, feeling the rock-hard peak of her nipple, then she drew back, her face aflame, her eyes cast down, the suspicion of tears quivering on her long black lashes. Her soft, hedge-berry mouth, full and moist, was trembling and she bit her bottom lip with even white teeth. God, she was glorious, perfect, the perfect woman and had he not meant to marry her as soon as he could he would have coaxed her to allow him more than these few chaste kisses they had exchanged. Her lovely skin was flushed at the cheekbone but the rest of her was the colour of pale gold. He could remember when he was small his nanny holding a buttercup under Amy's chin to see if "she liked butter". The reflection from the golden petals of the flower had turned a tiny spot of Amy's white flesh to a soft honey gold and that was the colour of Bryony's skin, but all over. Golden honey at her brow and chin and throat, dipping into the neck of her white dress and what would it be like beneath the dress, beneath those tantalising buttons which ran in a row down across her rounded breasts? Were they gold and what colour was the circle in which those tight nipples erupted? If only she would let him have one little peep, perhaps put his hand inside, hold them as he had held, fondled, crushed, sucked and bitten the full breasts of the cooperative farm girl . . .

Oh, Jesus God, but he was in agony!

"Tim . . . please, Tim, I must go . . . and perhaps it would be better if . . . if we didn't meet like this. My aunt and uncle would be . . . and think what your mama would say. I should never have agreed to come."

"No . . . no, don't say that."

"Tim, you know that a girl in my position should never allow herself to be alone with . . . with . . . but you are so . . ."

She turned away, ready to weep now and he took her hand eagerly, his own face very young and earnest.

"No, no, my darling, it is I who have . . . but you see . . . oh Bryony, I mean to marry you, you must know that . . ." and of course she did, for Sir Timothy Spencer was not the kind of young man who would play with the affections and reputation of a female of good family. A good girl to marry and a bad girl to kiss, she had heard Simeon say and she was a good girl and Tim must be made aware of it. As he was aware of it, naturally. They were too young now but she would be fifteen in March and many girls of her class married at fifteen. March, in March she would let him do whatever . . . well, whatever he had in mind and then no matter what his mama said, he would marry her. Just until March. Keep him off her until March. God in heaven, if only he didn't look like a frog with those eyes of his popping out of his head with excitement . . .

She turned her own softly golden, star-studded eyes up to his, her soft red lips up to his, but no longer allowing him to touch her with his hands.

"Tim, you mean we are . . .?" Her voice was breathless with wonder and he grinned, the grin of a man, a triumphant male who has won his woman. His woman!

"We are, Bryony, if you will have me. I shall speak to Mama tonight."

His young face glowed with rapture and pride and in his eyes was the beauty of a shy boy's first love, then a worried look clouded them and he chewed an anxious lip. "Or should I ask Uncle Jonas first, d'you think?"

She was aghast as she pushed him violently away, her own face losing its lovely colour, her eyes suddenly sharp and narrowed.

"No, oh no. We must tell no one, Tim." She tried to keep the urgency out of her voice. "They will say we are too young. Send you away probably, abroad or something and then I'll never see you. They would marry me to someone else and I could bear no man's hands on me . . . on my" – she allowed her eyes to fall to her heaving breasts – "only yours, Tim."

Appalled at the very idea of some other man having access to what was rightfully his, Tim Spencer's young mouth opened on a splutter of rage and, gratified by his reaction, Bryony began to weep with a desolation which was heart-rending. He reached for her but she twisted away, her eyes blind, her face contorted with her grief. His confusion was so great he began to babble, saying nothing that made sense, his face quite idiotic as it worked madly, slack-jawed with a mixture of lust, frustration, bewilderment and a justifiable male anger for she was driving him mad with desire. She was leading him on with her obvious reference to her . . . to her breasts, telling him she wanted only his hands to . . . Oh God, if she would just let him . . . but even as his thoughts rampaged towards the delight of what was under Bryony's immaculate bodice she sank to the autumn leaves in a boneless heap becoming distraught, her face in her hands and at once he was full of contrition.

"They'll take you away from me," she wept. "I wouldn't want to go on if I couldn't see you."

"No, no, my little love, never."

"But we are so young, Tim. You are not yet eighteen."

"I don't care, Bryony. We can wait."

"You won't tell anyone?"

"Never."

"So we can still meet like this." Somehow, though he was not awfully sure of it and told himself later that he had imagined it, she seemed to be promising that perhaps when she said "like this" she meant that she would allow him to . . . to . . .

"You promise?" she breathed, her full, soft mouth just below his.

"I promise."

"You'll keep this our secret?"

"I will, my little love."

"Oh Tim, I do love you."

"Do you, do you, Bryony?"

"Oh yes. You are so . . . so chivalrous."

"Well . . ." He smiled, feeling a surge of masculinity such as he had never before experienced.

"Kiss me, please Tim."

They exchanged a chaste and tender kiss.

The bombshell fell that very evening and it was himself who caused it to explode. They were at table, Lady Spencer, her son the baronet, Sir Timothy Spencer, and her daughter, Amy, who was his twin.

Daresbury Park was very old and very elegant. A beautifully turned staircase led out of the great hall which had seen generations of Spencers pass through it. There was carved oak with painted panels on the walls, a ballroom which Lady Spencer, with her father's money, had transformed into dazzling, mirrored splendour, huge stone fireplaces in which enormous logs were burned, deep armchairs, rich carpeting, modern kitchens, warmth, comfort, luxury, and chimneys which no longer billowed smoke back into the rooms. All achieved with her father's money, for Linnet Fielden had meant to entertain on a grand scale when she married the baronet and so she had until Sir Julian's death on the hunting field.

Now her aspirations lay with her children. Grand marriages for them both, of course, wealth perhaps, for the upkeep of Daresbury Park was not cheap and though she knew it meant handing over her rule of the lovely old house into another woman's hands it would not be for years yet. Tim was only seventeen and would marry when he chose but Amy, the same age of course, was already privately promised to a gentleman of good name from Northumberland. Very suitable he was and more to the point, he had become besotted with her daughter when visiting Sir Edward Faulkner, Lady Spencer's brother-in-law several months ago. He had approached herself only last week after speaking to Sir Edward. Of course Amy was quite exquisite, as Lady Spencer and her own twin had been at that age. Spun silver curls, a skin as beautiful and delicate as rare porcelain, cloudy blue-green eyes and a sweetly curved young girl's figure which it seemed Sir Robert Blenkinsopp could not wait to get his hands on. If the disgusting idea of a man of fifty or more having in his bed her innocent, not quite eighteen-year-old daughter distressed her, Lady Spencer showed no sign of it.

Signalling to the butler that they would take coffee in the drawing room where she meant to inform Amy of where her future lay, Lady Spencer rose to her feet, followed by her son and daughter.

They talked of this and that, the light chatter in which Lady Spencer excelled, having practised it since she had first entered society at the age of sixteen. She did not believe in ladies discussing what she called "gentlemen's business" which meant politics or indeed anything of a serious nature, preferring, as did her twin sister and their shared friends, to gossip about the affairs, the successes and adversities of those in their own circle, idle talk, meaningless, trivial, mostly harmless since they did not wish to be disturbed in their well-ordered lives by the unsavoury.

"And so your cousin Beth is to marry," she observed, smiling, "and to a . . . what is he? . . . an undertaker! Good heavens, one shudders to think of having such a dreadful occupation brought into one's home since one can only imagine that he will talk about it to his wife at the dinner table as gentlemen do. At least gentlemen of his class. What a gruesome subject. I wonder if he is prosperous, though I doubt Jonas Townley would allow any of his girls to marry where there is no money."

"No indeed, Mama." Amy sipped her coffee. The lamplight fell on the smooth, pale silver of her hair, shading it in places to gold and put a cream glow beneath the white surface of her skin. She sat on the sofa opposite her mother, an immaculate young woman with not a wrinkle in the well-fitted bodice of her ivory silk gown, her ivory silk skirt spreading all about her in what appeared to be symmetrically placed folds. She was composed, her smooth brow serene, a delight to the eye; many gentlemen had thought so, her air of quiet good breeding matching exactly that of her brother, though in looks they were not alike.

"Still, I suppose Nella and Jonas will be glad to have two off their hands," Lady Spencer went on mysteriously, "and he has prospects so my sister informs me."

"He seems an agreeable young man, Mama," Amy said, smiling at her mother, "and Beth is happy with him, or so she says."

"Well, and so she might but then she was always easy to please."

"Do you think so, Mama?"

"Indeed I do." Her mother lifted her head regally, indicating to the hovering butler that her cup needed refilling and he passed the message on with his eyes to the parlour maid who glided to her ladyship's bidding.

Amy continued the conversation in the way she knew her mama approved. "Well, she is at least to marry the gentleman of her choice which must be gratifying. Poor Florence Smithson has just become engaged to the nephew of a peer who, I suppose, most would agree was a wonderful match but the man can barely read. He has only one talent and that is to jump higher and ride faster and further on his hunter than any other gentleman of his circle. He had never heard of Shakespeare can you imagine it, Tim, and Florence says he can talk of nothing but withers and hocks. She is quite desolate and wonders how she is to spend the rest of her life joined to a man with so little intellect.'

Her brother pulled a face. "There are such men about, Amy. Men who care nothing for books or music. I was speaking to a fellow at the Faulkners' only last week who has never attended a concert or seen the inside of a library and though he had been to Italy couldn't remember whether he had been to Rome. The centre of wonderful museums and art galleries, all the things I would give my eye teeth to see and he could not even recall being there."

"I read in the newspaper the other day that . . ."

Amy's voice receded to a low, pleasant hum and Linnet Spencer closed her ears as the conversation steered its way towards what she called "bookish". Since her husband died it seemed to take place more and more frequently between her son and daughter and she did not care for it. The sooner Amy was married and involved in the duties of a wife the better. There would be no time for newspapers and Shakespeare when Sir Robert bore her off to the wilds of Northumberland. She often wondered where her children got their clever minds from since she and Julian, she was the first to admit, at least to herself, were not academically gifted. Tim had gone to a decent school, the public school all the Spencer males had attended and had, unlike his father, done well in everything classical, Latin, languages, English and he loved music, poetry and though he liked to ride had no particular interest in the hunting field. Amy had been educated by a governess who had imbued in her pupil all the skills thought necessary for a girl of her breeding which were little more than how to be the wife of a gentleman and mother to his children.

So here she was with a son and daughter who, though they were polite enough to indulge her in the pleasant and idle chit-chat she loved and which she and her sister and friends had been brought up to be good at and which passed time so delightfully, would rather discuss books and poetry and the latest news of the present government.

The thought made her tone cool as she brought their exchange to an abrupt halt.

"There is something I wish to discuss with you both. Well, hardly discuss since the matter is settled but there are arrangements to be made and the sooner they are in order the better."

Both her children turned politely in her direction. She placed her cup and saucer on the table beside her, indicated to the butler and maid that they might withdraw and when they had done so turned a frosty smile on her daughter.

"You will be pleased, I'm sure, to hear that you have been asked for by a very suitable gentleman, my dear. A true gentleman of breeding whose name goes back as far as our own. He approached your uncle first since you have no papa and Tim is somewhat young . . ."

"Uncle Jonas?" Amy's voice was anxious. Of course

many young ladies of her class had their marriages arranged for them since like must marry like, pedigree must match pedigree, for the blood of a thoroughbred, though often a drop of common blood helped to improve the strain, must on the whole remain pure. So was it to be the son of one of Uncle Jonas's manufacturing friends who—?

"Of course not Uncle Jonas." Her mother's voice was scathing, interrupting Amy's frantic thoughts. "You have another uncle, Amy. Uncle Edward speaks very highly of—"

"Unce Edward? This gentleman is the son of one of Uncle Edward's friends?"

"Amy, I would be obliged if you did not keep interrupting me in such an ill-bred fashion."

"I'm sorry, Mama," Amy straightened her back but Tim could see she was badly frightened. She was a quiet girl, somewhat like his own Bryony. She kept in the background, happy in her own company, or the company of the books which some more learned Spencer had built up in the library, and her piano. She was almost eighteen, an age when most of her friends were already married, some with a child but those gentlemen who had shown interest in her had not, it seemed, been considered appropriate for the daughter of a baronet.

"His name is Sir Robert Blenkinsopp. He has a large estate in Northumberland. This is a splendid match, Amy, and the family are very pleased about it. Especially your Uncle Edward who is a close friend of Sir Robert's."

"Sir Robert Blenkinsopp?" Tim looked perplexed. It was obvious from the expression on their faces that both Tim and Amy were casting frantically about in their minds to put a face, a form to the name of Sir Robert Blenkinsopp. A friend, a close friend of their Uncle's? Did not Mama mean the *son* of a close friend of Uncle Edward's since he himself was approaching fifty?

"Yes. He visited your aunt and uncle some months ago and was very taken with your sister."

"Taken with her?"

"Really, Timothy, you are getting as bad as Amy. Surely I have made myself quite clear. Sir Robert Blenkinsopp is a landowner from Northumberland, as I have said. He admires your sister and really we could not hope for a better match. He is in a position to give her every comfort. I'm sure he will be kind to her and . . ."

A dreadful suspicion reared itself in Tim's young and sensitive mind, a suspicion coloured by a memory of a party, a birthday party held at Faulkner Hall in honour of the heir, Blake Faulkner. A very grand affair with a celebration not only for the members of the family and their aristocratic friends but of the tenants of the estate Blake would one day inherit. A mixture of old and young, of the upper and lower orders and amongst the former had been Sir Robert Blenkinsopp, his wife and his three daughters, all of them older than Amy. He could put no clear face to Sir Robert, only an image of a vast frame, a mean mouth, enormous hands, one of which he had shaken and beside him four timid women who had smiled placatingly.

"But . . . he's married, Mama. I distinctly remember now . . ."

"No, darling, his wife . . . died."

"But that was only in June, the day of Blake's birthday. Do you mean to say that already, barely six months, even before she was dead he . . . Dear God, Mama, you cannot . . . cannot . . ."

Tim was beginning to babble now, the dreadful picture of his dainty sister who sat like stone beside him, clasped in the meaty arms . . . as he had imagined it with Bryony . . . those hands . . . fingers like fat hairy sausages on Amy's lovely . . . taking her clothes from her . . . Dear Christ, it was not to be borne . . .

"Yes, dear," his mother was saying placidly, apparently seeing nothing obscene in a man of fifty or more, a man only recently widowed having in his bed a girl young enough to be his granddaughter. "He will, naturally, wait for the proper period of his mourning to go by, but in the summer, perhaps June . . ."

Amy began to weep, prisms of reflected light shining in each separate tear as it rolled silently down her face and again Tim was reminded of his own sweet love. My God, women were such vulnerable, oppressed creatures, compelled by life, by their circumstances, to suffer indignities of the worst sort, forced to have men they did not love take their bodies and their minds, for there was no doubt in his that Amy would lose hers in the revulsion of being married to that old man. A coarse, hard-drinking, hard-riding man, ugly as sin and cruel, Tim was certain of that. Look how his womenfolk had cringed beside him.

"Please, Mama . . ." Amy put a trembling hand to her eyes, still straight-backed, still doing her best to be the well-bred young lady she had been brought up to be, to contain her tears, her fear, her disgust, though she herself could not exactly remember Sir Robert. He was old, as old as Uncle Edward, she knew that and a total stranger. She would be taken away up north by a total stranger who would own her, have her at his mercy with no one to run to, no friends, no brother whom she loved, forced to that act of which she knew so little but which would be hard enough to bear with a man she loved, she was sure. Tim knew him and look at the way *he* was acting, pleading with Mama . . .

"Please, Mama," she said again, her distress growing, "I don't know Sir Robert and . . . though I am sure he is . . . is a . . . I would rather not—"

"And I feel the same," Tim interrupted hotly. "I'm not

going to stand by and see Amy married to that dreadful old man."

"Tim, you are frightening your sister, and for nothing. Sir Robert is a perfectly respectable gentleman. A man of standing and wealth who, naturally, needs a son to carry on the—"

"Stop it, stop it, Mama," he shouted as his sister began to moan, both of them turning the pale yellow of old cheese, she in ignorance but instinctively guessing what it entailed, he with pictures of what he had done to the farm girl in her father's hay loft. The girl was sturdy and he himself young but the image of his fragile sister naked under that great red heaving . . . Jesus! oh Jesus!

"I won't stand by and watch it happen, Mama." His voice was clipped, decisive but already in his mind was the anguish of how he was to stop it. He was seventeen, under age, a boy really and the future of his sister lay with his mother and with his Uncle Edward who, since the death of his father, had taken it upon himself to guide and advise his own wife's sister. What could *he* do, short of running away with Amy and how could he, Sir Timothy Spencer, guardian of Daresbury Park, holder of an old, distinguished name, run away from his responsibilities? It was silly even to think about it and perhaps if he kept on remonstrating with Mama he might be able to persuade her to change her mind. There must be dozens of young men in the county who would be considered suitable and who would gladly marry his lovely sister. There were always guests at Faulkner Hall and here at Daresbury Park, young lordlings any one of whom his mother would accept as a suitor for Amy.

He tried to catch Amy's eye, willing her to stop weeping, to control herself for it did no good to anger Mama when she was set on something. Let a few days go by, talk to her calmly and make her see how revolting this was and Mama would come round to their way of thinking and see that it was not at all suitable for a young and innocent girl to be given to an offensive old man.

"Why are you doing this to me, Mama?" Amy mumbled, her tears dripping forlornly down her cheeks from where they splashed in great round patches on to the ivory silk of her gown. "I'd rather die than marry that man."

"My dear, don't be so dramatic. 'That man' as you call him, is madly in love with you . . ."

"Don't . . . don't, Mama." Amy shuddered visibly. "I cannot bear the thought of being . . . being hugged and kissed" – her ignorance of the sex act took her no further than this – "by a man I don't know and I beg you to reconsider. Please, please don't force me. How can you be so cruel and heartless? Have you no feelings . . . maternal . . . you're a woman, my mother . . . you loved Papa and . . ."

"Amy, take a hold of yourself."

". . . and Aunt Dove and Uncle Edward have a fondness for one another. Why must I marry a man older than . . . Please, Mama, please. Aunt Nella would not force her girls to a marriage of . . ."

Lady Spencer, stung by her daughter's reference to her own lack of feeling, laughed shortly.

"Your Aunt Nella will be lucky if she marries any of her girls properly. Oh, I grant she's done well with Jenna and I suppose an undertaker for Beth is better than no one but I'm surprised that he's asked for her. Her dowry must be enormous to have persuaded him. Let us hope the other two fare as well though the bastard won't be so lucky."

Both Amy and Tim became very still, their expressions identical, their eyes wide and bewildered as they stared at their mother.

"Oh yes," she spat, her usual control, badly eroded by

her son's defiance, slipping away completely. "I suspect Jonas Townley's bastards, particularly that girl Bryony, will find it difficult if not impossible to marry at all in these parts!"

Chapter Fifteen

The exchange between Sir Timothy Spencer and Bryony Townley took place on his eighteenth birthday just before Christmas and it was all he could do not to shed tears of childish tantrum. It was as though a toy he had coveted and had been promised was snatched from his extended hand at the last moment. To compensate himself for his loss he was unusually brutal as he told her exactly why their relationship which, she must realise, had contaminated him, coated him with the filth of her illegitimacy, must come at once to an end. He had considered, he said in his high, boyish voice, not even coming to explain but he was a gentleman and felt it was his duty. She had taken his boyhood, his youth, his dreams, his ideals, his heart and trampled them into the mud, changed him from an awkwardly shy, essentially kind boy into a disappointed man and though it was not her fault, strictly speaking, it was she who had thrust him into this torment.

Baldly and without remorse he did it, omitting nothing of what his mama had told him. He told her what she was and what he hoped would become of her since contact with her had tainted him and he could never forgive her for it. When it was over he did not look again into her yellowed, shocked face but turned his horse and cantered away.

Bryony Townley, who had schemed because she had been forced to it, who was cunning because she must look out for herself and Simeon, who was stealthy in her ways because she and her brother had been second-best all of their lives, was, for those first few minutes, quite devastated, blind, speechless and without defence. She had meant to put everything right for them both, of course, in the only way open to a female which was with a good marriage and how could she do it but by stealth and cunning but now she was for the first and only time in her life frozen, stunned, paralysed, unable to speak or even think properly as the dreadful tale was made clear to her. She shivered against the tree trunk, her eyes on the disappearing back of the young man who had just dealt her a fatal blow, her shocked state so total he had gone before she came to herself but his words still hovered in the biting air about her and she absorbed them slowly, agonisingly, still a young girl for that last moment, a young and frightened girl.

Bastard! That was the word he had used. She and Simeon were not the son and daughter of a respectably married, if somewhat mysterious second cousin of Uncle Jonas. Not the children of impoverished parents who had died in circumstances neither Bryony nor Simeon had understood or even bothered about overmuch since they had been brought up in a comfortable home with affection and in no apparent different state to the children of the house. They had known kindness, she realised that, but now, as she looked back, hindsight bringing understanding, she knew as she shivered against the tree that they had always been different, apart, essentially the same as Jenna, Beth, Nancy and Rose, but *not*! There had been many things not understood, or even noticed at the time for she and Simeon had only been children. Servants with a sly look on their faces, a word quickly hushed, an inclination for them to dawdle when given an order by herself or Simeon. The failure of Lady Spencer and Lady Faulkner to invite them, *any* of them, to Daresbury Park, to Faulkner Hall, though Tim and the others had attended parties at Bank House. Lady Spencer's tendency to look right through her, to act as though Bryony was simply not there; strange glances from older members of the community and the way Molly, their nanny, had favoured Jenna and the others. Kind she had been to Simeon and herself, but kind as though they, she and her brother, were the children of servants perhaps.

And now it was all clear! Uncle Jonas was not Uncle Jonas but their father, so Tim had told her in that tortured voice he had acquired. Even now Bryony was still not really aware of the pedestal on which young Tim Spencer had placed her, the true and idealised love with which he had loved her, the worship, the beauty of his adoration which his mother had sullied irretrievably with the coarse words flooding her mouth. Not only were Bryony Townley and Simeon, who did not of course matter, the illegitimate children of Jonas Townley, the most powerful and wealthy coal owner in the parish, their mother had been nothing more than a collier's daughter, he had told her cruelly. A pit brow lassie who had worn clogs and a shawl and had crawled, half-naked as these women had once done, along the roadways of the deep mine and God knew how many men had had her before Jonas Townley had taken a fancy to set her up in a house some miles from Marfield.

Filth! Tim Spencer's pure innocent angel had been bred of filth and he poured it over her as he told her of her beginnings, of his own pain which was unbearable, of his disappointment which had made him vicious.

She did not know at that precise moment what to do with this information which had been thrust so harshly upon her. She trembled violently inside the luxurious warmth of the lovely cloak her Aunt Nella – was she still an aunt? – had bought for her only last week. A Christmas present, she had said, though there would be something under the Christmas tree as well. She must pull herself together, really she must, dry her eyes – she hadn't realised she was crying – and find some way to get herself home, *home* – was Bank House her home? – and into her own room, was it her room any more? where she would plead an illness and then, when she was quiet and composed, turn over in her mind what she was to do. There was Simeon to be told and that must be done carefully so that he would not go shouting and swinging his fists all over the house and take away any advantage this might have for them both. And there must be an advantage somewhere. If it was true and it must be or Tim would not have . . . Lady Spencer would know, she would hardly tell such lies . . . if it was true then she and Simeon were the son and daughter of Jonas Townley. Simeon was his *son*, for God's sake and . . . Oh dear God, but she was so . . . so paralysed with shock . . . she hurt all over . . . her mind was confused . . . she had so wanted to be . . . had been *determined* to be Lady Spencer . . . now . . . now . . . but that could wait and so would Tim Spencer who would be made to pay for what he had said to Bryony Townley this day. Dearly he would pay!

For that last moment she allowed self-pity to over-whelm her, bending her glossy head in despair, then she lifted it and the softness had gone. Her girlhood had gone, leaving only a young woman of cool beauty, impassive, composed, strong but empty of anything that could be described as warmth. Life had taught her self-control and she employed it now. Life had taught her that you obtained from it only what you fought for, however discreetly. Life had taught her how to take and this last blow, this last abuse of her trust, had not altered her flesh, the look of her, only her mind, her shrewd mind which had learned early the advantage of knowing an advantage when it came!

*   *   *

It was two days later, just as they were about to celebrate Christmas, that Simeon and Bryony Townley struck. A savage blow they had planned together, or at least that she had planned and he had agreed to since at first he had been almost unmanageable, incapable of thought, let alone forming it into a decision on what they should do.

She had, before she told Simeon, been obsessed with the idea of trying to find out more about the family of this mother of theirs, this foul woman who had allowed their Uncle Jonas – Oh God, oh, dear sweet Jesus – her *father*, to do to her what Tim had wanted to do to her. She must have lived in Marfield, her family employed in one of Jonas Townley's mines. To come to his attention she would have had to be concerned in what he did each day. A picture of a woman, unclothed from the waist upwards, her body sweated and streaked with coal dust, her eyes and teeth gleaming in her black face, would keep imprinting itself behind her own eyelids. It was there, that picture, quite clear really, apart from the exact details of the face, but for the life of her she could not imagine Jonas Townley putting his hands on such a creature – her mother – Jonas Townley who was so handsome, so fastidious, always so immaculately dressed, who loved Nella Townley, you could see it, feel it, his hand everlastingly reaching for hers, and yet she must have known. Nella Townley must have known where she and Simeon came from or had Jonas Townley deceived her as well?

But she could hardly drag herself about Marfield questioning its inhabitants, could she?

"Excuse me, but do you happen to know who my mother was? The collier's family from which I and my brother sprang? Oh, yes, they lived and worked in the town but their name escapes me."

Perhaps, as she drove by in the Townley carriage she had passed one of her relatives, a grandmother, an aunt,

a cousin in his coal-blackened clothes? Averted her face
from a drunken brawl outside the Colliers Arms in which
her own, proper family were involved. The thought sick-
ened her but still the curiosity gnawed at her. No doubt
those women at Smithy Brow in which Nella Townley –
she found she could no longer call either of them, even
in her mind, aunt and uncle – took such an interest would
know and that was what was so amazing really. How in
God's name had the truth of it been kept from them for
fifteen or sixteen years? Simeon had just had his sixteenth
birthday and she herself would be fifteen in March and
in all that time not one whisper had ever reached their
ears, nor the ears, she presumed, of Jenna, Beth, Nancy
and Rose Townley with whom she and Simeon had been
brought up. If it had then there was no doubt it would
have exploded in their faces with a force which would
have rocked the foundations of this very house. Servants,
some of whom had worked at Bank House then, were
still here. Molly, who had been their nanny. Dolly, Mrs
Blaney and yet by not so much as a word out of place
had they divulged it. A certain slackness, yes, quickly
hidden, she could see that now but nothing to alert or
cause suspicion, at least to her who was a child.

Of course Lady Spencer and Lady Faulkner would
know and what pressure could Jonas Townley put on
them to keep them quiet, as he could on the servants?
Unless it was a financial one. That was a splendid and,
even to her inexperienced eye, a very expensive hunter
Chris Faulkner had just been given. Jonas Townley was
a man of influence in the town and, she presumed, could
make or break a tradesman who spoke out of turn. But a
whole town! Of course, she and the other girls had been
kept very close to home, closer than most, even in their
class and this age of over-protection of young girls who
grew up in it and Simeon had been away at school but
even so it must have taken a great deal of power, of

pressure on the part of Jonas Townley to keep a secret such as this from six young children.

So what were they to do, she and Simeon? How were they to find their rightful place, to get what was rightfully theirs since, though they were illegitimate, they were the son and daughter of Jonas Townley? What must she, Bryony Townley, do to . . .? Here she found herself brooding on what it was exactly she wanted for herself now that Tim Spencer was lost to her. She was finished here. There was nothing more certain than that since to an illegitimate girl, woman, every door would be closed. Every decent door, that is. There would be no good marriage for her now. No gentlemanly husband whom she could shape to her own ambitious ends. No fine house where the cream of society would gather and in which she would play gracious hostess. Not in Marfield. It would be different for Simeon. He was a man, the son of Jonas Townley and now that it was out, the black secret, the stigma of their birth, since there was no further need to keep it hidden, he would be drawn into the running of the collieries. Perhaps with even a proper share in them which wouldn't please the high and mighty Mrs Conal Macrae but which, if gone at the right way, would put power in the hands of Bryony Townley. Through Simeon! Simeon who had always come to her with his problems, his childish woes, his boyhood tribulations, despite the difference in their ages and she had never failed him, never. He loved her and she loved him in a way which went deeper than the affection between brother and sister, probably brought about by their orphaned state, or so she had thought but perhaps it was more than that now. She had guided him. He had protected her and surely, surely she could find for them, from the devastation of this tempest into which they had been flung, what they both deserved! What she needed!

They were word-perfect for she had gone over it

again and again with Simeon, once she had calmed him, soothed him, clung to him, screamed at him, hit out at him, then clung to him again as they both wept. She had chosen Seven Cows Wood to break it to him, some ironic demon in her needing to turn the knife in her own private wound. Her clever mind also told her she would need space and privacy to contain his shock, his disbelief, his mounting fury, and yes, his fear. He would want to hit out at someone for the brand of bastard was not one any man wished to carry, and best he hit out at her, the one who at that moment was branding him. He was a hasty, unthinking boy, no more than that really, pleasure-seeking, risk-taking, careless and secure in his world. He was eager to grasp some measure of authority in the collieries, resentful sometimes of what his cousin Jenna would have, but accepting it grudgingly since he had been led to believe he had no other option. It would be different now!

"I don't believe you," he had said at first. "Who told you this bloody rubbish?" twisting this way and that, looking, for the first time in his privileged young life like some awkward, gangling, arm-flinging schoolboy.

"I can't tell you," she answered flatly for if she did Simeon would probably take it into his head, knowing why, to ride over and beat Tim Spencer to pulp and what would that achieve? It did no good to close avenues which might be better kept open for some future date.

"Then I can't believe you."

"Simeon, have I ever, ever lied to you?"

"No." His tone was reluctant.

"Then why should I do it now and about such an appalling thing? What would be my purpose? I would hardly make it up, would I? God in heaven, do you think I want to be Jonas Townley's bastard? Have you any conception how this will . . . will affect my life, even more than yours?"

"Bryony . . . Bryony, it's absolutely unbelievable. I'm not saying you're lying, not deliberately but it's just not possible. Our parents were . . . were . . ." His face jerked and his fists clenched in anguish.

"Were what? Go on, tell me about them." Her young voice was hard.

"Well, I don't know . . . died . . . killed."

"How? Has anyone ever told you?"

"I've never asked."

"And would they have told us the truth if we had?"

"Oh Jesus, how could this have been kept from us all this time?"

"That's what I asked myself but he's . . . Jonas Townley's a powerful man."

"But her . . ." It seemed he was as reluctant as his sister to name the woman he had called Aunt for as long as he could remember. "Surely she wouldn't take in his children by another woman? By a . . . a . . . collier's daughter. Oh, Jesus . . ."

And it was then and for another hour that he had lost control, hurting himself and her in his shocked despair. At the end of it, sitting with her back to the rough trunk of a tree, she had cradled him in her arms, his wet face pressed into the curve of her throat beneath her chin, rocking him, soothing his quietening figure and when they stood up to face one another Simeon Townley was no longer that careless, heedless youth he had been an hour since.

"Tell me what we should do, Bryony. You'll know."

They sat down to dine several days later, the Townley family. Jonas, though he had not been well recently, suffering from the chesty cough which was the bane of all men who ventured underground, was looking better and looking forward, he said as he unfolded his napkin, to that fine haunch of doe venison Mrs Blaney had cooked for them and which he was about to carve. He was very partial to venison, he continued, particularly with cook's sweet sauce, made with red currant jelly and port wine, which went so superbly with it.

"I agree with you." Bryony's rich smile curved across her white teeth and her eyes, which were sometimes amber, sometimes the colour of treacle toffee, deepened almost to black in the soft, candle-glowed loveliness of her face. Her ebony hair was smoothly brushed and arranged at the back of her head in a dancing knot of curls tied with a white froth of ribbon. She looked far older than her almost fifteen years. She picked up the sauce boat, handing it to Rose. "I love sweet sauce with venison and so does Simeon. I wonder if either of our parents did? They say children often inherit not only the look of their parents but their tastes. Did our mother like venison, d'you suppose?"

It was as though Jonas Townley had been kicked in the belly, one of those low, what are called "below the belt" blows which take the breath from the lungs, the strength from the legs, even the blood from the brain. The carving knife fell from his hand with a loud clatter on to the enormous carving dish, splashing the good juices from the meat up and over the front of his clean white shirt.

"Papa," Rose said in dismay, the sauce boat still in her hand, "Oh Papa, you have marked your shirt front and . . . are you all right, Papa?" She turned from her papa to her mama, her father's suddenly stricken face frightening her but her mother's did nothing to reassure her and her eyes flew back and forth from one to the other, like disturbed and terrified birds.

Nella Townley rose to her feet and took a step towards her husband, her eyes never leaving the smoothly smiling face of Bryony Townley, but her husband raised his bowed head and smiled a ghastly smile, indicating that she was to sit down.

"I'm all right, Nella, really. Just a . . . a sudden

twinge," though what had "twinged" he didn't say and she didn't ask, both of them prepared to believe that the question had been an innocent one.

Nella sat down again and at the back of the room Dolly became unfrozen from her own suddenly paralysed state, clattering hot plates as though she had been stricken with palsy. But Bryony had only just begun.

"Simeon was only saying the other day how Jenna resembles you, Aunt Nella, weren't you, Simeon, wondering, as I suppose is only natural, which of our parents we take after."

"Yes indeed," Simeon continued as smooth as silk while at the head and the foot of the table Nella and Jonas Townley sat carved to stone. "Now does Bryony look like our mother? What was her name, by the way, Uncle Jonas? I don't believe we have ever heard it mentioned."

Nancy, Beth and Rose Townley, though each one sensed there was something in their midst which was not quite right, waited for their father to speak, their young faces, despite the odd tension, showing interest for, come to think of it, they themselves had never heard the names of Simeon and Bryony's parents. Shrouded in mystery their deaths seemed to have been, happening long ago, but still it was strange the way Mama and Papa never spoke of them to their children. It surely was only natural for a child to be curious about its dead parents but as far as any of them were aware Mama and Papa had never spoken of them.

Their papa, whose eyes clung desperately to those of their mama, appeared to have been struck quite dumb and they stared at him in growing alarm, but from her end of the table Mama spoke and the faces of the three girls turned as one towards her.

"Dearest, do carve the venison or it will be quite cold." Her voice was perfectly normal though her face was paper white except for the scatter of golden freckles which stood out across her nose. "And Dolly, pass the plates to the master and put the vegetables on the table. And not another word from anyone until we have eaten and that means you as well, Simeon."

But Simeon Townley, watched by his sister who had told him exactly what he was to say, did not mean to be silenced.

"Oh, please do carry on, sir. We must not spoil Mrs Blaney's superb venison."

Jonas Townley, the breath escaping from him on a slow sigh of relief, reached for the carving knife, had it in his hand, the sharp edge of the blade to the succulent meat, when Simeon spoke again.

"But we can talk as we eat, can't we? So to get back to the fascinating and quite mysterious matter of our parents . . ."

"Oh God, Nella," Jonas Townley said for some reason, groaning deep in his chest.

". . . who it seems," Simeon continued imperturbably, "must have died when we were very young since neither of us can remember them, can we, Bryony?"

"No, that's true, so won't you tell us what happened to them?" Bryony went on. "Was it Mama who . . . oh no, of course not. I was going to ask if it was our mother who was related to you but it must have been our papa since our surname is the same as yours."

Jonas Townley made a strangled sound in the back of his throat and beside the serving table Dolly set the plates carefully on to its surface then put her hand to her trembling mouth. Her mistress, her green cat's eyes narrowed in the strangest way, stared at Bryony as though she would dearly love to cut her throat with the knife she was holding.

"And how were you related? I know that you had a brother. Jenna told us some time ago when we were old enough to understand, an older brother who died before you married Aunt Nella. An unmarried brother so we know he couldn't be our father so perhaps there is another branch of the family which is unknown to us."

Bryony smiled her soft smile, a gentle smile, a golden shining smile. She sat straight-backed in her chair as she had been taught, turning politely from one adult to the other and from across the table her brother took up the questions.

"We wondered if they, our parents' family, I mean, perhaps our mother's family, were connected with the coal mining industry, as yours are, sir, and if so, was it in these parts?"

Nella Townley suddenly rose to her feet and moved round the table to her husband. She stood behind him, her hands on his slumped shoulders. He leaned on one elbow, his head in his hand. With the other he covered one of hers, gripping it fiercely as if, should he let it slip he might be dragged away into a world less disastrous than this and though he dearly would have liked to escape what had come upon them, he could not leave it, not again, for his wife to deal with.

"Jonas, my darling, why don't you go and lie down?" his wife said. "You have not been well," she added lovingly, "and this will wait for another time. Or I can . . . can answer Bryony's question. I know you hoped that . . . that it would not come to this, but it has and—"

"Nella, this is my doing and it must be I who—"

"No, sweetheart, we agreed, long ago . . ."

They might have been alone. It was as though the room was empty but for the two of them and for some reason best known to herself Dolly began to weep silently, then, just as silently, she crossed the room, opened the door and went out. No one appeared to notice.

"You have always been my . . . salvation, Nella. You

have been there, always, when I most needed you. When . . ."

"Hush, darling, hush . . ."

"But now . . . it seems . . . they must be told and I must tell them."

"Well . . ."

She lifted her head and turned to the three young girls who were still sitting frozen to their chairs in numbed horror. They didn't, of course, know what that horror was for there had been nothing said, no actual words spoken that could be described as frightening but they were frightened nevertheless. It was the sense of devastation, the distressed expression on the faces of their mama and papa, the strange and menacing manner of Simeon and Bryony, who were actually smiling, which filled them with sick trepidation.

"Go into the drawing-room, girls. Ring the bell and ask Dolly to bring you . . . well . . . coffee . . . whatever you want and Papa and I will be along presently to explain."

The three young girls rose obediently but Bryony's voice, not rising in any way, not shrill or protesting – just a shade of . . . what was it? Surely not sadness? – stopped them.

"Perhaps it might be as well if they were to know the truth, Aunt Nella. After all, this is a family matter and as family they should be told."

"Thank you, Bryony, but I think I will decide what my daughters should or should not be told." Nella Townley's voice was icy. She would not be browbeaten by some chit of a girl especially one, or so it appeared, she did not care for.

"Mama . . ." Beth quavered. She was trembling, longing to run away and she began to weep, not silently as Dolly had done, but noisily, sobbing like a child. "Mama, I don't understand what is happening."

"No, sweetheart, I know you don't but—"

"Surely, Aunt Nella, she has a right to know she is related to—"

Nella whipped back to stare angrily into Bryony's sweetly smiling face, her lip ready to lift in a snarl of protective defiance.

"Stop it, girl! Stop this at once. Your uncle and I have—"

"My *uncle*?"

There was a deep and dreadful silence and even Simeon, who had thought he shared his sister's bitter despair, her fury at what had been done to her, her smouldering black rage towards the man who had shattered her life, felt a thrill of apprehension at the virulence in her eyes. It was not an expression you would expect to see in a pretty, well-brought-up young girl of not quite fifteen, one who had lived comfortably, securely, in the bosom of a family who had given her nothing but kindness and affection. And yet she still smiled, her soft mouth curved, plump and girlish.

"What is it, Bryony? What is it you wish to say?" Jonas Townley's voice had strengthened and he lifted his head with a semblance of the arrogance which had once been a byword in Marfield. "You seem, without actually putting it into words, to be asking something of me. I know what it is and so does your . . . my wife, but before we . . . discuss it, since it seems the time has come for it to be discussed, I must insist that my daughters leave the room. This has nothing to do with them."

"Do you think so? Do you not think they should know what you—"

"Bryony! I'm warning you." Nella Townley's voice was like the crack of a whip and Simeon rose abruptly, moving to stand beside his sister. He placed a hand protectively on her shoulder and his young face was hard and suddenly older.

"Don't threaten her. Don't you dare threaten her. Not after what you two have done to us."

"This was not your aunt's doing, boy, it was—"

"My *aunt*! She's not my aunt. She's no relation to me. She's related to her daughters, but not to me, or my sister, as you are!"

"Oh, sweet, sweet Christ, don't, I beg you . . ." It was his wife who moaned. "Don't do this. Can we not . . .?"

"Can we not what, Mrs Townley? Keep it hidden from . . ."

"Not like this, please. They are only children. Don't . . ."

"Yes, children. His children." He flung a bitter look of contempt at Jonas Townley who reared back in his chair at the force of it. "*His* children, as we are. But who was our mother? Who was his bloody mistress, his whore, his woman. Oh, Jesus, why did you do this to us?"

He began to weep, a devastated boy again for that moment and, taking his arm gently, his sister, strong and indestructible, led him from the room.

Chapter Sixteen

Ewan Macrae was born exactly nine months from the day he was conceived in the guest bedroom of his father's house. Jenna had grumbled and fretted her way through the last eight weeks of her pregnancy when she had suddenly and rather alarmingly become, as she put it, the size of a whale and had sworn to her uncharacteristically patient husband that this was positively the last child she would ever have. If Conal was to come near her again, that's if he could ever get near her again, she would borrow Mrs Garnett's carving knife and personally cut off that part of his anatomy that had got her into this state in the first place. And would Marian, who seemed to have some experience of such things, put her mind at rest by telling her that she would, one day, be the shape she once was; that she would one day be able to walk, never mind run, as she once had done, and not be this waddling, top-heavy, graceless breeding animal she seemed to have been for ever!

She and Marian, or Conal when he was at home, with the dogs racing about them, lumbered about the gardens which stretched around the house, seriously embarrassing George and Eppy, who didn't know where to direct their gaze, George privately told Mrs Garnett, especially the lad, and if she sat down for a breather on the bench it was all she could do to get up again, Jenna moaned to her mother.

"Darling, be patient," her mother told her when she and Laura, who was now Jenna's sister-in-law, came to call at the end of November. She couldn't bring the girls, Mama added, not with Jenna as she was, particularly with Beth to be married in the early spring. The business of child-bearing was not one that should be "carried on" around young unmarried girls and though Nella Townley had always been contemptuous of such niceties, for what was more natural than a woman having a baby, she did not want Marfield and the young bachelors it contained to get the idea that her daughters had not been properly brought up.

"Mama, I am trying to be patient but really, if one more person tells me that I must, I swear I will go mad. Conal has the words on his lips constantly from morning till night but you can see his own patience is wearing thin. How you managed it four times I really don't know."

"I had little choice, my dear."

"Well, I don't mean to have another, not for a long while."

Her mother had smiled placidly, exchanging a wise glance with Laura. "Well, we'll see."

"There's no 'we'll see' about it, Mama. Conal has promised tha—"

Jenna bit off her words and again Nella and Laura exchanged glances for it did not seem to either of them that Conal Macrae was a man likely to forgo the pleasures of his connubial bed, nor the sweetness of his young wife in it. Both ladies, being enlightened and well-read women, knew of Richard Carlile's book published over thirty years ago on the subject of control over the conception of a child. *Every Woman's Book: or What Is Love* recommended several methods of preventing childbirth and since then there had been other publications describing several techniques but neither Nella Townley nor Laura Eason could imagine Conal Macrae allowing them to fall into his young wife's hands. Of course, it was nothing to do with them but did Jenna know what she was talking about with such airiness? Her mother steered the conversation to safer anchorage.

"And have you engaged a nurse yet, darling?"

"Yes. I believe Doctor Sterling is to bring her over tomorrow. Conal wanted her to come a week or two since but I put my foot down. Imagine having some old fool breathing down my neck every hour of the day for weeks on end, since I believe the doctor means her to stay on after the child is born."

"It is customary, Jenna," Laura murmured, sipping tea from Jenna's fine bone china. "Though I must admit I made do with the girl who worked in my kitchen and the help of the women at Smithy Brow."

"There you are then," Jenna crowed triumphantly.

"Jenna, Conal is a very different man to his brother. Mark was . . . well, not quite so . . ."

"Bloody-minded?"

"Jenna!"

"I'm sorry, Mama, but I feel like some prize cow from which the farmer hopes for a thoroughbred litter or am I mixing up my farm animals? They *all* watch me, Conal and the maidservants, the men in the stables."

"Jenna, you don't go to the stable yard?"

"I want to see Dory and Duff and my little mare, Amber. Do you realise I have never yet ridden her? Conal doesn't know I go there, of course, and I have sworn the grooms to secrecy. You won't tell him, will you? And I do have Marian and Campbell and George whose wife has ten children, hovering at my back the whole time. Dear God, I get so bored, Mama, so bored and can only long for the day when I can put this" – her hand on her jutting belly – "in the arms of Marian's cousin."

"Marian's cousin?"

"Mmm, she is to be nanny. Abigail, she's called and she knows of a good clean wet nurse so between them they should manage it nicely while I'm away."

Nella Townley, who did not care to be involved with these ominous words since she knew only too well what they implied, stood up and pronounced that they must be on their way. She did not envy Conal Macrae when the time came for him to tell his wife, her daughter, that she was to stay at home and look after her child, Nella's grandchild.

"Ewan," Conal said, holding his newborn son in possessive and curiously proficient arms. He lounged in a chair by his wife's bedside, grinning into the infant's yawning face, then looking up at his wife who, an hour after the boy's birth, was sitting up in bed spooning Mrs Garnett's delicious chicken soup into her mouth. Nurse Morris had bathed her, changed the bedclothes and her nightdress, brushed her long, knotted hair and tied it back with a bunch of white ribbons. She approved of Mrs Macrae, who did not lie about moaning as so many of her patients did, but declared she was hungry after her hours of hard work and would nurse find out what Mrs Garnett had in her pantry. Yes, the baby was very handsome, Mrs Macrae said. A boy, thank God for that and she meant to call him Jonas and would Nurse Morris send her husband in and here he was, proud as punch, and with the obvious intention of sitting beside his wife's bed and admiring her and the son she had given him and Mrs Macrae needing to rest.

"Ewan! Where on earth did that come from?"

"It is a family name. My father was Ewan and my grandfather Conal so this little blighter's son will be the same. Turn and turn about for generations it's been. My uncle will be next chief, of course, and he's Duncan, his son is Angus and so on. D'you see?"

"No, but it doesn't matter because that one is to be Jonas."

"Ewan." Conal looked down into his son's crumpled face then bent his head and to Jenna and the nurse's surprise put his lips tenderly to the baby's cheek, revealing for a moment that hidden facet of his nature which even his beloved wife had not yet seen.

"Ewan Macrae." He looked up then, his eyes the softest, purest golden brown and his wife could have sworn there were tears in them. Though she claimed she felt splendid and had eaten her soup, Jenna's own eyes were deep and tired in her pale face but nevertheless she sat up awkwardly and leaned towards her husband.

"I would like a kiss too, Conal," she said huskily.

He looked up from his dreaming contemplation of the baby in his arms then, laying the child neatly between them on the bed, he put his arms about his wife. He drew her against him with a gesture which was as possessive as the one he had used with his son. He smoothed her hair, then tipping up her face he kissed her lovingly. He smiled down at her, kissed her again, his lips lingering against hers then laid her back on her pillow, the child ignored.

"I love you, my bonnie lassie," he said simply, the truth of it plain to see. "But you're weary. You've done well with the boy though I suppose I did have a small part to play. He's a fine lad, Jenna Macrae, and I thank you for him. You've been a good girl while you've waited for him and as soon as you're on your feet we'll be away up north to show him to his family." He frowned down at the child. "He has only one fault that I can see."

Jenna and the nurse turned alarmed eyes on the calm infant on the bed.

"No, dinna worry, my lass. He's a fine, handsome boy. 'Tis just that he's no' like his mother at all. No' a trace of her colour, ye ken. So dark like his papa but he's a mutinous set to his jaw which tells me there's something of you in him!"

She was out of her bed in five days and out of her room in a week, clamouring to be allowed to visit her mother; to drive down to the Misses Yeoland or to Miss Renshaw's to be fitted for some new gowns; to walk in the fields with her dogs; to get on her mare and gallop into the breathless and icy world beyond the garden gate, showing little interest or concern in her son who, she had been told by the scandalised nurse, was doing well.

"Won't you go and see him, Mrs Macrae?" the good woman begged, "or will I bring him down to you? Nanny Abigail is—"

"Nanny Abigail?"

"Yes, madam, she's in charge of the nursery and would be glad of a visit from you. And please, Mrs Macrae, I do beg of you to remain in that chair, if not in your bed. Mr Macrae will not like it if he comes home and finds you up and about."

"Don't fuss, nurse. I am quite recovered," which was true. Her healthy, eighteen-year-old body, supple with youth and the active life she had, unlike her sisters, always led, had sprung rapidly back to its former energetic grace. Almost overnight she had regained her normal shape and ten days after Ewan's birth she was downstairs dining with her anxious husband who had been led to believe that ladies did not leave their beds for weeks after being confined. She was superbly gowned in one of her wedding trip creations, a dazzling thing of pale gold tissue from which her creamy shoulders and the magnificent swell of her breasts emerged as she leaned in the candlelight to tantalise Conal Macrae.

For the past month Conal had insisted that she sleep alone, ignoring her protests, saying that they needed to rest and neither could do so with her restless bulk disturbing them both. Now, it seemed, as she smiled at him in the hazed glow of candlelight and firelight, her turquoise eyes sending an urgent message that was unmistakable, she intended to sleep alone no longer and why could they not dismiss the servants and proceed to their bedroom at once, she asked him.

"Darling, there's nothing I'd like more," he murmured into her hair as they moved up the stairs together, Jenna leaning against him in a way that told him exactly what she planned. "But it is only ten days since Ewan's birth and really, should I no' give you a week or two to . . . to heal a wee bit? I admit I know little, if anything about childbirth and its after-effects but even I can imagine . . ."

"Conal, I love you, and I feel fine, fit and fully recovered and ready to take up my life again. And that means every aspect of it. I intend to ride Amber tomorrow and I intend that you should ride me tonight!"

They had reached the top of the stairs and were out of sight of the maidservants who, Conal was certain, would be nudging one another slyly, telling one another as they cleared the dinner table that there'd be another boy in the nursery in nine months' time at this rate. In his justifiable masculine excitement he appeared to have missed completely his wife's reference to riding her mare, the latter part of the statement having more significance for him at this moment. There was nothing he'd like more than to take his young and passionate wife to bed and make love to her as he had been unable to do for the past few weeks. Not that he and Jenna had practised celibacy as he had heard many couples did, probably at the insistence of the wife since not all women were made for loving as his Jenna was. She had taken to marriage and their marriage bed with a delight and eagerness not usual in what were known as nice women, or so he had heard, and her response to his lovemaking and her initiation of many of their sweet and passionate encounters had been most satisfying. Almost until the boy was born she had contrived to position herself into an arrangement of pillows and bolsters, sometimes so hilariously they had often found themselves so consumed with laughter they were not able to complete what they had started, but she had kept their closeness, their ardour a warm and pleasurable thing to them both despite her size.

What a joy she was! He still couldn't believe it sometimes, the delight she gave him and at his age too, an age when he had thought himself to be well beyond the capacity of a man to fall romantically in love. When he had made up his mind to settle, in a year or two, he would do so with some suitable, sensible young lady of good family he had told himself, one well trained by her upbringing to be the mistress of his home, the mother of the children he wanted. Dutiful, well-mannered, calm, a pale cream and ivory girl who would run his household and wait serenely in his bed for him at night. Cool, logical, unhurried, untroubled by anything but her duty to please him.

Look what he had got and look how it enchanted him! Jenna! His Jenna. With a spirit as fiery as the hair that tumbled down her back; with a wilfulness which would let nothing stand in her way; with a joy of living which seized on every obstacle to it and flung it imperiously to one side; with a belief in herself and her capacity to do as she pleased, an intensity of feeling which was glorious, which was, at least men supposed so, not felt by women; with dreams her tempestuous heart would never give up. Jenna! His Jenna. A passionate tawny girl, untroubled by anything but her absolute determination to get him into her bed this night. She had taken his life and his heart, twisting them about to suit herself, binding him to her and could he fail to love her? Christmas was almost here and she had not complained at her inability to attend the round of parties and dances which took place at this time of the year. Soon it would be the new year, surely a propitious time to begin their new roles as parents. He and his Jenna. His tawny rose!

"Darling, this is not like you," she murmured huskily, putting her lips against his throat, just above the collar of his shirt where his pulse beat rapidly. "You are normally as eager as I to . . ."

"Goddammit, Jenna, I'm bloody eager now, let me tell you and if you lift that arm any higher your breasts will fall out of your gown."

She lifted her arm higher and the twin globes of her breasts were exposed and his hands went to them at once as she had meant them to.

"There, my darling husband, is that not very pleasant?" smoothing her moist lips up the curve of his jaw, then across to his mouth.

"Dammit, Jenna . . . this can't be right. You're only just out of childbed." He reached to pull the bodice of her gown still lower and her breasts swelled eagerly into his hands. "Look, sweetheart, would it not be . . . more fitting if we were to get off this bloody landing?"

"That's what I plan to do, Conal Macrae."

"Jesus . . .!"

"Open the bedroom door . . ."

At the last he resisted her and at the last she had to agree with him. She was still somewhat sore, she admitted and besides, there were other . . . complications which she knew he would understand, to do with childbirth, but soon . . . soon . . . and in the meanwhile she would just . . . there, did he like that? . . . yes, she thought he would . . . and again? . . . very well, but if he imagined she was going to sleep alone after the pleasure she had just given him, then he could think again.

They slept in one another's arms, well pleased with this evening, this new start to the coming year, to the new decade, with their life together, with the unfolding of the good days ahead which they knew would be splendid, with their new son who slept in the nursery and sometimes awoke to cry for his mother who, though she saw him every day could not quite bring herself to pick him up.

"I suppose, nurse, we had best get him ready to take him over to meet his grandparents," Jenna said doubtfully a week later as she looked down at the sleeping baby. She and Marian had gone up to the nursery, a large, rather sombre room at the top of the house. It looked out over the garden at the back and towards the squares and oblongs of the neatly hedged fields. There was farmland between Beechfield Lodge and Walton on the Hill, dotted here and there with mansions such as their own, each one standing in four or five acres of well-tended garden, a bit of woodland, orchards and paddocks. There were farms whose tenants planted the fields and where cattle grazed the rich pastures. It was flat land, dissected by rambling lanes, by groves of trees and a hamlet or two. From the barred window of the nursery it appeared to be all set out like a chequerboard, neat and drab at this time of the year, quiet and unhurried with only the occasional slow movement on a lane of a horse and cart, a labourer readying a field for spring ploughing and immediately below in the paddock the figure of Percy standing in the centre exercising Amber on a long lead rein.

The mare had grown even more sleek and glossy, plump even, for it was more than six months since Conal had bought her. Since then she had not been ridden, only trotted round and round the paddock by Percy. Now her tail was up and swishing the air, a lovely silken banner of cream to match her mane, a pale contrast to the almost golden colour of her coat, the winter sun polishing it to gleaming splendour. She looked quite superb, her ears pricking, her eyes clear and intelligent as though she watched for her mistress, waiting for Jenna to rescue her from the tedious circle the groom had her in.

Jenna, who had moved from the cradle to the window, smiled at the sight of the animal and she let out her breath on a long sigh of delight. She leaned forward, her forehead pressed to the window pane and her breath misted the glass for it was the first day of January and cold outside. There had been a frost and where the sun's rays had not reached there was still a white shadow on the ground.

Jenna turned back to where Marian and Nanny Abigail hung over the cradle and she bit her lip, chewing it reflectively.

"He's a handsome lad, Miss Jenna," Marian said dotingly in that way women did, Jenna had noticed. It was strange, really, for though the boy was handsome, with his father's dark hair but curling where Conal's was straight and heavy; with his winged eyebrows and long dark lashes, even with Conal's scowling expression at times, Jenna had observed, he might have been Nanny Abigail's child for all the emotion he aroused in her. That first crumpled, elderly look he had at birth had gone now at almost three weeks old. His skin was clear and smooth, rich with good health, with rounded pink cheeks and a sweet little rosebud mouth which sucked and sucked even when he was asleep. His nose was no more than an unformed blob though his eyes had proved to be a brilliant blue, almost green, Conal said, just like hers. He was her child, her son, hers and Conal's, the result of that first enchanting love they had shared in the room just below this one and indeed there was no doubt he was a lovely child but she could go no further than that.

And she must take him over to Marfield, she really must. Her mama was itching to see him, she had said in a hasty letter she had sent after his birth though strangely she had asked Jenna to wait a week or two before she brought Ewan over to Bank House. She could not come to Liverpool herself, Mama had said, since Papa was troubled by a cough, the dread cough of colliers brought about by a mixture of damp and coal dust and which killed so many, though of course Papa was not much underground these days and was certainly not dying but if she should take her eyes off him for a moment he'd be up and away, hell bent on getting to his damned pit, Jenna would know what she meant. She would write and let Jenna know when Papa was feeling better but in the meantime perhaps it would be as well to keep the boy at home. Until Papa was well again.

Jenna had been uneasy, though she could not have said why, feeling a real need to see for herself how Papa was. It was not only to show off her fine son – he was fine, everyone told her so – and to see her papa who was not well but to get that first time over, the first time of knowing that all those she met would be studying her sturdy, obviously full-term child, and drawing their own conclusions. Not that she cared for herself, not really, but Papa would know, would realise what she and Conal had done and would blame Conal, particularly after all the trouble there had been last year when she had come over to Liverpool to see him. Papa would think Conal was no gentleman to have taken advantage of her even though they were now respectably married and she could hardly tell him that it was all her doing, could she? And she really did want to talk to Papa about her return to what she had begun before she and Conal were married and that was, of course, her work at the colliery. She had missed almost a year of what she liked to regard as her "training" for her future management of Townley, Fielden and Kenworth Collieries and though the complexities of how she was to get from Liverpool to Marfield and back again each day were a bit daunting she was sure she and Papa would work something out together.

She turned again to the window, aware that Marian and Nanny were exchanging glances and staring at her back. She badly wanted to leave the somewhat rarefied atmosphere in which it seemed an infant must be reared and indeed had already changed into her new, beautifully tailored riding habit the Misses Yeoland had designed and made for her. It was of dark, bottle green cloth with a well-fitting bodice, a cambric habit-shirt collar and a short basque jacket. The sleeves had turned-back cuffs edged in velvet and the skirt was full and long. She would wear a black beaver top hat and a veil, with riding trousers of chamois leather over which she would pull tall black riding boots with a high heel. She meant to ride astride though as yet Conal did not know!

She watched Percy for another few minutes while at her back Marian and Nanny fidgeted by the cradle. She pulled at her lip indecisively. She was strangely fixed on this compulsion that she really should ask Campbell to bring round the carriage to take her to Marfield and yet at the same time she badly wanted to leave it for another day. Leap up on Amber and put the mare through those first tentative paces a rider and an animal new to one another must go through. That's if her healing body would allow it, naturally, and she knew Marian had severe doubts about that. And yet . . . oh, she did wish Mama had not seemed so odd in her letter, a bit cryptic, was that the word she wanted, just as though there was something she was not saying, even as she wrote it.

"Oh damn and blast it!" she said, making both servants wince. "Run down and tell Campbell to bring the carriage, will you, Marian? I shall be ready in ten minutes and wrap the baby up, Nanny, we are going over to . . . what? . . . how long? I don't know. Does it matter? Oh yes, I'd forgotten that. Well, bring the woman along then. She can be put in the nursery with Molly . . . yes, at Bank House . . . and can feed the child there. Molly will be overjoyed. Oh, and Marian" – halting the trot her maid had broken into at the urgency of her mistress's voice –

"don't bother to put out my travelling outfit," for suddenly it seemed extremely important to get to Bank House at the earliest possible moment. "Just fetch my warm boots and my cloak with the fur lining and I'll go as I am."

It was almost noon when the carriage drew up at the steps to Bank House. The journey had been slow due to the icy state of some of the roads, no more than rutted lanes really, and Campbell was not going to chance his horse's fragile legs in some wild gallop across frozen pools and tracks, he told Mrs Macrae dourly. He thought the whole expedition to be insane, you could tell that by the grim set of his mouth and wasn't it just like a woman to take it into her head to go visiting a distance of nearly ten miles on a day like this? Mr Macrae'd have Campbell's balls when he heard about it and would want to know what Campbell had been thinking of allowing the mistress to be so wilful. But then the master knew full well that when Mrs Macrae got some daft scheme in her daft head there was no man on earth, and that included Mr Macrae, who'd the right to it as her husband, who could stop her.

Dolly's mouth fell open as she opened the door and saw the small assembly on the doorstep, her eyes going from one face to the other, the expression on her own changing rapidly in succession from dismay to pleasure, from pleasure back to dismay and then to softness as her glance fell on Miss Jenna's bairn.

"Eeh, Miss Jenna, we wasn't expecting you," she said, her manner becoming strained, making no attempt to open the door further.

"I can see that, Dolly and would it be too much to ask if we may come in? It's damned cold on this step."

"Eeh, Miss Jenna," Dolly said again, falling back from Miss Jenna's determined stride across the threshold. Her maid followed her and behind the maid was the new nanny carrying Miss Jenna's lad and behind her another female who had the clean, apple-cheeked goodness of a country woman written all over her. She was plump and smiling, ready to take the little one from nanny's arms, looking enquiringly at her mistress as she spoke.

"I'd best find t'nursery, ma'am," she said placidly. "Both me an' little 'un 'll feel better if tha' could just tell me . . ."

"Pardon?" Miss Jenna looked blankly at the woman but Marian, who had once worked at Bank House and was known by Dolly, took charge, bustling past the housemaid with the two women and the baby who had begun to wail, moving towards the foot of the stairs.

The door to the drawing-room opened a fraction as though the commotion in the hallway had disturbed those inside and a tired-looking woman peeped out. Yes, that was the word Jenna would have used to describe her action – peeped. Who was she? Familiar, of course. . . but no, it could not be . . . not be her . . .

"Mama?" she said hesitantly, incredulously, and then again, for it seemed so unlikely, "Mama?"

"Jenna, is that you, darling?" the woman – Mama? – asked anxiously. "Oh darling, is that really you?"

"Mama . . . Dear heavens, Mama, what is it?"

Papa! It must be Papa. That devilish thing called black spit had got him, that awful disease which filled a collier's lungs with a thick black liquid through which he could not breathe, and which, when it was coughed up, looked just like ink. He had been unwell for a week or two, Mama had said in her letter but why had they not sent for her, told her to hurry, that her papa, her beloved papa was . . . was . . . dear God!

"Is he dead, Mama?" she asked baldly.

"Who?"

"Is Papa dead?" for surely he must be to reduce her mother, her vital, her eternally strong mama to this pitiful, haunted wraith who quivered in the doorway. She and

Papa were . . . had been . . . held together by a bond that, should it break would leave the one that remained in much the state her mother was in. As she herself would be in if Conal was taken from her, she remembered thinking, then from behind her mama's back her papa spoke her name and she felt the relief pour into her and she wanted to laugh at her own absurdity.

"Oh Papa, there you are," she called, tossing her cloak to Dolly. The cloak slipped through Dolly's fingers and fell to the floor and strangely, Dolly made no attempt to pick it up. What was wrong with everyone today? Jenna thought irritably, moving towards where her mother still hovered in the doorway. Jenna smiled at her, then in a flood of almost tearful emotion, put her arms about her and hugged her. Really held her and hugged her for she loved her so much and there was this feeling . . . God knows what it was, but . . . Her mother felt thin, fragile bones where none had been before and yet it was only . . . when was it? . . . a couple of weeks before Ewan was born when Mama and Laura had sat beside her in her sitting-room and begged her to be patient. Told her, smilingly, that it would soon be over, both of them in the best of health, her father at the coal exchange, her mother had said, with no mention of anything wrong.

They were just about to have lunch, Mama said, her arm about her daughter's waist as they entered the drawing-room, and of course Jenna must join them and then . . . the boy, he was upstairs? Of course, they were longing to see him, the nurse could bring him down later. Papa was . . .

Papa sat in the deep and comfortable leather armchair which had been brought in from his study. It looked out of place, its masculinity contrasting sharply with the dainty, essentially feminine furniture of the drawing-room which was a place for ladies to relax. He was fully dressed in his usual well-fitting, immaculately pressed tail coat and trousers, his shirt front starched to perfection, his watch-chain bright across his waistcoat, his neckcloth, with its diamond pin, perfectly knotted. His hair was brushed and he was freshly shaved but somehow he looked crumpled, not quite right, slightly out of true as though the clothes he wore belonged to another man.

The fire leaped and crackled, the pretty clock on the mantelshelf ticked musically and Papa smiled at her and his smile was dreadful. False, twitching somehow as though it was taking a great effort on his part to lift the corners of his mouth. His knuckles were white as he gripped the arm of the chair. His face was a kind of mushroom grey, like the ashes in the grate when the fire is dead and there was a purple mottling beneath his shadowed eyes, his eyes which were, quite simply, or so it seemed to his daughter, ready to die as well.

Oh dear sweet God, what was it? What was wrong? What was wrong with her vigorously youthful mama and her powerfully indestructible papa who had always seemed to her to be as enduring, as deep-rooted as this house in which she had been born, in which generations of Fieldens including her mama had been born, had lived and prospered? What had happened since that week before her own child was born that had reduced her beloved mama and papa to this pitiful old couple who stared at her as if . . . as if they were waiting for her to . . . to issue a death sentence?

There was a movement from the outer edge of the room which, at this time of the year, before the lamps were lit, was always shadowed. By the windows and the door which led into the conservatory there was daylight, sharp, wintry, bright but to the side behind where Papa sat brooding into the fire the chairs which were placed there were barely more than dim shapes. They were occupied. Beth was there, silent and staring. Nancy, no more than a spectre in a pretty dress. Rose, Bryony, both like children placed by a disapproving parent and told to sit still and behave.

And Simeon!

He rose as she gaped in astonishment, too astonished at that moment even to wonder what he was doing home from the mine. Papa was unwell but Mr Eason, Mark as she was now expected to call him, was there to guide Simeon in Papa's absence. He sauntered towards her, his hands deep in his pockets and he smiled. She didn't know what was in that smile though she knew she didn't like it but before she had time to dwell on it, or to ask him what the devil he was up to, since it was certainly something, Bryony got to her feet and in that graceful way she had, swayed across the room to stand beside her brother. She put her hand in his and rested her cheek against his shoulder, the gesture binding the two of them together as no words could have done.

"Well, this is a surprise," Simeon drawled, his eyes sharp, narrowed, defiant. "We had not expected you, had we, papa? Do come and join us. Come and join our family circle, our close family circle. Now that we are all here perhaps we could bring out the champagne? What d'you think?"

"A splendid idea, brother . . . and sisters!" Bryony's eyes glowed like candles and Jenna felt a sudden tremor attack her though as yet she had no idea what was happening. Sisters?

"Ring the bell, Rose, there's a good girl and we shall have a celebration for it's not often a chap discovers he has not one sister but five."

"What are you drivelling on about, Simeon?" Jenna snapped contemptuously but Simeon began to laugh with every sign of great good humour.

"Oh, of course, you don't know, do you? Well, let me bring you the good news. It seems that you and I are not cousins as we had been led to believe but brother and sister and surely that is something worth celebrating. Yes, you may well stare. I did myself when I heard of it but it is true. Ask our papa there . . ." and from behind her Jenna heard her mother moan. Her papa sat, just as though he had not heard, his eyes on the cheerful flames which licked in the grate and beside Simeon, Bryony laughed softly.

Chapter Seventeen

She shivered in her husband's arms, his warm cloak wrapped about both of them but still she was cold. Her eyes were blank and unfocused, staring blindly from the bedroom window out over the frozen bleakness of the garden to where Seth, with the lad Dinty, was industriously gathering broken branches from the littered ground beneath the cedar trees. There had been a storm several weeks ago, a high winter wind which had howled out of the east, lashing the trees, snapping branches and the man and the boy had just got round to what Seth called "a bit o' tidying". Dinty was breaking up the branches, stacking them neatly in the wheelbarrow and Jenna could hear the crack of the wood as it broke.

It was almost dusk, the stark outline of denuded trees black against the ice blue paleness of the clear sky. It was quiet here now. After the screaming and the shouting, after the crying and the wailing, but it was not until Conal had come, sent for by her frantic mother, that the turmoil had eased. Like Simeon Townley – Townley? No, he wasn't a Townley, was he? What *was* his name? – she wouldn't believe it. He had laughed, genuine amusement on his smug and smiling face, and so had she, thinking this was one of Simeon's imbecile jokes, a schoolboy joke, the sort he was fond of, he and those wild young men with whom he had mixed at school. But then if it was a joke why were Papa and Mama not laughing?

Why were Nancy, Rose and Beth sitting huddled at the back of the drawing-room hiding, or so it seemed, from the light as though they were ashamed of something and must keep out of sight? And why was Bryony, who had always been in Jenna's opinion inclined to be uncommunicative, smiling in that strange triumphant way, clinging to Simeon as though they were lovers?

Her bewilderment, her apprehension, made her voice harsh.

"What in God's name are you drooling on about, Simeon? Have you been at Papa's port? And as for you, Bryony, what on earth does that inane look on your face mean? The pair of you should be banished to your rooms and made to stay there until you can talk sense, in my opinion, and the sooner the better. Upsetting Papa with your nasty jokes. Well, I for one am not laughing and neither is anyone else that I can see. Papa, don't you think this fool has gone too far this time?" She turned to her father. "Papa, are you not going to . . .?"

"Jenna, come and sit down by me, darling." Her mother had returned to the sofa from which she had risen as Jenna and her servants had entered the house, and she patted the seat, beseeching her daughter to join her. Papa sat opposite her, just as he had done since Jenna had arrived, his eyes still fixed on the fire and it was then she really began to be afraid.

"What is going on here?" She did her best to keep her voice light, for as long as she could pretend there was nothing wrong, then there was nothing wrong! "Won't someone tell me why this idiot" – throwing a scornful glance at Simeon and Bryony – "both these idiots are acting as they are? Really, it is too much. This is my first visit home since Ewan was born. I brought him over especially to meet you, Papa," smiling at her father as she offered him the gift of his grandson, the grandson who, though his name would be Macrae, was a Townley and would follow in her footsteps when the time came. The blood of Fieldens mixed with the blood of Townleys and now Macraes, but all the same blood in the veins of the child whose inheritance this all was.

"Your son, Ewan? Is that what you are to call him?" Bryony said, smiling a little.

Jenna turned to her coolly. "Yes, and have you something to say about that, too?"

"Oh no, a good name, I suppose."

"Well, thank you. It's nice to have your approval."

Her mother's voice was filled with pain as she spoke. "Jenna, dearest, will you not come and sit down beside me? Papa and I have something to—"

But Jenna, as though her instincts, the warning sense that lay buried deep beneath all her other senses, knew and was telling her that some devastation was to come and wanted no part of it, sauntered across to face Bryony.

"Just a moment, Mama, if you please. It seems Bryony had something to say about my son now. Dear God, if it's not him, it's her . . ."

"Jenna . . ."

"No, Mama, I really think the pair of them have gone too far. Simeon has always been obnoxious, right from being a child and now it seems—"

"Jenna, you are merely postponing what your mama has to say to you." Bryony was completely unruffled, her composure so. . . so complete Jenna felt a sudden urge to strike her across her smooth young face, to shatter, smash, break irrevocably whatever it was that was pleasing her so much. "It is quite important to us all, particularly to Simeon, so perhaps it might be as well if you went and sat down beside your mama."

"Don't you presume to give orders to me, Bryony Townley. I shall sit down when and where I please and if—"

"Jenna."

It was her papa who spoke. He still gazed, almost dreamily, into the fire, but his voice was firm, the one he used when he meant to let them know, all of them, that his word was law. He was pale, pale as death, but he was himself, Jonas Townley and he had had enough of the squabbling which was going on at his back.

But Jenna was still not prepared to listen. It appeared she was eager to do or say anything to delay that sense of terror which was slowly filtering through her veins.

"And what's the matter with you three, may I ask?" Whirling again she faced her sisters who cowered from her as though she had produced a bull-whip and was about to flay them with it. "What the dickens are you doing crouched against the wall in that peculiar manner? Why don't you come and sit by the fire with Mama and Papa, where it's warm?"

At almost the same moment Nancy and Beth began to weep, great tearing sobs which shook their girlish frames. Rose remained stony-faced and dry-eyed and Jenna stared at all three in astonishment.

Bryony sighed, turning her eyes ceilingward and Simeon shook his head as though the caprice of women never failed to amaze him.

"Jenna . . ." Her mother's voice was gentle.

"Mama . . .?" Her own was terrified.

"I think your mama has something to say to you, Jenna," Bryony said softly, turning to smile up at her brother.

"Bryony, will you stop this at once. Go and sit down, and you too, Simeon."

"Yes, Papa."

"And Jenna, come here, child. Sit beside your mother."

"Papa?"

"Yes, my dear, I know, I know, but it must be . . . brought out into the open."

"What?"

"Come and sit down."

It was soon told. A sordid tale which, had it not been her papa's tale, might have seemed, perhaps, romantic to a young woman who knew what it was to love a man and to be loved in return. A great love story in which a handsome prince carries off his beautiful princess to a fairy castle, fighting dragons – in this case society's conventions – so that they might live happily ever after. Of course, the prince had a wife and four daughters but when the princess died leaving her own two children behind, the prince's wife had forgiven him, another great love revealed, and then returned by the prince, and it was *they* who would live happily ever after.

So, here they were. The prince and his wife and their four daughters and the two cuckoos who had come to fill the nest, nourished, loved and protected by a woman so dreadfully wronged it did not seem possible to her daughter, who sat white-faced and straight-backed as the tale was told, that she could ever show forgiveness.

She could not! She said so, spitting in her father's face, hitting out at him, striking his unresisting figure again and again, screaming her hatred, her agony, her despair for how could she manage her life without the hub of it, the father she had adored, idolised, idealised, in its centre? He had gone now, the man she had loved for so long, faded away into the insignificance of other lesser men, buried beneath the filth he himself had created when he wallowed with the woman he had made his mistress.

"Who was she?" she had screamed. "Mama, who was she?"

"Darling, darling, she is dead."

"I hope she rots in hell!"

"Jenna, don't, don't . . . she was a good woman."

"You can say that after what they did to you?"

"Yes, she was . . . she was my friend."

"Your friend! He fornicated with your friend and you forgave him? Allowed him to bring these . . . these" – She turned to glare, hissing her loathing of the pair who were her half-brother and sister – "into your home . . . bastards . . . to live with your own children?"

It had gone on for more than an hour, perhaps two when, miraculously, Conal was there. He had pulled her away from Simeon whom she had backed up against a wall, and drawn her into his arms. There were scratches on Simeon's face and his sister, her calm deserting her, was huddled in a chair, her hair, through which Jenna Macrae's hands had dragged, hanging about her face. Her eyes were still filled with venom though, peering through the tangle of its ebony darkness. Beth was wailing since it seemed Frank Miller would not want to marry the sister of a bastard, *two* bastards, for he was bound to hear of it, and her sisters sat in a state of glazed shock, in the shocked state they had drifted about in since it had been revealed to them the exact nature of their relationship with Simeon and Bryony Townley.

Conal had put something to her lips and she drank it and when she awoke it was late afternoon. She was in her own bed, the one she had slept in for the first seventeen years of her life and Conal sat beside her. The fire burned in the grate and a candle-lamp glowed on the table and when she pushed back the coverlet and swung her legs over the side of the bed, he stood up at once, ready to catch her.

She began to cry, great, long shuddering cries of grief and pain and when he reached for his cloak and wrapped them both in it, she clung to him gratefully. She wept, sick and cold, in his arms until the sky outside was black with night, Seth and Dinty long gone to their own suppers and the warm fire beside which they each spent their evenings.

She sighed now, her face pressed into the hollow of her husband's shoulder. She still wore her elegant new riding outfit, sadly rumpled and she looked down at it, remembering, perhaps, the moment she had put it on a lifetime ago. Happy she had been at the prospect of riding Amber, happy, eager to show off her new son to her papa, and yet fearful. A seven-month baby could not be mistaken, and Ewan was certainly not that and what, her apprehensive mind had asked, would her papa have to say about it? Her fine, upstanding, noble papa whose opinion she had always sought and whose approval she had always prized. She had been worried that he might be stern with her, cool, shocked and she could not have borne it. Had it not been so tragic she might have laughed. What a farce life was!

"How did you know?" she said at last, her tone lethargic.

"Your mama sent a note begging me to come at once." He drew her even closer, tucking her head beneath his chin, his arms strong, telling her that no matter what happened here today, or in the past, *he* was here for her to lean on. "She was afraid for you, my darling."

"For Papa, not me. He means more to her than any of us."

"Is'na that how it should be? Between man and wife, I mean?"

"Yes, but it was not always so." Her voice was cold and bitter. "You know all about it, I suppose?"

"Aye, lassie. While you were asleep I had a word or two with your papa."

"I don't know how you could bring yourself to speak to him. Not after what he has done to me."

"He is devastated, Jenna. And it was not only done to you."

"Yes, I know, but the others didn't love him like I did."

"How do you know that, my love?" His voice was gentle as he lifted her chin to look into her eyes. He drew her across the room and seated her before the fire, wrapping his woollen cloak about her trembling shoulders, then knelt at her feet. She was still badly shocked, he knew that, but deep inside her was an icy core of rage which would need a great deal of love, of understanding, of gentleness and forgiveness on her part before it melted. He himself had known all about it, of course, long before he had married her. Not that Townley had told him, probably thinking it was none of Conal Macrae's business, and indeed Conal agreed with him but Mark had considered it his duty to tell him Jonas Townley's secret for it had seemed to him that Conal should know. Conal had not cared unduly. Jenna Townley was all he wanted and her link with the illegitimate children of her father would make no difference to their lives when he married her.

He wished, sadly, he could say the same about her three sisters. The stigma, the taint of bastardy fouled all those who came into contact with it, or so it was said, and like Bryony Townley before him, he wondered at the influence of a man who could sweep it all under the carpet for over fifteen years. But it would be out now, for the girl who shivered in the chair before him would shriek it from the rooftops in defence of her inheritance. She was Jonas Townley's heir, his true heir, which was what everyone had believed in the past since Simeon Townley was no more than a cousin of sorts. She was married. To him. They had a son. They lived in Liverpool where he himself was a respected ship owner and this revelation would do them no harm. But what of the three poor little snivelling creatures – at least Nancy and Beth, the two eldest, were snivelling – who were downstairs? What of them? Who would marry them now? Perhaps some struggling ambitious tradesman who would be willing to overlook their background in order to get his hands on their no doubt sizeable dowries, but certainly not one of the sons of the gentlemen with whom their parents now mixed. Or *had* mixed until this was out for everyone to gloat over. And what of Bryony Townley, herself a bastard? What would she do with herself? Beyond the pale, she was. On equal footing with her own mother who had been a whore and the best thing Bryony could do, they would say, the only thing she could do, was to put an end to herself and save her family a great deal of heartache.

But from what Conal had seen of her and her brother, with whom she had been whispering in the hall when he came through it on his way to his father-in-law's study, he doubted that either of them meant to suffer from this or else why had they divulged it? He wondered where they had learned of it.

"You must accept it, you know that, don't you, lassie? There's nothing to be gained from brooding about it. It was your father's . . . I suppose you would call it wrongdoing, and it happened a long time ago. Your mother forgave him and God knows how many women would have done it, *and* brought up his children for him. Not many, I suspect. But if she could do that surely you—"

"Oh, don't be so bloody sanctimonious, Conal. My mother was a damned fool. She, as well as him, brought this on us. They could have been farmed out with some decent family and no one the worse off. Not them and not us."

He was inclined to agree with her but to say so would not help to mend the great, fraying tear in Jenna's relationship with her father. The other girls, without her fierce spirit, her strong will, more malleable, would, if their future could be mended, forgive him but Jenna would be more difficult to persuade.

"Well, whatever should have been done we only have what is the result to deal with and I think it might be a good idea if we collected our son, who has been neglected enough already today and take him home. Poor little beggar! His first day out to visit his grandparents and nobody has shown the slightest interest in him. I think the best thing for all of us, you and your family, but particularly you, my darling, would be if you and I and the boy were to go away for a wee while. Up to Renfrewshire on the *Thistle*. She's sailing at the end of the week. It will give all this time to die down and then when we get back you and your papa can talk and, who knows, find a way to . . . to be friends again."

He smiled winningly into her face, doing his best to coax her from her shock and pain. Jenna continued to stare sullenly into the glowing heart of the fire, her chin on her folded arms, the cloak about her. She had drawn up her knees, throwing back the wide skirt of her riding habit, her arms wrapped about her trousered legs and her husband frowned, then he sighed. There was no point in taking her to task about the peculiar garment she wore, not at this moment. Let her come to terms with her father's deceit, the terrible wrong he had done his family which had, like all bad deeds do, so they say, come home to roost today. She could do without a lecture on her riding breeches, at least for now.

"Come on, lassie, you must speak to your mama before you go. She is very upset, you know."

"I think I had best have a word with my . . . with my father first," Jenna said abruptly and stood up. She flung his cloak to the floor and shook out her skirt. She gave every appearance of not having heard a word he said, or if she had, was not concerned with it.

"Your father is hardly—"

"He'll have to go, of course, for I'll not work with him."

"Who will have to go? What are you talking about?"

"The bastard, who else?"

"Jenna!"

"You don't seriously expect me still to work with him, do you? Papa will have to . . . God, I wouldn't care if he threw him out without a penny to his name, or her come to that. Did you see they way they were gloating, just as though they were to gain something from this? I suppose Simeon thought as Papa's son . . . Oh, Jesus Christ, it brings bile to my mouth even to say it. I suppose to be a . . . a son, even an illegitimate one, has more standing than a cousin, but by God, he'll learn his lesson and I mean to make sure Papa teaches it him."

"Jenna, Jenna darling, don't . . ."

"Get out of my way, Conal. Don't try to stop me. I know you think you have a right to protect me and I suppose you do but really, I don't need it."

"Is that so?" Conal's dark eyebrows dipped fiercely and his mouth set in a grim line, one which his employees, and men with whom he did business, knew well, but which, as yet, his young wife had not encountered. Since they had married she had been pregnant, forced, not by him but by her condition, to behave and so he had cherished her, spoiled her, loved her, indulged her. But she was his wife and if, even on this terrible day, she needed to be reminded of it, and of his mastery over her then he was perfectly willing to refresh her memory.

"Conal, Papa and I have certain matters which must be cleared up between us."

"Not now, Jenna." He tried to be gentle with her since she was still in a state of great distress.

"Yes, now, Conal. He cannot really believe that Simeon and I could still work together at the collieries, can he? Even if he and Simeon are . . ."

"Father and son."

"Don't, Conal, please don't . . ." Her cry was high and painful.

"But it's the truth, my darling." He moved towards her

with the intention of taking her in his arms, of kissing her and holding her, perhaps taking her to bed and drowning her in the passion of their shared love. The love in which she would forget for an hour all that had happened today. Each small forgetting eased the pain, allowed the mind and heart to heal a little and one day, as the moments of forgetting became longer and more frequent, it would grow easier. That was the miracle of nature's healing. Not a real forgetfulness, of course, but an acceptance and a lessening of grief.

"Simeon is your father's son, lassie, and there is no changing it," trying to draw her into his arms but she fought against him, pushing him away and again his face hardened. "You must accept—"

"I am his daughter. His legitimate child, Conal. He . . . the bastard has no name even. His mother . . ."

"He has a name, Jenna. He has had a name, your father's name, his father's name, ever since Jonas Townley adopted him, and Bryony, soon after their mother died."

It took several moments for his words to make any sense and he watched as the expression on her face changed to one of appalled horror as she understood.

"No!" Her voice rose to a shrill scream and Conal felt his heart squeeze in anguish for her. It made no difference, to him or to his wife, though she was not yet aware of it, what Jonas Townley and his son, Simeon Townley, did at the collieries which belonged to Jonas. Jonas could work them until he killed himself. He could sell them, blow them to kingdom come, give them to that belligerent lad who was his own blood and who, from what Conal had seen of him, would run the thriving business to a full stop within five years, it was of no concern to Jenna Macrae! She was his wife, the mother of his son, his future sons and though he had said nothing as yet to enlighten her, enjoying the months of euphoria her pregnancy had brought them, there was absolutely no way that he would allow her to be a coal owner. He had promised her nothing when they married, hoping marriage itself would fulfil her and so it might for he had no intention of hedging her about as other husbands did. He would allow her to take an interest in his business since her sharp intelligence, her shrewd, enquiring mind would need something to nourish it. Like her mother with that place of hers in Marfield, so his Jenna would be allowed to stretch and grow, expand her mind. He would take her on one of his ships, to Ireland, Scotland, down the coast to the southern ports of England when he went himself on business. They would travel, later, as the children came and grew, to Europe, perhaps America, a rich, exciting life for a woman, but he loved her and in his love he would give her a freedom, within his protection, naturally, never before known among the women of her class.

"What does it mean, Conal? Please, please tell me what it means," she babbled, clutching at the lapels of his coat, her face awash with agonised tears. "Surely he cannot take precedence over me! Over my sisters? He's illegitimate! A bastard! His father and mother weren't married so he can't . . . my father wouldn't, couldn't . . . Dear Christ . . ."

She turned and picked up his cloak, swinging it up and about her shoulders, rubbing her hand across her face to clear it of tears.

"Where are you going?" His voice was sharp. She did not answer him.

"I don't know where my handkerchief is," she murmured distractedly to herself and gave her face another swipe round with her hand. "Oh, dammit . . . dammit . . ."

His love for her at this moment of her defeat which she refused to recognise, at this blow which had knocked her to her knees but from which, painfully, she was pulling

herself, surged in his chest and throat and he felt a most
unmanly desire to weep for her. For her pain which he
would gladly have taken on himself, for her bravery, for
her stubbornness. In God's name, where was she going
now, wrapping herself up in his cloak which was far too
long for her and on which she kept tripping as she reached
for the bell beside the fireplace? Her hair, as it always did
in moments of excitement or emergency, or even in none
at all as it followed the will of Jenna Macrae, tumbled in
a mass of corkscrew curls down her back, a vivid blaze
of copper red against the dark material of his cloak.

"What do you intend, my darling?" he said more gently,
almost choking on his love for her, his pride in her, his
sadness that he must curb the magnificence of her spirit
if they were to make any sort of a life together.

"I must find out what it means, Conal. You do see that,
don't you?" She whirled to him, her face distorted with
anguish, the cloak and her hair flaring about her.

"Find out what what means, lassie?"

"Who would know, d'you think?" She put her hand to
her brow in an attitude of deep thought.

"Jenna, my dearest love, shall we not send for something to eat and then" – he glanced at the bed which was
meant only for one – "it's small . . ." He smiled. "But then
you and I always sleep close so I'm sure we'll manage. A
bath first . . . let me bathe you, my love, and then . . ."

"Oh blast it, where's that girl got to? I'd best go and
see to it myself, I suppose."

Conal's gentle expression changed, becoming bleak,
grim, all the softness, the warmth of his love slipping
away. The glow of golden brown in his eyes darkened
angrily.

"Would you mind telling me what the devil you think
you're doing, Jenna?"

"The carriage, Conal. Our carriage, I must get to—"

"The carriage? At this time of night?"

"What difference does that make? I must go at once to—"

"Jenna! Stop it. Calm down."

"Thomas Young. He's a solicitor. He'll know. He'll be able to tell me if that bastard has any claim on my father's collieries."

Chapter Eighteen

The first intimation of the dramatic turn of events at Bank House came when Jonas Townley introduced that lad he carted about with him to a new business acquaintance at the Coal Exchange.

"This is my son, Simeon," he said to the surprised gentleman who had not been aware that Townley had a son. "He is learning his trade, as you can see," he went on. "I started at the bottom, quite literally as it happens, at the pit face in my father's mine and Simeon means to do the same, don't you, lad?" He turned what the gentleman could see was a proud eye on the boy and, give the lad his due, he was everything any father could wish for, at least to look at. Tall and with an easy grace of movement which had nothing of the awkwardness of youth in it as he lounged, hands in his pockets, beside Jonas Townley. A handsome youth, the image of his father with eyes as brilliant as a turquoise in his smooth amber face and a cap of black curls falling over his eyebrows. Somewhat . . . well, the business gentleman would have described him as indolent, a touch of arrogance in him but then the older Townley had that in plenty now, and when he was young, so he had heard, so could you wonder it showed up in his lad?

The news spread like wildfire through the coal exchange but even those who had always known the real truth of it, of the Townley scandal which had taken place fifteen years ago, could scarcely believe it. Not after all these years. Fifteen years he had managed to keep it damped down, the smouldering heart of it buried beneath a thick layer of grey ash and now, not only had it flared into life, Townley was giving it a good stir round with a poker!

It was the same wherever he went, the lad striding at his side, not with diffidence but brazenly, and could you wonder at the change in him? If Jonas Townley was to recognise him openly as his son and without the slightest hint of guilt or embarrassment, then did that mean the boy was to take it all over when Jonas popped his clogs? And if that was the case, no wonder he looked so bloody cocky!

By nightfall, when all the gentlemen who were in coal had returned to the bosom of their families, it had reached St Helens and even as far as Manchester where Townley coal was used in the many industries which thrived there and, since Townley coal was shipped from there, in Liverpool.

They had ridden home in total silence, Jenna and Conal Macrae. Two carriages, Jenna and Conal in Conal's phaeton which he had driven himself, with the three maidservants and the baby in the second. She had not gone in to see her father again. Her violent determination to take the carriage over to Thomas Young's offices had been denied her by the sheer male strength of her husband who said he would tie her up if he had to and though she had cried, even shrieked out loud for someone to come and help her, no one had, of course, since what went on between husband and wife was nobody's business but theirs.

With Conal's hand cruelly gripping her arm she had kissed her mother at the front door who told her that Papa was lying down as he did not feel at all well.

"No, I suppose he wouldn't," was all Jenna said cruelly

before being helped, no, thrust, into the phaeton beside her husband.

It had turned icily cold again though the clear frosty sky had been bright with moonlight and starlight, making the roads easy to travel by.

For the first time since their marriage, though they shared a bed, Jenna did not fall asleep in her husband's arms. He had tried to draw her against him, wanting to break through that dreadful wall she had erected when it became clear to her that he was not going to allow her to drive into Marfield and call at the home of Thomas Young. The solicitor would have left the offices he rented in the centre of Marfield by now, Conal had said reasonably enough, and Jenna could hardly knock at the front door of his home at this time of night, could she? Besides which, the baby must be got home and the confused servants who, at least the nursemaids, had sat all day in the nursery with Molly, waiting to be summoned by Mr and Mrs Townley to fetch the infant down for inspection. Or at the very least for the baby's grandparents and his three aunts to come up and have a peep at him.

None had. There had been some commotion in the drawing-room in which Miss Jenna and Master Simeon were involved, which was nothing out of the ordinary and Dolly had been upset again as she had several nights ago when there had, apparently, been a set-to between Master Simeon, Miss Bryony and the mistress! What a family they were for falling out, apparently to do with some mystery in their past which, when it was revealed to them, had those who had not known of it rocking on their heels!

"We'd always known," Dolly admitted tearfully and Mrs Blaney, at that moment unable to wield the cane of her authority, figuratively speaking, being too upset to do more than sip the tea young Annie pressed into her hand

and dab at her eyes with a handkerchief, nodding her head in agreement. Several of the maidservants who had been there years ago when the two babies had been brought to the house by the master were married and gone now and some of the outside men like Absalom, the gardener, but there were a few of them left who remembered the dramatic events which had taken place then. The mistress had sworn them to secrecy and they'd stuck by her, her being such a good soul to them, and to the poor women, colliers' wives who lived in Marfield. Oh aye, everyone had known except those most involved in it. The children! Poor Miss Jenna who would, or so it appeared, be done out of her inheritance if what was being whispered, that the master had adopted Master Simeon and Miss Bryony, was true. Poor Miss Beth who was to have been married in the spring and would that be cancelled? All this talk of illegitimacy and – whispered behind discreet hands – bastards was enough to put off any bridegroom, no matter how ardent. And then there were the other two coming up. Miss Nancy and Miss Rose. Lord, oh Lord, where would it all end?

Conal Macrae watched his wife anxiously in those next few weeks, waiting for some indication of what she might do. He knew she was . . . well, he could only liken what she suffered to grieving, mourning the demise of the father she had loved. Her spirit appeared to have been quenched. Jonas Townley's actions in the past, despite that past being fifteen or more years ago and despite the close and loving relationship he and Jenna had shared since, had somehow taken him from her. Effectively as if he had died, he had left her, alone and mourning his loss and she would allow no one to comfort her. Not even her husband. She moved in a world of her own, a silent and cold world in which he, and their child, did not exist, her shocked state so deep he began to consider fetching a medical man to see her, for surely she was not well? She appeared to have swung, almost overnight, from a savage determination to make sure her inheritance, her son's inheritance was not threatened by this revelation of Simeon Townley's true parentage, to a numbed indifference which frightened her husband and he began to wonder if it would perhaps have been wiser to allow her to fight as she had at first wanted to. It was not like her to suffer pain or melancholy, joy or pleasure, in silence. Not that she had suffered a great deal of pain apart from the pangs of childbirth, and melancholy, as far as he knew, was something her papa, until now, had always protected her from.

Now she sat alone for hours on end on the wide window sill of her sitting-room, her dogs at her feet, her back against its deep frame, her knees drawn up to her chin, her gaze reaching pensively out over the garden at the front of the house. The wintry haze, iridescent with frost and the smoke from the cottage chimneys, hung on the air. The sky was a pale, pale blue but clear and the frost lay in stripes across the lawn. The path ran like a neutral grey ribbon across it and on the path walked Nanny Abigail pushing the brand-new perambulator in which Ewan Macrae slept. A splendid affair it was, not really suited to the needs of a small baby since it had a seat but Nanny, being a sensible young woman, had padded the interior with pillows and young Master Macrae, six weeks old and bound up like a parcel, lay amongst them unaware as yet that his mama sadly neglected him.

Conal didn't like it. He didn't like the way she treated her son's existence as casually as she might the arrival of a new kitten in the stable and he didn't like the way she drifted, that was the word he would have used, from the moment she got out of her bed, after he had left for Chapel Street, until she got into it again. Marian, as worried as he was, reported that Miss Jenna would stay there all day if she herself did not rally her to her bath, her toileting and

317

dressing. Obedient as a child, Marian said and though she ate, for he had seen her do so at the dinner table, she had become thinner, wraith-like somehow and was so withdrawn it was hard to get a word or two, a sensible word that is, from her. She jumped visibly when spoken to, just as though she had imagined herself to be alone and when she answered it was in a voice which was curiously toneless.

"No, thank you, Conal, I couldn't manage another mouthful."

"No, I have not called on anyone today."

"Pardon? No, nobody has called on me" – turning to the surprised Dora – "have they, Dora?"

"Ewan? Yes, he is well, I believe."

"I went for a short walk, Conal."

"I beg your pardon . . . the weather? Oh, of course, for January."

"The Misses Yeoland . . . yes, I intend ordering some new gowns for . . . when? Oh, soon."

She seemed only to communicate with her dogs who lay at her feet or padded quietly at her side wherever she went. For this reason he allowed it.

When he was not there he had her discreetly watched. Not, as he reassured the embarrassed Percy, to spy on her but because he wished to see her properly protected. She was not quite recovered from the birth of her son, he explained, and in her vulnerable state she must be guarded. He knew Percy would understand. Percy, whose Lily had given birth to seven children in as many years, dragging herself from her childbed the day after each was born, didn't, but he had the sense to keep his mouth shut. If the mistress wandered he was to watch her, from a distance, of course, and bring her home if she seemed . . . Well, here the master wasn't clear, saying he would leave it to Percy!

She would sometimes let herself out of the garden by

the side gate, Percy at a discreet distance behind and it said something for her state of mind that she did not even notice him though they were often the only two people on the path or lane. She would move slowly across the fields to the long tunnel of trees known as St Domingo Grove which stretched, arrow straight, from Beechfield Road where Beechfield Lodge lay to the parliamentary and municipal boundary, turning left on to the rough track which led to Walton Breck Road. St Domingo Grove had been planted by some long-forgotten horticulturist and she went there often, her dogs, now that they were out of the house, swirling about her booted feet, yapping at the scent of fox and rabbit. The rabbits themselves bobbed and nibbled, their little white scuts vanishing down invisible holes when Duff and Dory gave chase, barking furiously, and above their heads rooks rose in a great black cloud, rippling like a thrown fisherman's net.

She had caused quite a stir on one occasion when, moving like a sleepwalker, her dogs sedately at her heel, she had unaccountably left the garden by the front gate, turned left and made her unpredictable way to Breck Road and on into the village of Everton. Confused, or so it seemed, by the busy bustle of the small village on market day, she had paused like a doe which scents danger, almost sniffing the air, Percy reported later to the astonished servants. He had been about to go to her, take her arm and guide her home but she'd suddenly come to herself and proceeded back up Audley Street, past the rear of the Corporation Water Works and Reservoir and back along the lane which led to Beechfield Road. Odd, she was, and no wonder the master wanted her watched.

Sometimes she set out briskly, just as though she was off somewhere and must get there at the earliest possible opportunity, but her eyes seemed not to see and her direction would become uncertain. Once she had fetched up at the Zoological Gardens on West Derby Road. She'd

gone in, those two dogs of hers keeping very close to
her skirts for there were wild caged beasts there roaring
their displeasure. She'd stared in at the deer house and
at the animals in the menagerie and had hesitated at the
door of the concert room, Percy said to his employer,
studying the notices there which were concerned with
coming events. After a minute or two she had sighed
deeply, then made her way back to Boundary Lane
and on to Beechfield Road, Percy following faithfully
behind. He hadn't said so to anyone but he couldn't quite
believe in the reason his master had given him about Mrs
Macrae not being recovered from the birth of her son,
for hadn't she been as merry as a skylark just afterwards
with Marian complaining she and that there nurse were
having the devil's own job keeping her in her bed! Well,
the master had his own reasons, Percy supposed, and it
was not for him to question them.

"Where did you walk today, lassie?" Conal asked her
casually that evening at dinner.

She lifted her head and looked at him, her spoon which
she had been about to dip into her soup hovering on the
rim of her soup plate. He smiled at her to let her see
he meant no reproach, crumbling a piece of bread with
fingers which tried not to quiver. It was not that he was
nervous or in any way afraid, he told himself, but her
strangeness was something which worried him more and
more. She was looking at him with that startled air of
confusion which so often trembled on her face and he did
his best to appear unconcerned. To give the appearance
that her manner was in no way unusual but his heart ached
for her. Where had she gone, that wild and spirited young
woman who had glared up at him from her sprawl at his
feet on that day of their first meeting? Where was that
head-tossing imperious defiance, the flashing boldness
of her eyes, the furious explosion of her temper, her
flaunting belief she was always right, the challenge she

threw down to those who said she was not? She looked the same, apart from her loss of weight, for Marian saw to it that she was always dressed to suit the time of the day, that her hair was brushed and arranged as it should be. Tonight she was in a dinner gown of the palest, honey-gold velvet, plain but elegant and her creamy white shoulders gleamed like pearl as they rose from the décolletage of the bodice. Her hair was fastened in a loose and heavy knot at the nape of her neck, unadorned, needing no adornment since its colour and texture, the gloss which seemed to shimmer about her head were adornment enough.

"You did walk, I take it?" he continued, his voice calm.

"Yes, I took Duff and Dory to . . ." She faltered, then, her voice stronger, ". . . into Everton village."

"Really, and did you buy anything? I hear there is a . . ." Dear sweet God, what was there in Everton village which would attract a fashionable young woman such as his wife? What kind of shops? Were there any shops? And why had he started on this nightly conversation which he had found out in the last few weeks led absolutely nowhere, but somehow he must break through this carapace she had erected about herself to shut out the pain and sense of betrayal into which her father's deception had flung her.

"Did someone tell me there is a fine . . . er . . . bookshop" – that sounded safe – "where they sell old prints?" He raised an enquiring eyebrow.

"I did not see one." Her voice was dull and she applied herself once more to her soup.

"Did you perhaps pass by Rupert's House? It lies on Rupert Lane." He kept his voice pleasantly neutral, putting no pressure on her and was rewarded by a spark of something in her face. Not exactly interest but at least an awareness that she had heard him.

"Rupert?"

"Yes, Prince Rupert." He took a spoonful of soup then popped a piece of bread into his mouth.

"Prince Rupert?"

"Mmm, you've heard of Prince Rupert's brave onslaught on the town of Liverpool over two hundred years ago, haven't you? It was during the Parliamentary Wars. Now don't tell me your governess failed to mention the Roundheads and Royalists during your studies. If so it was very remiss of her." He grinned broadly and was rewarded by a faint answering smile.

"I believe she may have said something."

"Liverpool was for Parliament, you see, but while York was being defended against the Parliamentary army Prince Rupert, who was the King's nephew and a mere twenty-two or -three years of age, collected a considerable army of his own on this side of the country. He would take the town and fortress for his monarch, he declared, despite the strong fortifications which surrounded them. On finding that his attempts to carry the town on the level ground around it was to no avail he moved up here to Everton where he camped on what was the common and around the beacon. He made his headquarters at a cottage in the village and it is still there today."

"I must have walked right past it."

"Indeed, my love, you did." He was gratified and relieved by her interest.

"And what happened then?" Her soup spoon was lowered to her plate and she rested her elbows on the table and even Dora, at her post by the serving table, seemed to lean forward in anticipation. She'd been born in Everton and her mam still lived in Claremont Street and she'd never heard of no Prince Rupert!

"Well, they say if you walk along Shaw Street you can see where earth was thrown up to make a platform from which the brave young prince raised his battery. Unfortunately the distance was too great for his offensive so he moved by foot on the town. It took him many assaults but eventually his tenacity won him the day, and the battle, and the victorious Royalists marched into town. The Parliamentary troops surrendered and the prince took up quarters in the fortress. It was only six days after the surrender of Liverpool that the battle of Marston Moor was fought which clouded the hopes of King Charles for ever as you will remember from your history lessons."

"And what happened to Liverpool?"

"Oh, the Parliamentarians retook it and twenty pounds was distributed for the relief of the widows and children of all the men 'murthered and slayne' by Prince Rupert's forces. Of course, Everton was really nothing more than a wasteland then."

She leaned forward into the glow from the candle-lamp and he thought how beautiful she looked. So fine and drawn, frail almost, though there was a faint flush of tawny rose in her cheek.

"Really?"

"Oh yes, only one hundred and four persons lived in the parish."

"How do you know all this, Conal?" Her lips parted, a moist peach, and as she leaned forward her full, swelling breasts fell towards him, pushed up by her arms which she had crossed on the table and he felt the blood run warm in his veins and the heat of it moved to the pit of his belly. It was several months since he had made love to his wife, in the fullest sense of the words, and his breath quickened in his throat at the thought of it but he kept his voice light and steady.

"I take an interest in anything of the past, my darling. That is not to say I live in it, or dwell on it but I like to know what happened to make this town" – he shrugged – "this part of the country where I live, and indeed where I once lived in Scotland, as it is now. For instance, those inhabitants paid their manorial lord each year for the use of the wasteland. To graze their beasts, I suppose, and grow their crops. The area around here is called the Breck. Breck Road, Breckfield, Walton Breck and because of it the payment was known as Breck silver."

"And is it still levied, the Breck silver?"

He sat back in his chair, his eyes drawn again to her breasts, his smile deep, his interest in her quite plain for her to see. She seemed not to mind.

"It is, my love, though they call it by the much more mundane name of the income tax. We must take a walk up to Everton together one day. There is a very fine view from the brow of the hill and the mineral spring which flows there is said to be particularly ferruginous and ochreous!" He winked slyly.

"Conal!" She began to laugh. "What on earth does that mean? I believe you made it up."

"On my honour." He placed a hand on his heart. "Ferruginous means containing iron-rust and ochreous is a mineral, yellow in colour and used as a pigment. What the devil the water from the spring would do to one's inside I cannot imagine or perhaps one is supposed to bathe in it. Equally the thought of lowering oneself, naked of course, into its depths, is not something . . ."

"Conal, I don't believe a word of it but do go on, tell me some more."

He did and that night, for the first time since the birth of their son, they made love. It was tender love, slow and pensive and dreaming, as though any sudden or abrupt movement might shatter the calm acquiescence she had fallen into when their meal was ended.

They reached the privacy of their bedroom and his smile was barely more than a slight lifting at each corner of his mouth. His eyes were soft and musing as he drew down the bodice of her gown, lingering in absorbed concentration on her breasts, her arched throat, her shoulders and she appeared to bask in the warmth of his desire. His eyes told her she was a desirable woman and that he wanted her and she accepted it. She reached out and wound her arms about his neck, drawing his mouth down to her distended nipple, throwing back her head as his lips took first one, then the other, sucking, gently biting, tasting her flesh with his tongue and his lips, but slowly, waiting for her to set the tempo, ready to go at her pace, or to stop should she want to.

"Jenna, I love you. I don't always know why but I love you."

"And I love you, Conal."

And in their renewed delight it was as though this was their first time. A time of discovering, a slow wandering through the feel and taste and fragrances of love. The fall of her glorious hair as, the pins drawn from it, it cascaded about their naked bodies. The pleasure of studying at great length the quickening fall and rise of her full breasts, the hard, engorged peaking of her almond nipples, the rounded quivering of her white belly, the crisp, copper spring of curls at its base. He caressed her with his gaze, asking nothing of her but that she allow it. That she lie and drift and sigh, this way and that wherever he placed her, as he smoothed her chin, the point of her shoulder, the soft undercurve of her breast, the soft inner curve of her thigh, the length of her back and buttocks, with his hands, his fingers, his lips, his tongue. They were mindlessly content in their slow, slumbrous dance of love, the rhythm and music of it heard only by them as she stretched and turned for his delight and when, at last, at last, he pierced her, dissolving her body into his, overflowing with the joy of it, it was like a slow-moving summer stream in which they were immersed together. They were, in those hours, as content, as joyful, as loving with one another as they had ever before been and they both fell asleep smiling, love on their lips, his name on hers, hers on his.

But the next morning when he reached for her she turned away, presenting the graceful curve of her back to him.

"Jenna, my lovely lassie, will you no' kiss me at least?" He was pleading with her to be as she had been the previous night, mourning the loss of her all over again, pleading for a return of the sweetness, the fierceness, the delights and irritations, the laughter, the quarrels, the qualities of every sort which made up the whole complex structure of Jenna Macrae. Which made their marriage so glorious and so infuriating and which had been sadly missing since Jonas Townley's perfidy had been revealed.

"Darling." He moved round the bed to kneel at her side, pushing back the tangle of her love-tossed hair, smoothing her forehead, bending his head to look into her unfocused eyes. He had been patient with her, God knows, realising, because he loved her so deeply, exactly how this crushing blow had devastated her but really, they couldn't go on like this for much longer. Apart from himself there was the boy who, from what he could glean from his nursemaids, had neither sight nor sound of his mother from one day to the next and it must end, and soon.

"Not just now, Conal," she said listlessly. "I'm tired."

"Sweetheart, I know you are only weeks from the birth of our son and" – he smiled down lovingly into her face – "last night was . . . you did not get much sleep but you . . ."

She turned away from him abruptly, pulling the bed-clothes up around her shoulders, a rebuff so cutting his mouth whitened.

That night he wrote to Nella Townley.

Chapter Nineteen

The carriage drew up with a great flourish at the front door of Beechfield Lodge as though its occupant meant no one to miss its arrival, nor its splendour. It was as if the coachman had been ordered to make a grand entrance, and so he did, snapping his whip, shouting to the two matched greys to "whoa" in a voice so loud it might have been heard at the Pier Head. Or so George, who was working on a bit of rough digging in preparation for spring planting, muttered to Eppie who stared open-mouthed at the sight. The sunlight glinted on the brightly polished metal of the leather harness and on the scrupulously cleaned panels of the carriage. The horses were handsome and high-stepping and the lady who descended from the equipage was just as splendid.

Even before Nella Townley reached the bottom of the four wide, shallow steps which led up to the front door it opened briskly and Dora was there, smiling and bobbing and wishing her mistress's mama a very good morning, as relieved to see her as the eagerly awaited promise of spring after a particularly hard winter. Mrs Townley had not been to Beechfield Lodge since before the birth of Master Ewan and with the mistress in the doldrums as she had been lately perhaps a visit from her mama would cheer her up. There had been talk in the kitchen, strange talk about something to do with Mr Townley but as Mrs Garnett sternly pointed out to them it was nothing to do with them but it all added to the mystery somehow. It was not like the young mistress to be so low-spirited and it had not been caused by the birth of her son, neither, for she'd been chirpy as a cricket right after he was born. No, it was more recent than that so perhaps her mama would lift her out of it. There was the christening to see to, wasn't there? Here he was, the little lad, nearly eight weeks old now and not a word said to anyone about the religious service nor the reception which would follow it. Again it was none of their concern only in as much as he was their family, so to speak, and he was as strong as a little lion but sadly, what was vaguely termed as weakness, fever, a rash, convulsions, leading to death came to the strongest child, carrying them off before you had time to say "Spare him, Lord Jesus" and best get Master Ewan christened as soon as possible to be on the safe side.

"My daughter is at home, I trust . . . er . . ." Mrs Townley hesitated, turning her kindly smile on the parlourmaid as she handed her her warm cloak.

"Dora, madam," sketching another curtsey.

"Of course, Dora. I'm getting quite forgetful in my old age," and indeed, now she had a good look at her Mrs Townley was looking older. She could have sworn her hair was as bright a red as her daughter's but it was faded somehow, and her face looked worn and sad. Lively she'd been when she had last visited with Mrs Eason. Now she walked with a slight drag to her feet, her shoulders slumped and as she followed Dora up the stairs and along the first-floor landing to Mrs Macrae's sitting-room Dora heard her sigh deeply.

Dora knocked on the door, prepared to usher the visitor in, to announce her even if she was her mistress's mama but Mrs Townley nodded, dismissing her with a smile. Dora heard her murmur something under her breath then the door closed behind her.

Jenna was sitting in a chair by the window. It was

almost noon, a bright February day and so mild there were midges dancing about the unfolded leaves of the willow catkins hanging over the small stream which idled across the end of the garden. There had been a rapid thaw over the past few days and a battle was taking place on the soggy lawn for the possession of some tit-bit between a couple of sparrows and a dashing, red-breasted robin. Jenna appeared to be watching them but when, the fight over, they darted off among the bare branches of the trees which lay at the end of the garden she continued to stare at the spot in which they had just squabbled.

She was not yet dressed. Her nightdress could be seen, a shimmering silken thing in ecru, trimmed with lace over which she wore a matching peignoir. The garment was carelessly draped, hanging open and she sat, her arms about her waist, her legs crossed at the ankle, her bare feet propped on the window sill, the expression on her face one of deep preoccupation with her own brooding thoughts.

The dogs at her feet stood up and their tails moved lazily as they inspected the visitor. Reassured that there was no danger to their mistress from this woman they knew, they lay down again, watching her with somnolent dark eyes.

"Heavens, are you not well, child," her mother said lightly, "and if that's the case should you not be in your bed?"

Her daughter turned sharply towards her, then, putting her feet to the ground, she stood up drawing the silken wisp of her peignoir about her. Her face closed, hardened, and she squared her shoulders as though preparing herself for a set-to with some unwelcome intruder. Nella Townley's heart sank.

The last few weeks had been amongst the most difficult Nella had ever encountered in her less than easy life and Conal's summons to her, though he had, naturally, not put it quite like that, had been unwelcome. She had enough to contend with at home without driving over here to speak to her daughter as he had begged her to do. It probably needed no more than a word of reassurance from her father, he had said, if Jonas would care to come and give it, since she would not listen to him and Nella had been surprised. She had thought Jenna to be in good hands with the emphatically vital man who was her husband and the letter which had revealed his own great forbearance had quite amazed her. He had bundled her off to their home, Jenna spitting like an enraged kitten, shrieking that she must talk to her papa, that she must discuss this matter with Thomas Young, the solicitor, and find out how much Papa's indiscretion had damaged her own chances of inheriting what was rightfully hers; that she would seek out Simeon, presumably to blacken his eye; in fact there were not many persons, in and out of the house, with whom she did not have a quarrel and she would see Conal Macrae in hell if he didn't let go of her arm, put her down, take his bloody hands off her and let her get about her business.

He had got her into the carriage at last and they had driven off, followed by the nursemaids and Nella's grandson at whom she had got no more than the merest peek and since then not a word. Until now! But patient as it seemed he was with her, Conal certainly would not put up with such behaviour for long and his letter had intimated as much. It was this which had brought Nella over to Liverpool though she would have given a lot to avoid it. Jonas had wanted to come, longing to be reunited with his daughter, to reassure her of his everlasting devotion to her but Nella had begged him to wait a while, to let Jenna calm herself a little for they all knew how volatile she was and how, when time had passed, she would always come round. Nella would go in answer to Conal's letter, she had told Jonas and later, when Jenna was more . . . more resigned, Jonas could go himself. Jonas had been distraught, longing to explain, he told Nella, to beg Jenna to try and understand. Jenna had loved her father, passionately and blindly. Trusted him implicitly and there had been a strong bond of companionship between them which had existed with none of his other daughters. He could not bear the thought that that bond was damaged, he had agonised to his wife, perhaps broken irretrievably and he must set to and repair it at once. Like her daughter whom she had caught brooding cheerlessly by the window, Jonas had adopted the same melancholy manner, staring for hours into the fire, then jumping to his feet and shouting for Daniels to fetch the carriage to the door.

But he had not been at all well, his chest weakened by bouts of the coughing sickness, and the damp chill of the winter had not helped and Nella had persuaded him to stay at home. Her other daughters were in much the same sorry condition, drifting about Bank House, weeping and wailing, refusing to go out, even in the carriage, convinced, and probably with good reason, that fingers would be pointed at them, remarks whispered behind raised hands and sidelong, furtive glances cast in their direction. The negotiations between Jonas and Frank Miller were at a very delicate point since Frank, rightly so some said, could not be expected to marry a young lady, no matter how good her family, if that family had such a skeleton in its cupboard and surely two illegitimate members were enough to make that young lady somewhat of a liability as a wife? Jonas had wanted to "shoot the young sod", he had thundered, saying he'd have no dealings with a man who was prepared to make capital out of a family's misfortunes but then Beth had cried, moaning that no one would want her now, would want none of them and Jonas had retreated in defeat.

Only Simeon and Bryony thrived, the matter of their

unconventional beginnings discomfiting them not one bit. Simeon strutted about Bank House as though it already belonged to him, giving serious offence to the servants, and herself who had always been fond of him, with his high-handed orders and Bryony, well, who knew what Bryony thought, or did for that matter, since she often disappeared for hours on end with that big dog of hers, confiding to no one, unless it was her brother, where she had gone. In her childhood she had been uncommunicative, solitary, private but Nella had never thought of her as sly. Now she did, watching her whisper behind her hand to her brother, watching the two of them stroll about the garden deep in conversation, the girl directing her brother's behaviour, Nella was sure of it, and it was this, the girl's dominance over Simeon which surely did not bode well for the future, and it was her fear that somehow her own daughter, this girl who stared at her so coldly, would suffer for it, that had brought her here.

"Won't you get dressed, darling?" her mother said. "It's almost lunchtime and really, it does no good to loll about the house allowing the servants to think you are a careless mistress."

"Surely what I do in my own house and with my own servants is my concern, Mama?" Jenna's voice was cutting but then Nella Townley, whose daughter she was, could be just as sharp.

"Don't be ridiculous, Jenna. This is your home and these are your servants and I am also aware that you have had a hard knock recently but that is no reason to lounge about like one of those young women of whom I have heard you speak with such contempt."

Jenna looked surprised. "Which young women?"

"Spineless ninnies, I believe you called them. Those with no backbone to speak of and who cannot get through life unless they are clinging, like parasitic ivy, to some man's arm. I have heard you speak very disparagingly of them, swearing you would never do as they do. That you can stand on your own two feet and have no need of—"

Jenna glared at her mother. "There is no comparison between their imagined woes and what has happened, not only to me, Mama, but to our whole family."

"Of course, there isn't, but I am still amazed that you feel it necessary to punish people who have had no hand in it. If there is blame to be apportioned, surely it is I and your papa who must be the ones to—"

"Punish? Who am I punishing?" Jenna opened her arms wide in genuine astonishment.

"Your husband for one. Do you mean to tell me that this is the normal state of affairs in your home? While the master goes about his business the mistress is still not dressed at noon and the servants are no doubt lounging about in the kitchen telling one another what an easy life they are to have with young Mrs Macrae as lax as she is. Does Conal not deserve better than this—"

"What the devil has he been saying to you?"

"—since it is obvious he loves you, and I believe you love him."

"I do, but again, what has that to do with you?"

"And as for that child in the nursery . . ."

"Ewan?"

"Aah, you remember his name then?"

"Of course I remember his name. He is my son."

"Kindly remember that when you can bring yourself to get dressed since it is my belief that you do not have very much to do with him. When did you last visit him in the nursery?"

"Why, it was just . . . just the other day."

"The other day! You have a fine son of eight weeks and you cannot remember when you last saw him! Dear God in heaven, do you know how lucky you are? When I first married your father I would have given my right arm for a son and let me tell you this. If I had borne one none of this might have happened. It was my . . . my ability to give birth only to girls—"

"Mama!" Jenna's cry tore a great hole in the rampaging distress which had suddenly afflicted her mother and at once Nella Townley stopped speaking. She shivered her way across her daughter's fine sitting-room, lowering herself into the chair before the fire, holding her hands out to its warmth. Her head was bent but when her daughter knelt before her she allowed her to take them, to chafe them between her own.

"I'm sorry, dearest," her mother said at last. "I should not have said that. I wanted a son. All women want a son but I have loved all my daughters dearly, as your father has done. You know that. And you have been – I should not say it – the brightest. I suppose I saw myself in you. I was not loved overmuch as a child so I loved you all the more. As your father has done."

"Mama . . ."

"Before we talk, as talk we must, darling, will you not ask that maid of yours to fetch some tea?"

"Of course." Jenna made as though to stand up but Nella held her hands, keeping her on her knees. She cupped her face, kissed her cheek, then smiled. "And then get dressed."

She was in a simple morning gown, her hair brushed and tied in a ribbon at the back of her head when the tea was brought and mother and daughter sat opposite one another in silence for a while. Jenna was the first to speak.

"I don't know what to do, Mama. That is what is so unbearable. If I could be doing something it would help but I'm so ignorant about such matters that my lack of knowledge and my inability to . . . to set things straight is driving me to despair."

"What is it that you want to put right?"

Jenna sighed, placing her cup and saucer on the small

table beside her. "I want to . . . God, I don't even know that. I'm just so . . ."

"Would you like me to tell you about it? About Simeon and Bryony? About your father . . . and their mother?"

"Dear God, Mama" – she leaned forward, her face warm with her concern – "I don't wish to hurt you by bringing it all . . . you must have suffered so much when . . . well, when Papa was . . . Christ, I'll never forgive him, never!"

She drew away from her mother, throwing back her head, arching the long column of her throat, then she stood up and moved swiftly to the window. She spread her arms, putting a hand on each side of the window frame, resting her forehead on the cold glass while her dogs watched her anxiously. George and Eppy were still furiously digging, at least Eppy was, being young and strong, but George, though he put in the same long hours that Eppy did, worked steadily, turning over each forkful with practised neatness.

Nella watched her daughter as Jenna whirled to face her then began to pace restlessly about the room. She had folded her arms across her breast, a hand to each elbow and Nella was aware of the depths of her suffering. She had always been restless, her energy and dash joyfully filling and escaping from every room she entered. Though she often exasperated those in whose company she was they could not help but smile at her bright wit, her heated arguments, her humour which was sometimes sharp but never cruel.

"Sit down, Jenna and let me tell you something about your papa and . . . and Leah."

Jenna's head snapped round sharply as though the last name had suddenly brought to life the reality of the events of so long ago.

"Leah?"

"Yes, Simeon and Bryony's mother."

"I don't know how you can . . . can even speak of her, Mama. Not after what she did . . . to you . . . to us. And Papa . . ."

"Your father loves me, Jenna. You must know that for you are a woman who knows love now. He loves me and he loves you. But he also loved Leah. Some men are like that. They can love more than one woman, and at the same time. When she was killed . . ."

"Killed?"

"Yes, Leah was murdered."

"Murdered!"

"Yes, most . . . most dreadfully, so you see, this was no ordinary . . . well, when she died, Simeon and Bryony were no more than babies, and your father, though he had done a great wrong, to all of us, would not leave them. I forgave him, Jenna, and surely if I as . . . well, as what they call the wronged wife could forgive him, surely that is what matters most?"

"I have not your forbearance, Mama."

"Neither had I at your age but I learned because I loved my husband. That is all that matters in the long run, darling, love. You have loved Papa all your life and he has felt the same for you. And your forgiveness is part of love. Can you not . . .?"

"No."

"Jenna, listen to me."

"No, Mama, it is . . . too soon."

"I understand that, dearest, but give it some time. Don't let Bryony and Simeon win."

"Win?"

"Think about it, Jenna. You will know what I mean."

Conal was agreeably surprised when he returned home that evening to find his wife, elegantly dressed in one of the superb new gowns the Misses Yeoland had designed and made for her, waiting for him in the drawing-room.

The gown was of silk, its colour somewhere between the palest green and ivory. Hardly a colour at all, the bodice a merest wisp of gauze, or so it seemed to her delighted husband, cut low and worn with no jewellery. She had always favoured plain, pastel-tinted dresses, delicate creams, near whites, the palest coffee, usually with some exotic, richly patterned shawl slipping carelessly from her shoulders and this one was no exception. Her strong shoulders and the upper curve of her lovely breasts emerged unadorned from a froth of sea mist and candlelight touched her skin to tawny cream. There were bowls of spring flowers everywhere, hyacinths and daffodils and crocus scattered about on every table. The fire crackled pleasantly and when she rose to greet him there was a return of the warmth they had always known. She brought with her the fragrance of the perfume he had bought her in Paris and when she put her arms about his neck his senses delighted in her.

"Darling, this is very nice," he murmured, then after glancing behind him to make sure they were alone, he swept her into a close embrace, holding her tight against him, kissing her until she was flushed and breathless.

"Sometimes I wonder how you live with me," she said when she had got her breath.

"I wonder that too, lassie, only I know I couldn't live without you."

"I've been harassed and gloomy," she whispered against his lips, "and I'm sorry but Mama was here today and she made me see I wasn't being fair to you. It had nothing to do with you, she said, what my father did and I shouldn't have acted the way I did, at least with you."

"Jenna lassie, is this my wife talking?" As he spoke he raised one whimsical eyebrow but there was a softness in his eyes, a gladness in his voice. "And is she actually apologising for her behaviour?"

"Careful, Conal Macrae," smiling too.

He led her to the sofa from where she had risen. Sitting down he pulled her into the crook of his arm. He smiled down at her, then kissed her soundly again, trailing his fingers across the exposed swell of her breasts. "Can this be the Jenna Macrae who never admits to being wrong?"

"This is the Jenna Macrae who will put her fist into her husband's eye if he does not stop teasing her."

"Will she indeed? Well, we'll see about that, my bonny lass, but in the meantime let us continue with this delightful – what is it called? – greeting one's husband when he comes home from business? I find I like it. There, that's better, my darling, and I'm sure though your mama probably told you that it is part of a wife's duty to be agreeable on the return of her husband at the end of the day, she did not tell you to expect this . . . or even this?"

It was several pleasant minutes before the tap on the door came – with an exceptionally long pause before Dora entered to announce dinner. She had known which way the wind blew the minute the mistress drifted downstairs in her beautiful gown, she told Mrs Garnett, and she had no wish to embarrass the pair of them. Mrs Townley, God bless her, must have said something to Mrs Macrae, the Lord only knew what, but it had done the trick, she whispered when she returned to the kitchen. The pair of them sitting on the sofa, him with a smile on his face like a cat that's swallowed the cream and madam all starry-eyed. In Dora's opinion, for what it was worth, the pair of them would have that fine roast duckling Mrs Garnett had prepared inside them before the clock struck eight and then be upstairs to the privacy of their bedroom without waiting for coffee!

"An' Marian'll not be wanted neither," she added, winking at the mistress's maid, earning a sharp rebuke from Mrs Garnett who, though she privately agreed, having herself seen the dreaming expression in her young mistress's eyes earlier in the evening, did not like such talk in her kitchen.

Dora was not far wrong. It was, in fact, almost nine o'clock before Conal Macrae undressed his wife before the fire in their bedroom.

They had talked first. "What did your mama have to say?" he asked her casually, his narrowed eyes on the splendour of the full white breasts which his enquiring fingers had revealed. He put his lips first to one then the other as he drew her gown off her shoulders.

Her voice was husky as she answered. "She told me about . . . Papa's mistress." She pulled away from him a little. Her face became set and her eyes hardened to iced diamonds as she spoke the last two words.

"And?" Conal encouraged her.

"It was, so Mama said . . . well, she was the daughter of one of Papa's colliers, a hewer, and had herself worked in the pit before the bill of 1842 brought women and children from the mines. She was clever, Mama said, and beautiful. Kind. It was as if those characteristics in her made Papa's behaviour acceptable." She toyed with the buttons on Conal's shirt front, a brooding expression on her face and Conal lifted her chin to look into her eyes.

"Men, many men, have a mistress, my darling." His voice was gentle. "Not that I am condoning what your father did, let me add, since it must have pained your mother who has always struck me as a . . . a . . . worthwhile woman."

"She is! She's a saint, I'd say. She forgave him after the . . . woman died." She blinked rapidly as though tears were not far away. "She was murdered, did you know that, by some chap from the mine, in some particularly dreadful way though Mama would not say what it was. Papa was deranged for a while. I really cannot imagine

it. Papa deranged!" She shook herself as if someone had
trailed a cold finger down her spine. "If it hadn't been for
Mama, though she didn't say so, of course, it seems he
would not have recovered nor would the . . . the children
. . . his children have survived."

Absently pulling the gauze of her bodice about her she
gazed down into the fire, its vivid flames painting a glow
of apricot on her high cheekbones.

"And has your mama's visit helped you to understand, perhaps feel compassion, forgiveness even, for
your papa?"

"Oh no!" She looked up at him in surprise. "How can
you ask that? I can never forgive him. Not for what he
did to Mama, to my sisters, nor to me."

"But sweetheart, it happened so long ago now. There
is nothing you can do about it. And your father has never
been anything but kind and, from what I have seen of him,
loving towards you. Your papa was indiscreet. That, in
the eyes of many, was his only fault. He did not, as a
gentleman is supposed to do, keep his two lives decently
separate as—"

"You knew all about this?"

"My brother told me something of what happened and
dinna glare at me like that. I could hardly tell my wife
of her papa's . . . indiscretions, could I? He has tried to
do his best by all his children and though it is bound to
cause a certain amount of embarrassment to your sisters,
they will not be harmed by it. Not in the long run. I
dinna mean to sound cynical, lassie, but your father is
a wealthy and powerful man and this factor will smooth
the way towards acceptance. At least for them, though I
cannot vouch for Simeon and Bryony."

"Should I care about that?" Her voice was cruel and
her smooth young face set itself into lines of harsh and
unforgiving implacability.

"Jenna, my sweetheart. It is hardly their fault that

they were born, is it? Nor what has happened since?" He reached out for her but she stepped back, her face mutinous.

"Nor mine, Conal, but it seems I and my sisters are the ones who might lose what is rightfully ours. Mama did not say so but if Papa leaves a will in favour of the bastards . . ."

"Jenna, don't. It doesna suit you to be so relentless," for though Jenna Macrae's spirit was often hazardously obdurate at times, she was never spiteful nor cruel. "Come to bed, my love. Don't let's talk of wills and collieries and . . . and whatever is to come of it all. I would let nothing harm you, you know that. I will take care of you and your father will take care of your sisters. He's a stubborn man, my darling, and likes things his own way. Hell's teeth, any man who can manage what he has for the past sixteen years, forcing folk to accept . . . well . . ." He had been about to say "forcing folk to accept his bastards as though they were legitimate", but realised just in time that such a sentiment would not exactly please Jonas Townley's legitimate daughter. "He is resourceful, a man of wealth and standing and influence. The gentlemen of Marfield and the neighbouring parish look to him for financial support on the numerous local projects in which they are engaged and they are not going to overlook that fact when they are considering the matter of his . . . er . . . misdeeds. And your aunts. One is the wife, the other the widow of a baronet and that will count for something. Especially as Sir Edward and, or so I am reliably informed, Sir Timothy are very often strapped for cash. Deny them Jonas Townley's pocket and they would be in a poor way, I hear. No, he will overcome it, my love, and Marfield will overlook it. Now then, that bit of nonsense which goes by the name of a dinner gown, how does one get inside it? There . . . aah, yes . . . I see, and these buttons . . . very clever . . ."

341

As she yielded to her husband's knowing hands and lips, sighing her pleasure, preparing to abandon her troubled thoughts until later, Jenna Macrae's last one was concerned with the bitter understanding of whether she really cared for the idea of Simeon and Bryony Townley having their paths so easily smoothed out for them.

Chapter Twenty

She was on her way to the stables with the intention of saddling up Amber and riding out into the misted haze of the February morning when she heard the baby cry. The stairs which led up to the nursery floor lay to the right of their bedroom and across the wide landing, and though she was at perfect liberty to go up there and see her son whenever she wanted to, she rarely did so more than once a day. He was well cared for by Nanny Abigail, thriving, she had been told and the wet nurse, a clean, respectable woman from Everton village who had an infant a month or so older than Ewan and who had enough milk to satisfy another half-dozen, she cheerfully told Mrs Macrae, came up twice a day to feed him. She expressed great quantities of rich milk from her capacious breast which, when warmed up, was fed to young Ewan Macrae from a bottle fitted with a calf's teat but which, nanny informed the somewhat astonished Mrs Macrae, he did not care for as much as the nipple. Mrs Macrae felt a great urge to giggle at this, wondering what nanny would say to the remark "like father like son" but she refrained, doing her best to keep a straight face. The wet nurse could not, of course, be immediately available when Master Ewan was hungry since she had her own family to see to but this arrangement seemed to suit everyone concerned. He was taking a little oatmeal gruel now, Jenna had been told yesterday, very thin and smooth.

He had also been introduced to a reliable brand of what was known as "milk-food" which was dissolved in warm water and was, nanny said, nourishing and sustaining. He was contented and flourishing so if that was the case why was he crying so heart-rendingly? And why did not Nanny Abigail do . . . whatever it was she did to comfort him?

Well, someone would see to him, she told herself as she draped the skirt of her riding habit over her arm and strode along the landing towards the stairs which led down to the wide front hallway. That was what Conal paid them for! She had no need to concern herself with him for Nanny Abigail was to be trusted absolutely. That was why she and Conal had employed her and if she was allowing him to cry for the moment then there must be a good reason for it. They had to cry sometimes, it exercised their lungs she remembered hearing someone say. Babies often cried with temper for they soon learned how to assert their rights, finding that by crying they had their desires gratified, or so someone said, though again she could not remember who.

She was halfway down the stairs and she could still hear him and something, she didn't know quite what and was not awfully sure she cared for it, tugged at her insides, just in the centre of her chest. Dammit, why didn't that nurse attend to him? She really should not let him scream like that. He might do himself some mischief, strain something . . . or . . . be sick . . . or . . . well, she didn't know what babies did since she had had little to do with one but . . .

Dora came clattering through the green baize door which led from the kitchen, calling back to someone that she wouldn't be long and was well into the bright, fire-warmed hallway before she saw her mistress lurking, or so it seemed to Dora, halfway up the stairs. She gave a little shriek and almost dropped the tray of cut-glass decanters she had just cleaned and was about the replace in the master's study. She looked quite astonished for they had been told by Marian that Mrs Macrae was to go riding this morning and had heard her telling Percy that he was to saddle Amber and have her waiting in the stable yard by nine o'clock. Mrs Macrae had to use the stairs, of course, but what was she doing hovering about on them looking for all the world as though she didn't know whether to go up or come down when Dora had expected her to be halfway to Everton by now. A real funny look she had on her face, an' all. Sort of vacant, Dora would have said and not at all like the decisive expression her mistress usually wore. Dora set the tray on the small occasional table and advanced to the foot of the stairs.

"Is there something wrong, madam?" she enquired.

Mrs Macrae stared down at her for a moment or two then seemed to collect herself, shaking her head as though the sound which had been in it was gone.

"Oh no," she answered, but Dora could see she wasn't happy about something.

"Can I get you anything, Mrs Macrae? Did you fancy a hot drink before you set off on your ride, perhaps?"

"No, thank you, Dora." She hesitated before going on. "Tell me, is Nanny Abigail in the kitchen?"

Dora looked quite shocked. "Oh no, madam. She never leaves the nursery. If she wants anything she rings the bell and one of us goes up to her."

"Yes, of course. Well, thank you, Dora. Go on with what you were doing."

"Will I tell Percy you're on your way, madam?"

"Yes, please do. I'll . . . well . . . I find I've forgotten . . ." and with no more ado she turned on her heel and, still dragging her full skirt awkwardly over her arm, went back up the stairs.

It was as though there was a length of cord fastened to her chest, fastened right in its centre though where its other end was situated was as yet unknown to her. As she had moved away from the stairs which led up to the nursery it had stretched tighter and tighter, hurting her quite badly but now, as she walked hesitantly back towards them, it became easier. The baby still cried.

Her skirt hampered her and she moved very slowly up the nursery stairs and along the corridor which led to the day nursery. There were rows of closed doors on both sides, those at the front opening into the day nursery, the night nursery, nanny's room and the schoolroom, as yet unused, the bathroom and water closet installed for the servants' use. On the opposite side of the passage, looking out over the back, were the bedrooms which were occupied by the female servants. Mrs Garnett had the largest and most comfortable naturally, but each maidservant, even the lowliest scullery maid Margaret, had a small room to herself.

The baby cried on and on, his distress very evident, even to her inexperienced ears and with a muttered oath Jenna strode towards the closed door of the day nursery, flinging it open with such force it hit a chair which stood behind it, the noise of it startling the baby to such an extent he stopped his wailing but only for a moment before he took it up again.

The nursery, facing south-west, was, on a sunny day, a bright and cheerful room but today, with the sun still lurking in the folds of mist which hung as high as the rooftops, the light was dismal and the only glow came from a cheerful fire crackling behind the fireguard on which several small garments were airing. The room had recently been painted in white and yellow on Conal's orders and there were bowls of spring flowers on the window sills. There were two deep and comfortable chairs before the fire, an enormous nursery table set about with sturdy white cups and saucers and plates, a pot of marmalade and in the centre a jug of wild daffodils. Bright rugs were scattered about the floor. There were two white-painted chests of drawers and a big box which was open revealing a great multitude of soft toys. Jenna wondered how they came to be there. Pictures on the walls were cheerful, clowns and toy soldiers, puppies and kittens, children rolling hoops and in a corner was a wickerwork bassinet with a muslin-draped hood. It was from there that the cries of the baby came. There was no one else in the room.

"Where in hell is Nanny?" Jenna exclaimed out loud and at the sound of her voice the baby stopped crying again. Jenna, her hand still resting on the door knob peered round the big room, even peeping to the back of the door as though expecting to find Nanny hiding there. Her eyes turned fearfully again towards the bassinet for what in God's name was she to find there, she asked herself, she who had barely held the stranger who was her son in her arms. The nurse had put him there an hour or two after he was born, a neatly wrapped, scrupulously clean bundle of silk and lace from which wandering eyes had stared and a rosebud mouth had hopefully sucked. A pretty baby, she supposed, with a fluff of dark hair on his head and hands like pink shells, one of which had escaped the nurse's tight binding.

Leaving the door ajar, just as though her mind was concerned with beating a hasty retreat should it be necessary, she advanced slowly across the scattered rugs towards the bassinet. Inside it lay her son, wearing nothing but a tiny garment which reached no lower than his navel. There was a flurry of waving hands, kicking legs and bare feet and flaunting itself proudly, the tiniest, dearest little penis she had ever seen. Not that she had seen many, only Conal's which she had thought to be quite amazing in its rampant masculinity and, years ago, Simeon's, as Molly bathed him in front of the nursery fire, but this one belonging to her son was beautiful. She had not even known its name until Conal told her but now she did and her son had one which, some day, would be as magnificent as his father's!

The child became quite still as she hung over him, his eyes, which she saw with bewildering delight were exactly the same colour as her own, somewhere between blue and green and surrounded by long, fine, gold-tipped lashes, watching her with great solemnity. His face was rosy, flushed with the might of his exertions since he was not accustomed to being ignored and had let it be known. Across his neat skull was an astonishing tumble of dark curls.

"Well," she said, marvelling at this beautiful child she had come across and who, it seemed, nobody but her cared about. The baby waited.

She bent lower until her head was almost beneath the hood. "Well," she said again and began to smile. The baby still waited. Her eyes ran over him and she longed to touch the down-like skin of his legs and body and sweetly serious face. His brilliant eyes watched her every move and when, leaning closer, the feather on her hat touched his cheek he grinned, revealing a quivering, moist pink tongue and gums to match.

"Well," she said for the third time, grinning back at him for how did one address a baby, and then, for some reason, she felt a great urge to kiss his cheek. She didn't know why for though she visited him on most days, as was her duty as his mother, she had never felt the slightest urge to do so before. But why shouldn't she? He was her baby, wasn't he? It was soft and rounded beneath her lips and her heart moved in her breast in exquisite, painful pleasure. She moved her lips gently across his forehead and under his chuckling chin then, again she didn't know why, she laid them on his stomach and blew a raspberry. He loved it!

But what the devil was he doing here lying all alone and half naked, she raged, as she tossed her hat on to the table next to the marmalade and bent once more to this fascinating creature who was her son. Where was Nanny Abigail who was the most responsible of women and who would cut her own throat rather than allow harm to come to her charge? And what of the wet nurse – what was her name? – Mrs Duckworth, who usually came first thing to put Ewan Macrae to the breast? Well, wherever they had got themselves to they'd feel the length of her tongue when they returned for she'd have no one, no one neglecting this beautiful boy whom she had come across quite by accident, it seemed to her, and who was her son.

Before she knew she was even contemplating it her hands reached out, one under his back, the other beneath his head and she lifted him for the first time voluntarily into the crook of her arm. She looked at him, studying the winged shape of his eyebrows which reminded her, she was suddenly aware, of Conal's, the unformed blob of his small nose which again, despite its infant shape, was uncommonly like his father's. And would you look at that chin! Where had she seen that before? she asked herself, not realising that she looked at it every day in her mirror. The boy stared back at her unblinkingly, as fascinated with her as she was with him and once again, giving in to some instinct she could not prevent nor understand, she kissed him, a dozen light kisses on his cheeks which seemed to please him for he smiled amiably.

"Well, it's no good," she told him, "we can't have you hanging about in this dreadful state of undress, can we? It's not decent, is it?" grinning at him to let him know she cared nought for his nudity. "Where do those women keep your . . . well, whatever it is they put on you? And I suppose you'll need a napkin of sorts?" and as though to agree with her he urinated in a neat and sparkling arc all over the bodice of her riding habit.

"You little devil," she squealed, absolutely enchanted

with his cleverness. "You've quite ruined my new habit," and she bent her face to him, burying it in the soft, sweet-smelling curve of his neck.

It was Dora who found Nanny Abigail at the foot of the servants' stairs which led from the nursery floor to the passage at the back of the small parlour. The stairs were used only by the maidservants first thing in the morning when they came down to the kitchen and last thing at night as they returned to their beds. They had no reason to go upstairs during the day unless it was an emergency or Nanny Abigail rang the bell. Had Dora not been struck with the cramps which she knew were the onset of her monthlies and had she not slipped up to her room to get a clean square of the linen she used for the purpose, the poor woman, unconscious from the blow she had received as she fell, would have remained there until the servants' bedtime. Of course they would have eventually found her for a search party would have been sent out but no one knew she was missing. You could have knocked Dora and Maisie down with a feather, honestly you could, they told Mrs Garnett when, having discovered poor Nanny Abigail all of a heap at the bottom of the stairs, they had pounded up to the nursery, their hearts in their throats. God knows how long the precious mite had been all alone, but they found madam, her riding habit flung to the floor, sitting in her petticoats, her bare feet up on the fireguard with her son warmly wrapped in a shawl and fast asleep in her arms. She looked quite beautiful as she gazed down at him, her face rapt and wondering, her eyes soft and dreaming, just as though he was the most amazing thing she had ever come across, Dora was to say later, and if she hadn't seen it with her own eyes she'd never have believed it. Didn't Maisie agree? There was Percy still clomping up and down in the stable yard and the blasted animal raising hell, Percy said, wanting to be off and chasing across the misty fields and the one who'd ordered it sitting dreaming by the nursery fire in her drawers nursing her own son and looking half cracked as she did it!

Mind you, she'd come to herself as they knew her soon enough when she and Maisie had hurtled into the room, Dora added feelingly, spitting like a damned she-cat, she was.

"Where in hell's name is that nursemaid?" she'd hissed at them as she stood up. She'd put the boy in the bassinet first, thank God, before she'd started on them, which was sensible of her for as far as they could tell she knew nowt' about bairns and was just as likely to drop him in her fury. She'd calmed down quick enough when they told her what had happened and had even apologised though she'd wanted to know what the devil Nanny Abigail was doing on the back stairs. They couldn't tell her, not yet, though no doubt nanny would enlighten them when she came to. George had been sent for the doctor who was just arriving and if Mrs Macrae would like Dora to fetch Marian to help her . . .

"Yes, thank you, Dora. Tell Marian to bring my . . . well, whatever she thinks suitable for . . . I shall need something plain and . . ."

She grinned for some reason Dora did not understand. "Something washable, I would say, then I shall come down and see what needs to be done with poor nanny. Stay here with my son, Maisie, will you? I shall be back shortly."

And so she was. Nanny Abigail, apologising most piteously for the inconvenience she was causing her mistress, still somewhat dazed from the blow to her head, was put to bed in the room which was hers adjoining the night nursery. She had, miraculously, suffered nothing more than a slight concussion and would be as good as new by the end of the week, the doctor said, but she must be kept quiet and certainly must not be allowed to worry over Master Ewan. One of the housemaids, surely, could take over her duties?

"Don't worry, Doctor Sterling," Mrs Macrae told the astonished man, Mrs Garnett and the assembled servants who hung about, as servants do when excitement comes to break the tedium of their long day, "I shall look after my son myself. There is no need to trouble anyone else. George can fetch Mrs Duckworth from the village to show me the complexities of his feeds but the rest I can deal with myself."

Well, their jaws dropped and their mouths popped open, even Mrs Garnett's, and the thought which was in all their minds was plain to see. God help the poor little bugger! They'd never heard anything so daft in their lives. Their light-minded, high-spirited, rebellious young mistress hadn't the faintest notion of how to look after those two dogs of hers, never mind a baby, letting them sprawl about the lovely carpet in her upstairs sitting-room all the live long day, and he let her.

"Dora, you and Maisie will take care of Nurse Abigail in turns but one of you must be immediately available should I need you in the nursery. Sarah" – whisking around to the astonished kitchen maid – "you shall take over Dora's duties, that's if Mrs Garnett agrees. Oh, do forgive me, Mrs Garnett," she said with one of those endearing gestures which were so like her and which you couldn't help but take to, "you must of course arrange the servants to suit yourself but my husband and I will understand perfectly if, being somewhat at sixes and sevens, you cannot quite manage that miracle of perfection which is your usual standard."

Mrs Garnett preened then, looking troubled, asked her mistress if perhaps it might be more convenient, meaning safer for Master Ewan, if a temporary nursemaid was employed?

Mrs Macrae would not hear of it, she said, skipping

away up the stairs on light feet, singing, if you please, in her hurry to get to the child who, for the past nine weeks, she had barely acknowledged.

"Where's Dora?" Conal asked the awkward though neatly dressed maidservant who waited in the hall to take his hat and cloak that evening. He had never seen her before since the inside of his kitchen and the women who worked in it, apart from Mrs Garnett and Dora, and sometimes Maisie, were unknown to him.

"She . . . well, she'm . . . mumble . . . mumble . . . mumble . . ."

"I beg your pardon. Speak up, girl, where is Dora and may I ask who you are?"

"Sarah, sir," hanging her head, then bobbing a curtsey in apology.

"Sarah? Well, Sarah, would you mind telling me what's going on?"

"Dora be . . . nanny . . . mumble . . . stairs . . . mistress . . . accident . . ." but by now all the anxious Sarah could see of her master was his back and his long legs as he leaped up the stairs, taking them three at a time in his desperate need to get to the top.

"Jenna, Jenna," he was yelling, his voice hoarse with fear. The words the unfamiliar servant had muttered at him had made no sense, only two of them having any meaning for him and those two had filled him with terror.

Accident! Mistress!

"Jenna, where the devil are you?" he yelled, crashing open the door to the bedroom he shared with her, his heart pounding, his breath ragged in his chest, his face cold with sweat. The room was peaceful, warm and smelled faintly of the perfume he had bought her and which he liked her to wear for him, sometimes with nothing else! The fire sang cheerfully, making small popping noises as the sweet applewood with which it was fed broke in the flames. The candles were lit but the room was empty.

"Jenna, oh Jesus . . ." He turned frantically, his mind filled with pictures of such horror he wanted to smash his fist into the door frame but as he scrambled towards the head of the stairs again he heard a door open, coming from the nursery floor and a voice called softly to him.

"Darling, I'm up here," it said, "but do try to be quiet, will you? I've just got him off to sleep."

"Jenna?"

"Yes, Conal, do come up."

"But . . ."

"Conal, for God's sake stop dithering about like some dumbstruck schoolboy and come and . . ." Her words died away as though she had gone back into the room, the door of which he had heard open.

He was up the stairs and at the open door in three long strides, his face a study in bewilderment and when he reached it he came to such an abrupt stop it was as though he had come up against a barred gate.

She was by the bassinet, her arms crossed and resting along its side. She was gazing into it with such a look of awe, of wonderment, of deep and unquestioning love he felt himself tremble at the beauty of it.

"Look at him, Conal," she breathed. "Look at him sleep. Come here, darling, come and see our son. I've been watching him sleep for an hour now, I'm so afraid he might stop, you see."

"Stop what, lassie?" he asked her gently as he moved across the room to lean beside her. He looked at her, not at his son since his love for the boy had begun at the moment he came from his mother's womb. This was new. This was miraculous. This was what he had longed for.

"Breathing."

"He won't do that, my love. He's strong and brave and beautiful like his mother."

"I love him, Conal," she said wonderingly. "I didn't know it until today."

"And I love you."

"I've been looking after him. Nanny had an accident and I was here so . . . I took over." She said it with pride.

"He is your son, Jenna Macrae."

"Our son."

"Yes."

"He has the most enchanting little penis."

Conal Macrae began to roar with laughter, reaching for his wife with loving, demanding arms and in his bassinet Ewan Macrae stirred for a moment then settled again, unaware that beside him, on the nursery floor his mother and father were making love, with laughter, with passion, with understanding, with tenderness.

He was taken downstairs to sleep beside their bed that night, to Nanny Abigail's mortification for what would a splendid gentleman like Mr Macrae make of soiled napkins, of a crying baby and the tedious business of getting his wind up after his feed?

Mr and Mrs Macrae had never enjoyed anything so much in all their lives, they told one another as they took it in turns to hold their son, to kiss him, to watch him sleep and wake and smile at them. And while they waited for him to do it Mr Macrae made love to Mrs Macrae and by morning she was pregnant again though naturally Master Ewan was not aware of it and neither was his mama.

They bathed him together the next morning, just as though he was some new toy they had been given, Maisie said with some disgust since her ma had had fourteen and there was no fun in that. Still, it was lovely that Mrs Macrae had become attached to the little-un at last and as for him, meaning the master, he was made up with it, you could see that. Nanny Abigail had told her and Dora that he had always come up to the nursery twice a day, regular, and often sat for half an hour or more, just nursing the baby, looking into his face, even talking to him when he thought no one was listening. Now it was the two of them, whisking him off to their own rooms, even when nanny was better, taking him away to the garden, well wrapped up, of course, Nanny Abigail saw to that, and quite unable to bear him out of their sight, it seemed.

It had been a mouse, nanny told them, which had caused the accident though Mr Macrae was adamant that the creatures never stirred beyond the kitchen. No, she argued fiercely, for her reputation was at stake, it had darted across the landing and down the back stairs and when, deeply offended, she had gone to give it what for with the nursery poker, she had tripped on that bit of drugget on the bottom stair, striking her head on the frame of the door opposite as she went down.

Anyway, the result was a smooth marmalade kitten which came to live in the nursery, to Master Ewan's surprised delight, for Mrs Macrae couldn't bear the very idea of mice skittering about her beloved son and the stairs were newly carpeted so, all in all, Dora was often to say, it was an ill wind which blew nobody any good. As long as that blasted demon of a kitten behaved itself and didn't get into Master Ewan's bassinet, and how could it with someone watching the little pet all the live long day and night, everything had turned out just fine!

Chapter Twenty-one

The early spring sunshine was weak and hesitant, a pale silvery lemon lacing through the branches of the great trees which were silhoutted against the blue-white of the sky. The tops of the common yew trees were feathery with new growth but the heavier branches showed no sign of the foliage which was to come. The sunlight cast uncertain shadows across the carpet of wood sorrel which had sprouted up through the layer of mould created by last year's fallen leaves and where the sunshine struck, wild massed daffodils lifted their brave and cheerful heads.

The light had a translucent quality about it which would come at no other time of the year, bringing changes to the beech and hornbeam, bare all winter but which were now beginning to show bright green with their new leaf. The evergreen holly was flourishing with rapid growth and through the centre of the small wood a trickle of water sang merrily along the clear bed of the winding stream. It was no more than a ditch really, gouged out of the woodland floor, but its edges were starred with golden saxifrage, with the bright and glossy yellow of marsh marigold, a two-stranded ribbon cut by the constant flow of water over the centuries.

The sun was low, gleaming horizontally over the open glades and the worn paths of Seven Cows Wood, revealing in the peace and stillness a family of rabbits who had ventured bravely out to nibble on the new grass, and a pheasant, one of those hand-reared by Jonas Townley's gamekeeper for the sporting pleasure of Mr Townley's guests, called harshly from the shelter of a clump of fern. A robin swung sharply from the branch of a beech tree to the ground, remaining only a moment to peck at something which had caught its bright eye before darting back to safety. Its sweet warbling song broke the silence before it flew off on some important business of its own. A chaffinch took wing with a great flourish and from some way off the flute-like sound of a song thrush carried on the early morning air.

The sound of galloping hooves brought the whole multitude of woodland creatures to an instant frozen moment of silence before, magically, they vanished from sight. There was not a sound anywhere but the clamour of hoofbeats on ground layered with new growth, the creak of saddle leather, the rattle of bridle and stirrup, the snort of the horse's laboured breathing and the underlying gurgle of the stream. The animal came on, the sound growing louder and louder until the whole wood seemed to be filled with the tumult of its passing.

Horse and rider came to the stream and though it was no more than a foot wide and a few inches deep, the youth on the animal's back urged it up and up, encouraging it to jump as though it took a five-barred gate, or the overgrown hedge of the hunting field. The hunter took it cleanly, its eyes rolling and wild, the mass of foam at its soft mouth trailing back across its sweated neck. It was breathing hard and so was the youth on its back but they did not interrupt their wild gallop. Behind them a fine-looking English setter, its black and white body stretched out low across the woodland floor, did its best to keep up.

The girl stepped out from behind the enormous girth of an oak tree directly into the path of animal and rider and though, with a hoarse shout of white-faced horror, the youth did his best to avoid her, she was struck a glancing blow from his booted foot. It threw her backwards, crumpling her into a boneless heap of tumbled clothing on the bed of wood sorrel where she lay, silent and still.

"Jesus, oh Jesus . . ." the youth was babbling as he hauled on the reins, cutting cruelly into the tender mouth of his mount and almost before he had brought it to a rearing, bucking, whinnying halt he had freed his feet from the stirrup and leaped to the ground. The dog was sniffing at the quiet figure of the girl and the youth pushed it aside savagely as he knelt down beside her.

It was Bryony Townley.

"Bryony . . . oh Jesus God, Bryony, what the hell were you thinking of? I didn't see you. Are you mad to step out like that? Oh God, Bryony, speak to me . . ."

She continued to lie where his mad ride had flung her. There was no mark on her face which, even in his terror, Tim Spencer noticed had not taken on the pallor of the unconscious but remained that flushed golden amber which he remembered so well. She was breathing, thank God, his appalled mind comforted him, as the rapid rise and fall of her breasts testified but her eyes were closed, the fan of her long, silken lashes resting quietly in the hollow beneath her eyes. Had he been older and wiser he might have wondered why a female deep in an unconscious state could be so flushed and lovely, her breathing so deep and rapid. He did not!

He put a tentative hand to her brow, smoothing back the gleaming tumbled mass of her dark hair, then removed his riding glove so that he might more easily feel the pulse – was that the correct thing to do? – just below her jawline. His young face was strained with anguish as he stared down at her and his heart beat so thunderously he thought it might break free of his chest. What should he do? Dear God, what had he done? It was not his fault, of course, since he had been merely exercising his new hunter and had thought he had the woodland to himself. His Uncle Jonas owned this land and though there were acres of parkland about Daresbury, there was none as rough and wild and testing as Seven Cows Wood. Uncle Jonas had told him he was welcome to ride it whenever he chose providing he did not disturb the game, though recently, so he had heard, his Uncle Jonas had lost his enthusiasm for shooting and indeed anything at all beyond the responsibilities of his business.

He slipped his left arm beneath Bryony's shoulders, lifting her head a little from the ground, watching with fascinated and remembered pleasure the way, as her head fell back, the golden column of her throat arched and her breasts rose. He drew her gently to him, speaking sharply to the dog which was still showing a great deal of interest in the fallen girl. He slid his right arm beneath her knees, lifting her with some difficulty from the ground and into his arms since she was tall and no lightweight. He turned and looked about him distractedly. What in hell's name was he to do? He was not even sure he was doing the right thing in moving her and yet he couldn't very well leave her to lie on the cold, damp ground while he went for help, could he? If he could get her on to his horse's back, perhaps . . . but then the animal was no docile hack and should he get the thing to stand quietly, which would be damn near impossible, it would not take kindly to having a girl in a full skirt, unconscious to boot, flung across its back. And where was the bloody thing, anyway?

He looked about him desperately, searching for the hunter at which he had not even glanced since he had leaped from its back but it had vanished as neatly as a rabbit down a hole.

Bryony gave a small husky sigh then, without opening her eyes she turned her face into his neck, her mouth warm on his flesh, nestling against him with evident signs of relief and pleasure. His heart pounded even more as her soft breath moved against his chin and throat and without conscious thought he put his lips to her smooth brow, just at the hairline. Sitting down clumsily he rested his back against the rough tree trunk from behind which she had stepped and cradled her across his knee, holding her closely to him. The sun's rays caught her hair, turning its thick, silken darkness to tones of russet and chestnut as it drifted about her shoulders, curling loosely at its ends, springing back from her golden-skinned brow and Tim Spencer found his hand drawn to it, holding its living beauty in fingers which trembled. Again he kissed her, this time her cheek and chin and soft lips, the thrill of doing so while she was not conscious filling him with excited pleasure. She was so exquisitely lovely. Not like his mama and his sister were lovely, a delicate, insubstantial loveliness which had gentlemen fighting to fulfil their smallest wish, but a strong, graceful, exotic beauty which, though he had tried, he had never forgotten. Hers was not a fashionable beauty, that of the pink and white, the blue-eyed, golden-haired sort, but dark, gypsy-like, flaunting, glorious, unforgettable.

But hell's teeth, he could not sit here with her languishing across his knees, delicious as it was, when she might be . . . be damaged somewhere. Inside her, or . . . or underneath the fine, well-cut wool of her blue morning dress, the soft, fur-lined luxury of her matching cloak. Perhaps bruised, that golden skin which he longed, longed to . . . Oh, Lord, should he perhaps examine her for injury, loosen her clothing . . . see if she was hurt . . . perhaps a broken leg dangling beneath her full skirt? She was so frail and defenceless like this, lying in his arms, his to do with as he liked but, sweet Christ, it didn't seem right. He was a gentleman, but he would never forgive himself if . . . if she was hurt and . . .

He had untied the ribbons of her cloak and the first

half-dozen buttons of her gown, his gaze greedy, his hands fumbling and eager, when her eyes opened. Her breasts were half exposed – undamaged, it seemed – the areola about her nipples, the peaked nipples themselves, dark beneath the fine white lace of her chemise. Her eyes were soft and clouded, the eyelashes which surrounded them lifting and drooping slowly, sensuously. They met his sudden guilty gaze with the innocent candour of a child and, as she made no resistance, he slipped one hand inside her clothing and fondled the firm swell of her breast. She smiled in narrow-eyed pleasure. She put one hand to the back of his head and drew his mouth down to hers, her lips full and moist and warm. She moved them, parting his, the tip of her tongue teasing the soft, inner flesh of his mouth.

"Tim," she murmured huskily. "Is it really you? I have dreamed of this moment ever since you – " then, as violently as a leaf caught in a sudden gust of wind, she sat up and flung herself away from him, tearing herself from his clutching arms, dragging her bodice across her exposed breasts, stumbling shakily to her feet to lean against the tree trunk. She was shivering, her whole body moving in great distress and he could hear her breath as she dragged it desperately into her lungs.

"Oh God," she wept, "how could you do this to me? How could you who are supposed to be a gentleman? I only . . . only wanted to see you go by. I've watched you for weeks now. I couldn't forget you, you see . . ." She bent her head in a gesture of utter despair and her lovely hair hung in a heavy, dishevelled curtain across her face and down her back to her waist.

He sat there as though he was pole-axed, his mouth slack, his jaw drooping, his eyes wide and staring as his bemused mind did its best to untangle the meaning of her words. She was saying . . . she was saying that . . . that – what? – she had hung about in these woods where

362

only a few weeks ago he had called her names, dreadful names, coarse he had been in his description of her . . . her . . . status and now it appeared she was telling him that far from hating him for it she had been longing for him, watching for him, hiding behind trees just to get a glimpse of him. That she . . . she . . . loved him . . .

His young, male pride took an arrogant swing upwards from the somewhat guilty shame he had done his best to subdue in the weeks since he had last seen her. He could feel the triumph of it, of his mastery over this lovely, weeping female who loved him, Tim Spencer, and with the knowledge that his advances, though they were not right, were something special to her, that she, in fact, took pleasure in them and should he have a fancy to go further he was certain Bryony Townley was willing to go with him.

He stood up awkwardly, squaring his shoulders and assuming what he imagined to be a pose of careless male sophistication, just as though this sort of thing, women chucking themselves under the hooves of his spirited hunter, happened to him every day of the week, and under the curtain of her hair where her eyes missed nothing, Bryony smiled secretly.

"Tim," she whispered, "please . . . I'm so sorry. I should not have acted as I did. I might have caused an injury to your fine hunter" – which my father paid for, she might have added – "or worse still hurt you, perhaps seriously but you see I was not myself. The sight of you . . ."

A great sob tore through her, rippling her body, and her heavy hair swung in the most fascinating way, the sunlight caught in it like molten copper.

"Bryony, don't upset yourself," he said to her kindly, feeling very masterful, very manly. "There is no harm done, really there isn't. My hunter will be halfway home by now and when he gets there will terrify my mama who will be convinced I have taken a serious tumble. I should have been showing more care, really I should, galloping like some madman where I had no right to be. But as you can see, I am all of a piece. It is you who took the blow."

"No, Tim, please, don't try to shoulder the blame. I deliberately stepped out . . ."

"What!" The expression on his face was comical.

"Yes, it was wicked of me but I wanted to . . ."

"Yes?" He bent his tall frame in an effort to peer under the dense veil of her hair.

"I wanted you to take notice of me, you see." Her head drooped even lower and he felt his masculine pride and triumph puff up his chest even further, filling him with pleased delight.

"Bryony, it was rather a foolish way of doing it, wasn't it? Could you not have just . . .?"

"What, Tim?" For the first time she looked him full in the face, her own a lovely tawny gold, her eyes, brimming still with tears, her hedge-berry lips parted questioningly.

"I don't know, but I'm sure I would have . . ." He shrugged deprecatingly, the infallible male who understands and is willing to overlook the shortcomings of a hapless female.

"Oh Tim," she breathed, just as though the words he spoke were pearls of wisdom and she marvelled at them.

"Are you sure you're not hurt?" he asked commandingly.

"Really, I'm fine," she answered shyly, her eyes cast down in a way he found enchanting. "I caught a blow just here" – putting her hand to her ribs – "but it is nothing."

"Perhaps it might be as well to . . . examine it. Make sure there is no . . . serious damage." He gulped, doing his best to retain that air of masculine urbanity which her revelation had roused in him.

"Oh, I'm sure it is nothing," but she winced as she took a step towards him.

"Bryony, you may have . . . have cracked a rib or something and if so it should be bound up at once. It does not do to neglect these things, you know."

"Do you think so, Tim?"

"I do indeed."

"Well . . ." She bit her lip, evidently in a state of great indecision. They were just on the verge of becoming friends again, her soft young face said, their previous misunderstanding put behind them and how would it look if she was to . . . to bare her body to him in what he might think of as an invitation to . . . well, to consider her less than pure. At the same time she really was in pain, her wide eyes told him and if he could ease that pain a little, just until she got home . . .

"Whatever you think best, Tim," she said meekly, her voice breathless.

There was a purpling bruise as big as his hand just beneath her right breast. He knew its size exactly because his hand fitted when he placed it there to see if it was inflamed, he told her. He was dry-mouthed, his eyes wide and glittering as they devoured the innocent beauty of her high young breasts which stood out above the bruise but when he attempted to touch them she drew back nervously, hanging her head.

"You . . . have an . . . enormous bruise, Bryony." His voice was hoarse with longing and his body strained achingly inside his breeches.

"I'd best get home then. My . . . my aunt will have something to put on it," she whispered in that sweet downcast way he found he liked so much. She had, as yet, made no move to cover the bobbing thrust of her golden breasts and Tim Spencer could not take his eyes off them. She seemed to be telling him that they were his, as she was, for her actions spoke of her love, but at the same time there was a childish naivety about her, an inexperience in matters such as this which had no conception of what she was doing to him. God, she was exquisite. God, how he wanted her!

She turned away at last, doing up her bodice but allowing him one final delicious peep at the rose-tinted points of her nipples, sweeping her mass of hair back from her face, then turning about to search the ground beneath the tree.

"I had a ribbon," she murmured, then, when she found it, a scarlet knot tangled among the wild daffodils, allowing him to tie it in her hair. She stood with her back to him, docile and flushed while his awkward hands arranged it at the back of her head. For an exhilarating moment, as she leaned back against him his hands were allowed to cup her breasts, the nipples bursting between his fingers, then she turned, gazing up at him with every sign of worship. He bent his head to brush her lips with his, feeling every inch the worldly man of experience. Her eyes glowed and so did her full mouth before she bobbed her head. He was newly enchanted with her. Her admiration for his strength and the infallibility of his opinions awoke some emotion in him he had never before known. His every word appeared to fill her with adulation and her sweetness did the same in him. And then there was the way she had allowed him to handle her which surely boded well for the future.

"You're very beautiful, Bryony," he sighed.

"Do you think so, Tim?"

"You know I do and I hope . . ."

"What, Tim?" looking up at him, her eyes wide and depthless.

"I was wondering . . . perhaps we might meet again. I

know you don't ride but if you were to walk your dog this way . . ."

"Well . . ."

"Please, Bryony."

"Oh, I want to, more than anything but . . . well, last time . . . oh Tim, you hurt me so . . . your words were . . . were cruel." Her eyes were enormous in her face. Enormous and artless, just as though, even now, she was not really and truly aware of what he had meant when he had abused her.

He was appalled now as he remembered what he had said to her but at the same time, as she had meant him to be, he was immensely gratified that she had accepted them with no apparent ill feeling.

"Jesus, Bryony, how could I have been such a brute? To have said you were a . . ."

"No, no, Tim, don't . . . please don't."

"But you are so sweet and lovely. Just because you are a . . . Well, it was no excuse to speak to you as I did . . . so, shall we forget it? Shall we put it behind us and be friends again?"

"Oh yes, please, Tim."

"You do like me a little, don't you, Bryony?"

"I love you, Tim."

"Do you really?" He was so pleased with her he kissed her again, wondering why he had considered her worthless when the truth of her bastardy had been revealed to him. She was delightful and what's more she would provide him with endless pleasure in the future. Just because she was illegitimate did not make her any the less desirable. And she loved him so! It shone in her deep golden eyes, along with the promise she was ingenuously holding out to him.

"Perhaps . . . tomorrow, then?" His voice was casual, a man of the world voice, one he imagined all gentlemen used when they made an assignation with a pretty woman.

"Oh, yes please, Tim."

"Until tomorrow then."

"Until tomorrow."

He was to wonder later, much later, if he would not have been better served never to have set eyes on Bryony Townley. She awoke in him a hunger and a thirst which consumed him night and day until he could neither sleep nor eat and his mother worried herself and him into believing he was in the clutches of some dreadful wasting disease. He and Jonas Townley's illegitimate daughter met several days a week in Seven Cows Wood or Beggars Wood and each time she allowed him to believe that today, this very morning, despite the chill of the slowly developing spring, she would allow him to undress her and do with her as he wanted. He could have her, lying in the deep roots of the gigantic hornbeam, his cape spread on the soft velvet mosses which made their bed. Yes, today he could have her, her glowing, loving sensuously narrowed eyes told him. Yes, he would have her, his frenzied hands and lips and male body told her as he laid her down and lifted her skirt but at the last moment she would elude him, leaving him more famished, more thirsty, more furious, but more obsessed with his passionate need of her than ever.

She would allow him almost to strip her, bringing his mouth to her rose-tipped breast, her own hands busy among his own clothing. She made no objection when he removed one garment then another, revealing the point of a golden shoulder, smooth as satin, the length of her graceful back from the nape of her neck to the cleft of her buttocks. The silken flesh of her inner thigh just above her white stocking and a glimpse of the dark flowering mystery above it. She drove him to madness, to cursing obscenities, to a teeth-gritting, hair-rending condition which threatened her with violence but at the exact moment when he was about to sink his grateful body into hers she would roll from under him leaving him winded and foolish with his face in the roots of the tree.

Sometimes she wept, blindly, inconsolably so that his male virility was stirred to such protective love he would have done anything to pacify her. She was so sweet and lovely, so soft and frail, so childlike, so womanly, such a perfect foil for his rampant manhood, he could not resist her.

She threatened never to see him again, her bodice torn where he had forced it apart, her naked breasts heaving with an enticement his dazzled eyes could barely contain and this time he wept for he could not bear to be parted from her, he said, and this time she comforted him, allowing him to suck on her nipples as though he was a nursing infant. She had had a terrifying time with him that day, having to fight him tooth and nail as his strong, horseman's hands tore at her clothing, forcing her back on the bed beneath the tree, forcing her legs cruelly apart.

"Oh yes, this time, madam," he hissed. "I'll not be said no to this time. I've had enough, more than enough of your coyness but this time you've gone too far so let's have those drawers off, if you please."

She was clever. She scrabbled away from him, her back to the tree trunk, her eyes as wide and terrified as a cornered doe. Her hair lay about her in a curling, disordered mass and her soft mouth trembled like that of a defenceless child about to be abused by some brute.

"Oh please, Tim, don't hurt me," she whimpered. "You frighten me so when you are like this. I love you so much . . ."

"Then let me do it, Bryony," he pleaded, somewhat taken aback by her look of childish terror for no man wishes to force himself on a child.

"Tim, darling Tim, please don't force me."

"I won't . . . really I won't," and already he was drawing her skirts down, studiously avoiding the bewitching sight of the target of his desire between her legs.

"I want it as much as you, Tim." She cried in great, gusty sobs, her eyes running, her nose running, as a child's would and he was filled with shame by the brutality he had forced on his little love.

"Then why?" he moaned.

"Because once . . . once we have done it you won't want to see me again." Her voice was a mumble as she dropped her chin despairingly to her chest.

When he folded her tenderly in his arms she was as lovely as ever, tears gone, running nose dried up, soft and sweet-smelling in his weary arms, promising somehow that it would all come right. When she was like that he began to believe that her innocent awakening of his male passion was his fault, not hers but always she seemed to say that tomorrow, tomorrow he would be allowed to love her in the fierceness only she could arouse in him and only she could ease.

Tomorrow!

He was still smiling later that night, his eyes narrowed and dreaming, soft with his thoughts of the girl he loved as he moved up the silent staircase to his room and when the slight figure stepped out from the shadows he was considerably startled. And exasperated!

"Amy, what the devil are you doing? Mama and I thought you had gone to bed." He knew, of course, what this was about, what this was always about and he groaned inwardly. How many times had he gone through this? he thought with growing resentment. How many times had he been the unwilling spectator when Amy had begged Mama not to force her to marry Sir Robert Blenkinsopp and how many times had he himself done his best to intercede for her and all to no avail. Mama might be as fragile-looking as a porcelain figurine but underneath she was like steel and, like steel, she would neither bend nor break. The devil of it was, he could, without much effort, put himself in Amy's shoes and he had at first felt quite sick at the idea of his pretty young sister doing – or having done to her – what he and Bryony . . . but really, was there anything he could do about it? he asked himself and the answer was No. He was himself in love and just at this moment he wanted nothing more than to go to his room, lie on his bed and dream about Bryony, not be plagued by Amy's hopeless despair.

"I know it's almost settled, Tim," she whispered, "really I do, but please, I beg of you, please won't you have another word with Mama? She is so fond of you and will do anything to please you," which was true.

"Amy, you know I've tried."

She began to cry, again, and his heart sank. His nerves, which had been soothed and sighing in the aftermath of his encounter with Bryony, began to jangle and the irritation showed on his candlelit face. Something cold rose in the pit of his stomach to choke in his throat and he turned away.

"Oh, for God's sake, Amy, don't start that again . . ."

"Tim, please, for the last time."

"I can't, Amy, you know I can't." He turned back to her with a winning smile. "And perhaps it won't be so bad. He is enormously rich you know, and you will have everything a girl could wish for. Jewels and furs and . . . and . . ."

Her face, which had been convulsed with misery, altered at once, becoming smooth and still and if Tim had not seen it happen he would not have believed that tears could dry up so quickly.

She stepped back from him, enormously dignified in this, her last defeat.

"Of course, how foolish I am. Any girl would be pleased and grateful to have such a husband. I'm sorry to have troubled you, Tim. You have been very patient. I'll bid you good night and go and tell Mama that I am to be Lady Blenkinsopp. She will be pleased, I'm sure."

Chapter Twenty-two

It seemed that what Conal Macrae had said to his wife earlier in the year regarding her sisters and their future was to be proved right, at least to some degree, when he and Jenna, Jenna's mama and papa, with Beth, whose own wedding had been put back until the end of June, Nancy and Rose, were guests at the wedding of his wife's cousin Amy Spencer to Sir Robert Blenkinsopp. It took place in April when the air was becoming gentle and the flowerbeds of Daresbury Park were thrusting with pelargoniums, purple auriculas and golden-eyed pansies. The trees and grass had begun to sprout and the fountains, which were a spectacular feature of the ornamental gardens, splashed iridescently in the mild sunshine.

A most beautiful wedding, everyone agreed and was not the weather kind to them for April could be treacherous. A flood of golden sunshine as the bride and groom left the church was most welcome though, unhappily, it did accentuate the quite alarming contrast between the exquisitely lovely and visibly terrified young bride and the gloating triumph on the coarsened features of the elderly groom.

Sir Robert Blenkinsopp was a widower of not quite ten months which was, some said, indecently hasty when it came to the mourning of a dead wife. On the other hand he was a baronet, getting on in years, a man with a noble

373

name, an old title, a man of illustrious and unblemished character with three children, not one of them a son. A gentleman who would want to carry on his name and pedigree and how else was he to go about it unless he took to his bed a young wife? A wife with twenty breeding years ahead of her?

It was this last image which lingered in the minds of many long after Sir Robert and his shivering young wife had climbed into their wedding carriage and been driven to the station and the train to the north. No wedding journey for him and Lady Blenkinsopp, he smirked to his old friend, Sir Edward Faulkner, since he had no time for such "fol-de-rols". He'd done it all before with the first Lady Blenkinsopp and what he intended for his young bride could be accomplished just as easily and far more conveniently in his own bed in his own home in Northumberland. He had not put it quite so indelicately to Sir Edward for were they not both gentlemen and was he not talking of his wife, but a certain sly gleam in the eyes of both men, since Sir Edward was inclined to envy his old school friend the sweet and youthful flesh that was to be his, said that they understood one another.

Lady Spencer and her son, Sir Timothy, had done well by the girl, everyone agreed and how Christian-like of her ladyship to invite her sister, the one who had been so cruelly wronged, years ago, by that still handsome husband of hers. He was beside her, immaculate and straight-backed, no sign of his past debauchery, nor of the results of it, his bastards, though it was noticed he never left his wife's side from the moment they arrived until the moment they left. Their three unmarried daughters who, in different circumstances might have been expected to follow their lovely cousin down the aisle as attendant bridesmaids, were somewhat pale and nervous, keeping their eyes modestly lowered, at least the two older ones did though the youngest was inclined, they thought, to be as bold as her mother had once been. Miss Beth and Miss Nancy Townley though, shrank from anyone who spoke to them, the elder of the two clinging to the arm of a young man who, it was said, would be her husband in a month or two. There was a rumour that her father had been forced to pay out a great deal of money to overcome the reluctance of the prospective bridegroom who had not wished to ally his good name with the somewhat tarnished one of his fiancée.

But all in all the disgraced family were accepted amicably enough, for the gentlemen at least understood a man's need for a mistress. Of course, even the saintly Lady Spencer could not be expected to expose her friends, her family or her twin sister's family, who were all blameless, to the grossness of the illegitimate children of her brother-in-law who had not been invited.

The eldest girl, the one who had married a Scot, a grandson of a Laird of sorts, did not bend her head though. Not for her the downcast eyes and modest shrinking from contact with the other guests that her sisters showed. Laughing, she was, her fox red hair a tumble of curls drifting from beneath her extravagant hat, itself a marvel of cream and pastel pink silk roses. Her gown was quite breathtaking, in a shade of pink so pale it was almost white. It fitted to her splendid bosom in such a way it might have been painted there, clinging to her tiny waist and falling in a positive cloud of billowing gauze, frill after frill to her cream boots. Was her gown cream or was it white or was it pink which was an unusual colour to wear with hair the colour of hers. Her husband was in a fair way of business over in Liverpool, it was rumoured. Shipping, they had heard and he was inclined to give his young wife her head more than was good for her and with a baby in the nursery it didn't seem quite the thing to them. She drank the champagne her aunt, Lady Spencer, had provided, chatted and laughed with every one of the guests, whatever their rank or pedigree, embraced her sisters and her mama, and even, after the ceremony, was seen openly to kiss her own husband full on the mouth but not once did she address her father, so what were they to make of that? they asked one another.

The champagne flowed like a brimming waterfall. A small orchestra of violins played in the great hall since there was to be dancing later. Elegantly gowned ladies, many with titles, and immaculately tailored gentleman, also with titles, moved about the splendid rooms of Daresbury Park, the magnificence of them brought about by the money which had come with Lady Spencer on her marriage to the baronet and there was not one manufacturing gentleman among the guests unless one counted Jonas Townley and Conal Macrae.

Sir Robert Blenkinsopp's three unmarried daughters, all older than the bride and therefore, Lady Spencer considered, almost as unsuitable to be bridesmaids as the Townley cousins, spilled sentimental tears as the enormous girth of their father forced its way into the carriage beside his shrinking wife. It was perhaps unfortunate that the daughter of the manufacturing gentleman who was, of course, well known for her habit of speaking out, at least amongst her family, should at that moment have been overheard to remark on the shocking disparity, in age and appearance, of the bride and groom. They had all noticed it, naturally they had, the titled gentlemen told one another, but a man needed a son, didn't he and what was wrong with getting one from a girl, who though a generation or two back came from colliers, was the daughter of a baronet and very young and comely?

"I should not like to be in Amy's shoes tonight, darling," Mrs Macrae was heard to say to her husband who, to do him justice, did his best to quieten her.

"Jenna, behave yourself," those about the couple

heard him murmur though one or two, Sir Timothy Spencer among them, saw that he was himself inclined to smile at her.

"I only said—"

"We heard you, Jenna, and it is not mannerly to remark on it."

"You agree though, don't you, Conal?" She tipped a half-glass of champagne down her throat, turning to look about her for the footman. They were at the back of the large crowd which stood on the wide, shallow steps of Daresbury Park to wave off the happy couple. The carriage had tipped alarmingly to one side as the bridegroom climbed into it and the picture of the marriage bed which, one presumed, would do the same was in more than a few minds, both male and female. Lady Spencer, not an imaginative woman, was not among them, her only thought one of thankfulness that her only daughter had done so well. It had not been easy and even yet Amy still looked somewhat drawn after weeks of distraught protest and daily weeping but she had been brought to see sense at last.

Turning to her son, Lady Spencer took his arm, no doubt wishing the same good fortune for him. It would be pleasant to talk of "my daughter, Lady Blenkinsopp, my son, Sir Timothy" and it was only as the carriage drove away that the commotion behind her came to her ears.

"Jenna," she heard her brother-in-law, Jonas Townley, say quietly, "you have had more than enough champagne and perhaps it might be a good idea if you were to go with your mother to the—"

"I will decide when I have had enough champagne," her niece was hissing, "and if my husband makes no objection then what is it to do with you?"

About them a circle of high-bred, embarrassed faces turned away from such appalling manners, their expressions asking, nevertheless, what else could you expect from such people? The argument, if that was what it was, had obviously been going on for several minutes. Jenna's heated face, the blaze of what could only be called malevolence in her eyes, the unsteadiness of her step, her general air of dishevelment, told Lady Spencer that her sister's daughter was horrifyingly and indecently inebriated. Dear Lord in heaven, why did not that husband of hers watch her more closely? She had always been what Lady Spencer could only call undisciplined. She had never been sufficiently curbed, in Lady Spencer's opinion, a forceful child and young woman, as mettlesome as an unbroken colt. Her parents had humoured her, allowed her to run wild, to speak as she pleased and now she was doing just that. And to her papa who, though Lady Spencer was mortified by the show of bad manners on this day of all days, surely deserved it?

"Conal, I would advise you to take your wife home now," Jonas said calmly, though in his eyes was the anguish of a man who can hardly bear the pain he is being made to suffer.

"I mean to, sir. If you would ask one of the flunkeys to call our carriage . . ."

"Kindly remove your hands from me, Conal Macrae, and never mind the damn flunkey. This is between me and my . . . my father here. He has the gall to tell me how to behave when . . ."

"Jenna!" It was her mother's voice, high and despairing, her own torment, caused not only by the dreadful rift between father and daughter but by this public airing of it, written deep in her suddenly lined face.

"No, Mama, I will not be spoken to as if I was a naughty child who has misbehaved at a party. I will—"

"That is what you are, lassie," her husband said wryly, raising his shoulders in a shrug as he turned to his father-in-law. "I'm sorry, sir. I should have—"

"Don't you apologise for me," his wife screamed, and

cowering behind their parents, two of her sisters broke into harrowed weeping. The fiancé looked as though he wished the floor would open up and swallow him for this would do his blameless reputation no good and the youthful Sir Timothy, who only that morning in the misted beginning of the new day had fumbled in the bodice of Jonas Townley's illegitimate daughter, dithered at his mama's back, his eyes haunted with his indecision on what to do next. He was, technically, the host on this occasion. This was his home. It was his sister who had just been married and it was his mama who looked ready to faint in lovely confusion. It was his responsibility to deal with this terrible family quarrel and to do it with the calm good manners, the breeding and restraint his upbringing and education had taught him but he was not yet nineteen, somewhat diffident and unassuming and the thought of placing himself in the midst of his cousin Jenna, her husband and his Uncle Jonas, who were mature gentlemen, quite demoralised him. He was aware that his guests were looking to him to step smoothly forward, to usher the protagonists to some private sanctum where they might do as they pleased, but he continued to hesitate, putting a hand beneath the elbow of his swaying mama, pretending that she was his first concern.

"Jenna." Conal Macrae took his wife's arm in a firm grip. "Will you come with me to . . ." He turned courteously to Lady Spencer, his expression asking if there were some secluded place where his wife might be taken. Perhaps to lie down, a maid in attendance, cold compresses put to her head which surely must be spinning. His wife was not well, his smooth face said and he would be obliged if her ladyship would follow his example in this charade he had entered into. Those about him looked on approvingly. He was doing the correct thing, the only thing a gentleman could do in the circumstances and with a bit of firmness and cooperation on Lady Spencer's part the incident might be smoothed over and if not exactly forgotten, then hidden away.

"Of course, Mr Macrae." Lady Spencer recovered at once, relieved that Jenna's husband should show such refinement. Jonas and Nella were standing side by side, their eyes staring in painful concentration somewhere over the shoulder of their distraught daughter and were no good to anyone. They seemed to be incapable of making the decision of even walking away from her, of simply removing themselves so that Jenna would be left with nothing and no one on whom to vent her fury and at their backs, Nancy and Beth, so pretty in their wedding finery, wept silently and piteously while Rose, more like her eldest sister than the other two, stared grimly at nothing. The humiliation which their sister was heaping on them, not only by her imbibing of too much champagne but by her act of defiance against their father and her husband, had reduced them to the status of children.

Gesturing to a maidservant who was hovering in morbid fascination just inside the wide front door, Lady Spencer indicated that the girl was to show Mr and Mrs Macrae to a private room but Mrs Macrae had other ideas.

"Thank you, Aunt Linnet, but I don't think I wish to be sent to my room and again, this has nothing to do with anybody but my father and me. It seems he is embarrassed by my behaviour which is really quite amusing when one considers his own. I suppose I have taken rather more wine than is considered proper for a lady and I will apologise to you and your guests if I have offended you. It was rude of me to make the remark I did about Amy and her new husband but what I said was only what everyone else was thinking. It is quite . . . quite obscene to think of . . . of . . . dear God, I find it impossible to dwell on . . ."

She blinked rapidly, doing her best to control her distress but the tears spilled over her lashes and glided down her cheeks. She put up a hand and dashed them away and beside her her husband made as though to take her in his arms but she twitched away from him.

Voices from the broad gravel driveway, guests who had somewhat boisterously escorted the eager bridegroom and his pitiful little bride on their way towards the gate, could be heard asking one another what was to be done and there was a certain amount of polite pushing. It was still cool despite being a sunny April day and they were eager to get to the enormous fires Lady Spencer kept burning and the champagne which was bound to be still flowing.

"Jenna, this is absolutely unforgivable," Lady Spencer began icily.

"Oh, you agree with me, Aunt Linnet? Then why did you allow it?" Her furious disagreement with her father seemed to have been forgotten as the horror of Amy's predicament distracted her.

"I beg your pardon!"

"How could you give her to that monster?" Jenna shuddered as the disgusting images of what was to be done to Amy by her husband that night crowded her mind. "I know he is rich and has a title but . . ."

Her father came suddenly to life and only his wife knew what an effort it had cost him. His daughter whom he loved dearly had turned on him, making a public spectacle of them both and he had been thankful for several minutes when her anger had been turned away from him but now she was disgracing herself and her family, humiliating her aunt before her friends and it would not do. Jenna was Jenna. She had always been outspoken and no doubt would never change but there were limits to what she should be allowed. And the only way to turn her attack from her aunt was to deflect it back to himself.

"Jenna, that's enough. This has nothing to do with you or with anyone but—"

She whirled like a cornered animal which is being attacked from another quarter. "Oh, you would say that, wouldn't you? What people do is their own concern and they should go ahead and do it and hang the consequences. No matter who is hurt by it. I should think everyone in Marfield, in Lancashire knows your views on that. Your actions are not to be censured because you—"

"Jenna, *that is enough.*"

This time it was her husband who spoke. His face was the colour and hardness of grey stone and the warm dancing brown depths of his eyes, which not a few of the ladies present had thought to be very attractive, had become dark, flat and forbidding. On the last word his mouth clamped tight shut and there was a perilous white line about it. His fierce, knife-edged anger rippled out across the great hall and many of those ladies who had thought him to be so charming, shivered and were glad it was not directed at them. He gripped his wife's arm just above the elbow and as she turned, her own eyes livid slits of pure green rage in which was mixed her pain, she did her best to throw him off as he began to drag her quite deliberately towards the door which led to the drive. The guests, doing their best to pretend there was absolutely nothing untoward happening, parted before them.

"My carriage if you please, Lady Spencer," he said politely over his shoulder. "My wife and I will wait outside and may I say what a splendid wedding it was. Your daughter was quite lovely and a credit to her upbringing."

It was all over the township of Marfield by nightfall but by now they were becoming used to the goings-on of the Townley family, asking one another what else could you expect from the shaking foundations on which those children's lives had been built. That the eldest girl of theirs was as blunt and arrogant as her father had once been and a good thrashing is what she should have had years ago. Mind you, wasn't it only what Jonas Townley deserved after what he had done to that poor wife of his? As you sow, so shall you reap, it was said and by God, he was reaping his just deserts with the lot of them tearing one another apart. His girl speaking out of turn at a society wedding, calling her father all kinds of names which didn't bear repeating, or so Mrs Robert Gore's parlour maid, who had had it from Lady Spencer's parlour maid, had reported. Mind you, what that lass of his said, though they were not sure of her exact words, was true. Her father with his philandering was coming close to wrecking all their lives, if what the gossips said could be believed. One of his girls having a husband bought for her, and God only knew what was to become of the other two, comely as they were, though it was well known that a guinea or two could buy anything these days, for most men had their price.

And the other two! The boy and girl born out of wedlock. What was to happen to them? Oh, that lad would be right if he shaped himself for there was nothing Jonas Townley wouldn't do for a son of his. If he shaped himself. He was wild, if the tales which went about were to be believed. Not much past sixteen he was, and hadn't Bertie Blaney's lad, who shouldn't by rights have been there himself since old Bertie was strict Methody, seen him at the back of the Colliers Arms with several sons of his father's manufacturing friends? In the fenced area with scores of others they had been, eyes gleaming, faces flushed, howling as loudly as the rest of the mob as they tipped the landlord's best brandy down their throats. A dog-fight, illegal of course, bull dogs which would mangle and maim each other for the sporting pleasure of the spectators. Colliers, most of them, factory workers from St Helens, "travelling" gentlemen in the glass trade and a few sons of the gentry who were attracted to the blood sport, all of them ready to bet on their favourite, many of the former the very wages which were all they had to feed their hungry children. Aye, Simeon Townley, swaggering, it was rumoured, and not a little drunk, laughing mindlessly as he lost five guineas and where had he come by such a vast sum they wanted to know? Jonas Townley had been poorly lately, troubled by that cough of his, staying at home to be cosseted by his wife, leaving his son in his manager's hands and, give the lad his due, since the revelation of his parentage had been revealed to him, and the prospect, no doubt, that one day Jonas Townley's collieries might come into his hands, he had worked as hard as his father had done at his age.

A bad business then, though Jenna Macrae cared nothing for what her half-brother Simeon might be doing with himself when the day was done, only on how it might affect the efficient working of Kenworth, Fielden and Townley Collieries. She had been badly shocked by her father's gaunt appearance at Amy's wedding and it was perhaps this, her need not to feel compassion, not to be infected by his evident suffering which had made her drink glass after glass of champagne. It had been over three months since the day she had last seen him in January when she had taken Ewan to Bank House, on the day when Simeon had callously revealed to her their true relationship. When the invitation to go to Amy's wedding had arrived she had almost refused it and only Conal's intervention had stopped her.

"You cannot refuse," Conal had said. "You cannot stay away from every function at which your father might be present and why should you? If he is as wicked as you think he is then why should he be allowed to stop you from doing what you want to do? Don't let him spoil your enjoyment, Jenna," he had said, probably hoping, Jenna was aware, that the dreadful rift might be healed.

But it hadn't. It was worse than ever. She just could not forgive him for . . . well, though it had been her mama to whom he had been unfaithful, it was as though he had broken faith with her, with Jenna, his daughter who had adored him and that faith, that trust, that respect and love were gone. No, she thought sadly, the love was still there but love without the other feelings was worthless in her opinion and she would despise Jonas Townley to the end of her days. There was black and there was white. No grey areas in between. No areas which an older, wiser woman might have understood and so Jonas Townley was worthless. Unworthy of Jenna Macrae's love and honour.

But what of her inheritance? Up until that day in January, over three months ago now, though she had brooded on it, agonised over it, she had got no further than that since she had, quite simply, not known what to do. She would do something, of course, for there was no way she would allow Simeon and Bryony Townley to usurp her position as Jonas Townley's eldest daughter, to cheat her out of what was rightfully hers, but exactly what she didn't know. She had been distracted and rudderless, telling herself that something would occur to her, some great and marvellous scheme which would put Simeon Townley where he deserved to be, but nothing had come to her. Conal had promised to consult a lawyer, an acquaintance of his and the fellow had told Conal that he would look into it. A tricky business, he had said, if what Mrs Townley had told her daughter was true. He had heard of a man adopting his illegitimate son if he had no legitimate heir since a man must leave his name and property somewhere and who better than to a child of his blood but he would do his best, he had promised Conal.

The law moved slowly and she must be patient but eight

weeks ago Jenna had discovered the small personage of Ewan Macrae and, as he had grasped her heart, making it for ever his, her aimlessness had been directed to one purpose and that was towards what would one day be her son's inheritance. Certainly he would be a ship owner, an entrepreneur in the thriving port of Liverpool, as his father was. He would be an astute man of business with that instinct amounting almost to inspiration which Conal possessed, a brilliant man with a financial acumen equal not only to that of his father but that of his mother's Fielden antecedents. He would be at home in the docklands of Liverpool which Conal thrived in, the thicket of masts, the towering hulls, the smoke-blackened funnels, the graceful sails, the deafening roar of chains, the shanties of the seamen, the shouts of the dockies.

But what of his mining inheritance? He was the grandson, the great-grandson, the great-great-grandson of colliers, men who tunnelled in the earth for their wealth, men who dreamed of the black gold that was there; who had risked their fragile bodies, their very lives for what they sought and her son, her and Conal's son, was not to be tricked out of what was rightfully his just because his grandfather, Jonas Townley, could not resist the flaunting face and figure of Simeon Townley's mama. Her own mother had said she was lovely and good but Jenna cared nothing for that. It meant nothing to her, nor did the past now which included what she, the woman and Jenna's father had done together, but she'd be damned if she'd let their lust and the result of it cheat her son. He was a baby yet, a five-month-old delight to her and Conal, a merry scrap, the image of his father except for the bright, blue-green eyes which stared in wonder at the beautiful brightness of the flames in the fireplace. His father loved him and held him safe when he would have reached out his plump, enquiring fingers to it, and his mother tossed him in the air until he squealed, then kissed his satin cheek and cradled him to her in a passion of love. He was her pride and her joy and he was a Macrae but he was also a Townley and a Fielden and it was over his dark and sleepy head that she swore that what was his would be his!

Chapter Twenty-three

The banksman at Fielden Colliery almost let the cage carrying a dozen men to the surface crash down the shaft again as he watched the splendid carriage draw up outside the colliery office. The lady sitting in it waited for her coachman to hand her down, then, ignoring the foul coal dust which immediately soiled her expensive cream kid boots and the hem of her cream voile skirt, turned back to the woman who shared the carriage with her.

"I'll take him, nanny," the banksman heard her say crisply, reaching to retrieve what appeared to be a parcel of white ruffled lace and muslin from the second woman's lap and it was then, as she moved away from the carriage, the child in her arms, the sun capturing a glint of flame in her hair, that he recognised her.

Bloody 'ell, it were the maister's lass, her that had married an' gone to live away. Liverpool, he'd heard. Done right well for herself, she had, an' right well for her husband, an' all, giving him a brave lad a bare nine months after they was wed, or even sooner, some said. A rare one she'd been as a lass, always on at her faither to let her stick her nose into colliery affairs, hanging about the pit office, driving the men and the clerks to distraction with her everlasting questions and even begging to be allowed to go underground, so he'd heard. It was nearly twenty years since a woman had worked in the roadways of Mr Townley's pits, pushing and pulling the corves, the baskets in which the coal was heaped, from the pit face to the pit bottom and the idea that this one should be allowed to satisfy her female curiosity, which is all it was, was so bloody daft he was not surprised the maister had refused her.

Across the yard on the far side of the headgear which wound up the cages of men and coal, shawled women, pit brow lassies working in the open-sided screen-room on the moving picking-belts sorting coal, nudged one another, staring in astonishment. They knew who she was, of course, for didn't everyone in Marfield know the Townleys, especially since the old scandal had been reopened, and they watched her with great interest as though expecting the chain of events to have altered her in some way, whispering to one another on the mystery of what she was doing here.

"'Ay up, Lennie, what the 'ell d'yer think yer doin'?" an aggrieved voice called from the iron cage which had just brought the colliers from the pit bottom. "Asta fell asleep or is tha' goin' ter let us out've 'ere? In tha' own good time, o' course," the voice added sarcastically.

The banksman, Lenny Carter, was jolted from his open-mouthed contemplation of the maister's lass, returning hastily to his job which was to regulate the movement of men and materials up and down the shaft. An important job, for on him depended the safety of the hundreds of men and boys who worked in shifts at Fielden, bringing the coal from the black depths of the mine

"I were just wondering' what the 'ell she were up to," he said to the man who had complained, nodding his head in the direction of Jenna Macrae who was carrying her son up the steps to the office, "an' what the 'eck she's doin' fetchin' that bairn 'ere, of all places."

The men all stopped to stare, milling about like sheep. It was a pleasant day, the cold, damp drizzle which had plagued them for a fortnight gone almost overnight. The hawthorn hedges were in bloom, each field surrounding the town enclosed in a ribbon of white and where the streams ran tiny petals drifted, blown there by a breeze which was almost summery. There were bluebells in Seven Cows Wood making a hazed carpet of blue on which Tim Spencer did his best to make love to Bryony Townley while above them a thrush and a blackbird competed for who was the most accomplished songster.

The sun was warm and in the shining carriage which stood so incongruously in the cluttered and busy yard at Fielden Colliery, the plainly dressed woman fretted on how long her mistress was to keep the bairn in this dreadful place and had she known she was to sit out here with the sun's warmth beating down on her she would have left off her winter undergarments. The man on the coachman's seat straightened his back, keeping his eyes on his nervous horses, conscious of the stares and smirks of the colliers who were just changing shifts.

Consternation ran rife as Jenna entered the office, the clerks there staring in slack-jawed stupefaction at this breathtaking vision which had invaded their dim and dusty world. The sunlight laid slender fingers across high desks littered with papers and invaded stacks of ledgers, tin boxes, shelves on which books of a technical nature appertaining to the getting of coal from the ground lurched against one another. There were framed pictures on the walls of stern-faced gentlemen with whiskers and high collars, Jenna's ancestors since this colliery had opened by her mama's grandfather, or was it great-grandfather?

"Good morning, Mr Chalmers, Mr Andrews," she said airily just as though Jenna and Ewan Macrae were accustomed to entering this office every day of the week and as she spoke, remembering at last their manners, the two flabbergasted men and the lad who was their clerk sprang to their feet. They could not tear their eyes away from the wondrous flower garden of cream silk roses which was perched dashingly on Miss Jenna's head, the soft cream elegance of her voile morning gown though the hem was sadly stained. The skirt was wide, the bodice well fitted to her quite superb bosom and about her waist was a cream satin sash. Magnificent pearls glowed in her ears and they could not help but privately think that never in their lives had they seen anyone so sadly out of place as she was.

And the child! A fine boy dressed in the fashion with which those of the upper classes clothed even their sons. A beautifully smocked and embroidered dress of white muslin, long-sleeved with a deep, lace-edged yoke. He wore white stockings and tiny white kid boots, an enchanting lace-trimmed bonnet tied with broad satin ribbons. From beneath its brim his baby face beamed amiably at one and all. You could tell who his mother was at once, and his grandfather, with those piercing blue eyes though from what they could see under his bonnet he'd not the bright copper curls of their master's daughter.

"Nay, Miss Jenna," Mr Chalmers, who was head clerk, said disapprovingly, his demeanour telling her he was not at all pleased with her foolishness in coming here though there was nothing he could do about it, of course. She had a perfect right to do as she pleased, within reason, being the master's daughter and until the master told him differently Mr Chalmers could not refuse her entry to the office. This was no place for her though, especially dressed up as she was and, if she was forced to come, wouldn't you think she'd have had the good sense to wear a dark colour?

"Yes, Mr Chalmers?" she asked him calmly, "you have something you wished to say to me?" and in her arms the child turned to look at her, then reached up a plump hand to grab at her earrings.

She smiled at him. "No, darling, you cannot have

Mama's earrings," taking his wandering hand and kissing the palm. The clerks shuffled their feet and looked hastily away as though they had caught her out in something which was not quite respectable and her smile deepened.

"Mr Chalmers?" she asked enquiringly.

"Well, Miss Jenna . . . er . . . Mrs Macrae," remembering suddenly the name of her husband. "I was only wondering . . ."

"Yes?" She held her son's hand as he struggled to reach the roses on her hat.

"What tha' wanted?" Mr Chalmers finished lamely.

Her face, which had been warmly smiling at them and at her squirming son, instantly became aloof, lofty, distant and the baby, sensing something in her which alarmed him, became still, drawing away in her arms to stare into her face.

"Is my . . . my father in his office, Mr Chalmers? If so I would be glad of a word with him." The roses on her hat lifted and bobbed as she raised an imperious chin.

"No, not at the moment, Miss . . . Mrs Macrae. He's been called over to Kenworth, him an' Master Simeon."

The dreadful consideration of what had been revealed in the Townley family recently and this young woman's connection with it turned the flesh of Mr Chalmers's face to the livid purple of a plum as he spoke the name of his master's illegitimate son and he felt the need to apologise but it was nothing to do with him, was it? The lad's name must be spoken even if, as was evident, the master's daughter didn't like it. "There was some problem with an order," he continued, "so they went over there to deal with it. Mr Townley's teaching Master . . ."

Suddenly conscious that the two other clerks were still staring in fascinated admiration at their master's dashing daughter he turned to them and indicated sharply that they were to get on with their work which they did, though the lad was seen to peep under his brow a time or two when he thought no one was looking.

"When will he be back, Mr Chalmers? Or is he to remain at Kenworth for any length of time?" Master Simeon might never have been mentioned.

"Now that I couldn't say, Mrs Macrae. You never know how long these things are going to take."

It was as he spoke that the two horsemen rode into the yard and with the sinking sensation inside which had come with her all the way from Beechfield Lodge, Jenna recognised her father. Behind him was Simeon Townley.

"Aah, here he is now, Mrs Macrae," and if Mr Chalmers could have added "thank God" without appearing impertinent to his employer's daughter, he would have said it.

From the high window of the office Jenna watched the expressions chase one another across her father's face as he recognised her carriage and for a moment she felt her heart move with love for him, to soften and almost smile. It seemed so long since she had spoken to him with that affectionate humour they had once known between them. So long since she had been held in his arms, felt his kiss on her cheek and brow, seen him smile wryly at her outrageous behaviour, felt his protection, his support, the sheltering love he had always surrounded her with. Oh, he would still provide it had she allowed it but it could not be. Not now, not while that insolently smiling, devastatingly handsome youth whom he claimed to be his son was beside him.

Jonas Townley looked better than he had at Amy Spencer's wedding though his face was still strained, etched with the sorrow his daughter's hostility had caused in him. The coughing sickness, the clogged chest and difficult breathing which was the collier's affliction, had eased with the warmer weather. Though his wife begged him to give it up, to leave it to Mark Eason and his other efficient managers who could just as easily deal with it all, reporting to him at home and from where he could supervise it, he was obsessed with his need to teach his son, who would one day take it over, he told her, before he could himself retire. Before he died, he had been about to say which, of course, he would not do for a long time yet, but the lad was . . . well, young and high-spirited and though he had settled amazingly well since he had learned of his true parentage and was eager to learn, he must buckle down to the responsibility which would be his in due course. There was plenty of time but it could not be wasted with Jonas Townley lolling at home and getting fat, he had said to his wife, smiling.

He was smiling now as he bounded up the steps to the office, young again and eager, for he had seen her, his beloved daughter, his grandson in her arms, in the office window. His son moved swiftly at his back, the smile on his face the enigmatic one he had assumed when he had discovered that this young woman was not his cousin but his half-sister, that the man he called uncle, was in fact his father, and that the vast wealth of the Townley empire was, if he was clever, at his disposal. In his eyes was that gleam of triumph he could not hide whenever Jenna Macrae revealed the extent of her outrage, her pain, her bitterness and her hopeless determination to force her father to renounce him and Bryony which Simeon now knew he would never do.

Jenna saw it and her face was as cold and rigid as marble, bloodless except for the vivid apricot of her mouth, the glittering blue-green transparency of her eyes and the scatter of golden freckles across her nose. She held the baby so tightly he began to struggle, his face screwed into bright indignation and a wail erupted from his shining pink mouth in which two tiny teeth could be seen.

"Jenna . . ." Her father paused on the threshold of the office, his face filled with love and a dawning hope. He did not stop to wonder why she had come here and not to Bank House, nor why she had brought her son. It was enough that she had. That she was – surely – about to extend the olive branch, to speak of a reconciliation, an end to this terrible estrangement which had existed between them for almost six months. That she understood the dreadful dilemma in which he had found himself since. Simeon and Bryony were just as much his children as she, Beth, Nancy and Rose were. He had no idea what he would have done had the truth not been revealed and even now he could not get it out of Bryony who had revealed it to her. Of course, neither of his children by Leah Wood would have been neglected, financially that is, after his death but now, now that it was all out in the open, different arrangements could be made and he meant to discuss it with Jenna and Simeon. Explain it to them. What he wanted of them. What he expected of them. He meant to be fair, naturally and when Jenna heard what he had to say she would understand and forgive.

He put out a hand, his eyes going to the boy in her arms, a boy strangely like the one at his back. Dark, eyes of turquoise, handsome and very evidently strong-willed, even at his tender age.

"Papa." His daughter's voice was icy.

"It's good to see you, Jenna, and . . . and my grandson."

The men at their desks were wide-eyed and open-mouthed, each one with his pen poised in his hand waiting with bated breath to see what would happen next. They all knew how their employer doted on that bastard son of his and what would he, Master Simeon, make of this new contender for his father's affections? This bawling infant whose ancestry was so apparent.

Nothing, it seemed, or so Simeon Townley's indolently leaning figure suggested and the expression of
bored indifference on his face would have incensed his
father had he had eyes for anyone but his daughter and
his grandson. Simeon was smiling that sly smile of
self-congratulation which Mr Townley, usually so quick
to show his displeasure, did not appear to notice. The lad
flicked an imaginary speck of dust from his immaculate
jacket, of which he had many these days, and yawned
behind his hand.

"May I take him, Jenna?" Her papa's voice was
pleading and the expression on his face was one she
had never seen before.

"Perhaps we might go into your office, Papa?" she
answered civilly enough, holding her son more closely
to her but there was still ice in her voice, ice so cold and
painful her father could not fail to feel it.

"Of course." He swallowed painfully then moved
across the outer office, opening wide the door to his
own room in which a good fire blazed. It was a fine
room created by Jenna's great-grandfather as his fortunes
grew, with panelled walls and a vast stretch of deep carpet
leading to a splendid mahogany desk.

"Perhaps we might have some coffee, Chalmers," he
called over his shoulder as he ushered the stiff figure of
his daughter across the threshold. His son straightened
and with the arrogant grace of the young, made as though
to follow his father and half-sister into his father's office
for surely whatever Jenna had to say, which must be about
the collieries and his father's many business interests, was
of great concern, as his father's son, to himself, but she
turned her head sharply.

"Not you," she said scathingly, reducing him to the
status of the office boy who was scuttling to make
the coffee.

"But Jenna, Simeon is . . ." Her father's protests could

scarcely be heard above the sound of the yelling baby but they all heard her answer.

"He is nothing to *me*, Papa, and as far as I am concerned has as little right as your clerks to hear what I have to say to you. It is a family matter, *our* family, not his." There was a flush now beneath her fine creamy skin and her eyes were narrow, gleaming slits of pure hatred as she grabbed the door from her father and slammed it in Simeon's face.

"Jenna . . ."

"Papa, I have brought your grandson to visit you. The boy who will one day become the man to run your collieries. As you can see he is a fine boy. Take him. Hold him, he will not mind," and without further ado Ewan Macrae was placed in his grandfather's eager arms.

They drank coffee, awkward and, at least on Jenna's part, distantly aloof. The child eased things, squirming on his grandfather's lap, lively and doing his best to stand, to walk up his grandfather's chest on sturdy legs as Jonas's hands held him firmly under his armpits. He did his utmost to stuff his grandfather's gold hunter watch in his mouth, hauled on the chain which held it, banged on the desk with his fists and yelled his way into his grandfather's heart as his mother had intended, then . . .

"Will you send the boy to fetch Nanny Abigail, Papa? She can take him up to see Mama while you and I talk. Tell her to send the carriage back for me. I should be no more than an hour."

If he was disappointed to be deprived of his lively grandson so soon Jonas made no fuss about it. He was exultant that he and his girl were talking. That was all he wanted, a chance to explain, to ask for her understanding. She was a woman who loved a man and, it was very evident, that man loved her, so could she not now appreciate how love could take a man's –

and woman's – senses, his reason, his sanity and compel him to do things which he knew, even while he did them, were wrong, were to hurt others.

"Now then, Papa," she began when the boy and Nanny Abigail had been driven through the yard gate and the carriage turned in the direction of Bank House. "You have seen your grandson and . . . well . . . I have not yet told Conal so I would be obliged if you would keep it to yourself, but I have reason to believe I am to have another child."

"Jenna." He leaned joyfully towards her, giving the impression of great relief since with two children she could hardly take an active interest in the collieries which is what he had feared this visit was about. She had always argued vociferously that she could see no reason why a woman, herself in fact, could not run his business concerns as well as any man and he had allowed her, before her timely marriage to Conal Macrae, a certain amount of freedom, perhaps a half-formed belief that she might do so. It was different now, naturally, with Simeon proclaimed as his son and did not her words, her matter-of-fact acceptance of a second pregnancy, bear up his thoughts?

She drew back from his hand, her face closed and expressionless.

"Yes, I can see you understand, Papa. Two children . . ." Her face softened for a moment. "With two as lively and . . ." She began to smile. "Ewan is very dear to me and I find a great deal of satisfaction, content, in caring for him as much as I am able – in the nursery, I mean. With another my time will be even more . . . besides which, Conal would not allow me to . . ."

Her face lost its bemused expression of smiling contemplation, of what was evidently a great happiness within her and she drew herself together with a slight frown.

"However, there is still the matter of the bastards to consider."

"The . . ." Her father plunged backwards violently, his manner that of a man who thinks himself to be fondling a kitten only to find it is a full-grown and angry she-cat. "Jenna!"

"Oh yes, that is what they are, Papa, no matter how you wrap it up and tie on a gaily coloured ribbon. That is what they are to me and to the rest of Marfield and as such they have no entitlement to anything my grandfather Fielden built up and I am amazed that Mama, who was a Fielden, has not made that clear to you. This colliery and Kenworth were dug out of the ground by Fielden men. It is their sweat, their shrewdness, their strength and courage and willingness to gamble which made the wealth for you to do the same at Townley. Your father and brother ruined their pit and it was not until you married my mother that you could get your hands on the cash to reopen it. She did that for you. *My* mother, not Simeon's. I am not denigrating your efforts, Papa, far from it, for since that day you have regenerated Townley, gambled yourself, I have seen it, and made our family one of the wealthiest in Lancashire. Our family, not the . . . the colliers from where your . . . your bastards come. They have no right to it. None! I am fully aware . . . oh yes, how could I be otherwise since I have had my face rubbed in it with every sign of relish by that youth out there," tossing her head in bitter and contemptuous recrimination at the door behind which Simeon Townley still hung aimlessly about. "I am forcibly reminded at every turn that he and his sister are your children but I will be brutal . . ."

"You seem not to flinch from that, Jenna."

"And you have not, Papa? It is because of you that I am kept from my home and my . . ."

"No . . . no."

"Oh yes, but what I was about to say is this. If they

are your children and you don't deny it, they have no
Fielden blood in them. Yours, true, but then you are not
a Fielden. My son is!"

There was a long and painful silence in which the
cheerful ticking of the satin-wood pendulum clock on the
wall and the hiss and crackle of the flames in the hearth
were the only sounds within the room. From the yard
came the heavy strike of horses' hooves and the clangour
of the iron-rimmed wheels of the waggons they pulled
on the cobbles. Men shouted and the rhythmic sound
of the winding gear vied with the noise of the shunting
coal waggons as they were hauled along the track. A dog
barked and a male voice yelled at it to behave. That would
be Jem Pickup's brown and white whippet which went
everywhere with him. A gentle, affectionate dog, aloof
with strangers, indeed with anyone but Jem for whom he
waited at the end of each shift. There he would be where
Jem had placed him just before he went down, waiting for
his master to come up. It was almost as though he knew
the workings of the pit, standing up at the very moment
Jem stepped into the cage at the pit bottom, there waiting
for him as he stepped out of it, his bark growing more
ecstatic as the cage ascended.

"Aye up, lad," Jem would say and the dog would fall in
beside him as they made their way up to Colliers Row.

"Did you hear me, Papa?" Jenna asked calmly.

Jonas Townley frowned. "Aye, I did, lass."

"Then . . .?"

"What are you asking me, Jenna?"

"I think you know, Papa."

"I suppose I do but I'd be obliged if you would put it
into words."

"I am your daughter, Papa. Your eldest daughter. My
sisters and I would, had you not . . ."

"Sinned?"

"If you like."

"That is what you think so why not say it, Jenna?"

"You wronged Mama and your . . . your . . ."

"Mistress? You seem to be having trouble with your words today, lass. And you the one who always insisted we call a spade a bloody spade."

"Very well, Papa. You did us all a great wrong, and worse, did not seem to care about it."

"Did your mother say that?"

"No, I am saying it but I realise it cannot be undone. It could be made worse though, if you were to put that . . . that boy out there in charge of it all."

"And who do you suggest instead of him? That's if I intend to do it?"

"Don't you?"

"He is my son."

"I am your daughter." She held up her hand as he would have interrupted. "No, let me finish. This could go on for ever, I realise that. You feel you owe them, your . . ."

"Don't keep calling them by that name, Jenna. It does you no credit."

"Very well. Your *other* children. You feel you owe them something though I cannot agree. But we, your daughters, have a moral entitlement, surely, to what our Fielden grandfather built."

"What do you want, Jenna?" her father asked her wearily.

"I cannot stop you from making the . . . the others some sort of allowance. Something to get her married and I suppose he must have his fine jackets and horses and everything that goes with them. Perhaps you could set him up in a business which would provide them for him." Her voice was filled with her contemptuous loathing for her half-brother. "But as for the pits, I am asking you to put in trustworthy managers to run them, men who will give honest service. Experienced men with a good record. Bookkeepers and accountants who will not cheat you and all of them to be under the supervision of myself and my husband."

"And does Conal agree to this?"

"He will when I explain it to him."

"I see."

"From the profits, and there will be profits, myself and my sisters will receive our share."

"And is that all, Jenna?"

"No."

"I thought not."

"I want you to leave it all to my son. Your grandson, Ewan Macrae. To be his when he reaches the age of twenty-one. To tie it up in some sort of . . . well, the lawyers will know how to go about it. Just so that *they* cannot get their hands on it. I am willing to . . . to keep out of it if you will leave it all to Ewan."

"I see."

"And . . . and you agree?" She leaned forward eagerly.

"I will have to consider it. Talk it over with your mother."

"And if she agrees?"

"I am promising you nothing, child . . ."

"I am not a child, Papa, and I can promise you this. If that boy out there and his sister get one penny of what I consider to be my son's inheritance then you and I will never speak to one another again."

Chapter Twenty-four

Before she became too cumbersome and weary with their second child, Conal said to his wife, did she not think it would be pleasant and only polite to visit for the first time her new Scottish family in Renfrewshire? They had been married for over a year now and since their wedding day had not renewed her brief acquaintance with his grandfather who was a great age, his aunts and uncles and cousins and the multitude of the clan who were anxious for a "wee gleg" at this new relative of theirs. Two if you counted Ewan whom his great-grandfather would wish to inspect. The brig *Thistle*, his only sailing ship, was to sail to Clydeside during the last week in May with a cargo of pitch and resin for the shipyards at Whitehaven, salt to Maryport herring salteries, taking on iron ore from there to the Clyde. A journey of no more than three or four days, wind and weather permitting, naturally.

Jenna had been somewhat quiet and distracted ever since she had visited her father in Marfield, a visit about which she had been less than forthcoming, saying only that she "hoped to make matters right" between them. More than that she did not tell him but it seemed she was now waiting for Jonas Townley to make the next move. So while she waited might not a little trip do her good? He had been delighted with her news that she was to have another child, calling her a "good girl" not to make a fuss about it and promising that he would ensure she had no more for a year or two, or even three, smiling approvingly into her curiously passive face.

The ship had delighted her. One hundred and eighty tons burthen, Conal had told her, swift and graceful, a brigantine with one deck and two masts. She was small, but neat as a pin and scrubbed so clean the decking was almost white. Jenna had bounded up the gangway with the eagerness of a lad and her the mother of one and another to come, Conal had whispered in her ear. Nanny Abigail, with Ewan in her arms, was not so enthusiastic, conscious of the stares of the seamen who were craning to get a look at their employer's young wife, and of the dock labourers who swarmed at her back. Orders were barked and men jumped to obey them as preparation for *Thistle*'s sailing went ahead. Sacks and barrels were being unloaded from a waggon and heaved on to the backs of a line of labourers who were running them up on board. All about them was the most melodious din as the ship cast off and it was repeated at regular intervals along the whole of the dock frontage, sometimes in reverse as ships of all shapes and sizes, flying the flags of a dozen shipping companies prepared to sail, or dock. Ships of the Cunard Line, White Star Line and Hemingway Line.

The river beyond *Thistle* was crowded with so many vessels it was difficult to see how they managed to avoid colliding with one another. Conal stood beside her, his son in his arms, having taken pity on Nanny Abigail and sent her off to her tiny cabin, pointing out to Jenna and the wide-eyed boy the small, strongly built pilot boats which buffetted through many a fearful night and encountered many a fearful storm to escort the vessels which frequented the port. Packet ships to Philadelphia and New York; small, full-bodied merchant ships off to China and Australia; paddle steamers going no further than across the water to New Brighton. A brigantine very much like *Thistle* running on the flood to catch the tide into Garston. Four-masted barques and schooners, full-rigged clipper ships, so fast and beautiful they stopped the breath, frigates and the squat clumsiness of the Mersey lighter which was actually a sailing barge and used to carry freight from ship to shore.

Since early in the eighteenth century and even before, Conal explained to Jenna, and to his son who appeared to listen raptly, the River Mersey had been a highway for commercial expansion which had made Liverpool the great city it was, from the traffic in local produce at the beginning of the eighteenth century to the flooding of imports from the colonial empire in this great nineteenth century and the trade of a manufacturing nation which Britain had become. Salt, produced locally, had been the first merchandise to be traded for sheepskins, tallow, linen, flax and wool from Ireland. Ships began to go to Spain and France, bringing back soap, fruit and fine wine. The continent of India was next where coal and salt were taken and it was Liverpool which controlled the export trade for these two commodities and for the manufactured goods produced within a radius of one hundred miles from the port.

Jenna knew the rest for had he not told her of his own shipping enterprises, Conal said, as he smiled down into her enraptured face, his own alight with his love, not just for her and the crowing baby in his arms, but for this great river. This great city which, though it had not been his birthplace, was close to his heart. There was harbourage here for ships from North America, South America, the Indies, China, from Australia, New Zealand, Canada, Argentina, South Africa, Brazil and the nearer shores of the Mediterranean.

"And what is that far point, where the ferry is going?" she asked.

"That's New Brighton. Look, on a fine day such as this you can see from the Cheshire woods in the south . . . there . . . can you see where my finger is pointing?"

"Yes."

"You can see right along the whole line of the Cheshire coast from Eastham to New Brighton and the Irish Channel in the north. Beyond is Bootle Bay and the Rock Perch Lighthouse and Fort. When we come home I'll take you and the boy along the western wall which is on this side of the river. It's one of the longest marine parades in the kingdom, they say, with fine views. But let us first enjoy this one and then I'll show you where you and I will sleep. I think you'll like it. Not quite as spacious as what you are used to but very comfortable."

"Will I make a good sailor, Conal?" she asked anxiously as he guided her solicitously through a knot of respectful seamen who all wore what was known as a gansey, a fisherman's jersey of dark blue wool with an elaborate pattern of stitching, with trousers of oilskin.

"It willna be rough, lassie, not in coastal waters and if it is, knowing you as I do, I doubt you'll let it trouble you. *Thistle* can fly like a bird and skim the waves like a dolphin, no matter how tall," and Jenna, who had never clapped eyes on this wondrous creature, could only take his word for it.

She enjoyed every moment of the voyage right from the moment the order came to cast off and the graceful little ship edged out into the traffic and laid a course outward to the north of the river which was beyond the influence of the Gulf Stream, Conal explained. The homeward journey would bring them to the south in the strength of its current. He stood beside her aft of the deckhouse where their cabin was, and to starboard as she was to call it, so that she might watch first the vast and turbulent clamour of the docks and the ships on the right-hand shore, and then as they drew towards the river's mouth, the long golden sweep of the Bootle foreshore.

The Bootle Marks stood out from the shallow water close to the sands, two stone fingers seventy-five feet tall pointing heavenwards, the base of each surrounded by steps on which tiny figures sat dangling their feet in the water. It was a warm day, clear and sunny and the long stretch of beach was alive with small, foreshortened figures. Some were daring the cold waters of the sea, ladies dressed in what was known as the Zouave Marine Swimming Costume which consisted of a body and trousers in dark blue serge, cut all in one to preserve modesty and allow perfect liberty of action, or so the advertisement would have those who wore them believe.

There were bathing machines on wheels standing in neat rows for all the world like up-ended coffins with painted roofs and narrow doors at the front. A few were actually in the gently lapping water, drawn there by patient horses and from them modestly garbed females emerged to splash and scream. Horsemen galloped their mounts, hazarding the lives and limbs of strolling ladies and gentlemen and children with buckets and spades. Small rowing boats carried would-be sailors a few feet from the shore. It was like watching a play, Jenna thought, the players acting out their parts for the private entertainment of those who watched from the dipping bows of the passing ships.

On past the flat expanse of Southport, of Blackpool and the port of Fleetwood which was almost as crowded as Liverpool with its busy fishing fleet. Across Morecambe Bay to the tip of Cumberland where lay Millom and Haverigg; on to Ravenglass behind which rose the rugged majesty of Sca Fell and Caw Fell.

Was it not time she rested in her cabin, Conal asked her, or was she to stand enchanted like some mythical fairy princess, frozen to the rail for ever?

They came at last to the grey-faced cliffs which loomed

from the sea on the western shores of St Bees Head, the hardy splendour of the mountains beyond, green and brown and remote but becoming softer, gentler, smoother as they ran down to the clifftop at Whitehaven, its harbour as lively as that of Fleetwood and where *Thistle*'s cargo was unloaded and another taken on, the procedure repeated when they reached Maryport. On beyond the wide bay of the Solway Firth, flying up the misted coast clear of Girvan and Ayr until they entered the Firth of Clyde.

All about them were the green hills of Scotland, their grandeur reflected in the clear and shimmering waters of the River Clyde, incandescent in the morning light. The weather had continued fine for the whole of the voyage. It was so fine and clear Jenna could see the close-packed chimneys of what Conal told her was the town of Paisley and to the east the soaring rooftops and spires of Glasgow. Behind them and about them were the narrowing waters of the Clyde, crammed from shore to shore with hundreds of ships and to the water's edge rolled the dense mass of hills from as far away as the peaks of Argyll to the nearer slopes and ridges of Cowal.

Jenna's rapt contemplation of this fascinating scene was not to last much longer for no sooner had they entered the river, or so it seemed to her, than they were at their berth and from then on for the next week she was for ever surrounded by the softly spoken, good-humoured members of the clan Macrae.

Macrae of Glencairn was the head of the family and commanded the respect and loyalty of them all. For centuries chiefs had adopted the title in the manner of Conal's grandfather, Macrae of Glencairn but it was abbreviated now to merely the Macrae.

The Macrae was kind to her, showing a great interest in her lively son, approving with a respectful but thorough glance the slight thickening of her figure in her growing pregnancy. She was included in family parties and celebrations with the scattered members of the clan and given a plaid, the Macrae plaid, to wear over her shoulder. Conal would not let her ride but putting her up before him on a sturdy bay, he took her into the hills at the back of Paisley, setting her down gently to stand beside her to look down on the town, split through its centre by the gleaming silvery ribbon of the White Cart Water.

He was pleased with her. She had behaved impeccably with none of her usual outspoken frankness or restless vigour. She showed intelligent interest in the vast ramifications of the clan and what concerned them, most of whom appeared to be related to one another. She was never bored and when questioned on her own life answered pleasantly. She was proud of her son and let them see it and they liked that for was he not a Macrae from the tumble of his dark hair, his determined, scrabbling attempts to crawl, his fearless efforts to ride on the back of one of the enormous shaggy dogs which sprawled about the great hall of Glencairn Castle and his amiable acceptance of the bearded strangers who were his formidable relatives. She was a Sassenach, like Conal's mother but that could not be helped. The boy was a true Scot!

Conal took her to see the port of Glasgow from where ships had conveniently sailed across the Atlantic to the British colonies in North America carrying trade to the new world since the middle of the seventeenth century. He showed her many of the splendid things which were the proud heritage of a Scot, ranging from the vast splendour of the cathedral to the field at Langside on the south of the Clyde where the tragedy of Mary, Queen of Scots had ended.

They strolled on Glasgow Green, a public park beside the Clyde, from where Bonny Prince Charlie had reviewed his bedraggled army after its long march from Derby.

Jenna took a great deal of interest in his and his country's history, showing it in her eager questions each evening in the great hall of the castle and Conal's family showed their pleasure in her.

"You've won their approval, lassie," her husband told her as he stood at her back with his arms about her while they gazed down towards the bustling River Clyde. From where they stood they could see across to the Kilpatrick Hills and looking westward the glittering waters, not only of the river, but of Gare Loch and Loch Long which ran into it. To Greenock and Gourock and Rothesay and the wide firth which tomorrow would take them home.

"Will you be glad to see home, my love?" he asked, kissing the smooth skin at the nape of her neck.

"It has been lovely, Conal, but . . . yes." Her husband held her to him, her back to his chest, his hands clasped across the gentle swell of her belly within which his second child lay, sighing with great content at this gentler, softer lassie of his, gratified by her behaviour in the midst of the male members of the clan who liked their women soft-spoken and pliable. She would do well now, his Jenna, be the wife he needed, the mother of his growing family of children, the gracious hostess of his home. The scandal of her father's bastards and the furore it had caused in her family had done him some good, if no one else, he privately thought, since it had taken his wife's attention off the vexing question of how she was to learn to run her father's business when her turn came.

Now it was a matter of *who* was to run it. The boy, Simeon Townley, was, Conal was pretty certain, to be in control for wasn't that what every father planned for his son and Jenna must just accept it. And it appeared she had. Her calm manner, her maternal serenity and growing love for her son, her quiet acceptance of this second pregnancy so soon after the first confirmed it and he sighed with satisfaction. It had been grand to see his boyhood home again, to show off his lovely young wife, his sturdy son, his increasing success and prosperity but he was eager to be back at the helm of his bravely sailing and robustly growing business.

"Give me a kiss, my lass," he murmured into her hair, one brown hand cupping the soft swell of her breast. She turned willingly and offered him her lips, closing her eyes so that he might not see, and perhaps recognise, the unquenchable gleam of speculation in them.

She had been home no more than twenty-four hours when Dora tapped on the door of her upstairs sitting-room to tell her that Mrs Townley and the Misses Townley were downstairs enquiring if she was at home. She was writing letters of thanks to the female members of Conal's family, those who had shown her a kindly welcome and made her stay so pleasant. It was a tedious task and one she was glad to put down.

They would have tea on the lawn at the back of the house, she called to Dora as she ran lightly down the stairs to greet her mama and sisters, noting thankfully that Mama had had the good sense not to bring Bryony. Or perhaps Bryony, who was becoming more and more solitary as time went on, her mama's patient and frequent letters told her, had chosen not to come.

"And tell nanny to fetch Master Ewan down, Dora. His grandmama will not recognise him," which was not surprising since her mother had not seen the boy since her last visit in February when she had taken a peep at him in the nursery.

They arranged themselves in a charmingly pretty group about the white wrought-iron table in the comfortable white wicker chairs placed there for them by the smiling, bobbing housemaids. The long, sloping lawns had been freshly cut and watered only that morning and they still sparkled in the sunshine. Their edges were neat, the beds themselves a magnificent blaze of colour with lupins of every shade, French marigolds, their faces as bright as the sun itself, sweet alison and sweet william, larkspur and stock. Symmetrically clipped shrubs made a dense, dark green background for the flowers and a riot of white and pink honeysuckle exploded on every inch of bare wall. Trees planted just beyond the glassed verandah cast their shade over the matronly but still beautiful face and figure of the mother and her four lovely young daughters. All were in white.

It was as though away from the oppressive atmosphere which still pervaded Bank House, the unmarried Townley girls threw off that disillusioned heartache the revelation about Simeon and Bryony had brought them. It returned them to the brightness of spirit, the ease of mind they had so mistakenly taken for granted and they became again Jonas Townley's untroubled young daughters. The old house stood behind them, calm and benevolent, its mixture of cream, buff and grey stonework mellowed by time to the softness of a mature woman's skin. A bulwark of strength, its polished windows looking out benignly, without judgment, its dull, red slate roof willing, whatever might be its creatures' faults, to shelter and protect them.

They talked of Jenna's voyage, her sisters listening with wide-eyed admiration for did it not call for courage to take to the sea in a brigantine which smacked to them of pirates and cutlasses and buried treasure. And were Conal's people very grand? What of their dress and customs for being Scotsmen they would be as wild and fearsome as savages, surely?

They talked of Beth's coming marriage which was to take place at the end of the month and Beth's face grew sweet and flushed as a poppy for was this not the culmination of every young girl's dream and would not a married status give her the respectability she had lost recently? Jenna was married and, as the second daughter it was only right that she should be next. She was to put behind her the horror of . . . of . . . Jenna would know to what she alluded, casting a careful eye in her mama's direction. Every invitation which had been sent out had been accepted since she had made it her business to let it be known that . . . Jenna would know who she meant, with another careful glance at her mama, were not to be present. Papa had been . . . sad, but had agreed it was her day, hers and Frank's and it must be as perfect as she could make it.

And had Jenna heard that Amy, Lady Blenkinsopp no less, was already with child? Yes, married for no more than two months and she had written to her mama to ask if she might come home, "for a visit, she says", Beth went on, the expression on her face saying she was quite amazed at the idea since she could not bear to be parted from her Frank for a moment, she was certain, once they became man and wife.

As Beth spoke Jenna and her mother exchanged glances, the look of two women who, though they did not speak of it, naturally, were happy to be sheltered within the arms of the man they loved, to share a bed with him and bear his children. The dreadful images of the ethereal beauty, the fine, brittle-boned body of the gentle Amy being assaulted nightly by the coarse and bloated Sir Robert was more than they could bear to contemplate.

"Aah, here he comes," Nella Townley said, turning in smiling relief to her grandson's nanny who approached them across the lawn. She took the boy from the nursemaid's arms and placed him to face her on her beautifully gowned lap. He stared at her with big-eyed solemnity, his mouth a little open to reveal his two little teeth which his mama and papa thought so miraculous, then, quick as a flash, reached for his grandmother's fob watch, an exquisite thing bought for her by her husband. It

was of enamelled gold, the case decorated with a pastoral
scene and richly circled with rows of pearls. It hung on a
heavy gold chain about her neck and before she could put
out a hand to stop him it was in Master Ewan's mouth. He
grinned at her then stood up, supported by her hands, his
triumph so endearingly masculine they all laughed.

For half an hour he was passed from lap to lap, watched
by his anxious nursemaid. He had just been fed and his
small stomach was often unreliable and should he be sick
over one of the guests she would be mortified.

The dogs came, let out by George and Eppy who were
sowing leeks and radish, lettuce and beetroot in the
vegetable garden and were, in George's words, "fed up
to the bloody back teeth by their damnblasted howling".
Unused to being shut up the creatures were, having being
spoiled by the young mistress's laxity in allowing them
to sprawl about her sitting-room. George was unaware
that the ladies were enjoying the sunshine beyond the
high wall which separated the vegetable garden and
when Duff and Dory, who loved all and sundry with
equal abandonment, raced over to Master Ewan who
was doing his best to crawl across the grass, "bloody
pandemonium brukk loose" he said later to Percy, still
somewhat white-faced with shock. "Well, he'd thought
them bloody daft creatures were going to make off
wi't babby, didn't he, wi' that there barmy nursemaid
screamin' her bluddy daft head off, but babby had
thought it a grand game, hanging on to't dog's collar
and bein' dragged at great speed across bluddy grass!
Missis had laughed, you know 'er," he said to Percy,
"can't see danger when it bit her bluddy head off, but
it were a right to-do, choose how."

Peace was restored and Ewan, protesting loudly, had
been gathered up by a vastly relieved Nanny Abigail and
returned to the nursery. The visitors sat on, saying they
should really be going but the garden was so pleasant

and the sunshine a blessing. Beth hoped it would be like this for her wedding day, sighing rapturously, not only at the prospect of being the bride, which was all she had ever aspired to be, but the relief of knowing she was to leave the wretched misery of her father's house for her own dear little villa in Sandown Place. What went on at Bank House, which would now always hold bad memories for her despite her happy childhood, would no longer be her concern. Simeon and Bryony still lived there, showing no sign, now that the dreadful truth was known, of moving perhaps to another establishment which she at least thought to be only proper. It was quite dreadful at mealtimes when Papa tried so hard to keep some sort of conversation going but with herself and her sisters refusing to speak to Simeon and Bryony, and Bryony taking no interest anyway, it had all become too wearing. Bryony was for ever off with that great dog of hers, no one knew where and she refused to say, even when Mama demanded it of her, and of course Simeon dragged about at Papa's heels, so for the most part she and Nancy and Rose were left in peace.

Suddenly she turned to her mother, the shade of the pretty lace parasol she held dappling her pale amber skin with moving patterns of gold. Beneath the brim of her straw bonnet her green eyes snapped with excitement.

"Mama, we have not told Jenna the news." She opened wide her eyes and drew in her breath with such childish delight Jenna wondered somewhat cynically how this pretty little girl who had no thought in her but to play at "house", would take to the duties, in and out of her bed, but mostly in, when she married Frank Miller. Had she the faintest idea of what marriage entailed? She was wrapped up in her dreams of her green velvet curtains, her Wedgwood tea service, the splendour of her new carpet, so what Frank Miller might do to her on her wedding night and every night thereafter simply did not seem to occur to her. Still, she was no worse off than any other seventeen-year-old bride and certainly more fortunate than poor Amy! At least Frank was young and wholesome.

"What news, darling?" her mother asked her smilingly.

"You know, Mama. About . . . Oh, may I tell her, Mama, may I?"

"About what, Beth?" Her mother was genuinely puzzled.

"Oh, Mama, really." Beth, on whose mind one and one subject only was uppermost, was plainly exasperated.

"For heaven's sake, tell her," Rose groaned. Rose, at fifteen the most like her eldest sister in looks and in temperament and inclined to be somewhat frank and outspoken as Jenna was, was clearly bored now that the merry sweetness of her nephew and the two amusing dogs had been banished.

"There is no need to be rude, Rose," Beth reproved her. "Ladies do not—"

"If you don't tell her I will," Rose warned and Nancy, who always sided with Beth, tutted disapprovingly.

"Well if someone doesn't tell me I shall call for your carriage and send you all home," Jenna declared.

"I don't blame you, dearest, but really, for the life of me . . ."

"Mama! Such an important event and you have forgotten it already. Of course it won't be as . . . well, it is her *second* and of course . . ."

"Dear sweet heaven, save me from this," Jenna moaned.

"Well, if Mama can't say then I will." Beth lifted her head importantly.

"Go on then."

"It's Aunt Linnet—"

"Oh of course," Nella Townley interrupted. "You are

quite right, my dear. It is most remiss of me to forget
such a momentous and . . . well, happy occasion. After
all Julian has been dead for . . ."

"Mama!"

"I'm so sorry, Beth, do go on."

Beth, gratified by her status of storyteller, smiled,
turning once more to Jenna.

"Aunt Linnet is to marry again." She sat back, allowing
Jenna to digest this prodigious news, begging her to share
her own amazement, preening as though the whole thing
was her doing.

"Good God!"

"And not only that," Beth went on before anyone
else could take up the story, "she is to marry into the
peerage!"

"Good God," Jenna said again.

"Yes, you might well be astonished for we all were. He
is a viscount. A widower who has grown-up sons so Aunt
Linnet will not be expected to . . . well, have children,
but she will be a viscountess, Jenna, think of that."

"I am. My God, she will be even more unbearable."

"Jenna!"

"Well, she will, Mama, and you know it."

"Even if she is it will not trouble you, child, since
she is to live in Leicestershire or Warwickshire or
somewhere south."

"My God, Viscountess? What is her name to be?"

"Overton, I believe."

"The Viscountess Overton!"

"That is her social title. Formally she will be the Right
Honourable Viscountess Overton."

"My God, there'll be no living with her."

"It's poor Tim I'm sorry for. Rattling about all alone
in that enormous place and him not nineteen yet."

Chapter Twenty-five

The manservant stared in amazement at the lovely young girl who stood on the doorstep then his eyes moved over her shoulder to the long and empty driveway at the back of her. His expression changed through varying degrees of admiration, bewilderment, back to admiration and then to the slightly sneering expression his sort reserved for those who were not lower than him, but lower than those the footman served.

Looming protectively beside the girl was an enormous dog.

"Yes?" the footman said, raising his chin. He seemed to look somewhat to the side of her left ear as though she was not splendid enough to deserve his full gaze. He had at once understood the implication of the carriage-less drive-way and ladies, the ones who had called at Daresbury Park before his mistress Lady Spencer, now Viscountess Overton, had remarried, did not make their calls on foot with a dog at their side, nor did they themselves knock at the door. A groom, or at the very least a coachman did that for them, enquiring if the mistress of the house was at home. This one, though she was certainly good-looking in a dark and foreign way and was dressed as fashionably and as expensively as any he had seen come through this doorway, had neither carriage nor coachman and what interpretation could he put on that? She had a small bag with her.

"I wish to speak to Sir Timothy, if you please," the girl said, "and don't tell me he is not at home for I have just seen him take his hunter round to the stable yard."

"I beg your pardon?"

"I think you heard me. I will wait in the hall," she declared, and short of hustling her off the doorstep or closing the door in her face, there was nothing he could do except allow it.

"I'm not sure if . . ." He made one last effort to assert his authority, not awfully certain really why he should do so since she was quite presentable but she moved inside briskly, handing him her bag, then seated herself gracefully on a straight-backed chair directly opposite the cheerfully blazing log fire, the dog flopping to the floor beside her.

Though it was August it was not warm. The hall was vast, lofty and the warmth of the fire barely reached more than six feet from the fireplace but she placed herself within its orbit like a kitten settling itself on a hearth-rug. There were deep leather armchairs, a table on which an enormous copper bowl of late roses stood, but there were already, though the new viscountess had been gone no more than a few days, signs of slight neglect. Rose petals were scattered on the table top where they had fallen as the flowers had begun to droop. There was a fine layer of dust on the arms of the chair where the visitor sat, and on the mantelshelf above the fireplace. The hearth was littered with ash and the cushions on the chairs were still squashed where the last person to occupy them had sat.

"May I tell the master who is calling?" the manservant asked, doing his best to be supercilious.

"No, you may not," the girl answered and he was amazed at her hauteur for one did not come across it in a female so young.

"I'll wait here," she added, turning a cool stare on him which told him he'd best be on his way.

While she waited she allowed her eyes to travel critically about the room. She was well aware that Lady Spencer, as she had been then, had spent vast amounts of her father's money on Daresbury Park when she had married Sir Julian. It had been barren and comfortless, she had heard, but Lady Spencer had installed bathrooms and flush water closets, modernised the kitchens, redecorated every room and covered acres of stone floors with rich, deep-piled carpets. The old tapestries which had mouldered on the walls for generations had been unceremoniously thrown on to the gardeners' bonfire, the bare stone walls panelled in wood and fires lit in every room to draw out the chill of centuries. Here in the hall a grand piano had been placed with a fine fringed shawl thrown across it. There was a heavy oak writing desk for the use of guests, rich, bright rugs were scattered about, Chinese lacquer cabinets stood against the walls, a score of antique vases and even, looming at the foot of the stairs, a suit of well-polished armour.

She rose gracefully to her feet as Sir Timothy clattered down the wide staircase and had she not been here on serious business she might have laughed out loud at the expression of vacant bewilderment on his youthful face. He had just come in after riding his hunter over to his Faulkner cousins at Faulkner Hall where he had spent the morning in the pleasant but sometimes alarming pastime of wagering the prowess of his magnificent animal against those of Blake and Chris Faulkner and an assortment of wild-riding, mud-spattered young squireens who always hung about there. Young men with better ancestry than his own, or his cousins'. Young men whose pedigrees stretched back into the past in an unbroken line of aristocratic lineage.

Two posts, across which a pole had been placed, had been set up in the paddock at the back of the stables to be lowered or heightened according to the courage of the rider, the amount of the wager and the breeding of the mount he rode. Blake had declared his animal to be capable of jumping higher then Tim's coal black hunter and as for the hack his brother Chris rode, he might just as well take it now to the knacker's yard since it could not be expected to last the day, let alone jump the height he had ordered the grooms to set the pole.

Tim was a good horseman but the wild and reckless daring of his cousins, of Anthony Sharples and of Toby Lowe who would one day be Sir Toby Lowe and was expected to marry Lady Faulkner's twelve-year-old daughter Caro when she was of marriageable age, was not to Tim's liking. He was a mild-mannered youth and easily led since he yearned for nothing more than to be liked, but he was no hero and though there was no doubt Knight was the best bred animal there, Tim had not the spirit to match the hunter. In an hour he had lost twenty guineas which he could ill afford since his mother was still in charge of his allowance. The only man who could be relied on to help him out was his Uncle Jonas and the idea of riding over to Bank House to beg a loan was one he did not relish. He was feeling surly, inclined to kick at the furniture in the manner of a petulant child and the awareness that tomorrow an unmarried cousin of his dead father, a lady of vast years, was to arrive at Daresbury Park, ostensibly on a visit but, he suspected, to keep an eye on him for a year or two, did not help his temper.

His face lit up at the sight of Bryony Townley standing quietly by his fireside and he felt his heart quicken joyfully. In that first moment he did not question why she was here, or indeed feel anything but joy that she was. His man had said there was a young lady to see him but something in the way Richards had spoken the word lady told Tim she was really no such thing!

"Bryony, darling," he said, his hands reaching out to

her, ready to pull her into his arms as he had done in Seven Cows Wood only last week before his mama's pretty wedding. He had not seen her since then, being concerned with guests come from a distance who had lingered on at Daresbury Park for a day or two. With the absolutely appalling task of telling his hysterically weeping sister, who had come from Northumberland for her mama's wedding that she really must go back there with her husband, almost forcing her, with Sir Robert's vicious assistance, into the carriage.

It had been to recover from that distasteful scene that he had ridden over to Faulkner Hall this morning, wondering moodily as he rode back when he would see Bryony again and here she was looking shyly radiant, casting down her brown eyes in that way he loved for it seemed to tell him he was masterful, a true gentleman and that everything he said or did was, to her, a miracle of manly perfection.

Richards had followed him downstairs, his eyes agog with fascinated interest, wondering how long he could hang about to ascertain what this pretty little thing wanted with his master, but Sir Timothy, seeing where Bryony's eyes went, turned to him and indicated that he should go. He still had time though to hear Sir Timothy ask his visitor in a wondering voice what had brought her here, though unfortunately he was out of earshot before she answered.

"Don't let's speak of that for a moment, Tim." Her voice was soft as she stepped towards him. Her cloak fell back to reveal the fine jacconet of her light summer gown. It was in white with a broad, gold-coloured sash of silk, the neck modest with tiny puff sleeves and a full skirt. The bodice had a row of tiny pearl buttons down the front and from the knees the skirt was layered with a dozen frills, each one edged with a narrow band of the same gold-coloured silk. It was demure but its very demureness emphasised the curve of her full breast and the slenderness of her waist. The cloak had a hood which had dropped back and the rich fall of her dark hair was fastened with a simple golden ribbon. She wore white gloves and dainty white boots. Though Tim and the footman were unaware of it she had ridden in a hired cab from the gates of Bank House to the entrance of the park which surrounded Tim's home and from there she had walked.

She looked like a girl attending her first party, fresh from her maidservant's hand, young and innocent and very desirable.

"It's been more than a week, Tim," she said in her husky voice. "A whole week without seeing you. Will you not greet me? Make me welcome in your home?" Her arms went softly round his neck and the cloak which had somehow become unfastened slipped to the floor behind her with a smooth swishing sound. Her lips breathed against his and he took them eagerly. He was quite dazzled. He had discarded his jacket and he could feel the softness of her breasts move against his chest.

He was gasping, his face red and excited when she stood away from him but a movement behind her caught his eye. His mouth gaped and his eyes looked as though they were about to pop from their sockets.

"But . . . why have you brought Gilly?" he managed to breathe.

"I'll explain later, Tim," then she was at him again with her lips and her hands which did lovely, terrible things to him as she led him, like some floundering fish on the end of an angler's line, across the hall and up the first few steps of the staircase. Her kisses were like small flames as she took him up and up the stairs, burning him first in one place and then in another for Bryony Townley had learned the art of lovemaking in the months she had spent, first enticing, then resisting Tim Spencer. His mouth was captured and released.

The lobe of his ear taken between sharp white teeth, hurting him, enchanting him, her tongue doing exquisite things along the curve of his jaw, down his throat to his chest and nipples where his shirt had mysteriously come undone. Her own bodice was unbuttoned and the straining, heaving, glorious golden swell of her naked breasts were pressed feverishly against his bare chest and when her soft whispered breath enquired which was his room he led her there, blind, deaf, senseless, mindless for at last, at last he was to get what he had lusted after for over a year now.

When he had it, when he had it once, then twice, crying out with a shrill and boyish ecstasy that could be heard clear along the wide passage outside his room to where the footman hovered at the head of the stairs, he lay in her arms, hers, her subject, her slave, hers to do with as she pleased while she told him exactly what that was to be.

They dined together that night at his mama's elegant dining table in his mama's elegant dining-room. Candle-light and flowers, ordered by Sir Timothy Spencer for his love. He couldn't keep his eyes off her, nor his hands, the sour-faced footman and the embarrassed parlour maid reported but what could they do about it? He was their master, young as he was, the owner of this splendid old house and the land about it and if he wished to entertain a lady of dubious morals, for she must be that, then they must accept it. Sir Timothy Spencer who would be nineteen in December and Miss Bryony Townley, or so she had turned out to be, who was only just fifteen years and five months old. They drank a bottle of Sir Julian's vintage champagne come from the supply he had put down on the day his son was born in readiness for his coming of age. The blank-faced footman and the round-eyed parlour maid served Sir Timothy and his guest the fine dishes their master had ordered and before the strumpet ordered them away she was heard to say that they'd best make their plans for her father would be after her the moment he discovered where she was.

When they were alone they ate and drank and played like the two children they were, shrieking with laughter as they fell up the stairs, Sir Timothy more than a little befuddled by the wine he had taken. Indecent it was, the footman declared as the servants exchanged titillated glances, but the spinster cousin who was to arrive tomorrow would soon put a stop to it. You could hear them all the way along the passage, her half naked and Sir Timothy giggling like a child unwrapping a Christmas present, to be followed by a deep and revealing silence behind the closed door of his room.

Well, he for one, the footman said petulantly, unable to forget the way the baggage had ordered him about, was of the opinion that someone, preferably the groom, should ride over at once and fetch Mr Townley. That little madam needed a good thrashing and he'd like nothing better than to give her one, but short of that he'd like to be present to watch the man who'd turned out to be her father, give it to her.

They argued for an hour, the servants, saying it was nothing to do with them and besides, when Sir Julian's spinster cousin arrived tomorrow she'd soon show Miss Bryony Townley the door. Best wait until then, eh?

The young couple and the enormous dog were gone when the scullery maid put the first match to the kitchen fire at six thirty the following morning.

The only one who did not appear to be perturbed by the disappearance of Bryony Townley, her dog and several articles of her clothing, was her brother. It was not discovered until the following morning that she had gone since, she being a strange girl who cared for no one's company but his and her own, each member of the household presumed she was in her room. She had not appeared at dinner, but then that was nothing new since she often ate alone from a tray by her bedroom fire. Ever since it had become known whose daughter she really was and to spare her own children, Nella Townley had persuaded her husband to allow the girl as much freedom as possible, beseeching him to understand how difficult it was for Bryony with everyone against her, more so than for her brother who at least left the house each day with his father. Bryony had to contend not only with the sudden and dreadful knowledge of her illegitimacy but the bitter enmity of her half-sisters who, quite simply, could not bear to be in the same room with her. It was not her fault, Nella knew that and so, deep down, did Beth, Nancy and Rose but it made not the least difference. They saw her as a reminder of their own shame and so they avoided her whenever they could.

Simeon always ate with them. She didn't know why but she suspected that his motives, encouraged by his far cleverer sister, were self-serving. He was the son of the family now and winning his father's approval could make the difference between being manager and owner, or at least part owner of his father's business concerns. So he was gradually accepted at table by her own children and if they did not exactly greet him with enthusiasm, particularly Rose, at least some sort of peace had been restored. Beth's marriage had helped. It had been a small affair by Marfield's standards but everyone who had been invited – those who could not afford to alienate Jonas Townley mainly and a few good friends of Nella's – had come, and the day had been successful.

And if Beth could do it, so could Nancy and Rose when their turn came and Nancy at least – Rose saying she did not care anyway – was prepared to endure Simeon's presence at the table.

But Bryony, it seemed, was not content to be merely

tolerated, indeed did not concern herself one way or the other and until events were . . . well, not forgotten perhaps, but accepted, best let her have her own way, Nella advised her husband. It would blow over eventually and until then if Bryony preferred her own company or the company of the dog, Gilly, then let her have it.

It was Betsy, who had been nursery maid when the children were young, and then chambermaid for many years, who discovered Miss Bryony's bed had not been slept in. Nella Townley, when summoned, had sent the manservants to search the grounds and even the woods at the back of Bank House. She herself had looked everywhere in the house, following excited maidservants from room to room, even foolishly, she realised later, peering under beds and diving into cupboards as though it was a game of hide and seek, and it was not until her grey-faced husband was sent for that Bryony's overnight bag and several articles of clothing were found to be missing, undergarments, stockings, a new gown of sprigged muslin, another of jacconet, her hairbrush, a cloak and a pair of white kid boots.

There might have been more but with Bryony becoming so secretive who could say what she might have bought from Miss Sabrina Renshaw's smart little milliner's shop where she had been seen on several occasions and Nella could hardly slip along and question Miss Renshaw, could she, not without questions being asked of her?

But where had she gone? She had been walking her dog in the garden the previous morning, for Dinty had noticed her, he confessed when asked, but it seemed he was the last to do so. She had no friends to whom she could run, or stay with overnight, so where the bloody hell was she, her father thundered, reducing his two daughters, several maidservants and almost the gardener's lad, Dinty, to tears.

"We must send to everyone we can think of, darling," his frantic wife told him, frantic not for Bryony but for her husband who had the strange appearance of being red-faced with fury and grey-faced with terror at one and the same time, his flesh mottled with both colours, his eyes wild and staring.

Even Jenna, away over in Everton, was not left out though the possibility of the girl, whose very name she loathed, running to her was ludicrous.

"Perhaps the police, Jonas?" his wife trembled and he had been just about to send for the constable when the elderly groom from Daresbury Park had ridden up to the front door to say that Miss Bryony had spent the night at Sir Timothy's home.

Jonas Townley's grey face became even greyer and he blinked rapidly as though from a body blow. His voice was hoarse.

"And Sir Timothy?" for did not everyone, including Bryony Townley, know that Lady Spencer, the Viscountess Overton now, was in Warwickshire and what deadly game was this Jonas Townley's daughter was playing?

"He . . . were there, sir, but . . ."

"Yes?"

"They're both on 'em gone now."

"Gone? Gone where?"

"I dunno, sir."

"Did . . . was a . . . a note left to say where?"

"No, sir. Us don't know where they be but they took t'dog."

"The dog?"

"Aye, sir."

Master Simeon was sent for. If anyone knew of his sister's whereabouts it would be he, his father roared, eyeing his son as he lounged indolently against the window frame of the study, his hands in his pockets, a look of innocent bewilderment on his handsome young face.

"Sir, I am as perplexed as you, and as worried," he said in answer to his father's questions and in the midst of his anguish Jonas Townley wondered why this son of his, though he had been told he may do so, had never once after that first day called him Father.

"But surely, since you are so close you must have known there was some . . . association between her and Tim Spencer?"

"I can't say that I did, sir. As you know, since the" – Simeon's face assumed an expression of gravity – "the revelation about our birth . . ."

"Yes, yes . . ." His father wanted no reference to that to muddy the waters.

"Well, sir, she has been much alone. I have been busy with the collieries and so could not be with her as much as I would have liked and if she has made a friend of Tim who is equally at a loose end with both his sister and his mother gone, one can hardly blame her." He managed to look injured and yet at the same time not at all judgmental. "She was very lonely, I believe, though of course she did not complain."

"Good God, lad, she spent the night at Daresbury Park with a man, alone! I know he is her cousin . . . well, of sorts . . . yes, yes, I know not of blood, but, well never mind. She has jeopardised her reputation by . . ."

"Surely it is too late for that, sir?" Simeon's voice was cool but his face retained its expression of guileless good humour mixed with what he wished his father to recognise as anxiety. Jonas Townley felt the sense of desolation his son's words, so innocently spoken but so cutting, had induced in him. He bent his head, placing his forehead in his hand. His elbow was on his desk and he leaned on it, his face seamed with his agony of spirit. He had tried for so many years to do to the best of his ability all he could for his two illegitimate children while at the same time endeavouring not to harm his four daughters who had been born to his marriage. They were all dear to him, his six children, and he had tried to be fair and loving to each one but Simeon and Jenna had always held special places in his heart. In all this time he had, with his wealth and authority, kept them safe from harm and from the scandal which might, at any time, have broken and he had been only surprised that it had not come to this before now. A life of deceit he, and Nella at his insistence, had lived, protecting all of them, legitimate and illegitimate children alike. He had prayed, not to any God, but to the fates, that they might all be grown, be mature enough, perhaps safely married, the girls, his son firmly secure in his position with Jonas Townley, before the truth was revealed to them as he knew in his heart that it must. But, through his sister-in-law's loose and spiteful tongue, so he had at last learned, it had come out before he and they were ready for it. It had split the family, not just in two but into as many pieces as there were members of it. Jenna cold and hard and refusing to speak to him except on matters of business, *his* business which she was determined to have, if not for herself then for her son. His other daughters, Beth inclined to be obsessed with her position in society, nervous, demoralised to the extent she was willing to let that husband of hers dominate her life in any way he wished. Nancy on the defensive, treading warily wherever she went lest she be rebuffed by those she had once taken for granted as family friends. Rose becoming brash, corrosive even, tossing her head carelessly to show her indifference but hurting nevertheless. Only his son, who before he had become his son had been mettlesome and inclined to what looked dreadfully like boredom, being what his father had wanted. Pleasant, eager to learn, obedient, respectful with men who were older and more experienced than himself. He would make a fine coal owner one day, brave and strong when he went into the darkness of the pit and if he showed a certain belligerence when challenged would, when he matured, learn to curb it.

And Bryony. His lovely, dark-haired love child. A child of the love he had known for her mother and who was so like her to look at it was sometimes almost more than he could bear to do so. Always reserved, quiet as her mother had been, but turning cold now and withdrawn, introverted, standing aloof from those who would still have loved her. Staring at him and through him with frosty eyes, turning more and more to her own company, unbending her haughty and forbidding demeanour to nobody but her brother.

And Tim Spencer, it appeared.

"Surely you must have known of her . . . well, good God, lad, she must have been . . . been friendly with Tim for quite a while for it to come to this." He ran a distracted hand through his thick hair. The greyish tinge to his face had become more pronounced and for a moment Simeon Townley felt a throb of fear surge in his chest for if anything happened to this man while Bryony was away what in God's name should he do? She had assured him that if he stayed at his place – that was how she put it, his place – nothing could go wrong. He was merely to carry on exactly as he had always done and . . . but what if . . . ? He looked so awful . . . ill, old and broken up. Perhaps Bryony had made a miscalculation. Gone too far in her ruthless ambition to bring not only to herself but to him everything she had sworn was as much theirs as it was the others. She and Simeon were as much his children as the others and were as entitled to their share of what was his. They were not at fault, were they and should not be made to suffer for it, should they, and so . . . but Jonas Townley was speaking.

"Tell me the truth, son. Where are they?"

"I honestly don't know, sir."

"You knew of this . . . liaison?"

"I knew she went walking with Gilly in the woods, sir." Into Simeon's voice a little resentment crept and his father winced. "She was very lonely. She told me once or twice she had come across Tim riding his hunter. Apparently you had given your permission for it."

"Yes." Jonas sighed deeply. "But she must have said more than that. She's spent the . . . the night at Daresbury and you are old enough and man enough to know what that means."

"Yes, sir."

"Have you nothing further to say?"

"I don't know what else I can say." Simeon's face was endearingly crestfallen as though he would like nothing more than to help his father.

"And where d'you suppose they've run off to?"

"To Scotland, perhaps?"

"For what reason?"

"To be married, I would presume, sir. My sister is not a loose woman."

"Woman! She's but fifteen, lad." Jonas's voice was filled with despair. "And he is only a boy himself."

"Boy or not, Tim Spencer must marry her, sir." Simeon's face was suddenly as hard as granite, showing his true self and looking, despite his youth, the mirror image of the man who sat at the desk.

"You believe so? In other words you do know more than you're saying?"

"I'm only saying, sir, that Tim is a gentleman." The last word was spoken with a malicious sneer. "If he has . . . well . . ."

"Wronged her, is the expression, I believe, lad."

"If he has and does not marry her, then . . ."

"Then I believe he will be sorry, Simeon and I believe it is not me, nor you, that he should fear, but your sister!"

Chapter Twenty-six

Jenna's second son, Roderick, Roddy Macrae, as he was to be known, was born at the beginning of November and he was no more than an hour old before Jenna was sitting up, her hair brushed by Marian and tied in a knot of emerald green ribbons which were not as glorious a colour as her eyes, her jubilant husband told her, kissing her soundly. Her face was flushed with good health and the strength of her endeavour and she wanted strawberries and cream, she told him, she didn't care if it was November!

"You shall have them, my darling, and anything else you care to ask for. How about these to begin with, and perhaps this to match?" tossing a velvet box on to the bed before snatching up his new son into protective, possessive arms.

Inside the box were diamond ear-drops and a slender bracelet to match and she wore them to eat her dish of strawberries and cream which were hurried in to her within half an hour. The nurse was scandalised, protesting loudly that "mother" should rest but she might have shouted from the window to the birds which were just awakening, for all the notice that was taken of her. Indeed, before she could voice a further protest, young Master Ewan was produced, summoned by his exultant papa and within minutes was sprawled on the bed in his mama's embrace. He cared nought for the new boy, his truculent gaze told his father and at once Conal gave his second son to Nanny Abigail to hold, telling her not to go far for he wanted him back the moment he had had a game with his first.

Squealing, the eldest boy was, his laughter high and excited and could you wonder with a mama and papa such as he had, the nurse's expression said. Children should be kept in the nursery, not allowed to romp about in their parents' bedroom at daybreak. Still in his little nightshirt, he was, though his nanny had changed his soiled napkin. Not yet walking since he was but eleven months old and her with another already but could that surprise you, the way her husband acted with her? Even an hour or so ago, when Mrs Macrae was labouring to produce the child just born he'd the temerity to stride into the room and ask what the hell was going on. Of course Mrs Macrae was shouting her head off, cursing, to tell the truth, shocking both herself and Doctor Sterling, but Mr Macrae had come to her side and held her hand and told her to swear as much as she wanted for he'd swear himself in the same situation. Laughing, they'd both been when Master Roderick entered the world, their laughter the first sounds their son had heard.

"What a dreadful day for a wee man to be born," Conal told his second son while his first shared his mama's strawberries and cream. And so it was for the world beyond the fire-glowed luxury of the bedroom was still and white and cold, draped with November mists. The hard ground was thick with frost. Nothing moved. Frozen leaves lay across the lawn, crisp and curling, the few that remained on the trees' branches hanging motionless. The birdbath in the centre of the lawn, filled with water the day before by George since the "little chap" did so love to see the birds at their ablutions, was frozen solid. A plump-breasted, speckled hen thrush banged vigorously on the side of an empty flower pot, doing her best to shatter the shell of a snail in her beak. She dropped it and looked round, cocking her head, her eye wary, then resumed her patient forage for food.

"But just wait until the sun shines, my bonny wee laddie," Conal continued, "we'll be off to see the world then. Your brother and your clever mama shall come with us and you shall have a pony and one for Ewan . . ."

"Heavens, Conal, let's get the child walking before we put either of them up on a pony though I must admit to a longing to leap up on Amber's back after such a while."

"You take your time, lassie. No leaping about for you just yet. That end of you needs to heal before—"

"Before what, Conal?" interrupting him mischievously, smiling at her husband above the head of her elder son.

"Well, there's that too," he winked at her lewdly. "I'll not say no to havin' ma' wee wifie back wi' me again, you ken that fine."

"And so you shall, as soon as that woman's gone."

Roddy was six days old when Jenna insisted on getting up and though the shocked nurse threatened to lock up her clothes and send for her husband, Marian helped her to dress in a warm blue woollen gown, brushing back her hair and threading it with blue ribbon.

"You look about twelve years old, lassie, and far too young to be the mother of two strapping sons," her husband told her when he came home to find her sitting by her fireside, "and far, far too young to be kissing a gentleman like that. Nevertheless I'll have another one, or perhaps two and then it's back to bed with you, and no, I will not come with you. Really, Jenna Macrae, you are quite shameless."

His laughter was soft and the house in Beechfield Road was warmed in the love that was captured within its walls. It was a slow, peaceful time, a drowsing time of candlelight glowing in the dark November days. Of firelight and warmth in every winter-shrouded room. Of young things growing, learning, flowering in the love and laughter shared by its master and mistress. Companionship, and passion in their bed though he made sure she did not conceive again and the delight of watching the thriving of their sons. There was a great contentment in Conal's wife and he was well aware that it was something to do with a visit she had made to her father's office many months ago. She would not say what had transpired there, only that she and her papa had come to an understanding. Whatever it was Conal Macrae was inclined to bless it for Jenna appeared to bloom now in her life as his wife and the mother of her two handsome sons. She had done well by him and he was proud of her, pleased at the way she had settled, and surprised too, for he had been prepared to fight her on what he had thought would be her determination to interfere in her father's business interests.

In those days after the birth of her second son she glowed, soft and warm as a scented candle, staying close to her home, walking in the garden with the baby carriage, Ewan in one end of it, baby Roddy in the other, the wintry sun low in the sky above the trees. There was a heavy spell of frost then one night at the end of November, a thin fall of snow creating a white world of unbelievable loveliness. A clear cold rosiness to the sky, the few remaining leaves tinkling like crystal as a chill wind stirred them.

Master Ewan took his first steps, falling with great enchantment into his mother's waiting arms and when his father returned that evening, obligingly repeating the performance. The nursery was apricot-tinted from the fire that crackled in the hearth and on his rug before it Master Roddy watched his brother with admiring, blue-green eyes, ready to smile, his mother declared as she swooped him up in loving arms. His feathery cap of bright copper curls was smoothed and kissed and they watched as Roddy's father and brother threw themselves into some glorious game.

"I shall take them to see Mama tomorrow," Jenna murmured that night as she drowsed in her husband's arms. "Roddy is six weeks old and will be walking with Ewan if I don't go soon. You know how quickly they grow at this age and I'm longing to show them off."

And so it was that Jenna Macrae was drinking tea with Nella Townley in the firelit comfort of the drawing-room when the splendid carriage, which was very familiar to them both since it had once conveyed Lady Spencer hither and yon, drew up at the entrance to Bank House.

"Dear God in heaven, not Linnet again," Nella Townley murmured as she put down her cup and saucer. "I realise how devastated she is by Tim's continued absence but really, what on earth can I do about it? It's a wonder that new husband of hers doesn't have something to say about her continual absence from his ancestral home. After all, they have been married no more than three months, if that, and ever since Tim and Bryony went she has been up and down from Warwickshire as regularly as clockwork."

"Has nothing more been heard of them?" Jenna asked the question with no more than polite indifference since the scheming stratagems of Bryony Townley meant nothing to her. In one way her disappearance with Tim Spencer had, Jenna thought, put Bryony at a disadvantage in the eyes of Jonas Townley who would not approve of his illegitimate daughter's behaviour and therefore it would weigh heavily against her in any contest over the collieries. She had only herself to blame if Jonas cut himself off from her completely and if Tim, who was only just nineteen, should tire of junketing about the country with her, and surely he would for he knew he had duties at home, then where would she be? Jenna found she could not care, nor should she, for Bryony was the kind of girl, woman, who would always find some

441

way of landing on her own two steady feet. Clever she was and cunning and there was no doubt if she fell in a midden she would come out of it smelling of violets!

Her mother said, "Not since your father had a note from her saying they were in London and he was not to worry about her. Of course he does."

"Of course." Jenna lifted her chin and turned her head away to signify to her mother that she had not come here to talk of Bryony Townley. Indeed, now that her Aunt Linnet had arrived she thought she had best get home. The days were drawing in now as Christmas approached and if Ewan was not removed from the conservatory where his tumbling legs and inquisitive fingers had taken him, her mama's camellias would be quite devastated.

The tap on the door to announce the entrance of the new viscountess brought her to her feet but the crash, followed by a wail of shocked alarm plus an explosion of terrified bird twitterings had her across the drawing-room carpet and through the open glassed doors to the conservatory where, to her horror, chaos reigned. There were small, brightly plumed birds in varying degrees of annoyance and fear all over the place, some swooping and diving, others perched tremulously on swaying palm trees and on Nella Townley's prized gardenias and brilliant bougainvillaea. In their midst was Ewan Macrae, big-eyed and hiccoughing but already beginning to be entranced with the results of his meddling. He pointed to a dazzling parakeet which was ready, or so he believed, to perch on his shoulder. He grinned, showing a fine array of baby teeth.

"Mama," he chortled, following that with a babble of delighted chatter which not even his fond parent could decipher.

"Never mind Mama, you imp," his mother told him, snatching him up into her arms and soundly kissing his round cheek. "Grandmother will skin me alive when she sees this . . . no, no you may not play with the pretty birds. No darling, stop that now and let's go and find Nanny Abigail and Roddy. It's time we . . ."

She was almost halfway across the drawing-room, her son squealing his displeasure, her arms full of his furiously wriggling body, when she became aware of the two stiff figures who stood, several feet apart, on her mama's beautiful carpet. Nella Townley had evidently risen from her chair when the visitor entered, taking two or three steps towards her, then stopped, the visitor doing the same just inside the door.

It was Bryony Townley. No one spoke, only the boy who could see no reason why he should be clutched so fiercely in his mama's arms, and said so at great length, loudly and incomprehensibly.

Still no one spoke and the child, young as he was, appearing to sense the dramatic tension in the usually tranquil room, shrank against his mother's shoulder with solemn eyes. He put his thumb in his mouth and finding it of comfort, sucked it vigorously.

"Well, Jenna," Bryony said, completely at ease just as though she was a regular visitor to Nella Townley's drawing-room and in the habit of finding her half-sister there too. "A fine boy you have there. He reminds me of Simeon . . ."

"Never!" The word was spat from Jenna's mouth as though she had bitten on some rotten, putrefying matter which would surely poison her.

"I only meant his colouring." Bryony smiled condescendingly as though at the petulance of a child, putting Jenna in that category. She moved slowly towards the fire, throwing back the cloak she wore and it was only then that the mother and daughter became aware of the splendour of her gown. Her cloak, a rich, ruby red velvet, was lined with a soft grey fur and the hood was edged with it. Her gown, of the palest pearl grey merino wool, was simple but beautifully made and her boots were of the very finest grey kid. She looked absolutely glorious, dark and glossy and expensive and the perfume she wore was heady, obviously French and of the best quality. She was not yet sixteen but her composure, her worldliness, her unruffled beauty were incredible.

"Bryony." Nella cleared her throat and blinked as though to release herself from the tranced state into which the appearance of her husband's daughter had flung her. She took a hesitant step towards her, perhaps feeling she should embrace her but Bryony turned aside, her cool demeanour telling Nella she had no wish to be involved in a false show of family affection. Nella fumbled with the cameo at her neck, clearly discomfited, not sure how to continue with this charade Bryony appeared to have decided on. Her daughter had no such problem.

"What in hell's name do you want here?" she asked harshly. "Have you not done enough to this family, and Tim's, without flaunting yourself like some peacock in its fine feathers? And which, by the way, makes one wonder where you obtained the money to buy such finery."

"Really, Jenna, marriage and motherhood appear to have done nothing for your manners. As to what I have done to this family, surely it is what this family have done to me? Your father . . . oh yes, I suppose he is my father too, though having come by him so recently and so late in life I find it hard to think of him as such. As I was saying, your father's partiality for fornication and my mother's apparent lack of morals and her weakness in withstanding him, brought about mine and Simeon's existence. We had no hand in it, no choice as to whether we should be born bastards and yet it is not my mother, nor yet my father who are made to suffer for it."

Nella Townley made a small sound somewhere between a moan and hysterical laughter and Bryony and Jenna, despite their absolute absorption with one another, were compelled by its very strangeness to turn and look at her.

"Dear sweet Jesus, you know nothing, either of you, about suffering . . . Oh dear God in heaven . . . poor Leah, poor Leah."

"I beg your pardon," Bryony said frigidly but Nella turned away from them, her head bowed, her shoulders shaking and both girls returned ferociously to the attack. The baby cowered in his mother's arms, his growing terror unnoticed by her and when Nella reached for the bell again neither saw it.

"So you must excuse me if I appear resentful, Jenna," Bryony continued smoothly. "It is I, and Simeon, who seem to be the villains in this unsavoury melodrama, not the two who were its main actors but, strangely, I find I am not prepared to cower in the dark and bemoan my fate or even quietly to do away with myself as I believe it has been suggested would be the only decent thing to do in the circumstances."

She paused for breath, her eyes a deep and muddy brown, flat like the exposed reaches of the estuary when the tides receded. She did not turn when the door opened, nor did Jenna. She did not so much as blink her own narrowed, hating eyes as Nanny Abigail, with a distracted wave of Nella Townley's hand, silently took the child from Jenna's arms and just as silently left the room.

They were all aware, those in the kitchen and the nursery, what was happening in the drawing-room. When Miss Bryony had stepped imperiously down from the Spencer carriage, all velvet and furs and expensive French perfume, Dolly had almost tumbled head first down the front steps, she told them later, as the girl they had known all their lives had swept up and past her, marching along the hall and into the mistress's drawing-room as though she had as much right to do so as the mistress herself. They had heard the raised voices. Miss Jenna and Miss

Bryony had never exactly hit it off. They had not actually fought as Miss Jenna and Master Simeon had but now they were at it hammer and tongs and at the head of the stairs where Betsy's garbled message had drawn her, Nanny Abigail had wrung her hands, anguished over the little mite who was caught in the middle of it. Molly, the Townley children's old nanny, was contentedly nursing young Master Roddy by the nursery fire, glad, she said, to have a baby in her arms again. And when the bell was rung Nanny Abigail had her charge in her thankful arms and was out of the room before you could say "come along, Master Ewan". Happy to get out of it, he was, his baby arms clinging round her neck, hanging on like one of those little monkeys she had shown him in his nursery rhyme book.

"Mama . . . burble . . . burble . . . burble . . ." he hiccoughed tearlessly.

"Yes, yes, I know, my lamb," she soothed him, shocked by her own brief encounter with the hatred which filled the drawing-room. And Miss Jenna such a good mother usually!

"More's the pity," Jenna hissed in answer to Bryony's last remark. "You and Simeon both. It would have saved us all a great deal of trouble."

"I suppose it would. But you see that is what I live for now, Jenna. To make trouble for you and this family. In any way I know how. If I can embarrass you, then I shall. If I can hurt you, then I shall. If I can take anything from you, then I shall, whether I am entitled to it or not."

"You are entitled to nothing, not even our name and how you came by it I shall never know. Your mother was not only a whore and husband stealer—"

"Please . . . oh sweet Jesus, stop it . . . stop it. Jenna, Bryony, you don't know what you're talking about. None of this is . . ." but for all the notice her daughter, or her husband's daughter took of her, Nella Townley might have been one of the brightly plumaged birds which young Master Ewan had let out of their cage and which were now beginning to swoop about Nella's expensively elegant drawing-room.

"You are probably right, Jenna. My mother must have been all the things you say she is. No more than the foul muck in which she worked as a girl. The man who says he is my father told me all about her though he did not describe her as you have. An angel from heaven she was, in his opinion. They all worked in Jonas Townley's colliery, my mother and her mother, her father and brothers and they are all dead so there is nothing I can get from them, but by God, Jonas Townley is still living and I mean to see that Simeon and I have everything that is owed to us."

"Over my dead body." Jenna was half crouched, almost in the manner of a wrestler looking for a hold on his opponent. Her face was paper white and on it her golden freckles stood out like small showy coins. Her eyes glittered madly and her lips, almost as colourless as her face, were stretched tight across her bared teeth. "God knows where you came from," she spat, "and you can be sure I for one don't care. My father associated in some way with your mother, no doubt as a dog will mount a bitch on heat and from it you and that . . . that . . . bastard brother of yours came, but be sure of this. There is nothing here which belongs to either of you. My sons are—"

"Simeon is *his* son."

"Simeon and you can go to hell and the sooner the better. Now get out of my mother's drawing-room. Climb back in Tim Spencer's fancy carriage and go back to where you came from in it. Tell your lover to keep you wherever men keep their mistresses – my father should be able to advise you on that – for there is no place for you here."

Bryony, inwardly as lividly incensed as Jenna, had remained outwardly cool. It was always to be the one strong weapon with which she could outwit her opponents. As they became more and more heated, she had taught herself, because not only was it in her nature but because it was forced on her by her circumstances, to be unruffled, to be composed, inciting her tormentors to greater fury.

Now it stood her in good stead. Jenna was circling her, almost beyond reason in her dementia and Bryony turned with her, facing Jenna whichever way she moved. Though her heart was beating just as wildly, though her pulse raced just as madly, she smiled, almost amiably, as she spoke.

"You still don't understand, do you?"

"I understand this. If you don't get out of my father's house immediately I shall call the men to throw you out."

"Don't be ridiculous, Jenna. They would hardly dare to do that."

"Try me! Try them! They are my father's servants and would do as they're told."

"I don't think so, really I don't." Bryony's eyes flared now in triumph. "They are impressed, awed if you like, by the trappings of the gentry. Put a woman in an expensive gown and she becomes a lady, you see, and they would not dare lay hands on a lady. You were asking me a little while ago where I had the money to buy this fine cloak and gown. Well, you might be surprised to know that my mother bought them for me. Oh yes, apparently she became a lady in the fine things your father decked her in, or so he thought, amongst them various pieces of jewellery which were very costly. So you see it was not exactly a case of a dog mounting a bitch as you so quaintly put it. She did very well out of him. Diamonds, and other valuable gems which, poor fool, he thought, as her daughter, should come to me. I swear he had tears in his eyes as he said it. Well, to cut a long and harrowing story short . . . yes, I can see neither of you are pleased," turning to smile at Nella Townley who had sat down heavily and put her head in her hands. "It came in very handy, the money I realised from that jewellery. It had no sentiment attached to it, you see, at least for me though Mr Townley seemed to think it should. Anyway, it kept me and Tim in luxury all this time we have been away. It is quite amazing what money can do, is it not? You have only to slip a coin into a reluctant hand and at once the hand's owner jumps to your bidding. We had a glorious time, moving from place to place so that Jonas Townley could not find us. Finally, when we thought it safe to do so, we travelled over the border into Scotland. You have heard, I presume, of Gretna Green?" She smiled brilliantly and the awful, awful truth began to seep insidiously into Jenna's stunned mind.

"I see you have," Bryony continued softly, "so here I am, not, as you thought, Sir Timothy Spencer's mistress, but his wife. Yes, Lady Spencer now, Jenna, with far more influence than simple Bryony Townley. I am still the illegitimate daughter of Jonas Townley but far more importantly, and inclined to cancel that status out, I would say, is that I am now the wife of Sir Timothy Spencer. And perhaps of even more consequence, the mother of his unborn child."

Chapter Twenty-seven

Conal Macrae lounged carelessly on the small, rather uncomfortable velvet chair, a ladies' chair, that stood beside the fire in his wife's upstairs sitting-room. On one arm he nursed his younger son who had just been bathed, changed and fed in preparation for bedtime, while in his other he held his elder. Ewan was completely absorbed, as only a young child can be, with the intricate task of opening his papa's pocket watch, a gold hunter. His busy, baby fingers struggled valiantly with the enclosed case he was determined to get inside. He knew what was there when he did so, for his papa often let him look at the magical moving fingers and listen to the "tick-tock" and best of all to the lovely chiming sound it made every now and again.

His small pink tongue protruded from between his rosy lips and he breathed strenuously with the effort of his labours. At intervals he kindly showed it to his brother who smiled in great good humour.

"My darling, there is absolutely nothing to be done about it," the boys' papa said to their mama who was pacing up and down, up and down, a sheet of notepaper in her hand, across the soft, biscuit-coloured carpet, at each turn kicking back the hem of the long, trailing skirt of her peignoir. It was a lovely thing of misted grey, silvery pale where the light caught it, pewter where it fell in shaded folds with so much material in it it floated in a great billowing cloud about her as she walked. It had white lace ruffles on it and yards of silver grey satin ribbons and with her hair like a living mantle of copper flame falling to halfway down her back, her perfumed passage was quite glorious.

"It is really not our business, you know," Conal went on, hitching his younger son more closely to his chest, at the same time keeping an eye on his elder. Ewan might be only fifteen months old but he was a bright little beggar and if effort was rewarded he'd have the watch open before long. "I ken you're upset and I ken women are inclined to put themselves in another woman's place and imagine how they would feel if it was happening to them."

"Dear God, Conal, don't tell me you're going to trot out that old maxim about . . . well, whatever it is gentlemen say when ladies shudder in sympathy and horror at what has befallen another. I'm sure she will not get used to it. I know I couldn't. I said so when she married him."

"I know you did. In fact the whole of Marfield knows your opinion."

"And what does that mean?" Jenna turned to glare at her husband but the sight of him sitting contentedly nursing his sons, a fond and doting look on his face, a sure sign he was not taking a great deal of notice of what she was saying, brought a smile, exasperated, but a smile nevertheless, to her irritable face.

"May I invite her here then?" she asked, taking advantage of his preoccupation with their sons since the opportunity might not come her way again for a few days. These pleasant moments when the babies were brought in to be with her and Conal before bedtime did not occur every evening. Her husband was a busy man and sometimes did not get home before they were put to bed, a disappointment to them all, especially Jenna, and Ewan who would wail for Papa for a full hour. Roddy was still too young to understand, of course, and did not as yet miss his papa but the half-hour was a precious family moment to both parents and it certainly put Conal into a receptive state of mind for one of what he tolerantly called "another of Jenna's wild schemes".

"She and her baby will be no trouble," she went on hurriedly. "Amy will have her own nanny of course and probably a nursemaid as well. You know what the gentry are like." Her face for a moment assumed a somewhat scornful expression, aimed at all those society mothers who scarce knew one end of their own child from the other. Not like herself who could, if the need arose, care for her babies completely by herself and enjoy doing it.

"Her letter is quite distraught, darling. Well, you have read it, threatening all manner of things from suicide, murder and even self-mutilation if it would divert her husband's unwelcome and frequent advances. She loathes him and if she doesn't get away from him, even for a short while, I shudder to think what she might do. And she has nowhere now that Aunt Linnet has gone and that . . . that . . . upstart has taken over at Daresbury."

Jenna's face hardened, taking on that expression Conal had come to recognise and to dread. His own lost the look of tranquillity this time which his wife and sons always lit in him.

"I think we'll get these two back to nanny, don't you agree?" he said smoothly. "I have to bathe and change yet and the concert begins at eight. Ring the bell, will you, darling?"

He stood Ewan on his feet and at once the boy toddled across the hearth-rug, reaching up for the bell on the other side of the fireplace, the bell which summoned the servants.

"Me, Papa, me do," he shouted in the voice he used when he was determined on a task which he had just learned. "Ewan do."

They watched him, his parents, smiling the proud smile all parents assume when their child performs an act which an acquaintance might think to be nothing out of the ordinary. The bell was within his reach and was easy to pull but Jenna and Conal turned to smile at one another just as though their son had taken apart some intricate piece of mechanism and put it together again. The conversation which had been in progress, the subject matter of it and the growing outrage which would inevitably follow was forgotten in their shared love and pride in their handsome son.

Ewan Macrae was a sturdy, good-looking child, as naughty and mischievous as any healthy boy of his age. He was an eager, staggering, bold-eyed imp, blessed with his parents' loving protection and secure because of it. He was destructive if allowed to be, as most children are, determined to have his own way, as most children are, and though Conal sometimes frowned at his son's wilfulness and swore it was time he was disciplined it was obvious he delighted in the child's high spirits. He was more of a Townley than a Macrae with tousled, glossy, ebony curls as his grandfather's had once been and which no amount of nanny's brushing could keep tidy. When Mama or nanny were not looking his busy little fingers played havoc with the delightful objects, all crowded on low tables in his mama's sitting-room and just the right height for a boy such as he to reach.

His parents both laughed and, knowing they were pleased, he began to strut about, to show off his cleverness until nanny came and he was led away, complaining bitterly in the jumble of infant babble mixed with the one or two short sentences he could now manage. Roddy, who had fallen peacefully asleep in his father's arms, went with him.

The concert was held in St George's Hall and the moment they entered the foyer Conal Macrae and his elegantly stunning wife were surrounded, then separated by the numerous gentlemen with whom Conal did business and who were accompanied by their wives and daughters. Conal was fast becoming a wealthy man, his six coastal ships, among them the *Jenna Macrae*, carrying goods from and to Liverpool, calling in at ports and fishing villages as far afield as the Clyde in Scotland to Bristol and the south coast of Devon and Cornwall. Five steamers, a sailing ship and another steamer almost completed across the river in Birkenhead and to be called *Ewan Macrae* in honour of his older boy. There would be another soon named after his second son, it was rumoured. He had property in Scotland, left to him by his father who had come from up that way and had an interest in many small businesses. A vigorous man, Conal had worked hard to gain what he had. A man who, before his father died and himself no more than a lad of sixteen, had sailed the wild waters of the Irish Sea and the North Channel, along the coast to Scotland; of Cardigan Bay and the Bristol Channel; the English Channel to Plymouth. He had scrubbed decks, coiled ropes, climbed spars and rigging to reef and unfurl the sails of his father's sailing ships. His hands had bled and become hardened. He had eaten what the crew ate, slept as the crew slept and been beaten with no regard for who he was and he had earned what came to him on his father's death. A proud man, proud of his forebears, it was said, even if they had fought and lost against the English over a century ago. A fine house he had out at Everton and he had married the daughter of another wealthy man and was in a fair way to starting his own dynasty. A canny man. A man worth cultivating. A man with whom to do business. A shrewd man and, or so the ladies evidently thought, an attractive man about whom they twittered and smirked, vying with one another to catch his attention.

Mind you, the gentlemen evidently felt the same way

about his wife since the quite scandalously low-cut, shimmering gold tissue of her magnificent evening gown left little to the imagination.

Conal had thought so too and before they left home, had they not already been late, would have insisted she change into something less revealing, he growled at her hazardously.

"Any sudden movement will expose your nipples and though I'm the first to admit they are worthy of any man's inspection, I dinna care for the idea that every man there will be eyeing what is for my enjoyment only. Have you no' a scarf . . . or something which could be strategically draped?"

"A scarf! Good God, Conal, have you any idea what this gown cost and you expect me to shroud it with a scarf!"

"Well, a shawl then." His face was clouded with his displeasure.

"I am not a grandmother who needs a shawl draped about her shoulders to keep out the cold. This is the very latest style from Paris, Miss Yeoland informed me and—"

"Miss Yeoland is not to wear it. My wife is and I would be obliged if you would—"

"Look, sweetheart, if it will make you feel better I promise not to move a muscle. I shall be most circumspect. Besides, it's very cold and I doubt I shall remove my wrap, even inside the hall."

"Hmmph, that I cannot credit. You have on a gown for which I have presumably paid God knows how many guineas, a Paris creation and you expect me to believe that you have no desire to flaunt it in the faces of the young matrons of Liverpool's society?"

Of course she did exactly as he knew she would, carelessly handing her fur-lined mantle to an attendant and as they became separated in the hubbub of voices which greeted them before they took their seats for the concert he could hear her musical laugh above the sound of all the others. He searched for her across the heads of those about him over which his tall frame towered, his eyes drawn to the circle of immaculately clad young gentlemen where his wife's flamboyant fox red hair glowed like the sun. As he watched, the circle parted for a moment and he was furiously aware that every man in it had his eyes glued to his wife's swelling breasts which threatened to show themselves as she lifted her arms to demonstrate some point she was making. Her low décolletage dropped even lower. At any moment the coffee-coloured areola which surrounded her nipples would be revealed and the man who stood next to her was watching for that moment with an admiring expectancy which was very evident. He was young, tall, lean, well-bred, it seemed, as they all were and though not handsome, his face was engagingly cheerful and his watchful expression was filled with boyish charm. He whispered something in Jenna's ear and she smiled, casting down her eyes, her own charm quite magnetic, as was the unfettered loveliness of her half-revealed breasts. She was not shy or timid, as a wild creature is, but she gave the impression of being completely untamed, swift and light and free unlike any other woman at the concert. She moved boldly as though she was unhampered with anything as sophisticated as a petticoat or crinoline and she looked at the men about her, meeting their eyes with the directness one male will turn on another. Except for that one man whom Conal did not know. But despite her almost male directness she was magnificently, eternally female. His woman and he resented the way in which the grinning young man was eyeing her, and her response to it.

Conal felt his fury begin to burn in him and, with a muttered apology, he pushed his way through the throng, scattering the circle of young men as swiftly as a wolf dropping down amongst a group of amiable sheep. He took her arm, being careful not to pull at her too strenuously but despite his vigilance every male eye was drawn to the flaunting movement of her creamy breasts.

"The concert is about to begin, my dear," he said through gritted teeth, turning the fierce knife-edge of his jealous anger on the retreating gentlemen who all, to a man, discovered they had duties elsewhere and for a moment Mr and Mrs Conal Macrae found themselves alone.

"What the bloody hell d'you think you're up to?" he snarled, his well-cut lips curling back on his teeth in what he attempted to turn into a smile.

Jenna was astonished. She had been flirting mildly with Charlie Graham who was an old family friend and the nephew of her father's banker. He had been a guest on many occasions at Bank House, the last nearly two years ago at the girls' combined birthday party when she remembered he had kissed her with more soundness than was sensible. In fact she rather thought he had gone further than that which was why she had been inclined to glance downwards, for her mother's appalled face was part of that memory.

"What on earth is the matter, Conal?" she whispered irritably, conscious of the stares and raised eyebrows about them. "I was only . . ."

"I am quite well aware what you were doing, lassie, and what that dandy wished he were doing but I'll ask you to remember you're my wife and I dinna care to see my wife being ogled by half the degenerates in this hall. It's that bloody dress and believe me, madam, it's the last time you'll wear it."

"Conal! You're hurting my arm and if you don't stop this foolishness it will be all over Marfield, carried there by Charlie Graham, who is not a degenerate, that Conal Macrae ill-treats his wife, and in public."

"I presume that was Charlie Graham peering down the front of your gown?"

"Yes, and he was not peering . . ."

"He and every other bastard here."

They were both completely bewildered by the force of his sudden and uncontrollable jealousy. This was not the first time Jenna had been admired, flirted with and smiled at lustfully by the gentlemen who were often in their company, at concerts such as this, at balls and soirées and banquets they attended, for Conal was fast becoming socially prominent in Liverpool, helped, there was no doubt, by his marriage to such an attractive and wealthy young wife. They were entertained by, and entertained in their turn, men of the same industrious convictions as himself.

They had been guests at the Grand Conservative Ball, held at the Philharmonic Hall in honour of the Earl of Derby where many of Liverpool's socially élite had been invited. Jenna had danced with them all, being herself, being natural and completely unaffected by their greatness, even his lordship's. The gentlemen had clamoured for her dances, finding her refreshingly amusing and quite overwhelmingly good to look at in a gown just as revealing as the one she wore tonight. A rich, midnight blue velvet, stark and unadorned, against which her creamy skin had glowed like a pearl. Conal had watched her, smiling, delighted with her popularity, even the gentlemen's fascinated admiration amusing him since he knew that he could trust her, not only with his love and his life, but with his honour which was very dear to him.

They had been present at a bazaar presented under the patronage of the Countess of Sefton, held at the Queen's Hall and attended by the Mayor and Mayoress of Liverpool, not to mention every dignitary and worthy who, as Jenna put it, twinkling, "had a bob or two to spare" and from which they might be parted. A charity, the name of which had slipped Conal's mind, had benefited from it and the Mayoress had personally thanked Jenna for her help in it. She had been surrounded by gentlemen wishing to tell her of their admiration and Conal had smiled again as he watched her charm them all as she had at the banquet to celebrate the opening of the Birkenhead Street Railway. Six months pregnant she had been and not one of them had been aware of it as she smiled and flirted, her lovely graceful posture hiding her condition, then took her husband home and made love to him in the way only she knew how.

Somewhat larger she had been and, in the opinion of the other ladies present, best off at home, though she wouldn't have it, of course, when in October the new library and museum presented to the people of Liverpool by the philanthropist William Brown had been inaugurated. The day had been observed as a public holiday and every street was decorated with flags and bunting. A levée had been held at the town hall and prominent, in more ways than one, was the flushed, bright-eyed Mrs Conal Macrae, her arm through her husband's since she meant to miss not one exciting moment of this thrilling day. There was a procession with soldiers and a military band and men of, as the newspapers put it, "a nautical character". Mr Brown's speech was rapturously received by the crowds who became silent as he announced solemnly that his gift was for the "perpetual benefit of the public, and especially my fellow townsmen". Sir Robert Peel was amongst the honoured guests, quite astonished, those who were not so forward agreed, to be shaking the hand of the heavily pregnant wife of one of the town's more prosperous businessmen.

"I shan't go home until I've seen the fireworks display,

Conal," she had told him, and she didn't, standing near Parliament Fields on the top of Kensington Reservoir until the last one flared into the night sky, declaring how Ewan would have loved it all. Like a child herself with stars in her eyes, her capacity to enjoy herself reawakening in her husband such a wealth of joyous love it was all he could do not to embrace her before the assembled multitude.

Now, for some reason, some instinct, some uncanny sixth sense which told him to beware of the man who had whispered in his wife's ear and made her hide the expression in her eyes, he was insanely and unbelievably jealous. He cared not one iota what Marfield said about the Townley family for had not their doings been the sole topic of conversation, the sole source of scandalised gossip for the past twelve months? This last contretemps concerning Bryony and her elopement with Tim Spencer had almost killed the new Viscountess Overton, it was rumoured, for the mother of the baronet had been so incensed she had gone so far as to forget her breeding and set about her new daughter-in-law as though the pair of them were a couple of fishwives wrangling over their stalls at St John's Market, calling her bitch and worse, it was whispered, doing her best to pull the girl's lovely dark curls from her head in great handfuls and if Sir Timothy had not intervened, which was only right since Lady Spencer was with child, would have knocked her to the ground and kicked her where she lay. Great hopes the new viscountess had harboured for her son. An earl's daughter at least and look at what he had landed up with! The illegitimate daughter of a coal owner and a woman from Colliers Row, granddaughter of a common hewer and a whore into the bargain. That was what Bryony, Lady Spencer was, and she could sling her hook, or words to that effect and it was not until Lady Spencer had reminded Viscountess Overton that Daresbury Park belonged to

Lady Spencer's legal husband did the full horror of the situation strike the viscountess who stumbled back, defeated, to Warwickshire.

Jonas Townley had fared little better, ordered, the servants whispered, from his own daughter's doorstep as though he was no more than a tinker peddling his wares. He was quite broken by it all, they said, his family ripped apart, two daughters who had not a good word for him, his wife ailing with some nervous thing come upon her on the day Lady Spencer called at Bank House in her crested carriage, her eldest daughter cool with her, her second daughter, now married and inclined to deny her own parentage, and the other two willing to take any man who offered for them in order to be away from the dragging atmosphere of heartbreak which pervaded Bank House.

Only the lad, Simeon Townley, seemed willing to offer support to his father. He was always where he should be at Jonas Townley's side at Fielden, or Kenworth or Townley Colliery, serious and observant as he learned his trade, doing as he was bid, polite to one and all, especially Jonas who, after all, it was whispered, held the purse strings and the lad knew full well which side his bread was buttered!

Mr and Mrs Macrae sat together silently through the first half of the concert. A Grand Vocal and Instrumental Concert it had been advertised as, given by the local Choral Society in aid of the society itself. Miss Waldie and Mr Sharples were the principal vocal performers, both from Manchester, assisted by Messrs Thorneycroft, Lindsay and Coleman, amateur performers from Liverpool and the neighbourhood. There was an air, "Every Valley", from the Messiah and sung by Mr Sharples, followed by Mozart's "With Verdure Clad" with Miss Waldie in fine voice. A chorus, again by Mozart, something from Handel, the first part of the evening ending with his "Hallelujah Chorus".

Part two began with a glee, "Swiftly to the Mountain's Brow", sung by Miss Waldie, Mr Sharples, Mr Lindsay and Mr Coleman but by the time it ended, the seats for which Mr Macrae had paid half a guinea each were conspicuously empty and Mr and Mrs Macrae were in a passionate embrace in their closed carriage, Mrs Macrae's beautiful and controversial gown about her waist and her husband's mouth at her breast. She was shrouded in her cloak when he carried her through the front door of the house, held open by an anxious Dora who enquired if there was anything wrong with her mistress.

"No," her master answered shortly. Mrs Macrae was giggling, Dora distinctly heard her and she tutted as she returned to the kitchen, saying it was only "them two" up to their usual tricks again. The servants all knew exactly what she meant.

Conal made love to Jenna with a violence, almost a savagery he had never shown before just as though Charlie Graham's covetous eyes had put some mark on her which he must himself erase with his own body. His hands were hard, rough and hurting as he parted her legs, taking her with as little concern for her pleasure as a man might with some woman he has paid for. He came to a wild and shuddering climax, falling on her so heavily she lay trapped and winded beneath him until his hammering heart had slowed. She smoothed his sweated hair back from his brow, kissing it, soothing him with an understanding love that was almost maternal, holding him to her until he lifted himself on to his elbows to smile ruefully down into her face.

"I'm sorry, lassie. I was a wee bit rough wi' ye."

"You're a brute," she answered dreamily, lifting herself, raising her breasts for his further inspection.

"You know why?"

"Oh yes, but you know very well I was only flirting a little." She ran her hands down his body, her fingers an enquiring caress at the bush of dark springing hair at his crotch. He groaned a little.

"I know that full well, my darling. Had I not I would have beaten you, not made love to you."

"Is that what it was? A beating might have been gentler."

He was contrite but at the same time triumphantly masculine. A man who has just shown his woman to whom she belongs.

"Perhaps we might . . ." She smiled, then began to lick his shoulder, the pulse at his throat, the hard jut of his jaw and it was her turn then as he took her on a wild and joyful journey of love, holding back to allow her to travel it again and again until he went with her at last and then they slept. Charlie Graham was forgotten, if indeed he had existed for either of them for longer than those few moments when Jenna had flirted with him. Jenna's inexhaustible compulsion with Bryony Townley, Bryony Spencer now, was forgotten, as was her brother whose existence picked at Jenna's mind on and off for the best part of each day. The constant anxiety of what she now considered to be her sons' inheritance and how she was to keep it safe for them and away from the self-confessed avaricious hands of her half-brother and sister was obliterated in the enchantment as Jenna and Conal loved one another.

The lovely content and joy of it lingered over the next day, colouring the hours with a warm and rosy hue. With a vigour which delighted them both Conal renewed his possession of her over and over again, making love to her whenever they were alone and the plight of Tim Spencer's sister slipped from Jenna's mind in a haze of well-satisfied, deeply satisfying sensuality.

It was a week later when Dora tapped on her door, saying that there was a lady to see her and should she show her in.

"Who is it, Dora? Didn't she give her name?" Jenna

was just about to go up to the nursery to collect her
sons whom she meant to take to the stables to see the
horses. True to his word and like a child himself in his
excitement, Conal had bought two sturdy cobs, one for
each of his sons and already Ewan was clamouring to be
lifted on to the back of the one he had claimed as his.

"Mine!" he would say fiercely, the one word he used
frequently about everything in the nursery. Everything
there was "mine" from Nanny Abigail who nursed the
intruder called Roddy, to the rocking horse, the books,
the toys, even his bassinet which now rocked Roddy
to sleep.

They were to decide on a name for the pony today,
she and Ewan, for the gentle, sweet-tempered animal
which he decided was his and perhaps for the cob which
would one day be Roddy's. Jenna had racked her brain
and even studied his nursery rhyme books for suitable
names since the animals must be called by something
which was familiar to her son. A name easy for a child
of not yet eighteen months to put his tongue round. She
had been looking forward to this hour when, Roddy in
the baby carriage, her unafraid elder son held firmly by
the hand, they would enter what, to Ewan, was the most
exciting place in his small world.

"I'll come down," she told Dora, her vexation very
plain, hurrying since perhaps the woman, whoever she
was, could be dealt with quickly and sent on her way.

She was standing by the window of the drawing-room,
her back to the door as Jenna entered, a slight drooping
figure dressed in the fine, fur-lined cloak and expensive
boots only the very rich can afford.

"Yes?" Jenna murmured. "You wanted to see me?"

The woman turned. It was Amy Spencer.

Chapter Twenty-eight

Amy told a harrowing, brutal tale. Oh yes, she had managed the journey quite alone, she said to Jenna in a flat voice, and on foot for some of the way, running from her husband and his vast and comfortless house. Many wearying days it took and many wearying hours in the telling of it and of her life since her marriage ten months ago. Sir Robert's house was set high amongst the rough hills and moorland wastes of north-west Northumberland. It was really a fortified manor for it was from there in earlier days his forbears had guarded the border for their monarch against the marauding Scots. Alone and solitary, it stood just below Newton Law from where it got its name, the nearest town being Jedburgh, nineteen harsh miles away over the border in Scotland, the next nearest town Carlisle which was twenty miles distant and situated in Cumberland.

She had decided on Carlisle and, since it was a scant month since the birth of her child and though the snow was as deep as her waist in some places she had followed sheep tracks and old drove roads, careless of danger so great was her desperation to escape her life with Sir Robert. She had at last come to the lower, gentler land just south of Liddel Water and the village where she had rested for two days at the cottage of an elderly woman who had taken her in, and been kind to her, she said tonelessly.

She had been indifferent to the curious stares of the men and women whose language she could scarce understand so broad was their dialect. Her intentions were unclear. She had no hope left of a decent life with her son for he had been taken from her and put in the hands of a "sensible" woman who would not dandle him uselessly on her knee as Sir Robert had found his wife doing. His was a masculine world where her boy would be forced into the mould her husband thought fit and she was no more than her husband's plaything. She could not, or would not, describe the services she had performed for Sir Robert as his plaything, she told Jenna in a calm voice. She was his toy and the breeder of the future sons he meant to have from her and so she might as well be dead. If she died between Newton Law and Jenna's home – she could think of nowhere else to go – then what did it matter now? She had been bred as an ornament for a man's pleasure and had her husband treated her with a little affection and kindness she would, as most women did, have managed her aversion to his caresses but Sir Robert had availed himself of her body at every opportunity, the last time only the night before she left Newton Law which was why she had been forced to the decision that she must go. It was barely a month since her son's birth, her body not yet healed but her husband would not be denied, tearing into her delicate tissues with the mindless rapacity of a bull.

So she could stand it no longer and certainly meant to give him no more children to treat as savagely as he had treated her. Women were weak creatures, she knew that, but she had proved herself fertile and could she bear to be torn from another child as she had from her son? She had learned to love him in the short time he was in her arms and the thought of suffering the pain and heartache over and over again, year after year, was more than she was prepared to endure. It had broken her already wounded heart to leave him, Robert, Sir Robert had called him, but, aware that her husband would follow her if she took him and bring both of them back she had left him behind. If she could not guarantee her own life or even safety over those miles to Carlisle, how could she hazard his? Yes, she was well aware that Sir Robert could still come after her and try to force her to go back with him but if he did she would kill herself, and the way she looked at Jenna and spoke the words told Jenna that she meant it.

From Carlisle it had been easy, she continued in the lifeless monotone she had used throughout the whole horrifying narrative. She had stayed for several days in a large hotel in Port Carlisle, waiting for a steam packet for Liverpool and here she was, her manner saying that Jenna and Jenna's husband could do with her as they wished. She would stay only a day or two, if they would be so kind, and then she would be gone. She would, indeed had planned to stay with Tim, now that Mama was married again and living in Warwickshire, knowing full well that Lady Spencer, as she once had been, would have returned her at once to her husband, whose property Amy was, but now, with Tim married to . . . well, she was sure Jenna would understand.

"But where will you go?" Jenna asked her gently.

"I shall take lodgings in Liverpool."

"Lodgings? And do what?"

"I can sew and play the piano. I'm sure I could get work teaching. A governess, perhaps?"

"Really!"

"Oh please, Jenna, just a day or two then I . . ."

"I have never heard of anything so preposterous in my life. Really, Amy . . ."

"I won't go back to him, Jenna, I swear it, but if you cannot . . . well, give me half an hour and I shall be gone, but not back to . . . to . . . him!"

"You idiot! I meant, when I said preposterous, that you

could no more earn your own living than I could, at least by sewing or playing the piano. No, you will stay here with me as my friend, companion, cousin, whatever you care to call it for as long as you like. Conal and I will think of something. Just look at you . . ."

Amy's exquisite but fragile loveliness, inherited from her mother, was all but gone. She was thin, pallid, gaunt, the spun silver curls which had cascaded about her delicate skull faded and lifeless. The clouded blue-green of her eyes had an almost vacant look about them. She was like a woman – the girl long gone – who is no more than a bare inch or two away from reality. Of this world but not entirely, too numb and degraded to feel any more pain but knowing it was there, its teeth grinning in readiness to rip at her again. She was like a hunted creature brought to bay, ready to cower away, ready to die if needs be, all resources gone. All hope gone.

"God almighty," Conal said when he saw her that evening and she flinched away from him as though he was Sir Robert, falling against Jenna where they sat together on the drawing-room sofa. Jenna held her slumped body against her own strong one, her head high and defiant, her manner telling her husband quite clearly that she would defend this poor little waif with everything in her.

"She's come to stay, Conal," she pronounced firmly, remembering his reluctance when Amy's letter had come several days ago, brooking no argument, guarding her cousin, who surely needed it, from the authority of man.

"Has she indeed?" then he softened, both women seeing it, for who could not help but pity the child in Jenna's arms. She was no more than that, a child handed over to a gross and elderly man to be used and abused in any way he thought fit and Conal pitied her and the thousands of well-bred girls just like her who, for the sake of a "good" marriage, suffered the same fate. But she could not stay here and he told his wife so when

Lady Blenkinsopp had been led away by Marian and Dora, to be bathed and have her hair brushed, a clean, lavender-scented nightgown put on her and was tucked up in the warm bed of the best, fire-glowed guest-room.

"She cannot stay here, my darling. No matter how she has . . . suffered, she cannot stay here. We must take her back to her husband."

"No, never, I won't allow it," Jenna said very softly.

"You have nothing to do with it, and neither have I." Conal's voice was tight with authority since he was a husband with husband's rights, just like Sir Robert Blenkinsopp.

"She will stay here, Conal, for as long as she wants to. This is my home, I take it? Yes? Then she will stay in my home as my guest. I will not send her back to that cruel, perverted old man. Yes, yes, she has told me something of what he does to her in their marriage bed and I can assure you I would not—"

"It is not your concern."

"Then whose concern is it? Who is concerned with cruelty to children, for that is what she is, a child?"

"She is barely a year younger than you and you seem to be able—"

"Six months, I believe, but there is no comparison between Amy and myself. I love you, Conal, and find your attentions pleasing. What we do together is congenial to us both but can you imagine how it must be . . ."

"Not as a woman can, obviously, but you're right, of course. Nevertheless, she cannot be kept from her husband. He has rights, legal rights which cannot be tampered with."

He turned his back on her, the fingers of his left hand drumming against the shelf over the fire while with the other he pulled at his lip, then he turned again to face her.

"This I will do for her. I shall write and let her husband know she is here and quite safe. I will explain she is . . . unwell and ask his permission to keep her until she is recovered. So, until Sir Robert comes knocking on my door demanding the return of his wife she is welcome to stay."

"Thank you, Conal, that will do for now and then later perhaps we can come to some other arrangement. Conal . . ."

"Yes."

"I love you very much, do you know that?"

"Aye, I do, lassie and I must feel the same or I'd not let you twist me round your finger the way you do."

A note was sent to Sir Robert informing him of the whereabouts of his wife, that she was not quite herself and would be glad of a small holiday with her cousin. Both she and Jenna held their breath for several weeks, expecting Amy's husband by the minute but he did not come, nor even answer the note.

Amy began to recover. She looked more herself within two weeks of her arrival, due to Jenna's devoted care. Her hair, washed and brushed until it gleamed, sprang up about her head again in a mass of soft curls and there was a hint of colour beneath her porcelain skin. Her lovely eyes had lost that haunted look of terror and had become, if not exactly calm, then clearer, steadier. She had taken great pleasure in Roddy who, at three months old was ready to smile at anyone who gave him a word, and Jenna, with a warning shake of her head at Nanny Abigail, allowed her to nurse him, asleep or awake, his fluff of copper curls cradled against Amy's breast, his warm, baby softness filling her empty arms. She cried then, the only time Jenna saw her do so, her tears falling on the child's head, bowing her own in great agony but waving away Jenna's sympathy with a thin hand.

Several gowns of Jenna's had been hastily altered for

her and the colour of one, the palest apricot, suited her. She was painfully thin but she began to eat a little and slept the healing sleep nature gives to those in pain.

They were in Jenna's upstairs sitting-room a day or two later when the door was quietly opened, so quietly they did not at first notice Conal standing hesitantly on the threshold and when they did Jenna knew at once that something was dreadfully wrong. It was to do with Amy of course and if Conal imagined for one minute that she would allow her cousin to go back to that brute who was her husband then he was sadly mistaken.

At once she stood up, her arms outstretched in the manner of someone determined to protect a creature weaker than herself, her head already beginning to move in denial.

"No, oh no, Conal. I won't have it. She's . . . she's not well enough. Good heavens, you have only to look at her to see she needs weeks, months of care and . . ."

Conal didn't even glance at Amy. His face was ashen and his voice trembled as he spoke.

"It's not . . . no, darling, it's not Sir Robert," he murmured. Amy fell back into the small velvet chair from which she had attempted to rise, putting her face into her shaking hands and from beneath them a moan escaped. For a moment Jenna half turned to her, distracted from the expression of compassion and sorrow on Conal's face, wanting to be distracted, for it seemed that whatever it was he meant to speak of was to do with her.

"Darling," her husband said gently. "I have something to tell you. Will you no' sit down?"

"No, I won't," she answered him angrily, wanting already to hit out at him, do something, anything to stop him from saying what he seemed about to say. "Why should I sit down, tell me that? Oh God, don't . . ." She put her hand, shaking as uncontrollably as Amy's now, to her lips and began to back away from her husband. "No, no, Conal . . . I don't want to know, really . . ."

"Let me hold you then, my lassie, for you'll surely need to hold on to someone."

"What . . . what is it? What is it, Conal? The boys are safe in the nursery. I've just come from . . ."

"No, sweetheart, no . . ." and at last he had hold of her. She struggled, ready, in her fear, to strike him in any place she could in order to stop his kind and loving voice from telling her the dreadful news and when he did she screamed so loudly little Ewan Macrae in his nursery above heard her and ran to hide his face in Nanny Abigail's lap.

They had been coming to see her, Rose said brokenly. Papa had been so worried about Mama who had not been herself since the day Bryony had called at Bank House to boast of her marriage to Tim. Mama had always been the strong one, the anchor and support to whom they had all clung and this sudden and dreadful inclination of hers to stay in her room, quiet and silent and not at all like their energetic, good-humoured, blithe mama, had frightened them all. But particularly Papa. Papa was all-powerful, more than a match for any danger which came to threaten his family, his home or his collieries, but Mama's illness, for surely that was what ailed Mama, a malady of the spirit, had affected Papa, weakened him, aged him, made him into an old man who could not walk without the aid of a crutch. Mama had been his crutch, all through the past terrible year, and before that it seemed, though they, her daughters, knew little of that except it had brought Simeon and Bryony Townley to Bank House.

Papa had made up his mind, his youngest daughter told her brother-in-law, that only a visit to see Jenna and her two grandsons would put Mama on the road to recovery. And perhaps, she had overheard him say to Mama, this time Jenna might bring herself to forgive him. To put the past behind them. To become as once they had been, or at least talk about it.

"He loved her, you see. Jenna, I mean. She was different to us. She had a spirit he admired and her refusal to accept the bastards and his behaviour in the past, the hurt he had done Mama, grieved him deeply. But it seems he loved Simeon too, and would not give him up so, there they were, two stubborn characters, neither prepared to give way. Papa because he could not. Jenna because she would not and Mama was caught in the middle. So, he was determined to make another attempt to patch it up. Make it better for Mama, and for himself. And there was something he wished to discuss with Jenna, he said. Something to do with the collieries. He was better, as though a load had been lifted from his mind. I don't know what but . . . well, he was almost his old self, Conal, as he . . . as they . . ."

"He was a man torn in two, Rose dear. A man who made mistakes but was doing his best to . . . to right them."

"I know."

Rose, not quite sixteen, was the only one of Jonas Townley's daughters to retain some hold on herself and in the days that followed Conal was to remark to his brother, Mark Eason, that Rose Townley would, given the chance, become as strong and remarkable as his own Jenna. Beth and Nancy simply gave way to one wailing fit of self-pity after another but through it all Jenna was composed and dry-eyed and those who came to offer their condolences, and who remembered him, could not help but murmur to one another that she was the spit of old Ezra Fielden, her grandfather, who had been as hard and unbreakable as flint.

It was at the crossing of Tuebrook Lane and the Bootle Branch Line of the North Western Railway that it had happened. Daniels had stopped the carriage as the train approached even though the gates, in charge of the crossing-keeper, had unaccountably remained open. Afterwards it was revealed that the keeper, a conscientious and reliable man, had suffered some kind of an attack, a great pain in his chest and left arm, it was reported, and had been unable to struggle to the gates, the consequence of which he was never to forgive himself. When the great shrieking monster flung itself in front of Mr and Mrs Townley's carriage horses they panicked and before the horrified gaze of dozens of onlookers, simply charged at it. The animals, the helpless coachman, the carriage and its occupants who, it was reported in the newspapers, were on their way to visit their married daughter in Everton, were dragged along with, and then beneath the fast-moving train and all were dead, even the horses, when they could be got out.

It really was strange, Conal mused again to his brother, how things turned out. Just as though Jenna's tragedy had turned the focus of her mind away from her own, Amy Blenkinsopp was a tower of strength in the shattering days which followed, quietly taking charge of Jenna's household in a way that amazed Conal. She had drifted on the periphery of his conscious mind during the past weeks, a pale and lovely ghost, vanishing whenever she caught sight of him as though his dark, full-blooded maleness was something she could not, as yet, bear to contemplate She had barely registered her presence in Conal's world which was filled completely with his ships and his cargoes, with bills of lading and excise duty, with tides and weather conditions, with the price of this and the cost of that and the profit he would make on the other. From dawn to dusk they were his sole concern, and from dusk to dawn he lived in the comfortable world his wife had created for him, with his sons and their infant doings in the nursery, with the pleasure he and Jenna shared when the bedroom door was closed behind them.

Amy had intruded on none of this and now, suddenly, she seemed to be where she was most needed, taking over the domestic arrangements of Beechfield Lodge, quietly ordering the servants in a way she had been trained for as her mama's daughter. The nursery was just as it had always been with "Aimee" for the moment taking the place of Mama in the children's safe and unchanging world.

Jenna and Conal remained at Bank House. Jenna's presence was required to prevent her sisters from falling into a decline, she told Conal, though they both knew better, and Conal had no choice but to remain with her. Laura Eason had been quite willing to have Nancy and Rose to stay with her until further arrangements were made for them, she had offered and Simeon too, if he was . . . well, if there was nowhere else for him to go, meaning Daresbury Park, Conal knew. Beth, naturally, had returned to her husband's house, declaring that she could take no more. Indeed a woman in her condition, her child expected within the next few weeks, should not be asked to suffer this dreadful blow and if Jenna could not see that, then she should be ashamed of herself. Jenna was hard and hurtful and showed her no sympathy and how was Beth to manage without her mama and papa, would Jenna tell her that?

It was none of these things which concerned Jenna, Conal was quite well aware. She would remain at Bank House and chaperone her sisters, she declared quietly, her face averted from the lounging figure of Simeon Townley who had spent the two days since the accident going to and from Bank House to Kenworth, to Fielden and Townley as though the collieries were already his to direct as he thought fit, with no concession to the propriety nor the decencies which should be observed

477

when in mourning. Jenna could not stop him but she could remain at her father's house to guard what had been her father's and what would be her sons'. It was just as though Simeon, with no adult in charge of him, or at least no person of responsibility to watch him, would strip the house of its costly treasures and pawn them to pay the gambling debts it was rumoured he had. Simeon Townley, now that her father, his father, was gone, was an unwelcome interloper, nothing to do with them and why did he not take himself off to his sister's home which anyone could see was the only place for him, she told Conal.

Yet the lad was reliable enough, Conal found. Willing to run errands and convey messages to do with the funeral arrangements when he was not at the pit. He was restless, true, a certain streak of wildness in him, and Conal had also heard of his tendency to gamble with money he had not yet earned and Jonas had been a fond father and paid his debts. The lad needed a restraining hand for a year or two but there was nothing in him, or so it seemed to him, that was not in all young men of his age and upbringing. He was young, only just seventeen and God only knew who would have the handling of him until he became a man but given a gentle but firm guiding rein he would shape, as most did.

The funeral took place on a mild and pretty day in which the coming of spring seemed imminent. There were early primroses growing in great swathes, pushing through the grass beneath the bare spread of the trees in the churchyard. The winds which had blown steadily from the east, cutting winds from the plains of Siberia, had died away, what was left veering southwards. Daffodil spikes crowded against one another about every grave, the tips showing the yellow of their heads which were not yet out and the birds sang rapturously as Nella and Jonas Townley were laid to rest together.

There had never been, since anyone could remember, so many persons attending one funeral, though perhaps it counted as two, those who were there told one another sadly. And persons from every walk of life, every rank of life, every class of society. Jonas, though an arrogant, stubborn man in his early days and one who had been at the centre of the most notorious scandal ever to have been known in Marfield, had, despite this, been a good and fair employer. Twenty years ago he had brought the women and young children from working underground in his pits, the first coal owner in the district to do so. He had made those collieries as safe as any in the country, indeed had been accused of being soft by other coal owners because of it. The first to use safety lamps, and an enclosed cage to move his men up and down the shafts instead of cramming them together, six to a corve, so that they were in dire peril of tumbling out and down the deep and terrible shaft which many men had done in the past.

And Nella. What could be said about Nella Townley? There were young men and women who could read and write because of her. There were children who were straight of limb, clear of eye because of her. There were children who were alive who would have perished, families who would have gone under, women who walked with unbowed shoulders because of her.

The road leading to the churchyard was lined that day on both sides with silent mourners from Colliers Row, men, women and children, each one with a bit of something black about them, even if it was only a scrap of material on a sleeve. The women wept openly and the men bowed their heads in the deepest respect, if not for him, then for her who had been a great lady. A true lady. They could not get inside the church for it was packed with the grand folk who had done business with their maister. Black-garbed bankers, lawyers, coal owners, men of wealth and authority from St Helens, from Manchester and Liverpool and then there was the family. Nella Townley's two, tragically beautiful sisters with their aristocratic husbands and children. The Townley daughters, Jenna, Nancy and Rose though Mrs Frank Miller, being so close to her time, had not cared to hazard herself in the distress the occasion would undoubtedly bring. Jenna Townley, Mrs Conal Macrae stood tall and straight-backed, in black from head to foot naturally, though she did not wear a veil which was strange. Neither did she shed a tear or show even a measure of grief. Her husband, to whom they thought she might have clung, had her two sisters, one on each arm, supporting them most gallantly but his wife stared over her parents' grave directly and with iced hatred into the faces of Jonas Townley's bastards.

Simeon Townley and his sister, Lady Spencer, stood together and apart from the rest, hands clasped, it was noticed and really, could you feel anything but sorry for that husband of hers who didn't know in which camp to put his foot? Poor sod, finishing up in neither, for his mother turned her face from him and he just seemed to hang about, his young face white and strained as his wife and her brother, stony-faced and defiant, treated him as though he did not exist. They didn't weep, either, returning frigid stare for frigid stare with Mrs Conal Macrae and more than one mourner noticed, and remarked on it later that though their colouring was not at all the same, Jonas Townley's bastards and his eldest daughter had an astonishing likeness to one another. Perhaps it was in the expression but whatever it was it was not pleasant and those who thronged the churchyard, some heartlessly come only to see the show, speculated on the contents of Jonas Townley's will which would be read directly after the service.

Mrs Frank Miller explained as she clumsily took her

seat, in a whisper naturally, for one did not talk of such things out loud, that she felt able to bear this part of the appalling day. Sit, she could; stand, she could not, even with her husband's arm to support her. The lawyer, Mr Thomas Young, seated himself at the table provided in the shrouded drawing-room at Bank House, shuffling papers, clearing his throat, peering over his spectacles to make sure everyone who should be was present. There had been refreshments, many of the mourners having come some distance but gradually Jonas and Nella Townley's friends and neighbours, his customers, the minister and the doctor took the hands of the Townley girls, the legitimate ones, and left. Simeon and Bryony had been seen, still hand in hand, strolling in the mild sunshine of the garden, the stark black of their mourning sombre against the greening shrubs, the hazed mass of the daffodils which were almost out, and the lawn. Sir Timothy Spencer in other circumstances would have left with the gentry, his mama and aunt and their families who had no expectations but he could hardly desert his wife, could he? The tension in the house was electric and even in Marfield it was hard to find a conversation which did not concern Townley and where he had left his money, his pits, his lovely home and his large estate.

After the funeral Conal tried to take his wife's rigid figure in his arms as they were alone for a moment in the bedroom they had shared at Bank House since the accident but though she did not resist it was like embracing a plank of wood. She had been like this ever since he had told her, deep in the shock her parents' death had caused in her. Blank-eyed, frozen, rock-like, answering when spoken to, kind to her sisters but without warmth, entrenched in her need to hold on to herself until the reading of the will was over. Then she would grieve. Then she would turn to him for comfort, he, who knew her so well, was certain. Now she was clinging to some hidden resource of endurance which would hold her steady until the two people whom she hated with a ferocity which alarmed him could be exorcised from her life. Bryony's marriage had made it easy for her since Simeon could now make Daresbury Park his home. Her mama and papa would be hers again, hers and her sisters and she could mourn both of them, her mother and her father when, with his bastards out of her life, her father's mistakes, her father's sin could be decently buried with him.

Though he and his family had been friends of the Townleys for over twenty years the lawyer's voice was clipped and formal as he began to speak. There were the usual bequests to servants, most of whom had been in the Townley and even Fielden service for more than twenty years. There was a sum of money to be set aside annually for the upkeep of the shelter on Smithy Brow, now to be named the Nella Townley Shelter. A refuge for women and children, his wife had called it when she began it soon after he met her, and it had been dear to her heart. The women who had been in her employ were to be taken care of when they reached an age when they could no longer work and there were arrangements which Mr Young was to administer, to maintain the shelter until, if such a thing could happen, it was no longer needed.

"And now to the bulk of Mr Townley's estate," Mr Young said ponderously, glancing briefly over his spectacles but looking at no particular face. Conal, who did not, of course, have any expectations, sat close to Jenna just the same.

"I will read the next part out to you but let me explain that these are Mr Townley's own words, not mine. They are not in any sense written in what might be termed legal phrases since I wrote them as he dictated them but they are still legally binding nevertheless. The will was . . . was finalised only a week before his death."

The silence in the room was absolute, even the weighty ticking of the long-case clock appearing to be more subdued than usual. Mr Young turned a page and without looking up again began to read.

"'I am addressing this to my son and daughters and I want you all to know that after my beloved wife you are more dear to me than anything in this world and I beg you to understand that I must take care of you all to the best of my ability and in a way I think just. My wife is provided for but should she go before I do, God forbid, my estate is to be disposed of as follows:

"'With my devoted thanks for the many years of friendship, service and support they have given to me and my wife, I leave my home called Bank House, the land on which it stands and everything in it to Mark and Laura Eason with the following conditions.'"

There was a rippling gasp from several parts of the room and Mr Young paused for a moment, then went on.

"'The servants will remain, their wages taken care of from a fund I have set up. Mark and Laura are to live at Bank House on the understanding that my daughters, Nancy and Rose will have a home with them until they marry or wish to leave of their own accord at the age of twenty-one. If you, Mark and Laura, do not wish to take on this duty then you have only to say so and other arrangements which my solicitor knows of will be made.

"'Now to you, my son Simeon. I wish you to continue your training in the management of a colliery under the care and guidance of Mark Eason . . .'"

Conal watched Jenna but though her pallor deepened and her hands gripped one another even more ferociously she made no sign that this last had dismayed her. Behind him he was conscious of the held-in breath of Simeon Townley and his sister.

"'. . . and you will also be guaranteed a home at Bank House until you reach the age of twenty-one when, having gained your majority, you may live where you please. Work hard, my son, and don't disappoint me.

"'As to the rest, I have thought hard and long and have only this to say to all of you. When you have it, take care of what I bequeath to you. My son-in-law, Conal Macrae, who has, I suspect, as shrewd a head for business as myself, will guide you all.'"

Conal, who was still carefully watching his wife, ready to leap to her aid should she need it in any way, or perhaps to prevent her from whirling on Simeon as seemed likely from the tone of the will, turned to stare at the lawyer, his mouth dropping open in surprise, then, as each person present in the room turned to stare at him, closing it with a snap.

Mr Young continued: "'And until the time comes he is to be the sole administrator of my estate. With Mark Eason to manage and supervise the collieries as he thinks best, knowing I trust him implicitly, and Conal Macrae to manage and apportion the profits in the same way, may each one of you, my son and my daughters, prosper and be happy. Together or apart. I would naturally prefer it to be together. Now then, to my daughter, Jenna. Jenna, my darling'" – Mr Young cleared his throat in embarrassment but pressed on – "'you know this is how it must be though I am aware you wanted to be involved in the running of the pits but you are a wife and mother now and will lead a full and contented life under your husband's loving guidance. I pray you will one day come to understand that this is the only way it could be, and so, if you can, forgive me. I am a man of my time. You are a woman and a clever one so you will come to realise that this is for the best.

"'On the day my son, Simeon Townley, becomes twenty-one years of age, he, you, and your sisters,

Elizabeth Miller, Nancy and Rose Townley with Bryony Spencer, will each have a percentage of my estate, to control or do with as you please. Until that day you will each receive the profit on your share to be paid quarterly, the shares to be as follows: my daughters Elizabeth Miller, Nancy Townley, Rose Townley and Bryony Spencer will receive five per cent each. My daughter Jenna Macrae and my son Simeon Townley will receive forty per cent each. I beg of you to work wisely and in unison. If you fail in this the collieries and everything your forebears laboured for will be destroyed. In the event of the death of my son his share will go to my daughter Jenna and then to her son Ewan Macrae.

"'If there be a God, may he bless and keep you all.'"

Mr Young did not raise his eyes from the document spread out before him as, from the grave, Jonas Townley dealt his final blow to his daughter, Jenna Macrae.

Chapter Twenty-nine

She was going to make a spectacle of herself, she knew she was, but she could do nothing to stop it. She could do nothing to hold inside her the outrage and pain which fought to get out. As Mr Young spoke she had distinctly heard the hiss of triumph from behind her, knowing, of course, exactly who it came from and the clamp, the rigid curb of self-control she had imposed upon herself since the deaths of her mama and papa flew apart, ripped apart and became ungovernable. She could feel it all dissolving inside her, parts of her breaking away from others, an explosion of feeling which hurt her so badly she had no way of escaping from it. She was aware that Conal was beside her and that she had only to turn to him, give it to him and he would relieve her of it gladly. He would enclose her in his strong, invincible arms and, warding off the forces which were about to overwhelm her, would lead her from this place of anguish and take her to the safe, warm refuge of her home. To the home where her babies were, where her life was, where there was love and laughter and peace. Just that one small movement, of her hand, of her body, a turn of her head and he would make her safe, lead her away, keep them from her, place himself as he had always wanted to, between her and this campaign, this battle she had been fighting ever since she had learned the truth about her father's relationship to Simeon and Bryony. Conal was there. He loved her.

She could feel his love even now lapping about her but it made no difference. None at all.

Her father had acknowledged the bastards publicly!

It was like being bereaved twice. Just as though the moment of stunned shock and then, when realisation had come, of tearing, anguished grief when Conal had told her of the accident, was happening all over again. It was worse in a way for then the wound had been inflicted on unharmed flesh. Now a knife was being thrust into a newly savaged laceration, turned for a second time in a wound which could barely stand the agony of the first.

Her father had cheated her again, committed a breach of trust which, for a moment, took her senses, her voice, the breath from her body and she didn't know how to defend herself. She didn't want to believe it. Even now, with Thomas Young's last words droning in her head like a hive of angry bees, she couldn't believe it. It was not true . . . not, but it was . . . it was, and she could not bear it!

Her head was the first to move in slow denial. She still had on her plain black mourning hat, a spoon-bonnet which was the fashion and worn towards the back of the head. It had a broad, high brim with wide ribbons tied beneath her chin. Under it her face was like chalk and between her white forehead and the deep black of her hat the vivid red of her hair seemed almost indecent on this day. Marian had brushed it severely back from her face and arranged it in a massively heavy coil beneath the frill at the back of the bonnet where again it glowed like fire. The hat bobbed as she moved her head and upon her brow several curls escaped and sprang out in a lively manner.

She stood up and Conal stood with her and on her other side Beth moaned, turning frantically to search for her husband. She had really no clear idea of what was in her father's will. She knew she would get something, probably quite a lot for Papa had been a wealthy man and Frank was counting on it, she knew that too, but now, from the way Jenna was reacting, she could not help but realise that however it had been shared out Jenna was not pleased and was about to say so. Beth didn't think she could cope with a scene, not in her delicate condition. Hadn't she suffered enough already? First there had been the quite disgusting act which had taken place on her wedding night and which, it seemed, Frank expected of her every night. Not at all the romantic dream her imagination had told her to expect. It had led to this gross distortion of her slim body which she hated and which would go on until, in great pain she had been led to believe, the baby, which she wasn't even sure she wanted, was born. On top of all this suffering her mama and her papa had deserted her just when she needed them most and now here was Jenna about to add further torment, not only to Beth's unhappy condition but to the scandal which had almost ruined Beth's life. It was too bad of her sister to subject her to more humiliation. Where was Frank? He must get her away from the intensity of the hateful scene which was coming but it was too late for that.

"I'll destroy it all," Jenna pronounced, her words low but very clear to everyone in the quiet room, "every last shaft and tunnel and roadway before I'll let that bastard set foot in any of my father's pits again. D'you hear me?" She spoke directly to the solicitor as though it was all his doing. Her voice began to rise and she turned violently, throwing off Conal's restraining hand, ignoring the pitiful moans which mewed from her sister's mouth. Looking straight at the brother and sister who sat behind her, her searing gaze moving from one face to the other, she almost strangled on her words as she continued.

"I will personally see to it that dynamite is tossed down each shaft so that there is no way of getting to the coal face. I'll blow up every ventilation shaft and every building and the machinery inside it. I'll destroy the headgear, the trucks, the screens and railway tracks. I'll raze it to the ground. Townley Colliery, Kenworth and Fielden until there's nothing but rubble sooner than let either of you get your hands on a penny that belongs to the Townleys. Do you think I care if I destroy my own share as well, or my sisters'? I'll put every collier out of work, beggar the lot of them . . ."

"Jenna, God almighty, remember where you are." Conal, even knowing his wife as he did, was appalled. Not for a moment had he expected Jonas Townley to leave his pits to his eldest daughter nor to treat her as he would if she had been his eldest son. It was out of the question, foolish, he knew that and so would any sound businessman. To expect a woman, an inexperienced foolish woman, which all women were, in their opinion, to take over and run an empire, even a small one such as the collieries which had belonged to his father-in-law, was preposterous. Townley had done the only thing he could do in the circumstance and Conal admired him for it. He had covered every contingency in the proposed handling of his business, protected it and ensured its smooth and continued running until those to whom it would belong one day were mature enough and experienced enough to manage it themselves.

If that day ever came, he thought with a quick glance at . . . God in heaven, he'd almost called them the bastards himself. And yet, were they? Were they still bastards, illegitimate, if, as Jonas Townley had informed them when their origins had been revealed a year ago, he had adopted them, legalised their position and given his name to Simeon Townley and the then Bryony Townley? The legal perplexities were not clear but that did not seem to matter a great deal since the will just read by the lawyer left no doubt that they were his children and that they were to be recognised as such and share in the estate he had left.

But Jonas had been clear-sighted enough to make sure that his son was protected. Protected from himself and his own youth, his own inexperience and his own and his sister's possible greed. As the will stood Simeon could not squander what was his, nor give it to his sister whose own husband was scarcely more than a boy. He had provided his son with a home and guardianship until he was old enough to fend for himself, as he had his two unmarried daughters who also had an income for life and who better to watch over them, give them support and affection than Conal's own half-brother Mark, and Mark's kind and gentle wife, Laura?

And the Easons had not been left unrewarded, for Bank House and the land it stood on was worth a great deal of money. Another factor, though whether it was deliberate on Jonas Townley's part, was that Jenna could not run over to Bank House – interfering – whenever she felt the need since it was now no longer in her family's possession. Of course Laura, being Jenna's sister-in-law, would not deny Jenna if she asked for hospitality but it was not the same and Jenna would realise it.

He was divided somewhat on Jonas Townley's wisdom, though Jonas had evidently tried to be fair, in leaving Simeon and Jenna exactly the same share in his collieries. Neither had a majority vote in any board decision, not with forty per cent each, though it did seem to Conal that Jenna's sisters, over whom she would have a certain amount of influence, would more than likely vote with her, should it be needed. In which case Simeon and Bryony had forty-five per cent and Jenna and her sisters fifty-five and there was no doubt in his mind his wife would not be slow to take advantage of that! Jonas would have reasoned that Jenna, with her shrewdness, her driving energy and passionate concern for the collieries would do her best to see they did not fail. When the time came, which was not until young Master Simeon was twenty-one, she would guard her own, her sisters', and – fortuitously – Simeon's and his sister's interests like a tigress!

But that was almost four years away and until then he and Mark had had placed on their shoulders the burden of holding the complex, cumbersome and unwieldy concern together; at the same time he himself must keep his wife from not only doing violent harm to Simeon and Bryony who, behind him, were clutching at each other in smiling satisfaction but from destroying, if only to thwart them, the very thing she wanted most passionately. He had known of her ambitions ever since he had first become involved with Jenna and he had done little to dissuade her from them since the chances of her actually owning the collieries had been so remote. Jonas Townley had been a comparatively young man with perhaps ten or even twenty years ahead of him. By then Jenna herself would have become a mature woman of almost forty, her children – and he meant her to have more than two – growing about her, set in the pleasant pattern of the wife of a wealthy businessman, the very idea of being a coal owner in her own right quite foolishly laughable. Simeon would have settled to his place in life as the son of Jonas Townley and the next keeper of the pits and all that entailed, as capable as his father of holding the collieries in good heart and the business would have remained safe, the profits waiting to be passed on to the next generation. Jonas Townley's untimely death had changed all that and how was it to affect not only Simeon but Conal's wife?

Jenna swerved away from Conal's restraining hand, his set face no more than a vague image floating through the shadows of her enraged mind. There were other faces behind him, blurred and horror-stricken, but in the ripping, searing agony which clawed inside her, that was all they were. A blur. She knew they were all familiar to her. She had seen them follow in behind her, the servants hesitant, somewhat bewildered, not at all sure why they were here sitting down with their betters, which surely wasn't right? Mr and Mrs Eason, dignified and upright, Mrs Eason with reddened eyes and a tremble to her mouth for she and Jenna's mother had been close friends for years. Beth leaning heavily on the arm of her eager-faced husband though Frank was doing his best not to let his jubilation show. Whatever Beth got would instantly belong to him since that was the law of the land and he could not wait to get his hands on it. Nancy and Rose, still stunned, Nancy ready to weep at the very mention of Mama and Papa, and they were all staring at her, some with compassion, she could sense that, some with shocked amazement, and two, the two directly behind her, with ill-concealed triumph.

"Tell them, Conal," she appealed to him in a high voice. "Tell these two intruders that they have no place here. Not now. They never had. They had no right being in this house right from the start and now that my . . . my father is . . . is dead there is nothing . . . no one . . . no reason for them to stay . . ."

"Jenna darling, don't do this." Conal had a firm grip on her arm by now. His own face was harrowed and he did his best to draw her to him, his eyes over her shoulder conveying to the frozen figures about the room that she was not herself. She must be forgiven, for was not the shock of both a father and a mother's sudden and frightful death enough to unhinge the strongest mind? She would be calm again soon. When a little time had gone by for everyone knew that time was the only healer, but Jenna wanted no one's sympathy, nor compassion, she only wanted justice and revenge and the only way she saw it as being accomplished was by the swift removal of Simeon and Bryony from her father's house and from the sight of all those whose lives they had so horribly disrupted.

"Let go of me, Conal," she shrieked and behind her hand Lady Spencer murmured something to her brother and they both smiled. Jenna saw it.

"You whey-faced bitch," she hissed, "smirking and fawning over everybody you think might do you some good. Whispering behind your hand to that idiot brother of yours, imagining that you have at last got your grubby hands on my father's money. Oh, you may smile but everyone here knows—"

"Jenna, this must stop at once, do you hear? This is neither the time nor the place to be raking up—"

"Stay out of this, Conal."

The riveted company gasped and Conal Macrae's face became fixed in an expression of white-lipped anger. The rich brown of compassion in his eyes became flat and hard. He had been prepared, knowing her pain, to excuse his wife's demented outburst, to lead her gently from the room, from the house and take her home to her babies who would surely be a comfort to her. It was all over now. She had her part of the inheritance. A fair part, more than fair in many men's eyes and through him, her husband, she would receive what was due her. A very wealthy young woman was Jenna Macrae, Townley's lass, they would say but when this tempest got out, as it would, the old scandal would be dug up again and speculated over, which would not make his or Mark's task an easy one.

Which was another thing! How in God's name was he to run his own business which took up all of his time now at the same time keeping an eye on Townley's collieries? Of course he had the benefit of knowing that his brother could be trusted implicitly and with good men at a technical, administrative and financial level they would manage, but not if Jenna was going to prove bloody-minded, as it seemed she was. She had whirled back to Simeon and Bryony, the latter still with a faint and, even Conal acknowledged it, contemptuous smile about her lips.

Bryony, Lady Spencer looked very lovely. She was, as was proper, in the deepest black of mourning but everything she wore was the very best and latest in fashion, beautifully made and of the finest fabric. Her gown was a separate bodice and skirt, the bodice cut like a waistcoat, buttoned down the front and ending in two points below the waist. It had wide pagoda sleeves, across the lower half of which were half a dozen flounces of black lace, these repeated on the enormous skirt. Her hat was small and dainty, a spoon-bonnet like Jenna's but swathed most attractively with filmy black net. To hide the slight thickening of her figure she wore a fine cashmere shawl which she allowed to slip back from her shoulders to display the soft swell of her bosom. Her honey-tinted skin wore a lovely flush, one of triumph Conal supposed, and her golden brown eyes had a glow in them, a spark of something which told him, and presumably Jenna, that she was well pleased with the way her life had turned out. Her ebony hair was glossy, a hint of light which was almost but not quite chestnut in it and just where the wide satin ribbons of her bonnet crossed her dainty ears small curly tendrils wisped against her skin. She was very desirable, even Conal had to admit that for was he not a man? She would be sixteen years old next month!

But Conal had had more than enough. He knew his nature to be what was known as stubborn, strong-willed. He had a powerful streak of obstinacy which, when aroused, could be menacing. He had for the most part been indulgent of his new young wife, loving her, delighting in pleasing her but only when it did not interfere with what he considered to be her obligation to him and to her sons. He could be easy-going, smilingly good-natured but when his temper was sharpened he could be dangerous.

And Jenna's behaviour had sharpened it. He knew her father's past misdemeanours had hurt her badly but he had also been aware that in the back of her mind had been the almost instinctive belief that he would one day make amends. That he would recognise his own fall from grace and the torment his deceit had caused in his eldest daughter. That he would recognise her as his true child. That he would put it right! He had not done so. Just the reverse in fact, but she could not be allowed to continue this bitter exhibition of her disappointment and, more to the point, her corrosive hatred of her half-brother and sister. He must get her away.

"Come away with you, lassie," he commanded, doing his best to keep his voice gentle. "It's a long drive to Everton and we'd best be off. Make your farewells and we'll be away home. The children will have been missing their—"

"Stop it, Conal. I'm not a child to be cajoled into obedience."

"You're acting like one, Jenna." Conal's voice was very soft but very threatening and at the back of the drawing-room Laura Eason bent her head, resting her brow in one trembling hand.

"If you think so, Conal, then that is your privilege but I must make it plain to all these people present, those to whom my father has left . . . left bequests, that I will not accept that they are entitled to them. I do not, naturally, mean Mrs Blaney or . . . or Dolly . . . nor . . . well, they have been with us a long time and deserve to have their loyalty and service rewarded. I do not begrudge Mr and Mrs Eason – Mark and Laura – their right to . . . to take over what was my home for . . . for eighteen years, though it will be hard."

She blinked rapidly and Conal felt his heart move in pity for her. She lifted her head and squared her shoulders, trying to smile at his brother and sister-in-law to let them know that she really did mean what she said though the loss of the right to run back to Bank House whenever the fancy took her was a bitter blow. She had not really given much thought to what was to become of it, or of those who lived beneath its roof. It was her home, her childhood home, always there, warm and welcoming and even though her mama and papa were gone, it was there and always would be. Again she had just imagined Nancy and Rose remaining there with perhaps Miss Hammond, their governess, and Molly in the nursery as she had always been, to look after them. Simeon, of course, would go to live at Daresbury Park with his sister for where else had he to run to and as far as she was concerned the pair of them could go to the devil. In fact she rather hoped they would though God help that slack-faced boy who hung about now by the door to the drawing-room waiting to take his wife home.

But now that hope had all gone. It had blown up in her face, shattered and unmendable and she could scarcely comprehend, nor bear, what had happened to her. Bank House belonged to someone else and the plan she had nurtured for the past few days, the plan that had got her through them, that she would spend several days each week there in order to be nearer her collieries, was in tatters.

"No," she continued, in a small voice, "Bank House is yours now and I hope . . . I hope . . . I wish you joy in it but I have this to say. I shall do my best to make sure you find none with him."

She lifted a pointing finger to Simeon Townley, her eyes flashing so malevolently that, despite his inclination to swaggering self-importance, he found himself inching a little closer to his sister. He was grateful for his inheritance since he knew it gave himself and his sister a place in the world, something she had always craved. Bryony was elated that their father had, with this final act, told the world that she and Simeon were as much his children as Jenna and the others, particularly Jenna for whom she had always harboured a deep antipathy. She had position now. She had money now of her own, since her husband would not dare to interfere with what her father had left her and, through Simeon, a control in the future running of his father's collieries. Not an overall control but if he knew Bryony she would soon remedy that. Jenna could point a finger and curse at him as much as she liked as she was intent on doing now, it would do her no good. There was a world of difference between being Jonas Townley's bastard and being Jonas Townley's legal heir.

"I'll go to the highest court in the land with this," Jenna spat out, looking first at him then at Bryony but when he turned to glance at his sister he was reassured to see that she was still smiling though she continued to say nothing. Her silence, he was inclined to think, was more effective and certainly more dignified than Jenna's outraged threats.

"I am sure Mr Young will tell me how to go about it, won't you, Mr Young?"

Mr Young, on being appealed to by this passionate, forceful young woman, could only shrug his shoulders since as far as he could tell the will was unbreakable. He wished to God they would stop this dreadful and quite shameful battle over Jonas Townley's will which, in his opinion, was a perfectly decent one. To act like this when the poor fellow was scarcely cold in his grave was quite deplorable particularly on the part of Jenna Macrae and yet, could anyone blame her for being so acrimonious? Her father's misdeeds were not her fault and yet because of them she and her sisters had been forced to give up almost half of their birthright.

"There must be an answer to this farce and I intend to find it," Jenna went on, Mr Young's indecisive shrug not deterring her. "You shall neither of you benefit from my father's will, not if I have to use every penny he left to me to stop it happening. You may smirk, Lady Spencer, thinking you are beyond reproach as the wife of a baronet but you're not, believe me. You have always been double-tongued and two-faced, showing only your good side to my parents but your behaviour with that poor fool you call your husband only proves what you really are."

There was a hiss about the room and Beth Miller moaned and clung to her husband. Conal still gripped his wife's arm but it was inflexible, rigid beneath his fingers and short of forcibly dragging her across the room there was not much he could do. Besides, he found he had a certain sympathy with what she was saying. Bryony Spencer was undoubtedly a beautiful young woman but there was something deep and complex about her, an ambivalence which spoke of her determination to "get on" as it was called. Had not her shameless, or so he had heard, pursuit and seduction of young Tim Spencer shown what she was capable of? That she was prepared to go to any lengths, even if it blackened her own name – which could hardly matter in the circumstances – to achieve her own ends.

"And as for you," Jenna proclaimed, turning contemptuously to Simeon who did his best to follow his sister's lead, assuming a pose of lounging indifference, "why my father thought you have it in you to follow in his footsteps is beyond me. But then he proved himself to be a . . . a fool, more than that, when he took up with the whore who was your mother."

"Jenna, don't, Jenna . . ." The cry of anguish came from the back of the room and everyone turned in surprise for it rose from an unexpected quarter. It was a man's cry and Conal was astonished to see his sister-in-law put her arms about her husband's shoulders. Mark? What had he to do with this tragic spider's web of emotion in which hatred and love seemed to be equally mixed? His brother's head was bowed, his shoulders slumped and when Laura began to lead him from the room he went without a word.

"Come, Jenna." Conal held his wife's arm even more firmly and this time, dismayed and astounded by Mark Eason's apparent breakdown, she allowed him to draw her away towards the door. The servants stood back respectfully, half a dozen of them, those who had served Jonas Townley and benefited from it, one or two still not understanding what had happened, to them or the daughter of their dead master. Beth was heaved to her feet, her hand to her face and beside her her two younger sisters rose with her, Nancy weeping copiously, she didn't really know why except she felt so lost without Mama, Rose blank-faced and dry-eyed.

"Oh dear, I feel so poorly, Frank," Beth moaned, "I really think I should get home at once. Perhaps Doctor Chapel should be called. This has all been too much for me and . . ."

"Of course, my dear, but I'm afraid we shall have to wait for a carriage. If you remember those that were available were to take some of the mourners to the station at St Helens but I'm sure you could go and lie down."

"Really, Frank, can't you see that I'm not fit to . . ."

The petulant voice followed Jenna from the room though neither was really aware of it. Jenna's sister had always been thus, making a great deal of fuss about any small thing – and surely childbirth was perfectly natural – in order to draw attention to herself. In a family of children such as the one in which she had grown up she had often felt overlooked, first by her elder sister Jenna who had been bright and confident, then by Simeon whom she had resented since he was really no more than a second cousin, or so she had thought then, and so should Papa have made such a fuss of him? Now she was to have a child and she was very frightened. They called her fanciful, she knew that, and implored her to be calm but how could she when her mama and papa had just been killed in such a dreadful way? It was enough to make her miscarry and surely Frank should realise that? She wanted to go home to her own immaculate little house where she was safe. To her beautiful curtains, the ones she had chosen herself and the carpets which matched them. To her embroidered sofa cushions, the embroidery done by herself, naturally. To her silver teapot and her ormolu and enamel clock, in fact to the well-ordered, well-polished comfort her nature craved. Safety, the constant attention of her own servants which her papa's money had paid for and the softness of the bed which, for now, she had to herself and where, thankfully, her husband no longer wanted to maul her.

"Dearest, there is no way, at the moment . . ."

"Perhaps I can be of help, Beth." The voice was very sympathetic and when Beth's head turned sharply the girl who had spoken glanced down at her own body as though she and Beth shared a bond since they were in the same predicament so to speak!

Beth stared apprehensively at Bryony. "I don't see . . ." she began hesitantly.

"I know how difficult all this is," Bryony continued, looking suitably sad, "but surely it does not mean I cannot offer my assistance when it seems it is needed."

"Assistance? What . . .?"

"My carriage is at the door," waving a vague hand in the direction of the drawing-room window beyond which could be seen the splendid crested equipage which, as Lady Spencer, Viscountess Overton had felt was her due. "Tim and I would be only too glad to drop you off at your home."

"Well . . ." Beth allowed herself a tiny smile of pleasure since it could do no harm, could it? Personally, she herself had never understood Jenna's antipathy towards Bryony who, after all . . .

Chapter Thirty

The gossip continued in the weeks following Jonas and Nella Townley's deaths, including in it not only the Townleys' immediate family but those who were related to them, one of them Nella Townley's own niece.

It seemed Lady Blenkinsopp had come from Northumberland quite alone, those in Marfield who had known her as Amy Spencer discovered, which was doubly amazing since she had been delivered of a son at the beginning of the year and what was her husband, the baronet, thinking of to allow it? But the answer to that question was not forthcoming and those who whispered about it were forced to contain their curiosity.

There was no such secrecy about Rose Townley's actions for it was well known she and her sister Nancy did not get on and what was more natural than that she should spend time with her older sister, Mrs Conal Macrae?

Rose Townley, who became sixteen years of age several weeks after her parents' deaths, drove over to Beechfield Lodge on the day following her birthday. She was a young girl just entering a state of womanhood and though she had shared the same upbringing as her sisters was as different to Nancy and Beth as oil is to water. She had always been contemptuous of their maidenly blushes and had told them so, jeering at what she called their simpering, empty-headed habit of always deferring to what the gentlemen thought, declaring that she had a mind of her own and meant to use it, as Jenna did. She had a great admiration for her married sister and despite the four years' difference in their ages had always sided with her against their sisters who were much alike. She favoured Jenna in her colouring and looks though what in Jenna was a rich riotous flame of fox red hair and vivid turquoise eyes, was, in Rose, a soft-hued delicacy which was just as striking. Her hair was as thick and curling but it was a pale, almost apricot colour, flowing to her buttocks in a ripple which was reminiscent of sunlight caught beneath water at dusk. Her eyes were a clouded blue-green, light and starred with fine, gold brown lashes and her skin was pearl-like in texture and colour. She was very pretty but her mind was sharp and her tongue caustic and the young men who had been drawn to her by her looks and by her dowry, which would be prodigious, had so far received short shrift!

"I want someone with whom I can hold a decent conversation, Mama," she used to say before Nella's death, "a man who will give me credit for knowing somewhat more than how to sew a fine seam and sing a pretty song," and they had all been aware that she meant someone like her papa or Conal Macrae. A gentleman who would allow her to reveal that she had brains. One who would realise when she spoke of *The Vicar of Wakefield* that she was not referring to a parson from Yorkshire but the book by Goldsmith which she had enjoyed immensely. She had gone through her parents' extensive library by the time she was thirteen, devouring Shakespeare and Plato, Jane Austen, Balzac, Pushkin's *Eugene Onegin* and the stories contained in *The Fall of the House of Usher* by Poe, among many others since her taste was catholic. Her mama had been happy to discuss these books at dinner, having read them all herself though Papa was often fidgety when they did so.

The others had yawned, Simeon, Nancy and Beth, and

though Rose knew Bryony to be as avid a reader as herself, her cousin, as she had thought her to be then, who had always appeared indifferent, even withdrawn from the rest of them, had rarely voiced an opinion.

Rose could play the piano, quite well as it happened, but she liked the grand passion of the rebellious and liberal Ludwig van Beethoven whose elemental force appealed to her, crashing out great chords in what Nancy and Beth called "ear-splitting cacophony", none of which was considered proper or attractive for a young girl to demonstrate in company. Rose had not particularly cared whether she was asked to play in company or not, preferring her own to those her sisters favoured and when Jenna moved to Liverpool she had missed her older sister's delight in stirring up the air with her wilful and sometimes destructive resolution to have her own way. Rose would be the same when she was Jenna's age, she had decided, agreeing fervently that Jenna could run the collieries, if she wanted to, as well as any man and certainly a hundred per cent better than the arrogant and often undisciplined boy who was her cousin Simeon and who, it seemed, Papa was intent on as manager.

The events of the past year had been as devastating a shock to the youngest Townley daughter as they had to her sisters but her own nature, which had always been down-to-earth, able to stand firm where theirs had not, had made her self-contained and outwardly calm. Her sisters had accused her of being cruel, uncaring and selfish since she did not weep and fling herself about despairingly as they did but she had been aware that in that last year of her life, her mama had been quietly grateful for Rose's calmness, her support and acceptance of Papa's scandalous past despite her tender years.

But now it was all over. Now Mama and Papa were gone. Beth was married and two weeks ago had given birth to a daughter. Nancy, still inclined to snivel at the

slightest word, clung to Mrs Eason or was for ever at
Beth's, or, worse still, ready to be friends with Bryony
who had offered her carriage to them both if they cared
to call at Daresbury Park.

So Rose, with Laura Eason's approval, came to pay
her sister a visit.

"I just couldn't stand sharing a roof with Nancy a
moment longer," she declared bluntly. "She really is
insufferable now she has become what she thinks of as
a great heiress but if it's too much just say so and I'll be
off," she told Jenna, quite appalled by her sister's gaunt
and unnaturally quiet manner. Rose spoke with her usual
decisive candour. Take me or leave me, she seemed to
say. I can just as easily climb back in the carriage and be
on my way and Jenna's mouth trembled into an unwilling
smile as she drew her younger sister into her arms.

"Darling, you're always welcome and for as long as
you like."

"But will it not be too much with Amy as well?"

"I could not manage without her, Rose, not at the
moment. She is so good with the . . . well, I am not
quite . . . and . . . she has taken so much off my . . .
and now you will be able to help her, won't you?"

If Rose was surprised to hear her sister speak so . . .
well, to be blunt, more like Beth than Jenna, she did not
show it, settling in at Beechfield Lodge for what appeared
to be an indefinite stay.

Jenna Macrae was not right, not yet, she told herself
during those first weeks but she would be as soon as
she could pull herself from the black, dragging morass
of unhappiness into which her father's death and his
will had flung her. She could hardly contemplate a life
which did not contain her papa who, though she had
barely exchanged a word with him, and those she had
brusque and unpleasant, since the revelation of Simeon
and Bryony's birth, had been there, waiting in the wings,

so to speak, until Jenna was prepared to accept him again. Which she would have done, she had subconsciously known, if only he had not got himself killed. Even then, had he left his collieries to his grandsons, his death, though devastating, would have been sweetly, naturally mourned. And her mama. How could she manage a life in which her patient, humorous, tolerant mama was not there with her arms open wide to enfold her often troubled and unsteady daughter?

She had sworn on the day her papa's will was read to destroy the pits rather than let Simeon and Bryony benefit from them and she had meant it so great had been her horror. Conal had brought her home, held her firmly in his iron-hard arms, compelled her to calmness and now, she was not quite sure how it had happened, she couldn't creep out of it. She must get over to Marfield and see what sort of a mess that . . . that bastard was making of her father's concerns, show him who was in charge, let them all see that Jonas Townley was not dead, not while his daughter lived, and she would, she would when she felt more . . . more steady. It was as though she was lightly drugged, able to hear and speak and tiptoe about her room but everything was hazed and it was, for the moment, so much more comfortable that way. In a while she would come from that haze and see and feel things clearly and then she would set about the business of destroying the bastards.

Now, for the moment, she could not get to grips with herself, with life, with the day-to-day needs of her children, her household and her husband. Amy had stood as a bulwark between it all and though it had stirred her heart to a terrible sadness as she crouched over her sitting-room fire to hear her son shout for "Aimee . . . Aimee," instead of "Mama", she could not seem to escape from the drowning pool of misery in which she floundered.

She slept each night in Conal's arms, passive as a dove, and just as pale and lovely. No fire now, no passion, no response to his attempts at gentle, compassionate lovemaking. She dined opposite him each night, putting a morsel of this or that to her lips, dressed immaculately by her maid in gowns which had become too big for her, her hair smooth with none of that enchanting inclination it usually had to drift in long, shining corkscrews about her neck and ears. Amy on her right and, now, Rose on her left and if she saw her husband's glance fall admiringly and approvingly on her cousin she did not recognise it.

Amy, after the weeks she had spent at Beechfield Lodge with her husband's grudging and temporary permission, or so he said, had become again the serene, quite exquisite young woman she had been before her marriage to Sir Robert. In the healing joy of Jenna's children, the peace of the lovely rooms and the spring blooming gardens about the house, the gentle compassion of Conal Macrae who was unfailingly kind to her, she was recovering from the wounds inflicted on her by her husband. She longed for her own child naturally, but Jenna's son, with no mama to romp with him turned to "Aimee . . ." who, though she was not Mama, was a wonderful substitute. Amy was loved, needed. The servants liked, respected and obeyed her. She was content and if her eyes turned more than they should to her cousin Jenna's husband, Jenna certainly did not notice it. In the weeks following the death of Jonas and Nella Townley, Amy had, in all but one respect, become Jenna Macrae as she blossomed like some lovely rosebud opening into sunshine.

"Shall I serve coffee in the drawing-room, madam?" Dora would ask but it was not to Jenna that she looked for confirmation but to Amy. To give Amy her due she would always turn to Jenna, her expression enquiring but, as was usually the case, Jenna shrugged indifferently, and

Amy would direct the servants as she had done since the day of the accident.

"We must do something about her, Amy," Rose said when she had been at Beechfield a week. "It's over seven weeks since Mama and Papa . . . the day the will was read and though I don't expect her to have got over her grief . . . none of us have . . . no, really, I'm all right" – gulping back her own tears – "but she isn't even functioning as she should. She can't just drift on like this, taking no notice of her husband or her children. Thousands of women suffer grief and sadness . . . oh, I'm sorry, Amy, I am so thoughtless," as Amy bent her head for a moment, "you know I don't meant to . . . it's just that I'm bewildered by the way Jenna is allowing this to . . . to affect her. Perhaps if we got her out of black it might help. What do you think?"

"She can't discard her mourning, Rose. It wouldn't be proper." Even Amy was dressed in the deepest black for her aunt and uncle and it would be six months before Jenna could discard hers.

"Perhaps if she were to cry or something. Have you ever seen her weep?"

"No, but then . . . well, maybe when she is alone with Conal?"

Rose sighed, turning her eyes upwards as though she would pierce the ceiling above to Jenna's sitting-room where her sister was huddled in a chair by the window. Rose had put her there that morning so that she might watch Ewan play with her and Amy on the wide lawn, perhaps be compelled to run down and join them. Ewan was walking now, falling down and picking himself up with monotonous regularity which did not appear to discourage him in the slightest and from the baby carriage pushed by Nanny Abigail four-month-old Roddy had watched admiringly. They had seen her pale face at the window and had begged Ewan to wave to Mama which obligingly he did. She had waved back but had remained where she was and when, an hour later, they had all bustled into her room, rosy-cheeked and slightly dishevelled, even Roddy, she had merely smiled vaguely in their direction. Ewan, in that determined way he had, clambered on to his mama's lap since it was what he had always done as far back as his infant mind could remember. Her arms had gone round him and her cheek rested on his glowing curls but her quietness, her impassive reluctance to play as once she had, had soon bored him and he had lurched to the floor, taking Aimee's hand and demanding something of her with the unintelligible baby chatter in which only three or four short sentences had any meaning – except to him!

Jenna's gaze had returned to the garden, to the swaying carpet of daffodils which moved in the stiff March breeze and Rose and Amy exchanged defeated glances as they stood up at the child's insistence.

"Lunch will be ready soon, Jenna. There's salmon and . . ."

"I'm not very hungry, Rose. Just a little soup perhaps. On a tray by my fire."

"Jenna, please come down, darling. Conal won't like it if you hang about all day in your room."

"Rose, please, I thought you at least would understand that – well, at least not just yet – I cannot forget what happened to Mama and Papa, and the—"

"It happened to us all, Jenna," Rose interrupted fiercely. "Not just to you. Do you think I'm not . . . not . . ." The words stuck in Rose's throat and she turned away so that Jenna would not see the tears which flooded her face but Jenna at once leaped to her feet, moving to put her arms about her sister.

"I know, darling, dear God, I know, but . . . oh Rose, I'm sorry but I cannot . . . I just cannot seem able to forget what . . . what he did to us. It's here . . . here

. . . here" – thumping her chest with a violent fist – "the pain of knowing he has given what belonged to us, the Fieldens and the Townleys and now, the Macraes, *my* sons, to those . . . Oh dear God, what's the use, what's the use?"

Before Rose's eyes the brief fit of passionate anger was over and Jenna sank back into the apathy in which she found peace and where she hid from everyone, including her husband.

There were no social calls, naturally, since Mrs Macrae could not be expected to suffer visitors, nor indeed should do when she was in mourning for both of her parents. She was, after the first flurry of letters of condolence, left strictly alone which Rose regretted for might not visitors shake her out of this awful self-pity she had sunk into? Conal, of course, continued to attend to his business, going down to his offices each day in Chapel Street, leaving his young wife in the care of her sister, who, though only sixteen, was very capable, and her cousin. He was very often out of his home from early morning until late at night for not only did he have his own business to run but that of his wife's dead father, at least the financial side, and often, so the gossips whispered amongst themselves, did not see his wife and children for days on end.

This did not apply to his wife's lovely cousin, it was rumoured. On one occasion, at the end of April it was, a Sunday, the strollers who took their weekly constitutional on the Marine Parade, which ran beside the river like a grey ribbon from Princes Dock landing stage to the basin of Clarence Dock, were considerably startled, those who knew him and they were many, to see Conal Macrae sauntering along its length with an incredibly lovely young woman who clung to his arm with the appearance of having every right to do so. She was dressed in a gown of silvery grey grosgrain.

Her bonnet was the same colour, just a wisp of silk
and white ruched lace, the whole creation so simple,
so modest she was the focus of every eye. There were
soft roses in her cheeks and her eyes were filled with
pale blue stars. Her hair was smooth, like spun silver
with bobbing curls over her ears and it seemed Jenna
Macrae's husband could scarcely look away from her.
It was only the timely intervention of his own toddling
son who seemed intent on climbing through the railings
and plunging into the river that brought him from what
appeared to be dazzled appreciation of his companion's
charms, or so Mr and Mrs Edward Hainsworth thought
as they stared in fascinated and eager astonishment at the
couple's approach.

Edward Hainsworth was a rival ship owner and one
who would dearly have liked to see Macrae, his ships,
in fact his whole damned business at the bottom of the
Mersey and his wife was a gossip-monger of the worst
sort but their voices were hearty with good fellowship as
they hailed Conal Macrae and his beautiful companion.

"Good morning, Macrae. A fine day for a walk, is
it not?"

Conal turned and though the expression on his face
remained polite, it lost that look of smiling pleasure this
outing with Amy and Ewan was giving him. He had
promised Jenna only last year as they had sailed from
Liverpool to Glasgow that one day he would show her
the view of the river and its far side from this parade
but somehow they had never done it. Almost a whole
year which, until the death of Jonas Townley and his
wife, had been a good one for both him and Jenna.
They had been happy together, sharing a contented
rhythm of days and nights which had been further
fulfilled by the birth of their second son. It had ended
when the runaway horses had smashed the bodies of
Jenna's parents and, or so it seemed at the moment, any

chance of picking up the lovely pattern of the days they had known.

He had begged her only this morning to take a carriage ride with him. No one would take offence if she should be seen in public during her period of mourning, he had told her, and besides, when had Jenna Macrae ever cared about what people thought or said? He and she both knew how she grieved for her parents; what was in her heart, and that was all that mattered, surely, so why did they not take Ewan for an outing, he pleaded. The boy would enjoy the ships and it was a fine, bright day, just right for a stroll on the parade.

She had sighed, her face withdrawn, pale against the black of her gown.

"Not today, darling, perhaps when . . ." Her voice trailed away and Rose and Amy, who were sitting with her, doing their best to draw her into plans for a picnic by the small lake if the weather stayed as warm and spring-like as it was, turned to gaze anxiously at Conal.

"Perhaps when?" he asked coolly.

"Well, another day . . . soon."

"But I feel like a walk today, Jenna. Look at that sunshine."

"Yes."

"Please, my love, it will do us both good."

"I'd rather not, Conal, really. I'm poor company. Why don't you take Rose, or Amy?"

Someone should stay with her, they decided and so Conal, somewhat reluctantly, he didn't really know why, drove with his son and his wife's cousin to the river and found that Amy's shy interest, her smiling delight, her hesitant hand on his arm, her exquisite, fragile beauty filled him with a pleasure he had not known for months. She hung on to his every word, not like some giddy, unformed girl whose self-interest was immature and unattractive to a man such as himself, but with the genuinely warm regard of a woman who is out of the world she has always known. One who has been transported to one which is new, exotic and unbelievably wonderful. How could any man resist the appeal of such delicate loveliness? She was dainty, small-boned, her head no higher than his shoulder, a little silvery thing who looked as though the lightest blow might fell her. She was modest, her long, feathery lashes fanning her cheeks except when she gazed up at him as he explained the sights about them. She was as tender as a new flower, untouched and virginal and yet, from what Jenna had told him when Amy first came to Beechfield, her frail body had known more of sexual abuse than many a whore's. She had borne a child and, like a wounded, terror-stricken young doe, had fled from the man who had hurt her, abandoned her infant and made for safety. She had been in his home for almost two months now and each day he had become more conscious of her at the very periphery of his awareness. Conscious of her fragrance, her soft, almost childish beauty, her vulnerability, her quite enchanting shyness and at the same time her strong and unassertive running of his household while Jenna was . . . well, ill.

She was quite delightful and he was taking great pleasure in giving her pleasure when the voice broke into his enjoyment.

"Aah, good morning, Hainsworth," he answered, his voice courteous. "As you say, a fine day."

"Indeed, indeed. I was just saying to Mrs Hainsworth how warm the sun is for the time of the year."

"It certainly is." Conal would have walked on, Amy still holding his right arm, his son pulling on his left hand but Edward Hainsworth showed every sign of stopping to chat and besides, if he didn't introduce Amy and explain who she was it would be all over Liverpool that Conal Macrae had a mistress. Not that he would be likely to walk with her on a Sunday afternoon in full view of many of Liverpool's society, with his son at his side to boot but best satisfy Hainsworth's curiosity.

"You know my wife?" the man was saying, his eyes devouring Amy's flushed loveliness.

"Indeed, how pleasant to see you again, Mrs Hainsworth."

"Mr Macrae."

"And may I present Lady Blenkinsopp. My wife's cousin. She is staying with us until Jenna is . . . well, you will have heard of . . ."

"Oh, of course, poor Mrs Macrae. We were so sorry to hear of her loss but may I say how honoured we are to make your acquaintance, Lady Blenkinsopp."

"Mrs Hainsworth, Mr Hainsworth."

She was superb. She had been brought up in a privileged class, bred from birth to have that quiet air of natural grace and authority, despite her shyness, which is unconscious in those who have it. But at the same time she was without vanity. She held out her small gloved hand, smiling graciously then, quite unconsciously, moved closer to Conal, holding his arm so firmly he could feel the small swell of her breast press against it. He glanced down at her, taken by surprise by his own masculine response to what appeared to be a plea for protection. It was almost as though the large, well-fed frame of Edward Hainsworth had alarmed her, brought back memories perhaps of the brute who . . . who . . . Dear God, it was quite unbearable, the thought of this tender young creature being subjected to the cruel indignities Robert Blenkinsopp, by all accounts, had forced on her, her soft, young body degraded and brutally torn, her flower-like innocence despoiled . . . Jesus God, if he had the man within range he'd give him the biggest hiding of his life and he didn't care if he went to prison for it. She had accepted him now, but at first when she had come to Beechfield he had been aware that she could tolerate no man near her and unless

515

her husband, which seemed unlikely, changed completely or she was treated as a woman should be treated by some other man, she would remain afraid all her life. She needed champagne and flowers, little frivolities which women appreciated. She needed wooing! She needed to be physically loved by a man, a normal, decent man who would show her the difference between the brute who was her husband and . . . God in heaven, she needed a loving relationship, to learn to trust again . . . Hell's teeth, what was he thinking of . . . here, with his wife at home and his sons . . .

Horrified, he tore his gaze away from her and his eyes met those of Edward Hainsworth and in them was the knowing look one man will give to another where a woman is concerned. It said he understood, and envied Conal Macrae but at the same time, in Conal's place, he would be exactly the same. He knew nothing of Sir Robert Blenkinsopp, nor of Lady Blenkinsopp's tragic story but by God he wished Macrae luck in his pursuit of her. What a delicious child she was, his hooded, lascivious eyes told Conal. With her spun silver curls, the rich cream and rose of her skin, her ripe, glossy child's mouth she would be a catch for any man and the way she was gazing up at Conal Macrae with those great clouded blue eyes of hers it was obvious where her affections lay.

Conal turned cold and his brown eyes became dull and flat with his contained anger and guilty shame. His voice was distant and even his small son who had been tumbling and lurching on the end of his father's arm became still.

"We must get on, Amy," he said harshly and at once she obeyed, nodding coolly, politely at Mr and Mrs Hainsworth, aware that Conal had changed, that something had offended him, though she did not know what.

"I must get over to Marfield tomorrow," he remarked casually at dinner that night, more for something to say than any need to share his plans with his three female companions. Later he was to realise that it was the events of the afternoon and his own confused thoughts which had followed that brought about his carelessness. Rose and Amy, whose gaze he studiously avoided, turned politely to him and he felt compelled to go on.

"I promised Mark I would go to the coal exchange with him just to see what happens there. He tells me it is quite an experience. He has not been in the habit of going, of course, but since . . . well . . ." He felt himself begin to flounder but could not seem to control his own words, especially with Amy's gentle and . . . yes . . . loving eyes upon him. "He goes with young Simeon who, it appears, is applying himself most assiduously to being the young coal owner and is most enlightening, or so Mark . . . well . . ."

Jenna raised her head slowly. It was the first time Simeon Townley's name had been spoken, at least in her presence, since the day of the reading of the will and it was as though a match had been put to the end of a fuse, one which would, when it reached the dynamite, cause an explosion which would blow them all to Kingdom come. Her eyes came alive first, bright and glittering, and if the subject had been a different one Conal would have felt a great surge of thankful jubilation. Her lips parted as though on cue.

"I'll come with you," she said.

Chapter Thirty-one

They said "like father like son" but the good folk of Marfield were inclined to think, as April moved on, that the adage should have read "like father like daughter". Of course Jonas Townley was known to have been a ladies' man in the past and liked to gamble on occasion but give the fellow his due he had worked himself harder than any collier in his pits to get where he had and it seemed Jenna Macrae was to be the same, much to the resentment of that lad of his who had thought he was to be sole "maister".

Shrewd had been Jonas, and resourceful, and you'd only to look at the way he'd left his brass tied up and those girls of his safeguarded to agree he'd known exactly what he was doing. Jenna Macrae had not thought so, of course, and she'd said so after her father's will had been read and they wondered, those who watched her ride into the pit yard with her husband that morning, how they would manage, her and that lad of Jonas's to work alongside one another as it seemed they must. She'd told them all on the day of the funeral exactly how she felt about her half-brother and sister, and at great length and with even greater vigour, it was reported and had it not been for that husband of hers who was, in all but name controller of Townley's fortune, at least until the lad was twenty-one, would have put out the eyes of both of Townley's bastards. Naturally, Townley had not left it in the hands of a green girl, no man would, nor those of an untried lad, for how would either of them have shaped and who else was Townley to trust but a man, an astute businessman like himself, as it seemed this Conal Macrae was.

Simeon Townley's grandfather, Simeon Wood, had been a staunch Methodist, a fine, upstanding member of the colliers' community who, unlike those with whom he had worked, had never taken strong drink, nor another man's wife, neither had he gambled away the brutally hard-earned, pitifully meagre wage he and his family had been paid at the coal face. A decent man, a good man who, if he had a farthing to spare, or even if he had not, even if it meant he himself went hungry, would give it to the first starving woman or child who asked for it. A much loved, well-respected man of the people and yet not "holier than thou" as some religious men were. A man who preached of goodness because he believed in it, and of mercy, and practised it too. A man who liked a good rousing hymn and who often led his fellow workers in a sing-song when, at the end of their fourteen-hour shift they trudged wearily to the miserable hovels in Colliers Row which were home to them. A man who liked to laugh and who raised his voice to praise his Lord without the sanctimonious and false humility of some who considered the Almighty to be their own private property and so would not stoop to communicate with lesser mortals. He shared his God, did Simeon Wood and when he was killed in a pit explosion he was sincerely mourned by hundreds.

His wife was the same, good without a show of piety, ready to run hither and yon at any time of the day or night to help a needy neighbour. Their daughter Leah, the mother of Townley's bastards, as they were still called despite their inheritance, had been another kettle of fish altogether. Until she took up with Townley, though she was reserved, not exactly of them, if you like, she had been as staunch as her mother in her efforts to alleviate the privations the colliers' wives and children suffered. Though they'd not really warmed to her, her being so aloof, like, they'd respected her, been thankful for her ministrations and the many kindnesses she'd shown them and their bairns before the scandal overtook her.

So where had Simeon Townley and Bryony Spencer got their sharp, challenging and acquisitive nature from? the folk of Marfield asked one another and it could only be from the man who had fathered them, for the Woods had thrown away any spare cash they might have had like a man with no arms! That lad of Townley's was, nevertheless, shaping up to be a good coal man, or would when he had more experience, which was not surprising since it was in his blood on both sides. He was not as fair-minded as his father had been which was a pity but he was young yet. Under the guidance of Mr Eason and with Jenna Macrae's husband at his back he'd make a go of it since he knew what he wanted from life, as his sister had done. Well, she was Lady Spencer! Master Simeon was at the pithead every morning prompt at seven to see the shift change, riding in through the yard gate on his fine roan, Leander, which meant "lion-hearted", he witheringly told the lad who ran to hold the animal's head.

And it was as plain as the nose on your face that that lass of Townley's, Leah Wood's girl, was as shrewd as her brother. She had no hand to steady her but she was steady all the same, despite her extreme youth. Lady Spencer's husband seemed unable to control her, and her with child, and indeed, or so it was whispered from one servant to another, had long since given up trying. It was said he spent hours each day in the saddle with that tall, black and white English setter of his at his heels and the gamekeeper at Daresbury Park had told the gardener at Bank House with whom, on occasion, he drank a glass of ale, that he had heard Sir Timothy talk to the animal as though it was human. Algie he called it and it was a poor do when a man had no one to converse with but a damn dog. *They* conversed, brother and sister, by the bloody hour, the servants said, for he was never off the doorstep, reporting to her, it was rumoured, all that had happened at the pit that day.

They had money now to spend as they liked, Simeon Townley and his sister Lady Spencer, which was the only mistake Jonas Townley had made, in many folk's opinion. A quarterly allowance they received, as did Townley's other children, or so the solicitor, Thomas Young, had whispered in the ear of Charlie Graham, the banker's nephew, an allowance which was, due to the satisfying profitability of the Townley Collieries, often quite prodigious. A forty per cent share, forty-five if you counted hers, in this profit, though they could not, of course, touch the actual assets, the investments and property Jonas had left, was a lot of money to put in the hands of mere children. It would be Conal Macrae and Mark Eason who decided what that profit was to be since, under Mark Eason's expertise, a good deal of it would be ploughed back into the business, or invested as Conal Macrae thought fit. A colliery will not produce what it should, like any other concern, unless worn-out machinery is replaced and new technical developments introduced into it.

Lady Spencer was the motivator, there was no doubt of that, for she had enormous influence over her brother and would, it was said in business circles, be the making of him if her ability to spend money was anything to go by. A bottomless purse, she'd need. Those of a more radical leaning had even murmured that she could run the bloody collieries herself, her being so clever. They were strong, the Townley women, wielding enormous power over their men. You only had to remember Nella Townley to realise that, and yet Bryony Spencer was no blood of hers. Of course if Mrs Conal Macrae, Jenna Townley that was, had been able to carry out the promise she'd made at her father's death, the promise to make sure her half-brother and sister got nothing from Jonas Townley's mines, things might have been different. As it was the threat of fierce competition, of a challenge to the Townley bastards, put steel in their hearts and determination in their gut. A determination to set Simeon Townley in the "maister's" place at the pithead, to watch over his inheritance, to make sure Jenna was not "maister" in his place, but it seemed it was not necessary for the rumour was that Jenna Macrae had lost her will to fight and was to remain at home with her babies.

In the last week in April, along with her grim-faced husband, she turned up at Townley Colliery. She was still in the black of mourning but her eyes were clear, her back straight, her step steady. They were in the yard, Mark Eason and Simeon Townley, their heads together with the checkweigh man, the surface worker whose job it was to check the weight of the coal-filled tubs on behalf of the hewers who had cut it from the coal face. There seemed to be some dispute and Simeon, with the vigour of youth and inexperience, was being restrained by Mark's more moderate control. They all three turned as the Macrae carriage drew up and at once Simeon's already mutinous expression became even darker.

"Jenna, this is a pleasant surprise," her brother-in-law said, hurrying forward to kiss her cheek. "We were just off to the coal exchange but we can spare half an hour to . . ."

"No need, Mark, I am to come with you." She did not even glance at Simeon, let alone greet him. He might have been one of the fine horses which were waiting to take Mark's carriage to the coal exchange and into which he now climbed. He scowled at her but said nothing.

Mark glanced quickly at his brother but Conal only shrugged wearily. He had not wanted her to come, his

manner said, and had spent the last twelve hours cursing
his own stupidity in mentioning that he was to visit the
coal exchange, and particularly his incredible lack of
thought when he had spoken Simeon Townley's name.
But would he have wanted her to remain in that apathetic
state which had gripped her ever since the day of the
funeral? It had tried him sorely, stretching his patience
to the limit to see her drifting about the house like some
fretful ghost but at the same time his compassion and the
strength of his love for her had kept him from shaking
her soundly and telling her to pull herself together as he
longed to do.

Now, she had pulled herself together but with what
unacceptable results. It appeared Simeon or Bryony's
names had only to be mentioned and no matter what
she was involved in, no matter how unwell she might
be, no matter how unsuitable it was or how important
her duties as wife and mother, she would fling up her
head like some battle charger, a war horse which will
go galloping to the flag and the bugle, and fight to the
bitter end. Dammit, she was the most perverse woman
he had ever known. He loved her and was proud
of her, overjoyed to see the return of her spirit, her
self, but he wished to God it was some other cause
which had brought her back. Why could she not be
as other women were, women like . . . well . . . He
turned away to hide his expression as a flower-like face,
gentle and . . . swam into his vision. Dear sweet Christ,
what . . .?

"But surely, my dear," Mark was saying as Conal
turned back to him and Jenna, "in the circumstances –
you are still in mourning – we can do anything that needs
to be done at the exchange." Glancing at Simeon he made
the same fatal mistake his brother had made. "Simeon is
progressing splendidly—"

"Conal and I will go in our own carriage, Mark," Jenna

interrupted him smoothly, "but perhaps you might like to join us. It seems unnecessary to take two."

"Of course, whatever you say, Jenna, though with Simeon it might be . . ."

"Ours will easily seat three, won't it, Conal?" and it was made quite plain right from that first moment how it was going to be between Jenna Macrae and Simeon Townley. Simeon simply didn't exist as far as Jenna was concerned. He was as unimportant to the working of the pit, the management of the pit, as the lowliest, unskilled coal face worker who could be replaced immediately if he didn't suit. Simeon Townley didn't suit but he must, because of her father's will, be accepted but that didn't mean Jenna had to acknowledge his presence.

Mark Eason's heart sank. He it was who would be forced to work with these two protagonists. To spend the hours his brother allowed Jenna to dash up here to Marfield and the collieries, and the pair of them, Jonas Townley's children, were to be at each other's throats from the start, Jenna was making that very obvious. Simeon, as yet, had said nothing, probably taken aback by Jenna's unexpected arrival when he had thought her to be safely ensconced in her own wifely duties and the vapours she was reported to have fallen into the day of her father's funeral. Though she was intent on ignoring him at this moment it would not be long before the sparks flew, for Master Simeon in these last weeks had come to think of himself as the young prince stepping into the old King's shoes and would not be prepared to make way for the mere princess, the usurper.

Simeon's face was like thunder. He was remembering that first day, the day on which he had, in his own mind at least, taken over what was his, or as much his as this challenger whose glance passed so contemptuously over him. He and Bryony had come to the colliery together on the day following their father's funeral.

"I'm glad you decided to come, Bry," he had said to her. "Not that she's likely to be there or if she is, can do nothing beyond rant and rave as I seem to remember she is so bloody good at, but a show of force, a 'united front' if you like, right from the start will let her see what she has to contend with. You know what I mean?"

Bryony Spencer leaned forward to straighten her brother's cravat, then stood on tiptoe to place a kiss on his mouth, indifferent to the glances the butler and footman exchanged as they waited patiently by the open door of Daresbury Park where Simeon had spent the night.

"Of course I do and why shouldn't I? We own half of it, don't we?" She smiled lovingly. "You have been going there each day ever since you left school." Her smile broadened to a wide grin as she looked up into his face. "You did not go as the master but today you do and I want to share it with you."

And to stand beside you, to defend and support you for my mind is quicker than yours, she might have added, for none knew better than Bryony Spencer the weaknesses of her adored brother. He was stubborn, determined to make a success, to show them all that he was made of the stuff a good coal man needed, tough and ready to knock out of his way anyone who got in it. Many youths displayed a certain wildness, a reckless course which an older man would not dream of taking, an inclination to rear and buck against restraint, against the hands which controlled them and Simeon had been no exception. To show that they were men, in fact and had no need of the older generation to show them how things were done. But as they approached manhood this lively rebellion had a tendency to die away as the vulnerability of boyhood matured and strengthened. So Simeon would be. Responsibility accepted, with her beside him. Restrictions accepted – with her beside him – in exchange for the lighthearted carelessness of youth.

With the responsibility came advantage which made up for the loss of boyhood. Freedom and choice to do as each man pleased and Simeon Townley, her brother, would have all these things and, with her beside him, would manage and overcome Jenna Macrae, she knew that and she knew he did, too.

"Shall we ride in, d'you think, or use the carriage?" he had asked her, conscious of her advancing pregnancy. His handsome face was creased for he was determined to make an impression on the men who would now regard him, must regard him as a worthy successor to his father.

"Oh, ride, definitely! We want to make a show, don't we, and what better way then to go in side by side on those splendid new mounts I persuaded Tim to buy. That's why I have on my riding habit. A bit tight," smiling down at herself ruefully, again unconcerned with the straight-faced servants, "but who cares about that? Both of us in black. Both on black geldings. A symbol of what we are and what our world is."

Simeon's face assumed a slightly confused expression and Bryony took his arm, leading him down the steps and on to the smoothly raked gravel beyond, well out of hearing of the two menservants.

"We are a pair, my darling brother. A pair. A couple who cannot be parted. Together no one can beat us. We shall today dress exactly alike, ride matching horses as we go to claim our inheritance, which is black coal."

And they had, making a triumphant and incredible entry into the pit yard, the focus of every man and woman who worked on the surface and, indeed, halting pedestrians and traffic alike as they passed through the town. Townley's bastards come into their own at last!

And now she was here, the woman who was his half-sister but by God, he and Bryony would best her, let her see that she had no place here, that he, Simeon

Townley, was capable of taking up his father's crown, of wearing it, and of running these collieries as well as Jonas Townley had done. He would show her, they would show her that she should be at home with her sewing and her babies and all the paraphernalia married women surrounded themselves with.

Not once did it occur to him that Bryony was just such a married woman!

Mark watched the two faces, the two expressions which were so vastly alike and he sighed, wishing to God that Jonas Townley had been less generous with his fine house and his handsome son who were now both in the care and under the protection of himself. The times he had agonised to his Laura in the last weeks that he wished himself, her and their daughter Verity back in the less grand but inordinately more peaceful atmosphere of their old home on the far side of Beggars Wood where they had not realised how lucky they were. It was bad enough having the responsibility of young Master Townley who seemed to think he could spend the night whenever he cared to with his sister at Daresbury Park, but there were Nancy and Rose as well, for though Jonas had placed them beneath the protection of what was now Mark's roof, he had not given Mark the legal guardianship of them and there would soon come a time when they would defy his attempts to keep them at home as Jonas would have wished. Rose had already taken up what seemed to be permanent residence with her sister in Liverpool. Nancy was now seventeen and, ever since the news of her share of her father's fortune had got out, had been the target of what seemed dozens of eager young men who wished to marry it! She was an attractive girl with soft hazel eyes, bright red curls and a creamy freckled skin. Her nature was inclined to peevish self-importance and the trouble was, the moment her own eligibility in the marriage market was made clear to her she had become puffed up with her own good opinion of herself. Not for her a mere funeral undertaker like the one her sister had got and to whom, in March, she had borne a daughter. Nancy was now aiming higher than that and if she and her half-sister Lady Spencer, with whom she was now on amazingly friendly terms, had anything to do with it, no less than a baronet would do!

Rose was more sensible and was certainly destined to be the beauty of the family. Brains and beauty, a pretty devastating combination, Mark and Laura told one another anxiously, wondering what more they might be asked to do for Nella and Jonas Townley's children.

Well, at least one of them was not their responsibility, thank the good God, Mark declared fervently to his wife since she was the most stubborn, valiant and enduring but damned exasperating of the lot and why the hell, cursing in a way which was most unlike him, his brother didn't get her at once with another child, in which circumstances she would be forced to stay in her home and no longer trouble him, was a mystery to him. Left alone, Simeon was showing signs of making a decent coal owner but with Jenna for ever disagreeing with everything he said, every decision he might be asked to make, God alone knew how the mines were to fare.

Jenna Macrae! Dear Jenna, whom he and Laura had affectionately watched grow through wilful, happy childhood, through the years of temperamental and mercurial defiance in which only her inherent sweetness and love of her parents had kept her within the bounds of propriety. Not even that really as the birth of her son seven months after her marriage to Conal had proved.

Followed by Simeon on his fine gelding, Jenna engaging himself and her savage-faced husband in light conversation just as though her half-brother was no more than a passing horseman whom none of them knew, they made their way to the coal exchange.

From that day Jenna began to ride over from Everton with a teeth-gritting and provoking regularity. It seemed she was to defy her husband's express wish for her to stay at home and allow Mark and Simeon to continue the running of her father's pits, and though he was not privy to the arguments which surely must explode beneath his brother's roof, Mark could well imagine them. She continued to present herself at the colliery, very often with her elder son beside her, accompanied by his nursemaid, since she said it would all be his one day.

"Roddy for the shipping office and Ewan for the collieries," she would say, as though the whole thing was cut and dried and there was no denying, young as he was, Ewan Macrae seemed fascinated with the environment which had been his grandfather's before him. When his mama lifted him from the carriage he would embark as fast as his sturdy legs would carry him on a furious exploration of every exciting function in the pit yard. The enormous horses with their hooves the size of dinner plates did not alarm him in the least. Indeed he could not wait to study them at close quarters which he did until a white-faced yard man whisked him away to safety, the boy objecting strenuously and loudly. On his feet again he would make for an interesting heap of "nutty slack", to the detriment of his white, be-sashed dress and when the same labourer distractedly diverted him, set off towards the cage with every intention, it appeared, of going underground with the next shift.

"Don't you think you should fetch that boy of yours, Jenna?" Mark would be forced to say, appalled by the darting, tumble-legged mischief of his eighteen-month-old nephew who, his ebony curls bouncing on his constantly turning head, his bold eyes everywhere at once, caused men to shout hoarse-voiced warnings and reduced his nursemaid to a state of heaving shock.

Spring became summer, days of breathless warmth

when the headgear and winding engine and the score of buildings about the pit yard seemed to shimmer like gauze moved by a breeze. Jenna appeared not to notice the heat. On the drive from Everton the blackberry hedges were laden with frail white flowers above which small, yellow butterflies vibrated. There was a fragrance in the air, drifting into the open carriage, the fragrance of the buttercups standing in the meadows, of the myriad sweet-fern fronds growing in the ditches on each side of the lane, the leaves and buds and blossom of the wild flowers pushing from the sun-warmed earth. She would be in white, casting off her mourning earlier than was thought decent, and every male eye in the yard watched her covertly. White on cream afternoon gowns of organdie, light and dainty and feminine. A tight bodice, long-waisted to a point at the front, buttoning down the back from the high neck to the waist about which she wound a broad sash of pale pink silk. Sleeves tight to the wrist and fastened from the elbow with a dozen pearl buttons. The skirt would be full and the hem brushed her ankle bone revealing her white, low-heeled kid boots. She wore no bonnet, her striking hair held insecurely with a knot of ribbons to match her sash, and it tumbled carelessly about her neck and ears. Mark often wondered, his mouth agape, on the indulgence of his brother, indeed any man who would allow his wife to go about as Jenna was doing, knowing nothing, of course, of the state of affairs in his brother's home. Jenna looked quite magnificent, motherhood having matured her into a womanly loveliness which drew men's eyes to her like bees to a hive. She was quite unique in her complete disregard for the proper and respectable mode of dress which should be worn by a married woman and indeed for the unorthodox calls she made at the colliery office. She sometimes carried a fragile parasol with an ivory-mounted handle, a thing of spun delicacy made up of white lace and tulle rosettes which she would put up as she crossed the yard to the office. Her boots would sink into the spread of coal and muck but she seemed not to care or even notice, her attitude that of a woman who has no need to bother her head about cost.

So far Mark had managed to keep her and Simeon apart, sending the lad to Fielden if Jenna was to come to Townley, or underground on some pretence and as Simeon had no head for figures he was not concerned with the ledgers which lined the shelves at the main office, as Jenna was.

"I've come to take a look at the books, if I may, Mark," she would say quite airily, filling the stuffy office with the fragrance of French perfume, unsettling the clerks as she demanded ledgers and invoices and statements of profit made since her father had died, just as though she did not trust her husband, who kept them in immaculate order with the help of the bookkeeper and an accountant, to pay her her fair share of the profits. And if that was all she wanted why did she not ask Conal to fetch them home for her to study instead of driving over here several times a week and causing chaos in the smooth running of the pit? She was quite recovered, at least on the surface, from that strange detachment which had afflicted her after the death of her parents. Oh yes, Jenna, the old Jenna, was back with a vengeance!

Jenna had done her best to persuade Thomas Young to take the will her father had made to court, stating that it was her intention to contest it since there was no way she could accept that her father's bastards had a right to a share in what he had left. The solicitor and her husband had brought every argument to bear on her that they knew of, saying there were no grounds on which she could contest it since her father had been in his right mind when he made the will and since Simeon and Bryony had been adopted by Jonas Townley when they were children. At least, if that was not exactly true he had tied it all up in such complicated legal knots there was no way of untying them and disinheriting what were, as much as she and her sisters were, his children. He had said so in his will. She could go up to London if she so pleased, though Conal looked menacingly dangerous as he said it, and seek out the highest legal advice in the land but it would do her no good for without the permission of her husband there was not a barrister nor judge who would even see her, let alone listen to her, not without the presence of her husband to guide her and he flatly refused to accompany her. The untangling of this problem, as Jenna called it – even had he wanted it – could not be achieved without some man to help her, Conal told her stiffly. He had not a lot of experience of the law but Thomas Young had and she must know that a woman had no rights, only those her husband was disposed to bestow on her since she had no identity but his. In the law courts to which she might apply for redress of the wrong she thought had been done her and her sisters, the judges, magistrates, clerks, jurors and police were all men and she would stand alone in a man's world, a world where a man had a right to dispose of his possessions as he thought fit. As her father had done! It would therefore be a waste of time and though she had money from her share of the collieries even that, should Conal think fit, could be denied her for the sacrament of marriage had made her possessions his.

She still would not give up though, she told him furiously. There were years ahead of her until Simeon reached his twenty-first birthday and though she begrudged him and that wanton sister of his every farthing they took from the collieries, spending it with such profligacy they would bankrupt her father's business before the year was out, she would make sure they did not get their hands on the shares that had been bequeathed them and which belonged by right to her sons.

Had Conal heard of the high jinks which were now

taking place at Daresbury Park? Lady Spencer had given birth to a daughter whom she had called, contemptuous of opinion, by her dead mother's name of Leah and since then she and that brother of hers seemed intent on giving as many parties and balls and whatever else they could think up as they could cram into their frantic lives. And did Conal know how cosy Jenna's own sisters had become with Lady Spencer? They spent a great deal of their time at Daresbury Park, Miss Nancy Townley and Mrs Frank Miller, whose husband the funeral director was only too pleased to see his wife mixing with what he liked to call "a better class of customer". Sir Timothy and Lady Spencer were for ever entertaining, though their guests were often left wondering who their true host was since Lady Spencer's brother was often the one to stand beside her on the receiving line, or so Jenna had heard. Her husband was there, naturally, but it was felt it was merely to observe the proprieties though why that should trouble Lady Spencer was a mystery.

And in the nursery where Tim Spencer spent more and more of his lonely time, he held his daughter to him with the same adoring love he had once shown his wife.

Chapter Thirty-two

Jenna poured her husband a second cup of coffee, handed it to him with a smile, then leaned back in her chair, her legs outstretched and crossed at the ankle. It was almost ten o'clock and shortly they would begin the lovely prelude to what was almost a nightly occurrence, for their lovemaking, resumed now that she was herself again, was something they both found deeply fulfilling.

"Aren't you having one?" Conal asked mildly though the mildness was deceptive for he thought he knew what was coming.

Jenna gave a small laugh, then sat up again. "Oh, of course. What am I thinking of?" She reached for the coffee pot.

"Not about what you're doing apparently."

"No, my mind is on other things."

"Really." Conal sipped his coffee with a careful show of casualness, his eyes on his wife's brooding face.

"Yes, I was thinking how glad I am that we have two sons."

"Oh aye?"

"Yes."

Conal found he was holding his breath, wondering how she would broach the subject which was on her mind.

"Yes, lassie, and so . . .?"

"Well . . ."

"You're glad we have two sons because you want

no more, is that it?" His voice was still deceptively
mild.

"No, not exactly, I would like more children but . . ."

"You want no more at this moment? Is that what you're
saying?"

"Well . . ."

"Come now, Jenna, be honest with me."

Jenna Macrae was twenty years old and she and Conal
had been married for more than two years. They had, on
the whole, been deeply satisfying years, Conal admitted.
Exasperating, maddening years, as Jenna herself could
be at times for, against his wishes, she had taken to
going over to poke her nose into colliery business, taking
his elder son with her. Fortunately the circumstances of
Jonas Townley's will had prevented her from doing more,
but even that was too much for her husband. Saying
she no longer had the time, the energy – which was
nonsense – nor the inclination, she had abandoned all
the pastimes with which women of her age and class
occupied themselves. She no longer exchanged calls,
those she had made before the death of her parents,
avoided visits and parties with their friends and with
acquaintances of her own age and station in life. She and
Conal rarely attended dances and dinner parties nor gave
them in their own home since she was far too busy with
her inheritance. They no longer supported the theatre,
musical concerts, opera and ballet and the spectacular
firework displays which were put on to celebrate any
special occasion which might arise.

Sometimes she was seen shopping with her sister Rose
and her cousin Amy who was still with them, driving to
the shops in Bold Street to which the rich and fashionable
gave their custom, but what spare time she had, and
even that very little, was given to her children who,
her husband had been heard to declare darkly, would
forget who she was before long. It was that cousin of

hers, the one from Northumberland and Conal Macrae himself who spent hours with Jenna's small sons, and the nursery and garden echoed with high, childish laughter, with their father's deeper bellow, with "Aimee's" slightly off-key singing voice, with the barking of dogs and the mewing of kittens.

With marriage husband and wife became one person in law and that person was the husband. But though Conal had complete control over Jenna by law, he had decided early on in their marriage he would not bind her so tightly to him she would be strangled by it. She had always had a great deal more freedom than most women. Her own carriage and horses, a coachman whom she might call out whenever she pleased, her own mare to ride. He had told her he did not care for her journeys to Marfield a dozen times, unless it was to visit her sister, or her sister-in-law but he was well aware she disobeyed him and spent all her time at the colliery. He had done little to actually stop her, yet. She had been badly wounded, not only by her father's death but by the disposition of his will and Conal had known he must let her get over it in her own way which it seemed she had to a certain extent but that was not to say he must like what she was doing.

Jenna sighed sadly, knowing that what she had to say would not please her husband but what else was she to do? To some extent her reason for doing this had gone. She had wanted Papa's acclaim, Papa's approval. She had longed for him to be proud of her, as if she had been a son. Now, with Papa gone the full thrust of her purpose was gone, if she was honest. Except for Simeon. Since she had been a young girl she had wanted the collieries, not for themselves exactly, though that was there, but because . . . because she wished to show her papa that she could run them as well as any man. Guide them, manage the intricacies of the holdings, supervise the running of all her papa's concerns, as he had done and if she fought Conal every hard, weary step of the way she meant to save them. To save the pits from the havoc she was convinced Simeon Townley's guidance, or lack of it, would wreak on them. And she could not do it if she was tied to the pattern of fertility which was the lot of most married women.

"You know what I'm going to say, don't you, Conal?" She looked at him from beneath her lashes and Conal felt his own long sigh begin in his chest. She looked quite incredibly attractive in her dinner gown of layered lace. It was the colour of tawny amber, the lace so fine he had marvelled that it did not fall apart as she moved. Each drifting layer was edged with a narrow band of self-coloured satin and about her neck she wore a narrow ribbon of velvet to match. Her hair was brushed back and coiled in an enormous chignon in the centre of which was a tawny silk rose. Her skin was pure cream, smooth and flawless and her eyes had the deep, enigmatic brilliance of a sapphire. She was becoming a sophisticated woman, mature, quieter than once she had been and she was the pivot of Conal Macrae's life, but beneath it all she was the same whimsical, ever-changing, always diverting girl with whom he had fallen in love. Her nature was to be good-humoured, sweet-tempered but that nature fought with another which was rebellious, arrogant, suspicious, quick-tempered. For months now she had curbed her impatience, the ebb and flow of her bitterness at what had been done in the past, buried as best she could the longing and frustrations which clawed at her over her inability to get the law to overturn her father's will and now she meant to battle those who had benefited from it. Simeon and Bryony Townley.

"I suppose I do, but tell me anyway."

"You'll not like it."

"I shall have to know first before I decide that, lassie."

"Oh Conal, you know how I have longed to run Papa's collieries," she burst out, unable to maintain the demeanour of calm composure she had won for herself over the last weeks. "I've longed for it and yet at the same time I've dreaded it, but someone must watch over them." She paused, then, "I like being your wife, Conal. I enjoy it, what I do at Beechfield. I love being with my children and I find, though it surprised me at first that my . . . my work here, if you like, gives me a great deal of satisfaction. Satisfaction in knowing that I'm good at it. That I do it well. It is, as I said, a job, like any other, if you know what I mean."

"I think so, Jenna."

"I thought it would bore me, you see, this job which was to be mine."

"And it . . . it hasna?" Conal did his best to keep the small tremble out of his voice, her revelation touching him immeasurably. It was what he had always wanted to hear from her but now, it seemed, it was merely a preamble to something else. He knew what that was, naturally and he found that he hurt inside him for what he must do to her. It would take that shining look of anticipation from her eyes, and the soft and wondering expression her face had assumed when she had divulged her happiness and fulfilment as his wife.

"Not at all. I've proved my worth. I'm good at being a wife and mother and" – she grinned wickedly, her eyes becoming even more brilliant – "and at other aspects of our marriage too."

"I'll no' deny that, Jenna Macrae." His own mouth twisted in a wry grin.

"I find that . . . that I like to do things well, Conal. I take a pride in it." She gave herself a small shake and her smile was warm as she put out her hand to him.

He took it, leaning forward to look into her face. He must try just once more.

"My darling, do you not think that, given time, those in charge at the collieries will look after them as well as your father?" His voice was gentle. She drew back a little as though not quite understanding what he meant.

"I have only the reports my brother gives me," he went on, "but it seems – now promise you won't bite my head off but will allow me to speak – but it seems Simeon is very eager and in Mark's opinion . . ."

With a vicious flick she threw off his hand and reared back in her chair. Her face hardened and her mouth became a thin line of contempt.

"Don't be ridiculous, Conal. You know how wild he has been all his life."

"He was but a boy and is scarcely beyond that now but . . ."

"I can't believe this! You are expecting me to leave what is mine and our sons' in the hands of that reckless, greedy . . ."

"Jenna, he was only being what young men are inclined to be and at a time when he had no expectations of your father, of his father. Now that the responsibility rests with him, Mark and I believe he will face up to it. He is facing up to it and Mark tells me he is prepared to wager he will make a good job of it. He has a reason to buckle down to it, Jenna, and with his sister behind him, who is even more ambitious than he is, there is no need to fear."

"I fear nothing, Conal Macrae. Not Simeon Townley nor Bryony Spencer for neither of them will get a chance to interfere. I mean to run my father's collieries as well as I have run your home for the past two years and nothing you nor Mark can say will stop me."

She looked away from him, her eyes brimming with the tears she did not wish to shed and which even more she did not wish him to see. She had brooded for years on the fascinating prospect which now lay before her. It had come closer and closer during the past weeks with no apparent opposition from Simeon who was always elsewhere when she went to Fielden or Townley. Let him break his back underground, she didn't care for that was where his grandfather had laboured. It seemed fitting somehow and as long as he did not interfere with her decision-making that was all that mattered. She had drawn this moment towards her with the anticipatory excitement of a fisherman slowly reeling in a catch for which he had angled all his life. Now it was here. Just beneath the water's surface the fish was ready to leap up on the end of her line when she would be able to admire the splendour of it. Her pulses quickened and she drew in her breath in fearful and yet enchanted dread.

"I dinna think so, lassie," her husband said. As was usual with him when he was troubled he lapsed into the soft Scots brogue which had been his in childhood. His voice was quiet though, without tone, just as though he had been asked his opinion on the weather and was giving it.

For a moment Jenna was startled as though, thinking herself alone, she had spoken out loud the thoughts which were in her mind.

"Pardon?"

"I think ye heard, Jenna. I have been lenient with you since your parents died and since the day you first went to the colliery, glad that you were recovering and glad in a way that you had something to take your mind from the . . . the tragedy but I dinna wish my wife to concern herself with business, nor to spend most of her days away from her children and her home. There is no need—"

"I beg your pardon!"

"– of it since I am well able to support you and our sons in a way which many women would envy. We have had this conversation more than a few times during the past two years. I have told you on many occasions to stay away from Marfield but you chose to defy me and

I chose to ignore it then. Mark and I are looking after your inheritance, what you choose to call your sons' inheritance, though they have no need of it, keeping it in good heart and we have made a fair showing in profit even in so short a time. Simeon is eager to learn and works bloody hard and one day, before he is twenty-one, will make a good coal owner. Mark is a clever mining engineer and is teaching him everything he knows, which would be impossible with you for there is no way you could go down into the pit. I have a good head for business and, if Simeon Townley is willing, I can see no reason . . ."

"Simeon Townley is nothing to do with me or, as far as I'm concerned, with my father's collieries. I propose simply to ignore him and get on with—"

"Don't be a damned fool, Jenna. You canna 'simply ignore him' as you so quaintly put it. He owns forty per cent of the collieries and all the other investments, the stock your father purchased and from which there is a great deal of income. You can do nothing without his agreement and I would imagine he knows it. Now if I were—"

"I also own forty per cent, Conal, and my three sisters own five each so between us we should be able to outvote him and his sister on any decision which might have to be taken."

"I see you have been doing your homework, Jenna, and I agree. When it comes to voting it appears, *appears*, I say, as though it would go in your favour which is all well and good and when it comes to board meetings at which all the stockholders must attend you will be in a good position but that is not the issue here. Of course you will be included in board meetings, but that is all! The day-to-day running of the mine will be in the hands of Simeon Townley and my brother."

"No!"

"Oh yes, lassie, for Simeon will be a man soon enough

and this is a man's world and if you imagine for one moment that you can enter it . . ."

"I will! I mean to continue going there several days a week. Take Ewan for—"

"No, you will not, madam. My sons are to be shippers. That is what my business is and that is what they will be trained for."

"No, no, Conal. They will have coal mining in their blood, as my father and grandfather and his grandfather had." Her voice rose to an anguished shriek and in the kitchen where the servants were settling down to an after-dinner doze or a desultory chat before making their way to their beds, glances were exchanged. It was a while since Mr and Mrs Macrae had raised their voices to one another so what drama was taking place now?

In the drawing-room where they were also telling one another it was high time they were in their beds, Amy and Rose glanced apprehensively at the ceiling and Amy's heart began to drum in that strange rhythm anything to do with Conal Macrae seemed to rouse in her.

"They are my sons, Jenna, and will do as I think fit. You are my wife and have been for more than two years. You have been quite superb in the running of my home and the management of my children . . ."

"Your home! Your children!"

". . . and you will continue to do exactly, exactly that. You will take up making calls again and will be at home when your friends call on you. You may visit your sisters in Marfield and, I hope, continue to see Laura who, I know, is very fond of you. I should imagine Simeon will remain at Bank House but I'm sure you will be able to avoid him as it seems you wish to do. But when I come home—"

"You can go to hell, Conal Macrae, and take your orders with you for I shall not listen to them."

"– I expect to find you here, with your children."

"Oh, so they're my children now, are they?"

"With your children" – she might not have spoken for all the concern he showed – "in the nursery or here in your sitting-room where one would expect to find a lady."

"You bastard! You can't tell me what—"

"And if I hear, as I surely will for they will fall over themselves to tell me, that you have been within a mile of that bloody colliery, by God, I'll lock you up myself."

"You have no right . . ."

"Have I not? I have every right in the world since, as my wife, you really do not exist as a person."

"You cannot and will not keep me locked up for ever, Conal Macrae. I mean to run those—"

"No, you dinna, lassie. Ye'll gang yer ain gait if ye're let, but I'll not let ye."

"You can't . . ."

"Dinna keep saying that, Jenna. I can and I will."

He was at a pitch of baleful fury where sanity had escaped him and Jenna knew she was in the greatest danger but her own reason was gone and she would not give in and neither would he.

"I shall tell Campbell that he is to take you nowhere but to Liverpool."

"So! I am not allowed to visit my sisters then, nor—"

"As to that, something will be arranged until you have convinced me that you dinna mean to go near the mines."

"An armed guard, perhaps."

"Perhaps."

His voice was harsh and unambivalent and his brown eyes were livid, glowing coals, the whites streaked with the red of his fury. He was a different man to the one who had, fifteen minutes ago, felt his heart move in love when his wife had revealed her happiness in her life with him. A man Jenna had not known existed since he had always been, for the most part, indulgent, easy-going, good-humoured, pleased with her. This was a side to Conal she did not like but it made no difference to her plans. Tomorrow, if she could not order Campbell to take her to Marfield then she would get the groom to saddle her mare and ride over there or, failing that, take a public hansom cab! This was what she had wanted ever since her papa had died and she would not be denied it. She had hoped, long ago, to be in sole charge one day but the law and her father had denied her that but she would fight Simeon Townley and anyone else who tried to stop her for her right to take part, to have her voice listened to and to be the deciding vote, with Rose and Beth and Nancy, in any decision, whatever it was, in the running of the mines. Her papa's collieries were a sacred trust left by generations of Fieldens on her mama's side until they came to her and she meant to guard them against the ravages of Simeon Townley and his sister. The bastards!

"You mean to defy me, don't you, lassie?" Conal said, his voice quiet and menacing. "I can see it in your face. I once said to ye that it isna in ye to lie. Everything you think shows plainly in your face but let me tell ye this, Jenna Macrae, I can be an ugly bastard when I'm crossed and you'd do well to remember it. Now, come to bed and . . ."

"I'd sooner go to the furthest fires of hell than get into bed with you, Conal Macrae."

A dreadful blankness came into his eyes, dousing the furious flame of his rage and his mouth stretched in a savage smile across his bared teeth. Within him something seemed to die as he contemplated their future together for if she was like this now, even before it had really begun, how was it to be between them if she persisted? He had often taken great pleasure in her rebellious spirit, been proud of it, and of her. He had loved the way she fought him, over things that were of no real importance, he realised that now, exulting in her dash and fire. They had battled vigorously but in the end it had always finished in the sweet passion of their bed or, indeed, wherever they happened to be, sometimes in this very room before the fire.

But tonight, for the first time in their married life, it seemed they would not make peace in the fiery meeting of their flesh, for tonight, also for the first time in their married life except during the last month of her pregnancies they were to sleep apart. Her cold, ice-green eyes told him so.

His said differently. "I don't think so, my love. You are my wife and one of your functions, amongst the others which you do so well, is to please me in our marriage bed."

"If you think . . ." Her eyes, which had been so cold, burned like fire in a face which had lost every vestige of colour.

"Oh, I do not think, Jenna, I know," and he took a step towards her, grasping her arms with such force he was to leave five small bruises on each one the next day. Pulling her forcibly to her feet he dragged her into his arms and cruelly captured her mouth with his. She was so amazed she at first made no protest, in fact she was quite ready to respond. He was glorious in his masculine aggression, the epitome of what all women secretly long for in a man, narrow-eyed, ready to be cruel if it was needed to subdue her, his body hard and arrogant against hers. His hair, which had been smoothly brushed back as they, Rose and Amy had dined together, had pitched in a sweep of darkness over his forehead and he looked like a gypsy, bold, wild, fierce and very handsome. She hated him quite desperately and loved him with equal force.

She began to fight him, snapping and snarling, her teeth lethal on his chin and lips, her hands which had

been forced behind her, reaching for the back of his neck,
ready to rake him with her nails.

"Let . . . me . . . go, you filthy bastard, let go of me
or I swear I'll kill you."

"Really, well do your best, my darling, but first I mean
to take you into our room where I will strip you and lay
you on our bed. As I have said before you are my wife,
and wife you'll be tonight!"

With one vicious movement he tore the lovely lace
bodice of her gown down to the waist.

"Never . . . let go of me . . . take your hands off
me . . ."

"You like that, Jenna, you know you do," and the truth
was, she did. She was suddenly filled with an unbearable
excitement and deep in the pit of her belly a delightful and
very familiar intensity stirred. Conal was looking down
into her face but in his eyes there was no warmth, only
the hard certainty that this was his home, that she was
his wife and he would have his own way in the first and
with the second.

Her mouth tightened until it was no more than a slash
of apricot in her white face and her eyes blazed their
defiance. She would fight the weak, female melting
of her body which could be her undoing, and she
would fight him, even if she damaged them both in
the process. She would not give in, not over the mines
and her determination to do as she damn well pleased
with them, and not over this barbarity he was creating in
his attempt to put her in the place he thought she should
be, which was in their bed.

"Take your filth elsewhere, Conal," she said coldly,
glorying in the way he flinched, "for I want none of it
about me."

"Is that so? Then tell me why that mouth of yours,
which is quite luscious now that you have parted it so
invitingly, is so close to mine? And why, if you find it

so distasteful, you have not covered your breasts. I see, you are pretending you had not noticed that I had torn your gown, is that it, or is it that you really are waiting for me to put my mark on you, like this . . . and this? As you see, Jenna, my love, my hands are fully occupied so why don't you move away? My arms are no longer holding you to me so there is nothing to stop you, is there?"

"Conal . . ."

"Aye, lassie?" He put his mouth to her breast and she found her arms lifting and wrapping themselves about his head, clinging to him as the only steady rock in a world of lilting, tilting glory.

Later, in his arms, she slept, exhausted and, staring bleakly into the darkness Conal knew he had won the first small skirmish in the war ahead. She was physically weaker than he was and it was only his own male strength which had dominated and won her, that and their shared passion, but what of tomorrow, the next day and the next? What of next week, next month and all the months and years ahead for if there was one thing that was a certainty in this woman who was his wife, his love, his world it was that she would never give up what she considered was hers.

"Tell Campbell to have the carriage at the front door in fifteen minutes, will you, Marian?" Jenna said to her maid the next morning. "No, I won't wear that gown. Get out my dark green riding habit and boots. It's cool today so you'd best fetch my cloak at the same time. No, I can manage to dress myself and when you come back you can button me up. Off you go. I don't want to be late. There's something I want to discuss with Mr Eason and I believe he and . . . well, he is to go to Kenworth Colliery. Some problem underground from which I am excluded. Oh, and has my husband gone? He has, good. Please hurry, Marian."

She was doing her best to untangle the mass of tight

curls Conal's lovemaking of the night before had created when Marian sidled back into the room, a look of anxious uncertainty on her pleasant, homely face. Jenna turned enquiringly towards her, her heart already beginning to sink as though she knew exactly what Marian was going to say.

"Well?"

"Beg pardon, madam, but Campbell he says . . . well . . ." Marian began to pleat her apron with nervous fingers and on her face was an expression of desperate apology.

"Yes, what is it, Marian?"

"Well, he says that the master has . . . well . . ."

"Yes?"

"The master has given orders that . . ."

Oh dear God, he had meant it then, which thought, as it entered her head, was quite ludicrous when she considered what had happened last night. Could he have made it more plain exactly what he wanted of her, expected of her and of course, the answer was no! Stay at home and be my wife and mother to our children, he had told her, and so why should she be so stunned when Marian came traipsing back to inform her that Campbell, obeying the man who employed him, who paid his wages, was refusing to take her out in the carriage? To Liverpool, she supposed wearily, if she insisted upon it, but not across country to Marfield.

"What did Campbell say, Marian?"

"I'm that sorry, ma'am, an' so's he, but he said it would be more than his job's worth to . . . well . . . what he wants to know is where was you wishing to go because if . . ."

"Never mind, Marian." Jenna became brisk, returning to her mirror and the attack she was making on her hair. "Brush my hair and be quick about it, then do it up in my black lace hair-net. And pass me my hat. No, my riding hat. Thank you. There, that's better."

Under her maid's expert hand her hair was brushed free of its tangles and bound up neatly in the net at the back of her head. The hat next, dashing and exactly matching her riding habit. Her riding boots were drawn up her legs over her breeches, then she stood up and stamped her feet. Lifting the wide skirt of the habit she looped it over her arm and picked up her cloak.

"There, that will do," she said, studying herself in the full-length, cheval glass mirror, turning this way and that to get the full effect. She was pleased with what she saw.

"Right, Marian, I'm off. Tell Lady Blenkinsopp I shall be home for dinner and let Nanny Abigail know I won't be up to the nursery this morning, will you, but I'll be in to see the children as soon as I get home."

"Yes, ma'am." Marian bobbed a curtsey. "Are you . . . will you . . .?"

"I'm off to work, Marian, as usual, if that's what you're trying to say. To my work in my father's collieries as I have always intended." Marian was aware that her mistress was not really telling her but Mr Macrae who all the servants knew was absolutely against it.

"Oh ma'am," she trembled. She was afraid, not only for the peace of the house but for the safety of her mistress.

"Don't worry, Marian," Jenna comforted her, knowing what her maid was thinking. "You won't be blamed nor punished for it."

No, but you will, the maid thought as her mistress strode from the room.

Chapter Thirty-three

Six weeks had gone by and though they had been deeply satisfying weeks to the part of Jenna which had hungered to take control of her father's pits there was, nevertheless, a strange emptiness inside her which no amount of hard work could fill.

A muted shaft of sunlight lay across her bedroom carpet, lifting a soft finger to touch the corner of the tumbled coverlet on the bed and as it moved, warming her foot which she had pushed out from beneath the covers, it seemed to send a message to her brain.

What the devil are you doing lying in your bed, it was saying to her when beyond the window is the sort of day which would normally have you, with Conal beside you on his bay, away on Amber up to the summit of Everton Brow? Even as Conal had his bath and shaved you would have been jostling him to one side in the bathroom, splashing water on your own sleepy face, laughing and sharing kisses with him as you hurriedly threw on your riding habit, intent on a ride before the children woke. Your hair free and flying out like a pennant behind you, the wind whipping your flesh to wakefulness, the sun in your face, dazzling your eyes as it caught in the dew, diamonds in cobwebs, Amber and MacBrodie stretching out joyously . . .

Where had it gone? she sighed, turning over to stare at the window, almost tipping her breakfast tray to the floor. Where had that joy in life she and Conal had once shared, that wonderful feeling that each day was special, that something breathtaking was about to happen, where had it gone? She felt so . . . so . . . calm now, so settled since Conal had given up fighting her over her almost daily visits to the collieries and though it had been a relief when he did for it meant she could call up Campbell and the carriage whenever she pleased, somehow it did not seem to give her the . . . the satisfaction she had expected of it. Their life together was without . . . without fire in it, even in their bed for though Conal made love to her just as regularly and she responded, it had lost that zest, that spontaneous sensuality which, until it was gone, she had not recognised. Oh yes, on the surface the Macraes were as pleasant and polite with one another as any other happily married couple but that was the trouble. Conal and Jenna Macrae had never been polite and pleasant with one another. They had always said and done whatever they felt like saying, or doing, hiding nothing, especially their deep and satisfying love for one another.

She sighed and turned on to her back, staring up at the ceiling. It was Sunday and the pits were closed and soon she would get up and fetch the children, take them walking in the garden or perhaps up to the Zoological Gardens and the menagerie in Everton. It was not too far to push the baby carriage though nanny would be bound to disapprove. This was the only day of the week when she would have the children, uninterrupted, to herself. Where was Conal? Perhaps he would come with her or was he, as he appeared to be so often these days, even on Sunday, down at his shipping office in Chapel Street? He was very busy, he said smoothly, with a growing concern to watch over, as she was he added, and she did not argue. The days simply ran into one another and the weeks hurtled by and, despite her hopes that time would heal, things were no better between them. Summer was drawing to a close as August drifted towards September. Conal was civil with her, demanding nothing of her, certainly not her passion, the storms that once had raged about them: no great upheavals of emotion to disturb the calm ebb and flow of their days, he at his shipping office, she at her collieries.

Ewan's voice caught her attention and she turned her head towards the window. It was opened wide for already it was warm and the sound of squealing laughter drifted up to her, disturbing her calmness, dissipating her sad contemplation of her own peaceful existence. What was he doing? It was surely no more than . . . well, she really had no idea of the time and with a sigh and an unexpected pang she realised it could be halfway through the day for all she knew. Oh no, her breakfast tray was still here, she thought with guilty relief so it could not be that late. Marian always retrieved it about half an hour after she brought it up.

She sat up and the tray wobbled dangerously, then throwing back the covers she moved from the bed to the window, pushed back the curtains and looked out beyond the sill to the long, sloping lawn which led down to the woodland and the lake beside it.

Her husband was chasing Amy who ran like a fleet-foot deer down the slope, her skirts held up to her knees, her slim, white-stockinged legs flashing in the sunlight. They were both laughing, their heads thrown back, their mouths wide and behind them tumbled Jenna's son doing his best to catch up with them though it was clear, his legs being shorter and less certain then theirs, that he would not do so.

"Bring it back," Conal shouted, his voice lifting up into the flower-scented air and floating to where his wife watched from behind her bedroom curtains.

"Bwing it back, Aimee," Jenna's son echoed.

"No, you'll both have to catch me first." Amy's hair

had come free of its neat coils and it flew back from her rosy face, a sun-trapped mixture of silver and gold and pale streaked amber that Jenna had never seen before and so thick and curling it reached to her waist like a living curtain of silk. She wore white, a simple gown of muslin, the hem and modest neckline edged with ruffles of lace. There was a narrow silver ribbon about her waist, tied in a bow at the front. She was quite breathtakingly beautiful, her animation lighting her to a dazzle which quite bewildered Jenna. She had never seen Amy so . . . so alive, even before her disastrous marriage to Sir Robert. She had always been quite incredibly pretty in a serene, unruffled way, attracting gentlemen to her by the score for she was everything they wanted in a wife but she had never shown the slightest inclination to be giddy, vivacious, playful, as she was now.

"Papa . . . Aimee . . . wait . . ." Ewan yelled. He tripped on something, probably over his own whirling feet and crashed to the ground and Jenna winced, wishing Conal would turn back to him, pick him up, kiss him as she would but Conal was still in hot pursuit of something Amy seemed to promise and did not notice his son's fall.

The boy hoisted himself to his feet, his face flushed, ready to cry, not in pain but in temper as his papa and "Aimee" left him behind.

At the edge of the lake Conal caught up with Amy and Jenna heard his triumphant shout. Amy held something behind her back, dancing from side to side to avoid him, laughing, teasing, taunting him to help himself to whatever it was she had stolen. They were face to face, still laughing, as the boy caught up with them, his indignation erupting from him in such great waves Jenna could almost feel them from where she hid and in that strange, dream-like moment her cousin and her husband stopped laughing, stopped hopping about in what had obviously been some game in which Ewan was involved, and became quite still. They faced one another, no more than a foot apart, Amy's small breasts rising and falling with the exertion of her dash. Her hands fell slowly from behind her and settled at her side. One rose again, holding out to Conal whatever it was he had been after and he took it from her, still looking into her face, then, as though a spell had been broken, he tore his gaze away from her and knelt to his son.

"Here it is, laddie," Jenna heard him say. "Now it's your turn to throw the ball but dinna drop it. Amy shall . . ."

"No, really, I must go in, Conal. I have lunch to . . . so you and Ewan . . ."

"No, no . . . Aimee play," Ewan protested, turning to throw his arms about Amy's legs, burrowing his face into her skirt. "Aimee play with Papa an' Ewan."

"But I have things to do, darling." Amy gently disengaged Ewan's clinging arms, then picked him up, settling him on her hip, kissing his flushed cheek. She turned to smile apologetically at Conal. They stood in a small, tight group, Jenna's husband, her cousin and her son and it was at that moment that Jenna became aware of something happening inside her. Her husband's strong, handsome face was stern and uncompromising as he looked into Amy's. His eyebrows dipped as though he was angry and Amy stepped back from him then turned and threw a frantic look at the house. She said something in a low voice, thrust Ewan into his father's arms and ran up the incline of the lawn just as rapidly as she had run down though this time she was not laughing.

Conal and Ewan watched her go, the boy still protesting loudly, then, when she had vanished through the conservatory door, Conal turned away and, setting his son on his feet, held his hand as he led him towards the lake.

555

Jenna moved slowly away from the window and though she was in a pool of warm sunlight she felt cold. She shivered and her pretty nightgown moved about her body in drifting ripples. Her face was quite blank but in her eyes something stirred, deep down, like a fish which hugs the bed of a river but is moving towards the surface. It quivered, no more than a small flashing light then suddenly, as a salmon will break the water and leap into the sunlight, Jenna's eyes became alive.

Her thoughts were jumbled, ravelled together like knitting which has been interfered with by a playful kitten, stitches dropped with the wool left in great knotted loops. She couldn't seem to make sense of what she had just seen and way at the back of her mind she acknowledged that she really didn't want to. There was some strange danger at work, in her home and it had to do with . . . with what? She wasn't awfully sure. She was aware with some deeply buried, primeval female instinct which she could not quite understand that . . . that there was, could be, something threatening in the way Conal and Amy . . . Dear Lord, what was she thinking of? This was ludicrous and she was being absurd in even giving a passing thought to the idea that . . . that . . . what a fool she was to . . . Then why did she feel this accumulation of anxiety and fear and . . . and something else which she was not willing to put a name to? Amy was her cousin and a staunch friend who, until she returned to her husband, as soon she must, Jenna knew that, was giving her a brief breathing space, time to arrange her own busy life to everyone's satisfaction. Which Jenna would do soon if only Conal would be . . . understanding. That was what she needed. Time and understanding and then she and Conal would take up that sweet and lovely intimacy they had known before . . . before . . .

Jenna sighed, her mind once more absorbed with the complexities of her busy life in which she must learn to be wife, mother and coal owner at one and the same time.

Conal had Sir Robert Blenkinsopp's latest letter in his pocket as he strolled down the lawn in the gathering dusk later that evening, the smoke from his cigar wreathed about his neatly brushed head. He had dined well on roast duckling with vegetables grown in his own garden by his own gardener. The meal had been, as usual, superbly cooked by Mrs Garnett, the menu planned by Amy Blenkinsopp and discussed by her with the cook in Jenna Macrae's small back parlour which Amy had taken over on the day of Jonas and Nella Townley's deaths. The day when she had quietly assumed the management of Conal's household, and still did.

When exactly had it been, he wondered despairingly, that he had finally turned away from his wife and found, not unexpectedly, the sweet face, the clouded blue-grey eyes which revealed her feelings for him and the slender body of his wife's cousin filling his disillusioned vision? She had been with them at Beechfield for nearly six months but it could not last, both she and Conal were aware of it. Sir Robert had, for the moment, the son he wanted from his wife and would insist on more children before too long but, for the moment, it appeared, he was prepared to allow his young wife to remain with her cousin. He had given out to his wondering neighbours and friends that she had never quite recovered from the birth of her son, implying that she had developed the nervous condition sometimes found after childbirth in highly bred young mothers such as herself. She had, since her mother was now living in Warwickshire and her sister-in-law was a highly unsuitable sort of a person as everyone would agree, gone to her cousin in Liverpool to recuperate, so the story went but she would soon be taking her rightful place at his side.

Rose had returned to Bank House only the week before since her sister Nancy, when her period of mourning was over and which, unlike Jenna, she refused to discard until the proper time, was to marry in the spring. Her groom-to-be was a well-bred but penniless young man she had met at Daresbury Park, though she did not mention this last to her sister Jenna. His family were landowners and distinguished gentlemen and had been for centuries. No title unfortunately but two thousand acres of farmland and moorland which would benfit greatly from Jonas Townley's cash, and a park in which was set a gracious, mellowed old house which had been built in the reign of Queen Elizabeth. Nancy was in heaven, she had written to Rose, and nothing would do but that Rose should come home and help her prepare for her great day since Rose, naturally, would be her chief bridesmaid. There was so much to discuss, Rose must surely see that, and with Beth in the family way again and Jenna so dreadfully engrossed in their father's mines, who else could Nancy turn to but her younger sister?

So, reluctantly, Rose had gone, groaning out loud at the prospect of the tedious weeks and months ahead as the arrangements, which would be bound to be extensive, for Nancy's wedding swung into action. Already, though the wedding was several months away, Nancy was in that state of smug self-satisfaction brought about by her new and elevated status, particularly in view of the grandness of her bridegroom. And there was so much to do, wouldn't Rose agree? With dear Mama gone, shedding several of her easy tears, who else could she turn to for support but her unmarried sister? Of course, Mrs Eason was very sympathetic but Nancy needed someone – someone she could order about, Rose proclaimed – to be beside her while Nancy decided on her trousseau, her linen and china, her carpets and curtains for she meant to make many changes in the lovely but very ancient seat which was to be her future home. There was the list of wedding guests to be drawn up and the bridesmaids, of whom she wanted at least six, to be decided upon.

"There is you and Verity, of course, and Caro since we are cousins," and which, of course, would guarantee Sir Edward and Lady Faulkner as guests, "Frances Lockwood who is my dearest friend, and Alice Gore and I cannot leave out Susan Finch, Emily Hensall, Sarah Bradshaw and Louise Davies," all older than Nancy and still unmarried and could she forgo the pleasure of drifting, gloating, down the aisle with them behind her? "Oh dear, that's nine, isn't it and I can't leave anyone out and an odd one wouldn't do, would it?" positively glowing as she floated through her betrothed days on a blissful cloud of – in Rose's opinion – insufferable self-complacency.

Conal put his hand in his trouser pocket, fingering the letter which had come in the afternoon post from Northumberland. In it Sir Robert, his tone courteous for was he not a gentleman even if Macrae was not, being in trade, informed Macrae, man to man so to speak, that it was time his wife returned to her duties: he was sure Macrae would know what he meant. Macrae was a married man himself and the absence of his wife beside him was very trying and he had missed her sorely. It was not natural for husband and wife to be parted, not to mention their son who needed the attention of his mother. He was well aware that Lady Blenkinsopp had suffered a complete breakdown of her nervous system after the birth of her child but that was six months ago now and he felt it was time, since she must have recovered, for her to return to Newton Law. By the end of the month, if not before and he was writing to his wife to tell her so.

Conal was aware that Amy had received a letter from her husband in the same post as his own.

He felt her presence rather than heard her. He had walked the full length of the sloping lawn down which they had run so giddily earlier in the day, reaching the edge of what was known as the lake though it was scarcely larger than a village pond. It had been a warm day, still was warm, and midges hung in a buzzing cloud beneath the full branches of the oak tree beside the water. Crows crowded overhead making for their nests and a lonely dove called plaintively for her mate. There was a full moon and the garden and small wood was an enchanted place, all the heavily scented flowers, pink and red of roses, purple of honeysuckle, blue of buddleia, crimson of begonia, seemed white in its mysterious light. It was almost as bright as day, the water a silver shining beyond the trees and yet beneath the vast expanse of foliage, branch touching branch to form a secret canopy, the man and woman were hidden from the house.

A light burned in Jenna's sitting-room where, she had told Amy and Conal, she must go over some figures Mark had given her and which must be ready for the next day. She was sure they would excuse her.

"It smells of strawberries and cream," he said idly, expecting her to know what he meant for it seemed she always did.

"I know. It's the buddleia. The full sun of the day seems to bring it out."

"Strange. I wonder why it is?"

The sky, which had retained a flush of golden peach where the sun had left it was a pure silvery blue now. Her pale blue gown, like the flowers, looked white in the moonlight and as she moved past him to stand beside the broad oak tree whose feet were almost in the water she looked like some ethereal water sprite, insubstantial, dream-like, as this moment was. It was absolutely still, quiet, empty, no movement except in the gentle lap of the water against the weeds and water violets at the lake's edge. Her light perfume, as delicate as she was herself, reached his nostrils and he breathed it in deeply without knowing he was doing it.

"You have heard from my husband?" Her voice was low.

"Yes." His own sighed from him as though he was in torment.

"He said he was writing to tell you to return me to him."

"Godammit, Amy, I cannot bear to think of you with . . ." He seemed about to choke but she did not turn back to him.

"Don't, Conal, really, it does no good. I knew I had to go sometime. I am better, stronger . . ."

"Good God above! I know I have no right to . . . Oh Jesus . . ." Conal could feel the bile rise in his throat for the implication of her words was very clear. Months ago she had come to them, as fragile as the water violets at the edge of the lake, and upon which a man's foot had carelessly trampled, broken almost beyond repairing but she had healed, regained her fragrant beauty, become a valued part of his household and was loved by them all. By his sons, by his servants, by his wife and by . . . aah, yes . . . how did Conal Macrae who loved his wife beyond measuring feel about this gentle, ethereal creature? Was it no more than the compassionate outrage a decent man feels for the suffering of a woman abused by another, or was it more? She had the kind of tranquil innocence any man would surely feel the need to protect, to defend against hurt, an almost child-like loveliness that would be impossible to besmirch. A woman who would awaken that strong, protective instinct which is inherent in the male but which her husband had lacked. It would all happen again, that cruel and greedy lust and could Conal bear to see her returned to it? The careless handling, the nightly outrage Blenkinsopp's gross body would inflict on hers in their marriage bed, the total lack of human warmth and affection dousing her spirit which, in Conal Macrae's home, had burned so sweetly. Was that it? Was that how he felt? Pity, anger, revulsion at what she must endure, or was it more?

"If I . . . we could only keep you here." His voice was so soft it could barely be heard above the quiet night sounds which murmured on the air.

"It's not possible, you know that. I'm his wife and he has a right to . . ." She bowed her head, her back still to him and the fine whiteness of her neck caught the moonlight. She was like a slender column of silvered alabaster, pure and untouchable and yet he had an urgent need to touch her, to awaken some warmth in her, some emotion which had never been touched, some knowledge of how it would be with a man who loved her. Not the bestial demands of the elderly man she had married but one who respected her youth, her inexperience, which was strange in the light of what she had already known, her innocence, which again was a curious word to use, her gentle nature, and would guide her slowly to the true heights of the love she had never known. She would never know them now. She would go back to her swinish husband. For the sake of convention and her baby son she would, *must* learn to accept her marriage and all it entailed but would it not turn her sour, dry up her natural sweetness in the conflict in which she must learn to live? To survive it she must become hardened and the soft trembling awareness, the shy ardour, the trust and, though she was not aware she had revealed it to him, the desire in her eyes when she looked at him, would wither away and die.

"Amy," he said huskily.

"Don't, Conal, please. I cannot bear it, to go, I mean, but I must. If you are . . . are kind to me it will only make it worse. You and Jenna have . . . I don't know how to say this . . . without you, without your . . . friendship I doubt I would have survived. Perhaps it would have been better had I not. If I had perished on that journey down from Newton Law . . ."

"Don't, don't say that, my dear. We, Jenna and I, have done nothing . . . nothing, only . . . loved you."

He choked on this last, bending his head in true pain. He had to force himself to keep bringing Jenna's name into the tormented exchange though he was, in reality, speaking for himself alone. It seemed improper somehow for a married man to say these things to his wife's cousin and yet how foolish, how absurd, what a stupid, stupid way to describe it. In a way that was entirely divorced from his feelings for Jenna was the tremulous love in his heart for Amy. It had none of the fire, the passion, the equality of the love he and Jenna shared. It had none of the excitement, the high and feverish intensity Jenna aroused in him, none of the maddening aggravation, the sometimes rude humour, the laughter, the sweet companionship they had shared.

Had shared!

"Would you like me to write to . . . or perhaps if it came from Jenna, your husband would allow you some more time."

"No, oh no, Conal. I must leave here."

"But . . ."

"And there is my son, you see. I have neglected him long enough. I am . . . I cannot wait to see him . . . hold him."

"Of course, I had forgotten."

"As I had but now that I am stronger, I can perhaps . . . fight for him."

"My dear . . . my dearest . . ."

She turned then and with an almost soundless moan blundered into his arms. They rose to hold her tightly to him and he was conscious of the lightness of her, the fineness, the fragile bones beneath his hands which could so easily be broken. He felt the heat flame in his belly and was ashamed but at the same time he sensed the change in her. She lifted her tear-streaked face which had been pressed into the hollow beneath his chin and looked into his eyes. He put a finger gently to the sweet curve of her cheekbone where the tears were and watched in fascination as her lips parted and she moistened them with her small pink tongue, an unconsciously sensual gesture which further aroused his male ardour.

"You are so beautiful, Amy," he said dreamily and smoothed the back of his hand against her cheek then moved it to cup her chin. She turned her mouth into it, pressing her parted lips into the palm, a gesture so spontaneously loving he felt his heart move in his breast. He was confused, knowing he should draw back. They had done nothing that could not be . . . if not forgotten, then put away. They had not kissed and this embrace could easily be construed as friend comforting, saying farewell, to friend but she turned her face up to his again and his mouth drifted gently to hers in a soft brushing kiss which was no more than the touch of a butterfly's wing.

"Conal," she murmured against his mouth, her breath soft and sweet, pressing the slim length of her body closer to his. "Oh, Conal."

"My little love." His voice was unutterably tender. Her arms tightened about his waist. Her hands were flat against his back, frail and fine-boned but strong now for she wanted . . . what did she want? She was not sure, she only knew that in every encounter with her husband she had never known it. Conal's hands rose to cup her face and his mouth became warmer, more insistent on hers. He tried his best to hold back, knowing what she had suffered at the hands of another man, knowing, deep, deep in his inflamed mind that a voice, a voice he loved, was crying out to him sharply, despairingly to stop this madness.

He hesitated for a brief second but already his hands, of their own volition, had slipped from her face to the long slender column of her throat, to her bare shoulders which rose from the low décolletage of her dinner gown. The gown was of some soft gauzy stuff, short-sleeved with a pretty froth of tiny ruffles about the neckline and when his hands pushed it off her shoulders and down her arms she allowed it, indeed helped him for she was as dazed as he was. Her small, sweetly rounded breasts were as rich and white as milk tipped in dark rose.

"Oh God, Amy," he groaned, as though he was begging her to stop him but she was beyond any point where marriage vows, where friendship and trust and gratitude concerned her. She loved Conal Macrae, her cousin's husband, she had known it for many months now and she also knew that this was the first time she would be truly loved for herself, for Amy Spencer who had girlishly dreamed of this before she married the monster who was her husband. This was the first time, and it would be the last.

He undressed her, then himself, making a bed for them in the roots of the sheltering giant of the oak tree. He laid her on it, spreading her glorious moon-streaked hair out like a fan, then arranged it across her body so that only her rose-tipped breasts peeped out. He spent a mindless hour caressing her, making her purr like a cat and moan like a soul in purgatory, showing her the ways of love and when he took her he had to stop her cries with his mouth lest she wake those in the house.

Afterwards she was like a sleepy child in his arms, smiling and stretching her body this way and that, a sleepy child, but a true woman at last. They kissed tenderly when they were dressed, both knowing that this was the beginning, and the end, for Conal Macrae and Amy Spencer, Amy Blenkinsopp who, tomorrow, would go back to her husband.

Jenna was sitting on the broad window seat as he slipped silently into their bedroom and he did not see her at first for the room was in darkness. The moon shone across the pale carpet, throwing the furniture, and then her figure, into dark relief and when she spoke, her voice like the hoarse croaking of the ravens in the trees at the bottom of the garden, he wondered why he should be surprised.

"And what the hell have you been up to?" it asked him.

Chapter Thirty-four

She lay alone in her bed holding herself tightly, her arms
locked across her breast, holding in her breath, it seemed
to her, for she knew if she let it escape, let it have its way,
it would have her leaping from her bed and screaming at
the window of her pain and desolation. Quite simply, she
knew she couldn't stand it and yet at the same time she
knew she must.

After those first, harshly spoken words to her husband
and his failure to answer, to offer any explanation of
where he had been for the last two hours, she had
become cold and silent, unnaturally so, for she had
always believed, when the idle and preposterous thought
had occurred to her, that if she ever learned that Conal
had been unfaithful to her she would kick and scream and
rake his eyes before turning her attention to the woman
with whom he had deceived her. Not for Jenna Macrae
the impassive silence, the stony-faced acceptance of what
could not be altered, but shouting, violence, madness and
the need for revenge, but never, never in her wildest
imaginings had she dreamed that her husband would
make love to her gentle, sweet-faced cousin, and under
the same roof as his wife and children. Oh, she was aware
that . . . that it had happened elsewhere . . . in the garden
. . . or away from the house but it was the same thing.
His face had turned grey as ash when she spoke and for
a moment was strangely like that of his infant son when

he had been caught in some misdeed, then he had slowly straightened, saying nothing. There was no need, for did she not know him better than any woman alive and could hardly fail to recognise that certain unmistakable air of male fulfilment which she had given to him herself on occasions too numerous to count.

Conal watched her grow old before his eyes and wondered at his own insanity in doing what he had done. His wife stood up, like a woman afflicted with crippled joints, moving towards the warmth of the small fire which still burned in the grate. The words she had spat at him were the only ones she spoke. It was useless to deny what had happened between himself and Amy and could he belittle Jenna's intelligence by trying? He made no attempt to justify what he had done for there was no justification for it unless it was to bring to Amy the awareness of her own worth as a woman and surely that was sophistry, true as it might be. He had wanted her as much as she wanted him and though it was no excuse, he had, at that moment of compassion, loved her. Not as he loved this tall, unbending woman who was his wife. He could never love any woman as he loved Jenna but his heart had been touched by her cousin Amy nevertheless.

So, he could only be honest. Whatever it cost he could only be honest. Easily said and easily done, his inner self sneered, for only a fool will deny he is stealing when he has been caught with his hand in the money box.

Jenna held her hands to the last glowing of the fire. She did not ask why he had brought this devastation to them, not then, for it seemed she was caught fast in some kind of shocked state which would not allow her to speak and though Conal wanted nothing more than to go to her, put his arms about her, take the burden from her, comfort her, tell her of his love which was still hers and was in no way threatened by what he and Amy had done, he knew he couldn't. Shouldn't!

Quite the Sir Galahad, that voice sneered again, comforting first one woman then another, and what will you do now, having lost them both? The injury he had inflicted on his wife this night was unmendable, at least for now and tomorrow there was no doubt Sir Robert Blenkinsopp's wife would be on her way back to her husband. He supposed he should be thankful Jenna had not thought to order her out now, this minute, and he also supposed he would have to go and tell Amy what to expect. There was nothing he could say to Jenna. There was nothing, it appeared, she wished further to say to him. He turned on his heel and left the room as quietly as he had entered it.

The next day she ordered the removal of his clothes, all his personal possessions to a bedroom on the far side of the house, as far away as she could from the one they had shared for two and a half passionate, stormy, sweet and wonderful years and Conal faced the awful possibility that his marriage was over. She had no words for him. She did not look at him, moving round him as unfeelingly as she would a table or a chair which stood in her way. She did not go to the collieries that day as she organised the pattern of the life she now meant to live without him in it and from then on it was as though he had simply dropped off the edge of the world, ceased to exist for her. He had expected, as the shock wore off and the days moved on, that she would turn on him the venom of her loathing, lash out and try to hurt him as he had hurt her, to scream and strike him as had always been her way when tormented. With a devastated Amy gone north to her husband might Jenna not allow her desolation to erupt from her, allow her pain and rage and bewilderment to show? Allow him to talk, perhaps in some way to explain, listen to him, rage at him. If they could just speak to one another might it not be soothed, the dreadful wound he had delivered her, nursed gently, perhaps healed, at least to the extent where their marriage might be given a chance to work again? It would take months, years to pick up once more the durable threads which had made their relationship so strongly woven, the love and trust and delight, the friendship and passion they had shared. They had quarrelled. They had known sharp and bitter arguments in the past over her wilful determination to take up the reins her father had dropped but they had always stood together, in love, against the rest. He had tried to be tolerant for she was young, young and headstrong. She had done her best to see his point of view, understood his need to hold and protect her. But now it was all shattered, smashed by his tenderness, his pity, his concern, his gentle love for her damaged cousin whom he had wanted to repair.

Jenna's pain was so deep it came from a part of her she had not known existed. She had never experienced such despair, no, not even when the horror of her father's past had been revealed to her. It all seemed irrelevant now, foolish even, Papa's unfaithfulness, his deceit, the children he had brought into the family, his will which had favoured his illegitimate son. Unimportant beside this dreadful crisis which had ripped her life apart. Everything she had ever valued, truly valued, she realised it now, was in ruin and ashes and nothing would be the same again. Two men had destroyed it. She had lost faith, first with her papa, now with Conal. The husband she had loved, blindly, trustfully, the husband to whom she had given her life, who had given her life stability, comfort and truth and on whom, though she had not known it then, she had leaned for over two years, had lain with her cousin, the woman she had called friend and the pain was not to be borne. She had been crushed by her father's treachery, now she was crushed again by Conal's.

She could not sleep. Not that first night nor on any other and her bleak blue-green eyes stared from her face which had become gaunt. She looked very much as her mother had looked in the last catastrophic year of her life. The year the truth about Simeon and Bryony Townley had been revealed to her own children. Jenna could find no relief, even in her children, nor in the work she went to each day though she spent all her time with either one or the other. They said at the colliery that she must be ill, or losing her mind for she found no challenge in arguing over every decision, every word spoken, every order given by her half-brother Simeon Townley, and they were glad of it. Not that she was ill, or mad, but that at last she seemed willing to let him take her father's place since, under Mark Eason's guidance, the lad was making a decent fist of it. A bit cocky, but then weren't all young men, and bent on including that sister of his, whose daughter, born in June, hadn't kept her at home, in grandiose schemes he had planned – or that she had planned – but there were years yet to knock him into shape and he'd made a good beginning. What was up with Jenna Macrae, Jenna Townley that was, they couldn't fathom, murmuring amongst themselves on where that spunk she'd had in abundance had gone.

Sometimes she and Conal didn't see each other from one week's end to the next and if he should enter the nursery when she was there she simply put down what she was doing, perhaps a book she was reading to Ewan, or even Ewan himself, and quietly left the room. She was in a state she could only liken to the one she had known – only a thousand times greater – when her parents died. Bereaved, suffering a grief that was at times too much for her. She would sit, dry-eyed, for hours on end in her locked sitting-room, her arms clutched about her racked body, rocking herself as women do when they mourn. But for the most part she allowed herself to feel nothing.

571

To become an automaton, speaking only when spoken to for it was the only way she could get through this, and survive.

The servants were badly frightened. They had known the master and mistress have . . . well, they could only call them blazing rows, with her shouting and stamping her feet and saying she would do it – whatever it was! – and him yelling she'd do as she was told or else, but they'd been heated uproarious confrontations that had lasted no more than an hour and always ended with that silence which spoke for itself behind their closed bedroom door. When they began the servants would smile at one another, being used to it now, as though to say "will you listen to that?" or "it's them two again" but this was different. This was ugly. This was something they had never known before and it seemed to go on indefinitely. Day after day, week after week with the master in one bedroom and madam in another and what could it be about, they agonised? Lady Blenkinsopp, God bless her, had gone very suddenly but surely she couldn't be the cause of it? Not her, poor sweet soul, for who among them was not aware of the nasty old man she was married to, but it was all very upsetting. Him eating in his study off a tray on his desk, her in her upstairs sitting-room just as though neither of them could bear to be in one another's company and neither could face the dining-room alone.

Dora and Marian, both young and inclined towards the romantic, and being the two most in contact with Mr and Mrs Macrae, apart from Mrs Garnett who was older and more worldly wise, were often in tears, one setting the other off, Mrs Garnett was disposed to think.

Jenna was seated before her sitting-room fire, stoked up to comforting proportions for it was winter now and the evening was bitter cold, when there was a knock at her door.

"Come in," she answered tonelessly, not turning

towards it for she thought it was Marian. She wore the loose-fitting, filmy gown she put on before retiring, lace-trimmed and the colour of pale honey. Her hair was free and fell in a rippling cloak of tangled curls down her back awaiting Marian's ministrations. Her face was unutterably sad but it had a hue of rosy colour about it in the dancing gold and orange reflection of the flames. Duff and Dory were sprawled at her feet, panting in the heat of the fire and both lifted their heads for a moment, then dropped them when they saw who had entered. Two tails thumped on the carpet then were still as the dogs dropped back into a light doze.

She turned then. Conal stood just inside the door but did not close it behind him and her face which had been soft and pensive, hardened at once. Her eyes turned to blue-green ice and her head lifted as she stared contemptuously across the room.

"Yes?" Her voice was as cold as her eyes.

"This willna take long," he answered woodenly.

"Good."

"I'm going away for Christmas. Up to Scotland."

"Should that concern me?"

"I dinna suppose so but I thought it best to tell you since I'm taking the children."

Her eyes turned to fire then and her teeth shone white between her straining lips as she glared at him, ready to spit and snarl as she stood up.

"Oh no! Oh no, you are not! Over my dead body shall you take my—"

The dogs, alarmed, leapt to their feet and moved warily to the far side of the room, their ears and tails down.

"Save your breath, Jenna," Conal interrupted her wearily. "I am going and they are going with me. Tomorrow."

Her heart twisted and thumped in her breast and her breath threatened to choke her and she wanted to leap across the room and tear at his flesh. He and Amy had almost destroyed her. They had torn and trampled on that part of her life, any woman's life, which is sacred to her. A woman's love for her man, his for her, the things they did in the privacy of that love must be shared with no other, exclusive to them alone. Conal had shattered the solid foundation of their marriage when he had made love to Amy, exposed Jenna and her trusting heart to a torment she found almost impossible to endure and made a mockery of what had been precious and she could forgive neither of them. Now he was to torture her further by the removal of her children but she would not stand for it. Not for this. She had no choice over the other, the . . . the loathsome images of Conal and . . . and Amy, but this, this she could stop and she would.

Conal watched her and though his own heart was racked with pain and sorrow and compassion for his wife he did not show it, nor did he back down.

"I can see you're about to give me an argument, Jenna." He sighed deeply. "But really, it would be a waste of time. We are still . . . husband and wife."

"Never, never! I am no longer your wife."

"And the law says I am the custodian of our children . . ."

"No! No!"

". . . and I have the right to do with them as I please. Take them where I please. I find I canna bear this house and its . . ."

"You cannot bear . . ."

". . . and so I shall go away for a few weeks. Nanny Abigail will come with me to care for the boys and . . ."

"No . . ."

". . . we shall be back in the new year. I had hoped you and I might perhaps talk . . . all these months . . . you might allow me to . . . but you have turned away . . . your collieries consume all your time so you will not . . . well, that is all."

Without another word he turned and left the room, closing the door quietly behind him.

The letter came just after the new year. It was three weeks since Conal and the children had gone and Jenna, quite simply, thought she would lose her mind. The house was like a house in mourning with servants tiptoeing about the place as though a corpse lay in its coffin in the close-curtained drawing-room. They spoke in whispers, moving about on the edge of her conscious mind like black-garbed ghosts. She wondered, in the depth of her misery, why they were in black, then remembered that Her Majesty's husband, Prince Albert, had died very suddenly just before Christmas and the whole nation had taken to mourning in respect for the prince and sympathy for their poor Queen who, it was said, had a broken heart. The sadness was universal, even the poorest wearing some show of black and of course Mrs Garnett, herself a model of convention and propriety, would insist on those under her doing the same. The general miasma of sorrow blended in very well with Jenna's own.

The letter was on her breakfast tray. The writing was unfamiliar and even the address, written neatly in clear copperplate at the top right-hand corner of the expensive notepaper failed to register in Jenna's frozen mind. Newton Law and the date was two days previously.

'*Dearest Jenna,*' it said. '*It has taken me many weeks to find the courage to write to you for even at so great a distance your loathing of me and what I did to you is something which fills me with anguish and guilt . . .*'

Jenna began to shake, the notepaper in her hand trembling as though it was trapped in a tunnel through which the wind rushed. Her eyes blurred, not with tears but with an all-consuming rage and hatred and her heart banged cruelly inside her ribcage. She gasped for breath, the feeling in her one of a runner who has gone beyond her endurance and she threw back her head, gritting her teeth at the agony the touch of this paper carved into her. It was from her. Oh, sweet God, how could she? How could she write, after all this time, after what she has done? She couldn't read it, really she couldn't . . . couldn't bear to have it in her hand knowing she had touched it . . . the words . . . the words . . . Dear God . . .

'*I know my torment is as nothing compared to yours,*' it went on, '*but I have something to say and say it I must . . .*'

I don't want to hear it. I don't want to know what she has to tell me for surely she has done enough, she and Conal, without this attempt to justify . . . is that what it is?

Conal loves you, Jenna. He and I . . . well, my dearest, there is no he and I for though we did you a grave wrong it was only on that one occasion and it was my doing. Conal is a fine man, a kind and compassionate man despite his masculinity and the simple truth is that he felt sorry for me. For what had been done to me in the past. You have known the joy of love, intimate, physical love, Jenna, and it has fulfilled you as a woman. You and Conal have loved one another in every sense of the word and I believe, though it was never spoken, that he wanted to show me that all men are not as my husband is. Conal does not love me, Jenna, and never has. Oh, I love him, I won't deny it, for he is a man easy to love but his heart is yours and always will be, my dear. But he is a man, Jenna, and you are his wife and though I must be brutal, what happened between Conal and I would not have happened had you been there. You were in his house and in his bed, I grant you, but you were not there. Your mining business and your obsession with the Townleys is the true cause of your estrangement from your husband and well you know

*it. He turned to me in compassion and loneliness. So
don't, I beg you, throw it all away for one mistake.
Hold him and hold your children to you for what you
have is more precious than anything in the world. I
wish it was mine, Jenna, but it is not. It is yours. Take
it, hold it, keep it.*

The letter was signed, Amy.

She sat for hours, the letter still in her hand. Marian
came in and spoke to her and, getting no answer, went out
again. Maisie tapped on the door bringing a fresh scuttle
of coal, repaired the fire and left, reporting to the rest
of the servants that Mrs Macrae was looking real badly
and did Mrs Garnett think they should send for Doctor
Sterling?

It began to snow at noon, a light fall which dusted the
garden and trees in white and glittering enchantment.
Snowflakes tapped softly on Jenna's window but she
did not hear or see anything beyond the words Amy had
written. They were burning in her brain as though they
were branded there and slowly, little by little the pain
of them, the bravery of them, the simple honest truth of
them moved in her heart and she began to weep.

Dear God! Dear God! What had she done? What had
she done to him, the husband she loved more than anyone
else in the world, to her beloved children who, it seemed,
had turned to Amy's warmth when Jenna's had been
preoccupied with how to best Simeon Townley? She had
been – what was the expression? – the wronged wife but
by God, had Conal not been the deserted husband? In his
despair he had turned to her cousin who was, though not
exactly waiting for him, there just when she was most
needed, and he had needed her.

But why had she, Jenna, not seen it? Why had she not
been aware of . . . and yet, she had, she had. The day
. . . the day on which she had watched them play ball

with Ewan . . . summer it had been then, the garden exploding with colour and Amy in a white dress with her hair down her back, Conal laughing as he had once laughed with Jenna. She had sensed in some depth she had not recognised that there was danger but her mind, as it had done for years, had been too concerned with Simeon Townley and her obsessive need to keep him from her father's mines, *his* father's mines . . . aah, that was the first time . . . Dear sweet Christ, it was the first time she had ever admitted that Jonas Townley, her beloved papa, and she did love him, she always had, was also Simeon's father and could she change that? Did she want to? Was it worth it? Was it? Conal . . . Amy was right. Oh, Amy, I do love my husband. Conal, Conal . . .

The tears began to pour from her eyes, from the pores of her flesh it seemed, a great waterfall of grief that escaped from her frozen heart and eased it a little. The aching anguish diminished, she leaned forward in her chair, reading Amy's letter again by the light of the fire's flames.

They were all surprised in the kitchen when, despite the snow which still fell in light and graceful eddies, Mrs Macrae ordered her carriage to be brought round to the front door.

"I shall be gone no more than an hour or so, Dora," she said to the parlour maid who stood anxiously holding the door open for her. "I am only going as far as Marfield, you know, not the North Pole."

"Oh, madam," Dora sighed, aware that nothing any of them said would make the slightest difference to this strong-minded mistress of theirs.

Simeon could not hide the expression of amazement which came over his face as her snow-blurred image emerged across the pit yard and proceeded up the steps to the office. He was alone, sitting in his father's chair, her father's chair, studying a sheet of paper on which were lines of figures and she marvelled at the sense of indifference the sight aroused in her.

He stood up slowly, his face closing in that wary way she knew so well, expecting trouble, arguments, fisticuffs even, for was that not what always took place between him and his half-sister?

His voice was cautious. "Jenna, this is a surprise," though not a pleasant one, he implied. "The weather being what it is I hardly expected—"

"I'm sure," she interrupted him, "but I have not come to discuss the weather."

"What have you come to discuss?" His caution had turned to truculence

"The future."

"The future?" He was clearly mystified

"Yes, the future of the collieries which I have decided to commit into your care." Her voice was crisp, decisive, though she felt a great desire to laugh at the slack-jawed bewilderment on Simeon's face. "Not that my shares will be unsupervised, of course, and I shall present myself regularly at board meetings but the day-to-day running of the pits will, when you are twenty-one, be completely in your hands."

"Jenna . . . My God!"

"Yes, I thought you would be surprised but don't think that I am to be your friend, or you mine, because of this. That could never be. It is not through any . . . any family sense of kinship that I am doing this. Far from it, but I have been told that you are . . . are . . . well, my father would have called it shaping in your role as coal owner and though you will never be the man he was I believe that . . . that you care about the mines as he did. My family need me, Simeon" – calling him by his name for the first time in years – "and I . . . well, I have this to say. Look after my father's pits. Keep them safe for . . . for future owners . . . as . . . as *he* did."

His voice was soft and strangely moved as he answered. "I will, Jenna."

Without speaking again she turned and retraced her steps to her carriage.

It was mid-afternoon when she moved to the window, her face more tranquil than it had been for months. Strain was still written there and pain had etched two faint lines at each side of her mouth but her eyes were clear and steady.

It had stopped snowing and somehow she was not surprised when she saw them. Conal was walking slowly up the snow-covered slope of the garden, his head down, his expression hidden from her but there was a certain slump to his shoulders which she recognised and which told her he was troubled. He normally walked so gracefully, tall, with the long confident stride of an athlete, his head set arrogantly, his step purposeful but now, his son chattering at his heels, he seemed to have fallen in on himself, burrowed deep in a silence which tormented him unutterably. Behind him and the boy were two sets of footprints leading from where they had evidently got out of the carriage, Ewan's small and blurred where he had run and kicked, Conal's long and firm and paced.

The carriage stood at the wide front steps of the house and from it Nanny Abigail was descending with Roddy in her arms, wriggling to get down and join his father and brother for he had begun to walk while he was away. Campbell and Percy were fussing with bags and boxes. The horses' breath steamed about their heads and round from the corner of the house Dory and Duff raced to leap about Ewan in delighted greeting. The boy fell over in the snow, laughing, then gathered a handful, throwing it in the air in what he thought of as a snowball. Conal turned to smile then moved back to his son.

"Come on then, laddie, we'll make a snowman, shall we?" he said and Jenna knew without knowing how she knew that the last thing he wanted was to come into the house.

They were back, those she loved. They were back and they were hers!

Without consciously thinking of what she was doing, acting purely on the instinct, that impetuous disregard for consequences which had always been the heart of Jenna Macrae, she flung the window open wide and leaned out, the snow on the sill bathing her in its reflected silvery white haze. The sound of the window opening lifted the heads of her husband and son. She grinned, her old grin of devilment, of wicked delight and to her joy both their faces lit up with pleasure.

"What on earth is all this noise about?" she called out in mock complaint. "Can a lady not enjoy a moment of peace but that her menfolk lark about beneath her window and disturb her?"

"Jenna . . . lassie . . .?" In Conal's voice was a question just as though he could not quite believe that it was really she at the window and not some figment of his tired disillusion.

"Mama, Mama . . . snow, Mama . . . Papa play snowman with . . ." Ewan was so excited to see his own pretty mama laughing at him as she had always done he lapsed into an unintelligible string of infant gabble in which only one word in four was recognisable.

"Yes, darling, yes," she laughed back at him since she was his mother and knew exactly what he meant.

"You're . . . well, Jenna?" Her husband's face was careful, afraid to disturb what seemed to be her glad welcome of him, but at the same time it shone with his love for her, and his eyes, she could see it, even from where she leaned in the bedroom window, glowed a steady, warm, adoring brown which only she, of all women, had ever aroused in him

"I'm better, Conal. Well enough to put on a coat and

come and join you. Fetch Roddy from nanny, will you, and we'll make that snowman you promised and perhaps later . . ."

"Aye, lassie?" Conal's voice deepened and his eyes narrowed with that expression she knew so well and which, deliberately, she was telling him she welcomed.

"Wait and see, Conal Macrae."

"I dinna think I care to wait and see, Jenna Macrae. In fact I've half a mind to climb that handy drainpipe and come up right now."

"Only half a mind!"

They shined and glowed into one another's eyes and the child babbled happily in the background. He clutched a handful of snow and hopped about and the two dogs began to bark, excited by the merriment which had been so sadly lacking of late. It was many months since they had heard their mistress's voice as it was now and they found they liked it.

It was bedlam when, having hurriedly thrown on her coat and boots, she moved down the lawn towards her husband and sons. The dogs swirled about Conal and Ewan's legs. Dory snatched at every snowball the boy threw in his frantic joy, snapping at the fragmented lumps of snow. Ewan ran to his mama as she approached and she picked him up, burying her face in the sweet curve of his neck then tossed him in the air until he screamed with delight.

From the steps Campbell and Percy paused to watch them, making no attempt to hide their satisfaction. Behind them Dora and Marian, and even Nanny Abigail who should have had more sense, clutched at one another in fearful hope, Dora and Marian ready to cry tears of joy.

They turned to one another at last. Conal made no attempt to touch her. He stood, straight-backed as though at attention on a parade ground and she knew he was afraid. He was thinner, his face drawn and haggard and as she looked at him, saw him for the first time in almost five months, she knew he had suffered as much as she had. His eyes clung to hers and they were steadfast with the power of his never-ending love for her. Hers were clear, sure, and bright with the same emotion.

"Conal," she said softly.

It was enough. His arms rose to take her and she moved into them. It would be hard. She didn't know how they were to return to its original strength the substance of their marriage. It would be hard and they might fall back two steps for one taken but it would surely be worth the trying. It was all right, her mind sang joyfully. It was all right now and she would work to keep it so. They had begun. She was at home where she belonged, with Conal. This was where she was meant to be, here where her husband was, where her sons were and – dear God, why had she not known it sooner? – where love was.